ALSO BY E L JAMES

Darker
Grey
Fifty Shades Freed
Fifty Shades Darker
Fifty Shades of Grey

THE MISTER

THE MISTER

E L James

VINTAGE BOOKS

A Division of Penguin Random House LLC | *New York*

For Tia Elba
Thank you for your wisdom, strength, good humour, and sanity,
but most of all for your love

THE MISTER

daily

/ˈdālī/

noun
informal

1. a newspaper published every day except Sunday
"The trial was reported in all the popular *dailies*."

   BRITISH *dated*

2. a woman who is employed to clean someone else's house on a regular basis
"My *daily* comes every day ..."

Prologue

No. No. No. Not the black. Not the choking dark. Not the plastic bag. Panic overwhelms her, forcing the air from her lungs. *I can't breathe. I can't breathe.* The metallic taste of fear rises in her throat. *I need to do this. It's the only way. Be still. Be calm. Breathe slow. Breathe shallow. Just like he said. This will be over soon. It will be over, and then I will be free. Free. Free.*

Go. Now. Run. Run. Run. Go. She runs hard and fast but doesn't look back. Fear drives her forward as she dodges a few late-night shoppers in her quest to flee. Luck is with her: the automatic doors are open. She flies under the gaudy holiday decorations and through the entrance into the parking lot. On and on she runs. Between the parked cars and into the woods. She runs for her life, down a small dirt path, through brambles, small branches slapping her face. She runs until her lungs are bursting. *Go. Go. Go. Don't stop.*

· · ·

Cold. Cold. Too cold. Fatigue fogs her brain. Fatigue and the cold. The wind howls through the trees, through her clothes, and into her bones. She huddles beneath a bush and gathers the fallen leaves to build a nest with numb hands. *Sleep.* She needs sleep. She lies down on the cold, hard ground, too tired to be afraid and too tired to weep. *The others. Did they get away?* She closes her eyes. *Did they escape? Let them be free. Let them be warm . . . How did it come to this?*

She wakes. She's lying between trash cans, wrapped in newspapers and cardboard. She's shivering. She's so cold. But she needs to move on. She has an address. She thanks her nana's God for the address. With shaking fingers she unfurls the paper. This is where she needs to go. Now. Now. *Now.*

One foot in front of the other. Walk. It's all she can do. Walk. Walk. *Walk.* Sleep in a doorway. Wake and walk on. Walk. She drinks water from the sink at the McDonald's. The food smells enticing.

She's cold. Hunger claws at her stomach. And she walks and walks, following the map. A stolen map. Stolen from a store. A store with twinkling lights and Christmas music. She holds the scrap of paper with what little strength she has left. It's worn and torn from so many days hidden in her boot. *Tired.* So tired. *Dirty.* So dirty and cold and frightened. This place is her only hope. She raises her trembling hand and presses the doorbell.

Magda is expecting her. Her mother wrote and told her. She welcomes her with open arms. And then backs away quickly. *Jesus, child. What's happened to you? I was expecting you last week!*

Chapter One

Mindless sex—there's a lot to be said for it. No commitments, no expectations, and no disappointments; I just have to remember their names. Who was it last time? Jojo? Jeanne? Jody? Whatever. She was some nameless fuck who moaned a great deal both in and out of bed. I lie staring at the rippling reflections from the Thames on my ceiling, unable to sleep. Too restless to sleep.

Tonight it's Caroline. She doesn't fit the nameless-fuck category. She'll never fit. What the hell was I thinking? Closing my eyes, I try to silence the still, small voice that is questioning the wisdom of bedding my best friend . . . again. She slumbers beside me, her sleek body bathed in the silver light of the January moon, her long legs entwined with mine, and her head on my chest.

This is wrong, so wrong. I rub my face, trying to erase my self-loathing, and she stirs and shifts, waking from her doze. One manicured fingernail skims down my stomach and over my abdominal muscles, then circles my navel. I sense her sleepy smile as her fingers slip toward my pubic hair. Catching her hand, I bring it to my lips. "Haven't we done enough damage for one night, Caro?" I kiss each finger in turn to take the sting out of the rejection. I'm tired and disheartened by the nagging, unwelcome guilt that gnaws at my gut. This is Caroline, for heaven's sake, my best friend and my brother's wife. Ex-wife.

No. Not ex-wife. His widow.

It's a sad, lonely word for a sad, lonely circumstance.

"Oh, Maxim, please. Make me forget," she whispers, and plants a warm, wet kiss on my chest. Tossing her fair hair away from her face, she gazes up at me through long lashes, her eyes shining with need and grief.

I cup her lovely face and shake my head. "We shouldn't."

"Don't." She places her fingers on my lips, silencing me. "Please. I need it."

I groan. I'm going to hell.

"Please," she begs.

Shit, this is hell.

And because I'm hurting, too—because I miss him, too—and Caroline is my connection to him, my lips find hers and I ease her onto her back.

When I wake, the room is flooded with bright winter sunshine that makes me squint. Turning over, I'm relieved to see that Caroline has gone, leaving behind a lingering trace of regret—and a note on my pillow:

> *Dinner Tonight with Daddy & the Stepsow?*
> *Please come.*
> *They are mourning, too.*
> > > > *ILY x*

Fuck.

This is not what I want. I close my eyes, grateful to be alone in my own bed and glad, despite our nocturnal activities, that we decided to come back to London two days after the funeral.

How the hell did this get so out of hand?

Just a nightcap, she'd said, and I'd gazed into her big blue eyes, brimming with sorrow, and known what she wanted. It was the same look she'd given me the night we learned of Kit's accident and untimely death. A look I couldn't resist then. We'd almost danced the dance so many times, but that night I resigned myself to fate, and with an unerring inevitability I fucked my brother's wife.

And now we'd done it again, with Kit laid to rest only two days ago.

I scowl at the ceiling. I am, without doubt, a pathetic excuse for a human. But then so is Caroline. At least she has an excuse: she's in mourning, scared for her future, and I'm her best friend. Who else could she turn to in her hour of need? I'd just pushed the envelope on *comforting* the grieving widow.

Frowning, I crumple her note and toss it to the wooden floor, where it skitters to a stop under the sofa that's piled with my clothes. The watery shadows float above me, the light and dark seeming to taunt me. I close my eyes to shut them out.

Kit was a good man.

Kit. Dear Kit. Everyone's favorite—even Caroline's; she did choose him, after all. A vision of Kit's desolate, broken body lying beneath a sheet at the hospital mortuary appears unbidden in my mind. I take a deep breath, trying to dispel the memory, as a knot forms in my throat. He deserved better than dear Caro and me—his wastrel brother. He didn't deserve this . . . betrayal.

Fuck.

Who am I kidding?

Caroline and I deserve each other. She scratched my itch, and I scratched hers. We're both consenting and *technically* free adults. She likes it. I like it, and it's what I do best, fucking some eager, attractive woman into the small hours of the morning. It's my favorite recreational activity and gives me something to do— someone to do. Fucking keeps me fit, and in the throes of passion

I learn all I need to know about a woman—how to make her sweat and if she screams or cries when she comes.

Caroline is a crier.

Caroline has just lost her husband.

Shit.

And I've lost my big brother, my only guiding light for the last few years.

Shit.

Closing my eyes, I see Kit's pale, dead face once more, and his loss is a yawning space within me.

An irreplaceable loss.

Why the hell was he riding his motorcycle on that bleak and icy night? It's beyond comprehension. Kit is—*was*—the sane one, the safe pair of hands, Lord Reliable himself. Between the two of us, it was Kit who brought honor to our family name, upheld its reputation, and behaved responsibly. He held down a job in the City and managed the substantial family business as well. He didn't make rash decisions, he didn't drive like a madman. He was the sensible brother. He stepped up, not down. He was not the prodigal mess that I am. No, I'm the other side of Kit's coin. My specialty is being the black sheep of the family. No one has any expectations of me, I make sure of that. Always.

I sit up, my mood grim in the harsh morning light. It's time to hit the basement gym. Running, fucking, and fencing, they all keep me in shape.

With dance music hammering in my ears and sweat rolling down my back, I drag air into my lungs. The pounding of my feet on the treadmill clears my mind as I concentrate on pushing my body to its limits. Usually when I run, I'm focused and grateful that at last I feel *something*—even if it's just the pain of bursting lungs and limbs. Today I don't want to feel anything, not after this fuck-awful week. All I want is the physical pain of exertion and endurance. Not the pain of loss.

Run. Breathe. Run. Breathe.

Don't think about Kit. Don't think about Caroline.
Run. Run. Run.

As I cool down, the treadmill slows, and I jog through the final stretch of my five-mile sprint, allowing my feverish thoughts to return. For the first time in a long time, I have a great deal to do.

Before Kit's demise my days were spent recovering from the night before and planning the next night's entertainment. And that was about it. That was my life. I don't like to shine a light on the vacuity of my existence. But deep down I know how bloody useless I am. Access to a healthy trust fund since I turned twenty-one means I've never done a serious day's work in my life. Unlike my older brother. He worked hard, but then again he had no choice.

Today, however, will be different. I'm the executor of Kit's will, which is a joke. Choosing *me* was his last laugh, I'm sure—but now that he's interred in the family vault, the will has to be read and . . . well, executed.

And Kit died leaving no heirs.

I shudder as the treadmill comes to a stop. I don't want to think about the implications. I'm not ready.

Grabbing my iPhone, I swing a towel around my neck and jog back upstairs to my flat on the sixth floor.

Stripping off my clothes, I discard them in the bedroom and head into the en suite bathroom. Beneath the shower, as I wash my hair, I consider how to deal with Caroline. We've known each other since our early schooldays. We each recognized a kindred spirit, and it drew us together, two thirteen-year-old boarders with divorced parents. I was the new boy and she took me under her wing. We became inseparable. She is and always will be my first love, my first fuck . . . my disastrous first fuck. And years later she'd chosen my brother, not me. But in spite of all that, we managed to remain good friends and keep our hands off each other—until Kit's death.

Shit. It has to stop. I don't want or need the complication. As I shave, solemn green eyes blaze back at me. *Don't fuck it up with*

Caroline. She's one of your few friends. She's your best friend. Talk to her. Reason with her. She knows we're incompatible. I nod at my reflection, feeling more resolved about her, and wipe my face free of foam. Tossing the towel onto the floor, I head into the dressing room. There I gather up my black jeans, which are embedded in a pile on one of the shelves, and I'm relieved to find hanging a newly pressed white shirt and a dry-cleaned black blazer. Today I have lunch with the family solicitors. I slip on my boots and grab a coat to defend myself from the cold outside.

Shit, it's Monday.

I remember that Krystyna, my ancient Polish daily, is due later this morning to clean. Taking out my wallet, I deposit some cash on the console table in the hall, set the alarm, then stroll out the front door. Locking up behind me, I forgo the lift and take the stairs.

Once I'm outside on Chelsea Embankment, the air is clear and crisp, marred only by the vapor of my frozen breath. I stare beyond the gloomy, gray Thames on the other side of the street to the Peace Pagoda on the opposite bank. That's what I want, some peace, but that may be a long time coming. I hope to have some questions answered over lunch. Raising an arm, I hail a cab and order the driver to take me to Mayfair.

Housed in the Georgian splendor of Brook Street, the firm of Pavel, Marmont and Hoffman has been the family's solicitors since 1775. "Time to be a grown-up," I mutter to myself as I push open the ornate wooden door.

"Good afternoon, sir." The young receptionist beams, a flush staining her olive skin. She's pretty, in an understated way. If these were normal circumstances I'd have her number within five minutes of conversation, but that's not why I'm here.

"I have an appointment to see Mr. Rajah."

"Your name?"

"Maxim Trevelyan."

Her eyes scan her computer screen, and she shakes her head and frowns. "Please take a seat." She waves toward two brown leather chesterfields that are situated in the paneled hall, and I slump into the nearer one picking up that morning's edition of the *Financial Times*. The receptionist is talking on the phone with some urgency while I peruse the front page of the paper but take nothing in. When I glance up, Rajah is coming to greet me himself, striding through the double doors with an outstretched hand.

I stand.

"Lord Trevethick, may I offer you my sincere condolences for your loss," Rajah says as we shake hands.

"Trevethick, please," I reply. "I've yet to get used to my brother's title."

My title . . . now.

"Of course." Mr. Rajah nods with a polite deference that I find irritating. "Would you like to come with me? We're having lunch in the partners' dining room, and I must say we have one of the finest cellars in London."

Mesmerized, I stare at the dancing flames of the fire at my club in Mayfair.

Earl of Trevethick.

That's me. Now.

It's inconceivable. It's devastating.

How I envied my brother's title and his position in the family when I was younger. Kit had been the favored child since birth, especially with my mother, but then he was the heir, not the spare. Known as Viscount Porthtowan since he was born, Kit had become the twelfth Earl of Trevethick at the age of twenty upon our father's sudden death. At twenty-eight I'm lucky number thirteen. And though I've coveted the title and all that goes with it, now that it's mine, I feel like I'm intruding on my brother's domain.

You fucked his countess last night. That's more than intruding.

I take a slug of the Glenrothes I'm drinking and raise my glass. "A toast to the Ghost," I whisper, and smile at the irony. The Glenrothes was my father's whisky of choice, and my brother's—and from today this 1992 vintage will be mine.

I can't pinpoint the moment I made peace with Kit's inheritance and with Kit himself, but it happened sometime in my late teens. He had the title, he'd won the girl, and I had to accept that. But now everything is mine. Everything.

Even your wife. Well, for last night at least.

But the irony is that Kit has made no provision for Caroline in his will.

Nothing.

This is what she feared.

How could he have been so remiss? He'd drawn a new will four months ago but he hadn't made provisions for her. They'd only been married for two years....

What was he thinking?

Of course, she may challenge it. And who would blame her?

I rub my face.

What am I going to do?

My phone buzzes.

WHERE ARE YOU?

It's a text from Caroline.

I switch off my phone and order another drink. I don't want to see her tonight. I want to lose myself in someone else. Someone new. Someone with no strings attached, and I think I'll score some blow, too. I pull out my phone and open Tinder.

"Maxim, this is a stunning flat." She gazes out over the murky water of the Thames that glimmers with light from the Peace Pagoda. I take her jacket and drape it over the back of the sofa.

"Drink or something stronger?" I offer. We are not going to be in the drawing room for long. On cue she flicks her shining black hair over her shoulder. Her hazel eyes, framed with kohl, are intent on me.

Licking painted lips, she arches a brow and asks, "Something stronger?" Her tone is seductive. "What are you drinking?"

Ah . . . she's not taking the hint, so no coke, then, but she's way ahead of me. I step closer so that she has to angle her head to look up at me. I'm careful not to touch her.

"I'm not thirsty, Heather." I pitch my voice low, pleased that I've remembered her name. She swallows, and her lips part.

"Me neither," she whispers, and her provocative smile reaches her eyes.

"What do you want?" I watch as her gaze moves to my mouth. It's an invitation. I pause for a moment, just to make sure I'm reading her correctly, then lean down and kiss her. It's the briefest touch: lips on lips, then nothing.

"I think you know what I want." She reaches up to run her fingers through my hair and pull me back to her warm and willing mouth. She tastes of brandy with a faint hint of cigarettes. The taste is distracting. I don't remember seeing her smoke at the club. I pull her hard against me, one hand at her waist while the other travels down over her lush curves. She has a small waist and large, firm breasts, which she presses enticingly against me. I wonder if they'll taste as good as they feel. My hand skims down to her backside as I deepen the kiss, exploring her eager mouth.

"What do *you* want?" I whisper against her lips.

"You." Her voice is breathy and urgent. She's turned on. Big time. She begins to unbutton my shirt. I hold still as she eases it off my shoulders and lets it fall to the floor.

Do I take her here or in my bed? Comfort wins and I grab her hand. "Come with me." I tug her gently, and she follows me out of the drawing room and down the hall, into the bedroom.

The room is tidy, as I knew it would be.

God bless Krystyna.

I switch the bedside lights on from the wall and walk her to the bed. "Turn around."

Heather does as she's told but sways a little in her high heels. "Steady." I clasp her shoulders and pull her tight against me, then turn her head toward me so I can see her eyes. They're intent on my lips, but she looks up at me. Eyes bright. Clear. Focused. Sober enough. I nuzzle her neck, tasting her soft, fragrant skin with my tongue. "I think it's time to lie down." I unzip her short red dress and peel it over her shoulders, pausing as I expose the tops of her breasts concealed by a red bra. I skim my thumbs across the surface of the lacy fabric. She groans and arches her back, pushing her breasts into my hands.

Oh, yes.

My thumbs dip beneath the delicate material and circle her hardening nipples as she gropes behind her for the button on my jeans. "We have all night," I murmur, and release her before stepping back so that her dress slides down her body and pools at her feet.

A red thong reveals her shapely behind.

"Turn around. I want to see you."

Heather tosses her hair over her shoulder as she turns and gives me a searing look from beneath her lashes. She has the most magnificent breasts.

I smile. She smiles.

This is going to be fun.

Reaching forward, she grabs the waistband of my jeans and tugs sharply so her glorious tits are once more pressed against my chest. "Kiss me," she growls, her voice low and demanding. She runs her tongue over her top teeth, and my body responds, my groin tightening.

"Only too happy to oblige, madam."

I clasp her head, my fingers in her silky hair, and kiss her more roughly this time. She responds, her hands grabbing fistfuls of my hair as our tongues lock. She stops and looks up at me with a salacious glint in her eyes, as if finally seeing me and liking what she sees. Then her lips are once more feverish against mine.

Man, she really wants this.

Nimble fingers find the top button of my jeans, and she pulls. Laughing, I grab her hands and push her gently so we both fall onto the bed.

Heather. Her name is Heather, and she's fast asleep beside me. I glance at my bedside clock; it's 5:15 A.M. She's a good fuck, no doubt about it. But now I want her gone. How long will I have to lie here listening to the soft sound of her breathing? Perhaps I should have gone to her flat instead, so then I could leave. But my place was nearer—and we were both impatient. As I stare at the ceiling, I mentally run through our evening, trying to remember what, if any, details I've learned about her. She works in television—or "telly," as she calls it—and she has to be at work in the morning, which means she has to leave soon, surely? She lives in Putney. She's hot. And willing. Yes, very willing. She likes to be on her front during intercourse, she's quiet when she comes, and she has a talented mouth that knows exactly how to revive a spent man. My cock stirs at the memory, and I contemplate waking her up for more. Her dark hair is fanned out on the pillow, and her expression is serene in sleep. I ignore the pang of envy that her serenity inspires and wonder if I got to know her better, would I find the same peace?

Oh, for fuck's sake. I want her gone.

You have intimacy issues. Caroline's nagging voice reverberates through my mind.

Caroline. Shit.

Three whining texts and several missed calls from Caroline have pissed me off. My jeans lie on the floor in a crumpled heap. From the back pocket, I retrieve my phone. Checking on the sleeping form beside me—no, she hasn't stirred—I read my messages from Caroline.

WHERE RU?

CALL ME!

POUTING

What is her problem?

She knows the deal; she's known me long enough. A quick tumble between the sheets isn't going to change how I feel about her. I love her . . . in my own way, but as a friend, a good friend.

I scowl. I haven't called her. I don't want to. I don't know what to say.

Coward. The voice of my conscience whispers. I need to put this right. Above me the shimmers from the Thames bob and weave, free and easy. Taunting me. Reminding me of what I've lost.

Freedom.

And what I have now.

Responsibility.

Shit.

Guilt overwhelms me. It's an unfamiliar and unwelcome feeling—Kit has bequeathed everything to me. *Everything.* And Caroline has nothing from his estate. She's my brother's wife. And we fucked. No wonder I feel guilty. And deep down I know she feels it, too. That's why she left in the middle of the night without waking me, without saying good-bye. If only the girl beside me would do the same.

I quickly type out a text to Caro.

Busy today. You OK?

It's five in the morning. Caroline will be asleep. I'm safe. I'll deal with her later today . . . or tomorrow.

Heather stirs, and her eyelids flitter open.

"Hi." She gives me a tentative smile. I reciprocate, but her smile fades. "I should go," she says.

"Go?" Hope swells in my chest. "You don't have to go." I manage not to sound disingenuous.

"I do. I have to work, and I don't think my red dress will cut it in the office." She sits up, clutching the silk quilt to conceal her curves. "That was . . . good, Maxim. If I leave my number, will you call me? I'd rather speak on the phone than message on Tinder."

"Of course," I lie smoothly. I pull her face to mine and kiss her tenderly. Her smile is bashful. Rising, she wraps the quilt securely around her body and starts to gather her clothes from the floor.

"Shall I call you a cab?" I ask.

"I can Uber."

"I'll do it."

"Okay, thank you. I'm going to Putney."

She tells me her address, I get up, slip on my discarded jeans, and taking my phone, leave the bedroom to give her some privacy. It's strange how some women behave the morning after: shy and quiet. She's no longer the lascivious, demanding siren of the night before.

Once I've ordered a car I wait, staring out across the dark Thames. When she finally appears, she hands me a scrap of paper. "My number."

"Thanks." I slip it into the back pocket of my jeans. "Your car will be here in five minutes."

She stands awkwardly, her postcoital shyness taking hold. As the silence stretches between us, she surveys the room, looking anywhere but at me.

"This is a lovely flat. Airy," she says, and I know that we've resorted to chitchat to fill the awkwardness. She spots my guitar and the piano. "You play?" She walks over to the baby grand.

"Yes."

"That's why you're so good with your hands," she says. Then

frowns as if she's realized that she's spoken aloud, and her cheeks flush a fetching pink.

"Do you play?" I ask, ignoring her comment.

"No—I never made it further than recorder group in year two." Relief softens her features, probably because I ignored her comment about my hands. "And all that?" She points to my decks and the iMac on a desk in the corner of the room.

"I DJ."

"Oh?"

"Yes. Couple of times a month at a club in Hoxton."

"Hence all the vinyl." She glances at the shelved wall housing my record collection.

I nod.

"And the photography?" She waves a hand at the black-and-white landscapes that hang on large canvases in the drawing room.

"Yes. And occasionally on the other side of the camera."

She looks confused.

"Modeling. Editorial, mainly."

"Oh, that makes sense. You really are a man of many parts." She grins, feeling a little more confident. She should. She's a goddess.

"Jack of all trades," I reply with a self-deprecating smile, and her grin vanishes, replaced by a puzzled frown.

"Is something wrong?" she asks.

Wrong? What the hell is she talking about? "No. Nothing." My phone buzzes, and it's a text to let me know her car has arrived. "I'll call you," I say as I pick up her jacket and hold it open for her to shrug on.

"No you won't. But don't worry. That's Tinder for you. I had fun."

"Me, too." I'm not about to contradict her.

I follow her to the front door. "Do you want me to walk you down?"

"No thanks. I'm a big girl. Good-bye, Maxim. It was nice knowing you."

"Same here . . . Heather."

"Well done." She beams, pleased that I've remembered her name, and it's impossible not to return her smile. "That's better," she says. "I hope you find what you're looking for." Reaching up, she gives me a chaste kiss on the cheek. She turns and teeters on her high heels toward the lifts. I frown at her departing figure, watching her fine arse move beneath her red dress.

Find what I'm looking for? What the hell does that mean?

I've got all this. I've just had you. It will be someone else tomorrow. What more do I need?

For some unknown reason, her words irritate me, but I shake them off and head back to bed, relieved that she's gone. As I strip off my jeans and slip between the sheets, her challenging parting words echo through my mind.

I hope you find what you're looking for.

Where the fuck did that come from?

I've just inherited a vast estate in Cornwall, an estate in Oxfordshire, another in Northumberland, and a small portion of London—but at what cost?

Kit's pale, lifeless face surfaces in my imagination.

Shit.

So many people are now relying on me, too many, far too many: tenant farmers, estate workers, household staff in four houses, the developers in Mayfair. . . .

Hell.

Fuck you, Kit. Fuck you for dying.

I close my eyes as I fight back unshed tears, and with Heather's parting words ringing in my head I fall into a stupor.

Chapter Two

Alessia digs her hands farther into the pockets of Michal's old anorak in a vain attempt to warm her cold fingers. Huddled in her scarf, she trudges through the freezing winter drizzle toward the apartment block on Chelsea Embankment. Today is Wednesday, her second day here without Krystyna, and she is heading back to the big apartment with the piano.

In spite of the weather, she's feeling a sense of achievement because she's survived the cramped and crowded train journey without her usual anxiety. She's beginning to understand that this is what London is like. There are too many people, too much noise, and too much traffic. But worst of all, no one speaks to anyone else, except to say "Excuse me" if they jostle her or "Move down the carriage, please." Everyone hides behind their free newspaper or listens to music on headphones or stares at their phones or electronic books, avoiding all eye contact.

That morning Alessia had been lucky enough to find a seat on the train, but the woman beside her had spent much of the journey shrieking into her phone about her unsuccessful date the night before. Alessia had ignored her and read the free newspaper to improve her English, but she'd wished she could listen to music through headphones and not this woman's loud whining. Once she finished the paper, she'd closed her eyes and daydreamed of majestic mountains dotted with snow and pastures where the air was scented with thyme and filled with the hum of honeybees. She misses home. She misses the peace and quiet. She misses her mother, and she misses her piano.

Her fingers flex in her pockets as she recalls her warm-up piece, hearing the notes loud and clear in her mind and seeing them in blazing color. How long has it been since she played? Her excitement builds as she thinks of the piano waiting for her in the apartment.

She makes her way through the entrance of the old building toward the elevator, barely able to contain her enthusiasm, and then up to the top-floor apartment. For a few hours on Mondays, Wednesdays, and Fridays, this wonderful place with its large airy rooms, dark wooden floors, and baby grand piano is all hers. She unlocks the door, poised to switch off the alarm, but to her surprise there's no warning tone. Perhaps the system's broken or it's not been set. Or . . . *No.* She realizes to her horror that the owner must be at home. Listening hard, trying to detect any signs of life, she stands in the wide hallway that's hung with black-and-white photographic landscapes. She hears nothing.

Mirë.

No. "Good." English. Think in English. Whoever lives here must have gone to work and forgotten to set the alarm. She's never met the man, but she knows he has a good job, because the apartment is huge. How else can he afford it? She sighs. He might be rich, but he's a complete slob. She's been here three times already, twice with Krystyna, and each time the apartment is a mess and requires hours of tidying and cleaning.

The gray day is seeping through the skylight at the end of the hall, so Alessia flicks the switch and the crystal chandelier above her bursts into life, illuminating the hallway. She peels off her woolen scarf and hangs it up with her anorak in the closet beside the front door. From her plastic shopping bag, she pulls out the old sneakers that Magda has given her, and after taking off her wet boots and socks she slips them on, grateful that they are dry so her frozen feet can warm up. Her thin jersey top and T-shirt are no match for the cold. She rubs her arms briskly to bring some life back into them as she makes her way through the kitchen into the laundry room. There she dumps her shopping bag on the counter. Out of it she pulls the ill-fitting nylon housecoat that Krystyna bequeathed her and puts it on, then fastens a pale blue scarf around her head in an effort to keep her thick braid in check. From the cupboard beneath the sink, she takes out the cleaning caddy, and from the top of the washing machine she grabs the laundry basket and heads straight to *his* bedroom. If she hurries, she can finish the apartment before it's time to leave and the piano will be hers for a short while.

She opens the door but freezes on the threshold of the room.

He's here.

The man!

Fast asleep facedown and sprawled naked across the large bed. She stands, shocked and fascinated at once, her feet rooted to the wooden floor as she stares. He's stretched across the length of the bed, tangled in his duvet but naked . . . very naked. His face is turned toward her but covered by unkempt brown hair. One arm is beneath the pillow that supports his head, the other extended toward her. He has broad, defined shoulders, and on his biceps is an elaborate tattoo that is partially hidden by the bedding. His back is sun-kissed with a tan that fades as his hips narrow to dimples and to a pale, taut backside.

Backside.

He's naked!

Lakuriq!

Zot!

His long, muscular legs disappear beneath a knot of gray duvet and silver silk bedspread, though his foot sticks out over the edge of the mattress. He stirs, the muscles in his back rippling, and his eyelids flicker open to reveal unfocused but brilliant green eyes. Alessia stops breathing, convinced he'll be angry that she's woken him. Their eyes meet, but he shifts and turns his face away. He settles down and goes back to sleep. Relieved, she exhales a deep breath.

Shyqyr Zotit!

Flushed with mortification, she tiptoes out of his bedroom and bolts up the long hall and into the living room, where she sets the cleaning caddy on the floor and begins to gather his discarded clothes.

He's here? How can he still be in bed? At this hour?

Surely he's late for work.

She glances at the piano, feeling cheated. Today was the day she was going to play. She didn't have the nerve on Monday, and she longs to play. Today would have been the first time! In her head she hears Bach's Prelude in C Minor. Her fingers tap out the notes in anger, and the melody resonates inside her head, in bright reds, yellows, and oranges, a perfect accompaniment to her resentment. The piece reaches its climax and then diminishes to a close as she throws a discarded T-shirt into the laundry basket.

Why does he have to be here?

She knows that her disappointment is irrational. This is his home. But focusing on her disappointment distracts her from thinking about *him*. He's the first naked man she's ever seen, a naked man with vivid green eyes—eyes the color of the still, deep waters of the Drin on a summer's day. She frowns, not wanting the reminder of home. He had looked directly at her. Thank God he didn't wake. Taking the laundry basket, she tiptoes to his half-open bedroom door and pauses to see if he's still asleep. She hears the sound of the shower in the bathroom.

He's awake!

She contemplates leaving the apartment but dismisses the idea. She needs this job, and if she were to leave, he might fire her.

Cautiously she opens the door and listens to the tuneless humming that echoes from his en suite bathroom. Heart racing, she ducks into the bedroom to collect his clothes that are scattered over the floor, then hurries back to the safety of the laundry room wondering why her heart is pounding.

She takes a deep, calming breath. It was a surprise finding him here asleep. Yes. That's it. That's all. It has nothing to do with the fact that she has seen him naked. It has nothing to do with a fine face, a straight nose, full lips, broad shoulders . . . muscular arms. Nothing. It was a shock. She never expected to encounter the owner of the apartment, and to see him like that is unsettling.

Yes. He's handsome.

All of him. His hair, his hands, his legs, his backside . . .

Really handsome. And he had looked directly at her with such clear green eyes.

A darker memory surfaces in her mind. A memory from home: ice-blue eyes flinty with anger, fury raining down on her.

No. Don't think of him*!*

She puts her head in her hands and rubs her forehead.

No. No. No.

She fled. She's here. She's in London. She's safe. She will never see *him* again.

Kneeling down, she loads the dirty clothes from the laundry basket into the washing machine, as Krystyna showed her. She goes through the pockets of his black jeans and pulls out the loose change and the customary condom that he seems to carry in all his pants. In the back pocket, she finds a scrap of paper with a phone number and the name Heather scrawled on it. She slips it with the change and the condom into her pocket, tosses one of the detergent capsules into the wash, and switches on the machine.

Next she unloads the dryer and sets up the iron. Today she'll start with the ironing and stay hidden in the laundry room until he's gone.

What if he doesn't go?

And why is she hiding from him? He's her employer. Perhaps she should introduce herself. She's met all her other employers, and they aren't a problem, apart from Mrs. Kingsbury, who follows her around critiquing her cleaning methods. She sighs. The truth is, all the people she works for are women—except him, and she's wary of men.

"Bye, Krystyna!" he calls, startling her from her thoughts and the shirt collar she's ironing. The front door closes with a muffled bang, and all is quiet. He's gone. She is on her own, and she sags with relief against the ironing board.

Krystyna? Doesn't he know that she's taken Krystyna's place? Magda's friend Agatha organized this job. Hasn't Agatha told him about the change of staff? Alessia resolves to check this evening if the owner of this apartment has been informed. She finishes another shirt, hangs it on a clothes hanger, then goes to check the console table in the hall and finds he has left her money. Surely that means he won't be returning?

Her day brightens immediately, and with renewed purpose she runs back to the laundry room and grabs the pile of freshly ironed clothes and his shirts and heads to his bedroom.

The master suite is the only nonwhite room in the apartment: all gray walls and dark wood. A large gilt mirror hangs above the biggest wooden bed that Alessia has ever seen. And on the wall facing the bed, there are two large black-and-white photographs of women, their naked backs to camera. Turning away from the photography, she assesses the room. It is in complete disarray. Quickly she hangs his shirts in the closet—a closet that is bigger than her bedroom—and places the folded items on one of the shelves. The closet is still a mess, and it's been like this since she started here with Krystyna last week. Krystyna always ignored the mess, and though Alessia wants to fold and put away all the clothes, it's a big project, and she doesn't have time now, not if she wants to play the piano.

Back in his room, she opens the curtains and glances through the floor-to-ceiling windows at the Thames. It's stopped raining, but the day is gray; the street, the river, the trees in the park beyond are all muted grays, so unlike her home.

No. Home is here now. She ignores the sadness that rises like a tide within her and places the items that she retrieved from his pockets into a dish on the nightstand. She then begins to clean and tidy his room.

The last job in the bedroom is emptying the wastebasket. She tries to avoid looking at the used condoms as she dumps the contents into a black plastic trash bag. It was a shock the first time she did this, and it's still a shock now. How can one man use so many? Ugh!

Alessia moves through the rest of the apartment, cleaning, dusting, and polishing, but avoiding the one room she's not allowed to enter. Fleetingly she wonders what's behind the closed door, but she doesn't try to open it. Krystyna was very clear that the room is off-limits.

She finishes mopping the floors with half an hour to spare. She puts the cleaning caddy away in the laundry room and transfers the washed clothes into the dryer. She removes her housecoat and undoes her blue scarf, stuffing it into the back pocket of her jeans.

Carrying the black bag full of trash, she deposits it by the front door. She'll take it to the dumpsters in the designated area in the alley beside the apartment block when she leaves. Anxiously, she opens the front door and checks up and down the hallway. There's no sign of him. She can do this. She wasn't brave enough the first time she cleaned here alone. She was afraid he might return. But since he left and said good-bye, she'll take the risk.

She rushes down the hallway into the living room and sits at the piano, pausing to enjoy the moment. Black and shiny, it's lit up by the impressive chandelier that hangs above it. Her fingers trace the golden lyre logo and the words beneath.

STEINWAY & SONS

On the rest there's a pencil and the same half-finished composition that has been sitting there since the first day she came to the apartment with Krystyna. As she studies the pages, the notes sound through her head, a sad lament, lonely and full of melancholy, unresolved and unfinished in hues of pale blue and gray. She tries to connect the profound and reflective tune to the indolent but handsome naked man she saw that morning. Perhaps he's a composer. She glances across the wide room to the antique desk in the corner cluttered with his computer, a synthesizer, and what might be a couple of sound mixers. Yes, they look like they belong to a composer. And then there's the wall of old records that she has to dust; he's certainly an avid music collector.

She pushes these thoughts aside as she stares down at the keys. How long has it been since she last played? Weeks? Months? A sudden, acute feeling of anguish steals the air from her lungs, making her gasp, and tears form in her eyes.

No. Not here. She will not break down here. She clutches the piano in an effort to fight off her heartache and her homesickness, realizing it's been more than a month since she last played. So much has happened since then.

She shudders and takes a deep breath, forcing a feeling of calm. She stretches her fingers and strokes the keys.

White. Black.

The mere touch soothes her. She wants to savor this precious moment and lose herself in her music. Gently, she pushes down the keys, sounding an E-minor chord. The sound rings clear and strong, a bold and verdant green, the color of the Mister's eyes, and Alessia's heart fills with hope. The Steinway is tuned to perfection. She launches into her warm-up piece, "Le Coucou"; the keys move with ease and a smooth, fluid action. Her fingers fly across the keyboard vivace, and the stress, fear, and sorrow of the last few weeks fade and finally mute as she loses herself in the colors of the music.

One of the Trevelyan London homes is on Cheyne Walk, a brisk stroll from my flat. Built in 1771 by Robert Adam, Trevelyan House had been Kit's home since our father died. For me it holds many childhood memories—some happy, some less so—and now it's mine to do with as I wish. Well, it's held in trust for me. Faced once more with my new reality, I shake my head and pull the collar of my coat up to fight the biting cold, cold that seems to emanate not from outside but from within me.

What the hell am I supposed to do with this house?

It's been two days since I saw Caroline, and I know she's furious with me, but I will have to face her sooner or later. Standing on the doorstep, I contemplate whether or not to use my key. I've always had a key to the house, but to burst in unannounced feels like an intrusion.

Taking a deep breath, I knock twice. After a few moments, the front door opens and Blake, the family's butler since before I was born, answers the door.

"Lord Trevethick," he says, bowing his balding head and holding open the door.

"Is that really necessary, Blake?" I ask as I stride into the entrance hall. Blake remains mute as he takes my coat. "How's Mrs. Blake?"

"She's well, my lord. Greatly saddened by recent events, though."

"As are we all. Is Caroline at home?"

"Yes, my lord. I believe Lady Trevethick is in the drawing room."

"Thank you. I'll see myself up."

"Of course. Would you like some coffee?"

"Yes, please. Oh, and, Blake, as I said last week, 'sir' will suffice."

Blake pauses, then gives me a nod. "Yes, sir. Thank you, sir."

I want to roll my eyes. I was the Honourable Maxim Trevelyan and referred to as "Master Maxim" here. "Lord" applied only to my father, then my brother. It will take me some time to get accustomed to my new title.

I bound up the wide staircase and along the landing into the drawing room. It's empty except for the overstuffed sofas and elegant Queen Anne furniture that has been in the family for generations. The drawing room opens onto a conservatory that has a spectacular view of the Thames, Cadogan Pier, and Albert Bridge. There I find Caroline, nestled in an armchair, wrapped in a cashmere shawl, and staring out the windows. She clutches a small blue handkerchief.

"Hi," I say as I stride in. Caroline turns a tearstained face toward me, her eyes red and puffy.

Shit.

"Where the fuck have you been?" she snaps.

"Caro," I begin, ready to placate her.

"Don't Caro me, you wanker," she snarls as she stands up, fists clenched.

Shit. She is really angry.

"What have I done now?"

"You know what you've done. Why haven't you answered my calls? It's been two days!"

"I've had a lot to think about, and I've been busy."

"You? Busy? Maxim, you wouldn't know busy if you tripped and stuck your dick in it."

I blanch and then laugh at the image.

Caroline relaxes a little. "Don't make me laugh when I'm angry with you." Her lips form a pout.

"You have a way with words." I open my arms, and she walks into my embrace.

"Why didn't you call?" she asks as she hugs me back, her anger dissipating.

"It's a lot to take on board," I whisper as I hold her. "I needed time to think."

"Alone?"

I don't answer. I don't want to lie. Monday night I was with, um . . . Heather, and last night it was . . . What was her name? Dawn.

Caroline sniffs and steps out of my arms. "I thought as much. I know you too well, Maxim. What was she like?"

I shrug as an image of Heather's lips around my cock comes to mind.

Caroline sighs. "You're such a whore," she says with her usual disdain.

How can I deny it?

Caroline of all people knows about my nocturnal pursuits. She has a collection of choice epithets to describe me and regularly berates me for my promiscuity.

Yet she still went to bed with me.

"You're whoring your way through your grief while I had to endure dinner with Daddy and the Stepsow alone. It was awful," she quips. "And last night I was lonely."

"I'm sorry," I answer, because I can't think of what else to say.

"You saw the lawyers?" She changes the subject, giving me a direct look.

I nod, and I have to acknowledge that this is another reason I've been avoiding her.

"Oh, no," she whimpers. "You look so grave. I've got nothing, have I?" Her eyes are wide with fear and grief.

I place my hands on her shoulders and break it to her gently. "Everything is in trust for me as heir."

Caroline lets out a sob and covers her mouth as tears fill her eyes. "Damn him," she whispers.

"Don't worry, we'll work something out," I murmur, and hold her once more.

"I loved him," she says, her voice small and quiet, like a child's.

"I know. We both did." Though I know she also loved Kit's title and his wealth.

"You're not going to evict me?"

I take the handkerchief from her hand and wipe each of her eyes. "No, of course not. You're my brother's widow and my best friend."

"But that's all?" She gives me a watery but bitter smile, and I kiss her forehead in lieu of answering her question.

"Your coffee, sir," Blake says from the entrance to the conservatory.

Immediately I drop my arms and step away from Caroline. Blake enters, his face expressionless, and he's holding a tray laden with cups, milk, a silver coffeepot, and my favorite biscuits—plain chocolate digestives.

"Thank you, Blake," I respond, trying to ignore the slow flush I feel creeping up my neck.

Brazen this out.

Blake places the tray on the table beside the sofa. "Will that be all, sir?"

"For now, thank you." My tone is sharper than I intended.

Blake exits the room, and Caroline pours the coffee. My shoulders slump with relief at Blake's departure. And I hear my mother's voice ringing in my head: *Not in front of the staff.*

I'm still holding Caroline's damp handkerchief. I stare at it and frown, recalling a fragment from a dream I had last night—or was it this morning? A young woman, an angel? Possibly the Virgin Mary or a nun in blue standing in my bedroom doorway watching over me as I slept.

What the hell does that mean?

I'm not religious.

"What?" asks Caroline.

I shake my head. "Nothing," I murmur, taking the cup of coffee she offers and giving her back her handkerchief.

"Well, I might be pregnant," she says.

What? I blanch.

"Kit. Not you. You're too bloody careful."

Damn right. The ground seems to shift beneath my feet.

Kit's heir!

Could this be any more complicated?

"Well, if you are, we'll figure out what to do," I reply, feeling at once a moment of relief that all this responsibility might pass to Kit's child, but also a sudden and overwhelming sense of loss.

The earldom is mine. For now.

Shit. Could this be any more confusing?

Chapter Three

My phone buzzes as I'm in the back of a black cab on my way to the office. It's Joe.

"Mate," he says. "How's it going?" He sounds somber, and I know he's referring to my frame of mind since Kit's death. I've not seen him since the funeral.

"I'm surviving."

"Fancy a bout?"

"I'd love to. But I can't. I have meetings all day."

"Earl shit?"

I laugh. "Yes. Earl shit."

"Maybe later in the week? My épée is getting rusty."

"Yes. I'd like that. Or perhaps a drink."

"Yeah, I'll see if Tom's around."

"Cool. Thanks, Joe."

"No worries, mate."

I hang up. My mood morose. I miss being able to do what the fuck I like. If I wanted to fence in the middle of the day, I could.

Joe is my sparring partner and one of my closest friends. Instead I have to go into the office and do some bloody work for a change.

Kit. I blame you.

The music is pounding at Loulou's. The bass reverberates through my chest. I like it this way. The noise level cuts down on unnecessary conversation. I make my way through the crowd to the bar. I need a drink and a warm, willing body.

I have spent the last day and a half in tedious meetings with the two fund managers who oversee the considerable Trevethick investment portfolio and the charitable trust; the estate managers from Cornwall, Oxfordshire, and Northumberland; the managing agent who handles the London properties; and with the developer who's remodeling the three mansion blocks in Mayfair. Oliver Macmillan, Kit's chief operating officer and his right-hand man, has attended all of them with me. Oliver and Kit had been friends since Eton; they'd both gone to the London School of Economics, until Kit dropped out to fulfill his aristocratic duty following the death of our father.

Oliver is slight, with a shock of unruly blond hair and eyes of an indeterminate color that miss nothing. I have never warmed to him. He's ruthless and ambitious, but he knows his way around a balance sheet and can deal with the numerous personnel who answer to the Earl of Trevethick.

I don't know how Kit managed it all and held down a fund-manager job in the City. But he was a smart, slick bastard.

Funny, too.

I miss him.

I order a Grey Goose and tonic. Maybe he succeeded because Macmillan had his back, and I wonder if Oliver's loyalty will extend to me or if he might take advantage of my naïveté while I try to come to terms with all my new responsibilities. I just don't know. But the fact is, I don't trust him, and I make a mental note to stay circumspect in my dealings with him.

The one bright spot in the last couple of days was a call from my agent telling me I have a job next week. I'd taken a great deal of pleasure in telling the old gorgon that for the foreseeable future I would no longer be available for modeling work.

Would I miss it?

I wasn't sure. Modeling could be mind-numbingly boring, but after I was sent down from Oxford, the work had gotten me out of bed and given me an excuse to stay in shape. I also got to meet hot, skinny women.

I take a slug of my drink and scan the room. That's what I want now: a hot, willing woman, skinny or otherwise.

It's Let's Fuck Thursday.

Her raucous laugh catches my attention, and our eyes meet. I see the appreciation and challenge in her gaze, and my cock stirs in anticipation. She has pretty hazel eyes, long brown glossy hair, and she's drinking shots. What's more, she looks sensational in the leather minidress and her thigh-high stiletto boots.

Yes. She'll do.

It's two in the morning when I let us both into my flat. I take Leticia's coat, and she turns immediately and wraps her arms around my neck. "Let's go to bed, Posh Boy," she whispers, and kisses me. Hard. No preliminaries. Her coat is still in my hands, and I have to steady myself against the wall to stop us both from falling. Her attack takes me by surprise. Perhaps she's more pissed than I thought. She tastes of lipstick and Jägermeister—an intriguing combination. I thread my fingers through her hair and tug, freeing my mouth.

"All good things, sweetheart," I chide against her lips. "Let me put your coat down."

"Fuck my coat," she says, and kisses me again. All tongue.

I'd rather fuck you.

"We're not going to make it to the bedroom at this rate." I put my hands on her shoulders and gently push her away.

"Let me see your place, then, model-slash-photographer-slash-DJ," she teases, her soft Irish accent a complete contrast to her direct manner. I wonder if she'll be as forthright in bed as I follow her down the hallway into the drawing room, her heels clicking on the wooden floor.

"Do you act, too? Great view, by the way," she says as she glances through the wall of glass that looks out over the Thames. "Nice piano," she adds, and turns to face me, her eyes alight with excitement. "Have you fucked on it?"

Lord, she has a foul mouth.

"Not recently." I dump her coat on the sofa. "Not sure I want to right now. I'd rather bed you." I ignore her jibe about my current lack of a stable career. I haven't told her I have an empire to run. She smiles, her lipstick smudged and no doubt smeared over my mouth. The thought displeases me, and I run my fingers over my lips. She saunters toward me and tugs the lapels of my jacket, forcing me forward.

"Okay, Posh Boy, show me what you can do." She puts her hands on my chest and rakes her nails over my sternum to the edge of my jacket.

Shit! It's almost painful. She has scarlet talons, not nails, talons that match her lipstick. She slides my jacket off my shoulders, letting it fall to the floor, and starts undoing the buttons on my shirt. The mood she's in, I'm relieved that she takes her time and doesn't just rip my shirt open—I like this shirt! Slipping it off me, she lets it fall to my feet and digs her nails into my shoulders. Deliberately.

"Ah!" I hiss in pain.

"Cool ink," she says as her hands travel from my shoulders down my arms and toward the waistband of my jeans, her nails leaving tracks across my stomach.

Ow! Boy, she's aggressive.

I grab her hand and tug her into my arms, kissing her roughly. "Let's go to bed," I say against her mouth, and before she can answer, I take her hand and haul her after me to the bedroom.

There she pushes me toward the bed and again rakes her nails over my belly as her fingers find the top button of my jeans.

Fuck! She likes it rough.

I flinch and catch her hands in front of her in a viselike grip, but in reality I'm avoiding her nails.

You want to play rough? I can, too.

"Play nice," I warn. "And you first!" I release her, moving her away so I have a good view. "Strip. Now," I order.

Tossing her hair over her shoulder, she puts her hands on her hips, her mouth set in an amused challenge.

"Go on," I urge.

Leticia's eyes darken, and she pauses. "Say please," she whispers.

I smirk. "Please."

She laughs. "I love your posh accent."

"It's just an accident of birth, sweetheart. Keep your boots on," I add.

She returns my smirk, reaches behind her, and casually unzips her tight leather dress. Wriggling her hips from side to side, she shimmies out of the dress and lets it slip down the length of her boots. I smile. She looks incredible. Slim, with small, firm breasts, she's wearing black French knickers and a matching bra and the thigh-high boots. Stepping out of her dress, she sashays toward me with a beckoning, sexy smile and grabs my hand. With surprising force she tugs me to the bed, then places her hands on my chest and pushes me hard so that I sprawl on top of the quilt.

"Take them off," she commands, and points to my trousers as she stands over me, placing her feet wide apart.

"You do it," I mouth.

She needs no further prompting and crawls up the bed to sit astride me, grinding down on my crotch. She drags her nails down my abdomen toward my fly.

Ow!

Fuck this! She's dangerous.

I sit up suddenly, taking her by surprise, and flip her onto her back, straddling her and pinning her arms down on either side of her head. She struggles beneath me, attempting to buck me off.

"Hey!" she protests, glaring up at me.

"I think you need to be restrained. You're dangerous." My voice is soft as I gauge her reaction.

This could go either way.

Her eyes widen, and I'm not sure if it's fear or excitement.

"Are you?" she whispers.

"Dangerous? Me? No. Not nearly as much as you." Releasing her, I reach over to the bedside cabinet and from a drawer take out a long silk restraint and a pair of leather cuffs. "Do you want to play?" I ask, holding up both implements. "Your choice."

She gazes up at me, pupils large with lust and anxiety.

"I won't hurt you," I reassure her. That's not my scene. "I'll just keep you in line." But the truth is, I'm worried she's going to hurt me.

A teasing, seductive smile tugs at her mouth. "The silk," she says.

I smile and toss the cuffs onto the floor: dominance as a form of self-defense. "Pick a safe word."

"Chelsea."

"Good choice."

I tie the silk around her left wrist and thread it through the slats of the bed's headboard, and then, taking her right hand, I deftly tie her right wrist to the other end of the restraint. With her arms outstretched, her nails are rendered harmless, and she looks fantastic.

"If you really misbehave, I'll blindfold you, too," I murmur.

She squirms. "Will you spank me?" Her voice is less than a whisper.

"If you play nice."

Oh, this is going to be fun.

• • •

She comes quickly and loudly. Screaming and straining against the silken straps.

I sit up between her thighs, my mouth slick and wet, and I flip her over and slap her arse.

"Hang in there," I mutter, and slip on a condom.

"Hurry up!"

Fuck, is she demanding!

"As you wish," I growl, and thrust inside her.

I watch the rise and fall of her breasts as she sleeps. Out of habit I go through my ritual of recalling everything I know about the woman I've just fucked. Twice. Leticia. Human-rights lawyer, sexually aggressive. Older than me. Likes to be restrained. Likes it a lot. But forthright, assertive women typically do, in my experience. She's a biter, screams on orgasm. Vocal. Diverting. . . . Exhausting.

I wake with a start. In my dream I'd been searching for something elusive, a vision that keeps appearing and disappearing, an ethereal vision in blue. Then, just as I'd glimpsed it, I'd fallen into a wide, deep abyss. I shudder.

What the hell was that about?

The pallid winter sun seeps through the windows as reflections from the Thames play on the ceiling. What has woken me?

Leticia.

Boy, she's an animal. She isn't asleep beside me, and I can't hear anyone in the shower. Perhaps she's left already. I listen carefully for any noise within the flat.

It's quiet. I grin. No awkward small talk. The day is looking up until I remember I have a lunch appointment with my mother and my sister. I groan and pull the covers over my head. They'll want to discuss the will.

Bloody hell.

"The Dowager," as Kit referred to her, is a formidable woman.

Why the fuck she hasn't gone back to New York, I don't know. Her life is based there, not here.

Something clatters to the floor somewhere in the apartment. I sit up.

Shit. Leticia is still here.

That means conversation. Reluctantly I haul myself out of bed, drag on my nearest pair of jeans, and go to find out if she's as wild in broad daylight as she is in the dark.

I pad down the hallway in my bare feet, but there's no one in the drawing room or the kitchen.

What the fuck?

I turn around at the kitchen entrance and halt. I'm expecting to see Leticia, but a slight young woman stands in the hallway staring at me. Her eyes are large and dark, reminding me of a startled doe, but she's dressed in a ghastly blue housecoat, cheap overwashed jeans, old trainers, and a blue headscarf that conceals her hair.

She says nothing.

"Hi. Who the hell are you?" I ask.

Chapter Four

Zot! He is here, and he is mad.

Alessia freezes as his blazing green eyes meet hers. Tall, lean, and half naked, he towers over her. His hair is an unruly chestnut mess with gold highlights that glint beneath the chandelier in the hallway. He is as broad-shouldered as she remembers, but the tattoo on his upper arm is far more intricate than she recalls; all she can distinguish is a wing. A smattering of hair on his chest tapers down over a toned stomach. Then resumes beneath his navel and travels farther down into his jeans. The tight black denim is ripped at the knee. But it's the hard line of his full lips and his eyes, the color of spring, in a handsome, unshaven face that make her look away. Her mouth dries, and she doesn't know if it's from nerves or . . . or . . . from the look of him.

He is so attractive!

Too attractive.

And he's half naked! But why is he so mad? Did she wake him?

No! He will send her away from the piano.

Panicked, she drops her gaze to the floor as she flounders for something to say and clutches the handle of the broom to keep her upright.

W ho the hell is this timid creature standing in my hall-way? I'm completely bemused. Have I seen her before? An image from a forgotten dream develops like a Polaroid in my memory, an angel in blue hovering at my bedside. But that was days ago. Could it have been her? And now she's here, rooted to the hallway floor, her impish face pale, her eyes downcast. Her knuckles grow whiter as she clasps the broom handle tighter and tighter, as if it's anchoring her to the Earth. The headscarf conceals her hair, and an oversize, old-fashioned nylon housecoat swamps her small frame. She looks totally out of place.

"Who are you?" I ask again, but in a softer tone, not wanting to alarm her. Wide eyes, the color of a fine espresso and framed by the longest lashes I've ever seen, look up at me, then back at the floor.

Shit!

One peek from her dark, fathomless eyes and I'm . . . unsettled. She's at least a head shorter than me, perhaps five feet five to my six feet two. Her features are delicate: high cheekbones, an upturned nose, clear fair skin, and pale lips. She looks like she needs a few days in the sun and a good hearty meal.

It's obvious that she's cleaning. But why her? Why here? Has she replaced my old daily? "Where's Krystyna?" I ask, growing a little frustrated at her silence. Perhaps she's Krystyna's daughter—or granddaughter.

She continues to stare at the floor, her brow furrowed. Her even white teeth chew at her upper lip as she refuses to meet my gaze.

Look at me, I will her. I want to reach forward and tilt her chin up, but as if she reads my mind, she raises her head. Her eyes meet mine, and her tongue darts out, and nervously she licks her upper lip. My whole body tightens in a hot, heavy rush as desire hits me like a demolition ball.

Fuck a duck!

I narrow my eyes as annoyance swiftly follows my desire. What the hell is wrong with me? Why does a woman I've never met have such an effect on me? It's irritating. Beneath fine arched brows, her eyes grow wider, and she takes a step back, fumbling with the broom so that it falls from her hands and clatters onto the floor. She bends with easy, economic grace to pick it up, and when she's standing once more, she fixates on the handle, a slow flush staining her cheeks as she mumbles something unintelligible.

Bloody hell! Am I intimidating the poor girl?

I don't mean to.

I'm annoyed at myself. Not her.

Or maybe it's another reason. "Perhaps you don't understand me," I say, more to myself, and I run a hand through my hair as I bring my body to heel. Krystyna's mastery of English extended to the words "yes" and "here," which often meant lots of gesticulating on my part when I needed her to undertake tasks that went beyond her usual cleaning routine. This girl is probably Polish, too.

"I am cleaner, Mister," she whispers, her eyes still downcast and her eyelashes fanned out above her luminous cheeks.

"Where's Krystyna?"

"She has returned to Poland."

"When?"

"Since last week."

This is news. Why the hell did I not know this? I liked Krystyna. She'd cleaned for me for three years and knew all my dirty little secrets. And I never got to say good-bye.

Maybe it's temporary. "Is she coming back?" I ask. The lines in the girl's forehead deepen, but she says nothing, though her eyes flick to my feet. For some unknown reason, this makes me feel self-conscious. Placing both hands on my hips, I step backward as my bewilderment grows. "How long have you been here?"

She responds in a breathless, barely audible voice. "In England?"

"Look at me, please," I ask. Why is she so reluctant to look up?

Her slim fingers tighten around the broom again, as if she might brandish it as a weapon, then she swallows and raises her head, regarding me with large, liquid brown eyes. Eyes I could drown in. My mouth dries as my body comes to attention again.

Fuck!

"I have been in England since three weeks." Her voice is clearer and stronger, with an accent I don't recognize, and as she speaks, she pushes her small chin toward me in defiance. Her lips are now rosy, her bottom lip plumper than her top, and she licks the upper one again.

Hell!

I'm aroused once more. I take another step away from her. "Three weeks?" I mumble, baffled by my reaction to her.

Why is this happening to me?

What is it about her?

She's fucking exquisite, the still, small voice roars in my head.

Yes. For a woman dressed in a nylon housecoat, she's hot.

Concentrate. She hasn't answered my question. "No. I meant how long have you been here in my flat."

Where does this girl come from? I rack my brain. Mrs. Blake had organized Krystyna through some contact she had. But Krystyna's replacement remains silent.

"You speak English?" I ask, willing her to speak. "What's your name?"

She frowns, looking at me like I'm an idiot. "Yes. I speak English. My name is Alessia Demachi. I have been in your apartment since ten o'clock this morning."

Wow. She really does speak English.

"Right. Well. How do you do, Alessia Demachi. My name is . . ."

What should I say? Trevethick? Trevelyan?

"Maxim."

She gives me a brief nod, and for a moment I think she might curtsy, but she stands still, grasping the broom and stripping me naked with her anxious gaze.

Suddenly I feel like the walls of the hallway are closing in and suffocating me. I want to flee from this stranger and her soul-searching eyes. "Well, good to meet you, Alessia. You'd better get on and clean, then." As an afterthought, I add, "In fact, you can change the sheets on my bed." I wave in the general direction of my bedroom. "You know where the linen is kept, don't you?"

She nods again but still doesn't move.

"I'm going to the gym," I mutter, though why I'm explaining myself to her I don't know.

As he stalks back down the hallway toward his bedroom, Alessia wilts against the broom and takes a deep, relieved breath. She watches the flex and pull of the muscles on his back—right down to the two dimples that show just above the waistband of his jeans. It's a distracting sight—very distracting. He's even more distracting upright than when he was lying down. He disappears into his room and she closes her eyes, her heart sinking.

He didn't ask her to leave, but he may call Magda's friend Agatha and ask her to find someone else to clean his place. He seemed so cross that she had disturbed him, and then he became angrier still.

Why?

Alessia frowns and tries to quell her rising panic as she glances into the living room at the piano.

No. That cannot happen. She will beg him to let her stay if she must. She doesn't want to leave. She can't leave. The piano is her one source of escape. Her only happiness.

And then there's the Mister himself. His honed stomach, his bare feet, and his intense eyes sear her imagination. He has the face of an angel, the body of . . . well . . . She blushes. She should not think of such things.

He's so handsome.

No. Stop. Concentrate.

With frantic strokes she continues to sweep the wooden floor of nonexistent dirt. She will have to be the best cleaner he's ever had, so he won't want to replace her. With her mind resolved, she goes into the living room to sweep, tidy, and polish.

Ten minutes later she hears the front door slam as she finishes plumping the black cushions on the L-shaped couch.

Good. He has gone.

She goes straight to his bedroom to strip the bed. The room is untidy as usual—clothes and strange cuffs on the floor, curtains half open, and the bedding a tangled mess—but she collects all the clothes and strips the bed quickly. She wonders why there's a wide silk ribbon tied to the headboard but unwinds it and places it on his nightstand next to the cuffs. As she throws a clean white sheet on the bed, she wonders what these items are for. She has no idea and doesn't want to hazard a guess. She makes the rest of the bed, then ventures into his bathroom to clean.

I run like I've never run before. I complete my five miles on the treadmill in record time, but I can't stop playing the conversation with the new daily in my mind.

Bugger. Bugger. Bugger.

I bend down and place my hands on my knees, trying to catch my breath. I am running from my fucking daily—cleaner, whatever she calls herself—escaping from her big brown eyes.

No. I'm running from my reaction to her.

Those eyes are going to haunt me for the rest of the day. Standing, I wipe the sweat from my brow, and a vision of her in that headscarf on her knees in front of me comes unwelcome to my mind.

My body clenches.

Again.

And this is just at the thought of her.

Fuck.

Angrily, I rub the sweat off my face with a towel and decide to do some weights. Yes. That should get her out of my mind. I pick up two of the heavier dumbbells and start my routine.

Of course, doing weights gives me space to think. In all honesty, I'm confused by my reaction to her. I can't remember meeting anyone who's had that kind of effect on me.

Perhaps it's stress.

Yes. That's the most logical explanation. I'm grieving Kit's loss and dealing with the aftermath.

Kit, you're a bastard for leaving me with all this responsibility.

It's overwhelming. *Fucking overwhelming.*

I push all thoughts of Kit and *her* out of my mind as I concentrate on my workout and count through my biceps curls.

And I've got lunch with my mother in two hours.

Shit.

Alessia is in the laundry room moving wet clothes into the dryer when she hears the front door slam again.

No! He is back.

Glad that she's hidden away in the smallest room in the apartment, she sets up the ironing board and starts ironing the few garments that are ready. Surely he will not come in here. When she finishes the fifth shirt, she hears the door slam again, and she knows that she's on her own once more. It irks her that he's not shouted a good-bye like he did when he thought she was Krystyna, but she shakes off the feeling and finishes the ironing as quickly as she can.

Once done, she goes to check his bedroom to see if he has left it in a mess. Sure enough, his gym clothes are scattered on the floor. Gingerly, she picks up each item. They are all damp with his sweat, but to her surprise she doesn't find this as repellent as she did before she met him. She places the items in his laundry basket and checks the bathroom. The fresh, clean scent of his soap hangs in the air. Closing her eyes, she inhales, and suddenly she's transported back to the tall evergreens that surround her parents' house in Kukës. She savors the fragrance, ignoring her pang of homesickness. London is her home now.

She wipes down the sink and is finished with half an hour to spare. She runs straight to the living room and sits down in front of the piano. As her fingers caress the keys, the strains of Bach's Prelude in C-sharp Major fill the apartment, the notes dancing in vibrant colors into the corners of the room and soothing her troubled soul.

I stride into my mother's favorite restaurant on Aldwych. I'm early, but I don't give a fuck. I need a drink, not only to forget my brush with the new daily but I need some liquid fortification to face my mother.

"Maxim!" I turn, and behind me is the one woman in the world I adore. Maryanne, my younger sister by a year, is walking through the foyer. Her eyes, the same shade as mine, light up when I turn to face her, and she throws her arms around my neck, her red hair flying into my face because she's only a few inches shorter than me.

"Hey, M.A., I've missed you," I say as I hug her.

"Maxie." Her voice catches in her throat.

Shit. Not here.

I hug her harder, willing her not to cry, and I'm surprised by the raw emotion that burns my throat. She sniffs, and her eyes are red-rimmed when I release her. This is not like her. She usually takes after our mother, who keeps her emotions under ruthless control. "I still can't believe he's gone," she says as she clutches a tissue.

"I know, me neither. Let's sit and get a drink." I take her elbow, and we follow the hostess into the large wood-paneled restaurant. The place has a classic old-fashioned feel: brass lamps, dark green leather upholstery, crisp white linen, and sparkling crystal glasses. The atmosphere buzzes with the chatter of businessmen and -women and the clatter of cutlery on fine china. I focus on the sight of the hostess's shapely backside swathed in a tight pencil skirt and the sound of her stiletto heels clicking on the polished tiled floor as she shows us to our table. I hold out Maryanne's chair, and we sit down.

"Two Bloody Marys," I say to the hostess as she hands us each a menu and gives me a coy look, which I don't return. She might have a fine arse and a cute smile, but I'm not in the mood to play. I'm preoccupied by my encounter with my daily and the memory of anxious dark eyes. I frown, dismissing the thought and turn my full attention to my sister as the hostess leaves with a disappointed pout.

"When did you get back from Cornwall?" I ask.

"Yesterday."

"How's the Dowager?"

"Maxim! You know she hates that term."

I give her an exaggerated sigh. "Okay, how's the Mothership?"

Maryanne glares at me for a moment, but then her face falls. *Shit.*

"Sorry," I mumble, chastened.

"She's really shaken up, but it's hard to tell. You know what she's like." Maryanne's eyes cloud, and she looks troubled. "I think there's something she's not telling us."

I nod. I know only too well. My mother rarely reveals a chink in her polished armor. She hadn't wept at Kit's funeral; she'd been the epitome of grace under fire. Brittle but gracious, as always. I hadn't wept either. I'd been too busy nursing one hell of a hangover.

I swallow and change the subject. "When do you go back to work?"

"Monday," Maryanne answers with a small, sad twist of her mouth.

Of all the Trevelyan children, it's Maryanne who has excelled academically. From Wycombe Abbey School, she'd gone up to read medicine at Corpus Christi, Oxford, and is now a junior doctor at the Royal Brompton Hospital, specializing in cardio-thoracic medicine. She had followed her vocation, a calling that was born the day our father suffered a massive coronary and died from a heart attack. She was fifteen years old—and she wanted to save him. Our father's death rocked each of us differently, and Kit most of all, given that he'd had to drop out of college and assume the earldom. Me, I lost my only parental ally.

"How's Caro?" she asks.

"Grieving. Pissed off that Kit didn't leave her anything in his will, stupid bastard," I growl.

"Who's a stupid bastard?" A clipped mid-Atlantic voice demands. Rowena, Dowager Countess of Trevethick, towers above us, auburn-haired, groomed, and composed in her immaculate navy Chanel suit and pearls.

I stand. "Rowena," I say, and give her a detached peck on her upturned cheek, then hold out her chair for her to sit.

"Is that any way to greet your grieving mother, Maxim?" Rowena scolds as she sits down and places her Birkin handbag on the floor beside her. She reaches across the table and clasps Maryanne's hand. "Hello, darling, I didn't hear you go out."

"I just needed some fresh air, Mother," Maryanne replies as she returns our mother's squeeze.

Rowena, Countess of Trevethick, kept her title in spite of her divorce from our father. She spends most of her time between New York, where she lives and likes to play, and London where she edits *Dernier Cri*, the glossy women's magazine.

"I'll have a glass of the Chablis," she says to the waiter as he delivers two Bloody Marys to the table. She arches a brow in disapproval as we both take long sips.

She is still impossibly slim and impossibly beautiful, especially through a lens. She was the "It Girl" of her generation and had become the muse of many a photographer, including my father, the Eleventh Earl of Trevethick. He was devoted to her; his title and money had seduced her into marriage, but when she left him, he never recovered. Four years after their divorce, he died of a broken heart.

I study her through hooded eyes. Her face is baby smooth—no doubt as a result of her latest chemical peel. The woman is obsessed with maintaining her youth, and she only deviates from her rigorous diet of vegetable juices or whatever her latest food fad is with the odd glass of wine. There is no doubting that my mother is beautiful, but she's as duplicitous as she is stunning— and my poor father paid the price.

"I understand you've met with Rajah," she says directly to me.

"Yes."

"And?" She glares at me in her slightly myopic way, because she's far too vain to wear glasses.

"It's all in trust to me."

"And Caroline?"

"Nothing."

"I see. Well, we can't let the poor girl starve."

"We?" I ask.

Rowena flushes. "You," she says, her voice frigid. "You can't let the poor girl starve. On the other hand, she has her trust fund, and when her father shuffles off his mortal coil, she'll inherit a fortune. Kit chose wisely in that regard."

"Unless her stepmother disinherits her," I retort, and take another much-needed sip of Bloody Mary.

My mother purses her lips. "Why don't you set her to work— maybe the Mayfair development? She has a good eye for interior design, and she'll need the distraction."

"I think we should let Caroline decide what she wants to do." I fail to keep the resentment out of my voice. This is my mother's usual high-handed manner in dealing with the family that she deserted many years ago.

"Are you happy with her staying at Trevelyan House?" she asks, ignoring my tone.

"Rowena, I'm not about to make her homeless."

"Maximilian, would you mind addressing me as 'Mother'!"

"When you start behaving like one, I'll take it into consideration."

"Maxim," Maryanne warns, and her eyes flash a fiery green. Feeling like a rebuked child, I clamp my mouth shut and scrutinize the menu before I say something I'll regret.

Rowena continues, ignoring my rudeness, "We'll need to finalize all the details for the memorial service. I was thinking we could do this just before Easter. I'll get one of my lead writers to do Kit's eulogy, unless—" She pauses as her voice cracks, causing both me and Maryanne to look up from our menus in surprise. Her eyes grow moist, and for the first time since she buried her eldest child, she looks her age. She clutches a monogrammed handkerchief and brings it to her lips as she composes herself.

Bugger.

I feel like a shit. She's lost her eldest son . . . her favorite child.

"Unless?" I prompt.

"You or Maryanne could write it," she whispers with an uncharacteristic, beseeching look at both of us.

"Sure," Maryanne says. "I'll do it."

"No. I should do it. I'll expand on the eulogy I did for his funeral. Shall we order lunch?" I ask, wanting to change the subject and feeling uncomfortable at my mother's unusual display of emotion.

Rowena picks at her salad while Maryanne chases the last of her omelet around her plate with her knife and fork.

"Caroline said she might be pregnant," I announce as I take another mouthful of chateaubriand.

Rowena's head comes up quickly, and she narrows her eyes.

"She did say they were trying," Maryanne adds.

"Well, if she is, it might be the only chance I get to have a grandchild and for this family to secure the earldom for another generation." Rowena casts an accusing look at both of us.

"That would make you a grandmother," I say dryly, disregarding the rest of her comment. "How will that go down with your latest cute conquest in New York?"

Rowena's propensity for young men, sometimes younger than her youngest son, is renowned. She glowers at me as I take another bite of my steak, but I hold her glare, daring her to say anything. Strangely, for the first time ever, I feel as though I have the upper hand with my mother. It's a novelty; so much of my adolescence was spent striving and failing to gain her approval.

Maryanne scowls at me. I shrug and slice another piece of delicious steak and pop it into my mouth.

"Neither you nor Maryanne shows any sign of settling down, and God forbid that the estates should pass to your father's brother. Cameron's a lost cause," Rowena grumbles, choosing to ignore my insolence. My encounter with Alessia Demachi springs unbidden into my head, and I frown. I glance at Maryanne, and she's frowning, too, and staring at her uneaten food.

Oh?

"What about the young man you met when you were skiing in Whistler?" Rowena asks Maryanne.

It's dusk when I return to my flat. Drained and a little drunk, I have endured a forensic cross-examination from my mother on the status of all the estates, the London leasehold and rental properties, and the apartment refurbishment in Mayfair, not to mention the value of the Trevethick portfolio. I wanted to remind her that it's none of her fucking business, but I feel a novel sense of pride that I was able to answer each of her questions in detail. Even Maryanne was impressed. Oliver Macmillan had briefed me well.

As I flop down on the sofa in front of the large TV in my spotless, empty flat, my mind wanders as it has all day, back to the conversation I had this morning with the dark-eyed daily.

Where is she now?

How long will she be in the UK?

What does she look like without the shapeless housecoat on?
What color is her hair? Dark like her eyebrows?
How old is she? She looks young. Too young, maybe.
Too young for what?

I shift uncomfortably in my seat and click through the TV channels. Perhaps my reaction to her was a one-off. I mean, she looked like a nun. Maybe I have a thing for nuns. I laugh to myself at the ridiculous thought. My phone buzzes, and it's a text from Caroline.

How was lunch?

Tiring. The Dowager
was her usual self.

I'll be the dowager if you get married!

Why is she telling me this? Besides, I have no interest in marrying anyone. Well . . . not at the moment. My mother's tirade about grandchildren comes to mind, and I shake my head. Kids. No. Just no. Not yet anyway.

That's not happening anytime soon!

Good.
What are you doing?

Home watching TV.

Are you OK?
Can I come over?

The last thing I want or need is Caroline messing with my head or any other part of my anatomy.

I'm not alone.

It's a small white lie.

You're still whoring, I see. :P

You know me well.
Good night, Caro.

I stare at the phone waiting for her response, but it remains silent so I turn my attention back to the television, only to find there's nothing I want to watch. I switch it off.

Restless, I sit down at my desk and open Mail on the iMac. There are a few e-mails from Oliver about various estate issues that I don't want to deal with on a Friday evening. They can wait until Monday. I check the time, and I'm surprised that it's only 8:00 P.M., too early to go out, and the thought of a crowded club doesn't appeal to me right now.

Feeling cooped up but reluctant to leave my flat, I wander over to the piano and take a seat. A composition I'd started weeks and weeks ago sits neglected on the rest. I follow the notes, the melody sounding in my head, and before I know it, my fingers are pressing the keys and playing the tune. The image of a young girl in blue with dark, dark eyes that strip me bare pops into my head. New notes form in a flurry, and I continue to improvise, playing beyond where my composition had stalled.

Bloody hell!

In a rare rush of excitement, I stop, fish my phone out of my pocket, and find the voice-memo app. Hitting the RECORD button, I begin again. The notes ring out through the room. Evocative. Melancholic. Stirring me. Inspiring me.

I am cleaner, Mister.

Yes. I speak English. My name is Alessia Demachi.

Alessia.

When I look at my watch, it's after midnight. Stretching my arms above my head, I examine the manuscript in front of me. It's complete. I've written a whole piece, and I am overwhelmed with a sense of achievement. How long have I been trying to do this? And all it took was meeting my new daily. I shake my head, and for once I go to bed early and alone.

Chapter Five

It's with trepidation that Alessia unlocks the door to the apartment with the piano. Her heart sinks when she's met with the unnerving silence of the alarm. The hush means that the confusing, green-eyed Mister is in residence. He has invaded her dreams ever since she'd seen him sprawled naked on his bed. But during her weekend, in quiet moments, all she'd been able to think about was him. She doesn't understand why, though perhaps it's the brief, penetrating stare he gave her when he towered over her in the hallway or because he's handsome and tall and lean, with dimples on his back, above his muscled, athletic behind—

Stop!

Her wayward thoughts are out of control.

Quietly, she slips off her wet boots and socks, then scampers in her bare feet down the hallway through the kitchen. The counter is littered with beer bottles and takeaway boxes, but Alessia scuttles into the safety of the laundry room. She props her boots on the radiator along with her socks in the hope they might dry out before she leaves.

Peeling off her wet hat and gloves, she hangs them on the hook beside the boiler, then removes the anorak that Magda gave her. She places it on the same hook and frowns as water drips onto the tiled floor. Her jeans are soaked from the torrential rain, too. She shivers as she removes them and struggles into her housecoat, grateful that the plastic bag has kept it dry. The hem falls to below her knees, so that she's not immodest without her jeans. Peeking into the kitchen, she checks that he's not there. He's probably still asleep, so she pops her sodden jeans into the dryer and switches it on. At least they'll be dry when she goes home. Her feet are red and itch with cold, so she grabs a dry towel from the pile of clean laundry and rubs them both vigorously, massaging life back into her toes. Once they're warm, she slips on her sneakers.

"Alessia?"

Zot!

The Mister is awake! What does he want?

As quickly as her chilled fingers will let her, she pulls her scarf from the plastic bag and ties it around her head, conscious that her braided hair is also wet. Taking a deep breath, she exits the laundry room to find him standing in the kitchen. She wraps her arms around herself, trying to find some warmth.

"Hi," he says, and smiles.

Alessia glances at him. His smile is dazzling, lighting up his handsome face and his emerald eyes. She looks away, blinded by his good looks and embarrassed by her creeping blush.

But she feels a little warmer.

He had been so cross the last time she saw him—what has brought about this change of heart?

"Alessia?" he says again.

"Yes, Mister," she answers, keeping her eyes lowered. At least he is dressed this time.

"I just wanted to say hi."

She peeks up at him but doesn't understand what he wants. His smile isn't as broad this time, and his brow is furrowed.

"Hi," she says, uncertain what's expected of her.

He nods and shuffles from one foot to the other, hesitant. She thinks he might say something further, but he turns and leaves the kitchen.

W hat an idiot I am! I mimic "Hi" to myself in ridicule. I've thought of nothing but this girl all weekend, and the best I can come up with is, "I just wanted to say hi?"

What the fuck is wrong with me?

I wander back to my bedroom and notice a trail of wet footprints on the hallway floor.

Did she walk barefoot in the rain? Surely not!

My room is gloomy, and the view across the Thames is drab and uninspiring. The rain is lashing down outside. It had been pelting against the window early this morning and the noise had woken me. *Shit.* She must have walked through this atrocious weather. Again I wonder where she lives and how far she has to come. I had hoped to engage her in some conversation this morning to find out these details, but I can tell I make her uncomfortable.

Is it me or is it men in general?

It's a troubling thought. Maybe *I'm* the one who's uncomfortable. After all, she chased me out of the flat last week and the idea that I fled to avoid her is disconcerting. I resolve not to let it happen again.

The fact is, she's inspired me. The whole weekend I've immersed myself in my music. It's provided a distraction from all my newfound and unwanted responsibility and a respite from my grief—or maybe I've found a way to channel my grief . . . I don't know. I have three pieces completed, sketchy ideas for two more, and I'm tempted to put lyrics to one of them. I've ignored my

phone, my e-mail—everyone, and for once in my life I've found
solace in my own company. It's been a revelation. Who knew I
could be so productive? What I don't understand is why she's
affected me like this when we've only exchanged a few words. It
doesn't make sense to me, but I don't want to overthink it.

I pick up my phone from the bedside table and look down at
the bed. The bedding is in complete disarray.

Bloody hell, I'm a slob.

Hastily, I make the bed. From the pile of clothes discarded on
my sofa, I grab a black-hooded sweatshirt and slip it on over my
T-shirt. It's chilly. With wet feet she's probably cold, too. In the
hallway I stop and turn the thermostat up by a few degrees. I don't
like the idea of her feeling the cold.

She comes out of the kitchen carrying an empty laundry basket and a plastic caddy full of cleaning fluids and cloths. Head
down, she walks right past me toward my bedroom. I regard her
retreating figure in the shapeless housecoat: long pale legs, a gentle sway of slim hips . . . are those bright pink underpants I can see
through the nylon? From beneath the headscarf a rich brunette
plait snakes down her back to just above the line of her pink
underwear, and it swings from side to side as she walks. I know
I should look away, but I'm distracted by her underwear. They
cover her backside and come up to her waist. They are possibly
the largest knickers I've seen on a woman. And my body stirs like
I'm a thirteen-year-old boy.

Fuck! I groan inwardly, feeling like a pervert, and resist the
urge to follow her. Instead I head into the drawing room, where I
sit down at my computer to work through my e-mails from Oliver
and ignore my lust and my daily, Alessia Demachi.

Alessia is surprised to find that his bed has been made. Every
time she's been to his apartment, this room has always been
a mess. There is still a pile of clothes on the sofa, but it looks

tidier than she's ever seen it. She opens the curtains fully and stares out at the river. "Thames." She whispers the word aloud, her voice wavering a little.

It's dark and gray like the naked trees on the opposite bank . . . not like the Drin. Not like home. Here it's urban and crowded, so crowded. Back at home she was surrounded by fertile countryside and snowcapped mountains. She sweeps away the painful thought of home. She is here to do a job—a job she wants because it comes with the added bonus of the piano. She wonders if he's going to be here all day, and the thought that he might bothers her. His presence will keep her from playing her favorite pieces.

But on the plus side, she gets to see him.

The man who's been dominating her dreams.

She has to stop thinking about him. *Now.* With a heavy heart, she begins to hang some of the scattered clothes in his walk-in closet. Those that she thinks need washing she places in the laundry basket.

The aroma of evergreen and sandalwood lingers in his bathroom. It's a pleasant, masculine scent. She takes a moment to inhale deeply and savor it like she did before. His striking eyes come to mind . . . and his broad shoulders . . . and flat belly. She sprays the bathroom mirror with Windolene and rubs energetically.

Stop! Stop! Stop!

He's her employer, and he would never be interested in her. After all, she's just his cleaner.

Her last job in his bedroom is to empty the trash. To her disbelief she finds the basket empty. There are no used condoms. She places it back beside his nightstand, and for some inexplicable reason the empty basket makes her smile.

Gathering up the laundry and her cleaning materials, she gazes for a moment at the two monochrome photographs on the wall. Both are nudes. In one a woman is kneeling, her skin pale and translucent. The soles of her feet, her behind, and the graceful curve of her back are all visible, and she holds her blond hair piled up on her head; a few stray tresses kiss her neck. The model, from this angle anyway, is beautiful. The second photograph is a close-up and shows the contour of a woman's neck, her hair swept aside, and the arch of her spine from the first few vertebrae down to her backside. Her ebony skin is luminous, caressed by the light. She's stunning. Alessia sighs. Judging by these photographs, he must like women, and she wonders if he is the photographer. Maybe one day he might take her photograph. She shakes her head at her fanciful thoughts and returns to the kitchen to tackle the chaos of take-away boxes, empty beer bottles, and washing-up.

I've set aside all the condolence letters and e-mails to answer at a later date—I cannot face them yet. And how the fuck did Kit manage to get his head around farming subsidies and animal husbandry and all the other crap that goes with cultivating and grazing thousands of acres of land? For a fleeting moment, I wish I'd taken farm management or business studies at university, rather than fine art and music.

Kit had been reading economics at the LSE when our father died. Ever the dutiful son, he'd dropped out of the LSE and enrolled in the Duchy of Cornwall's university to study farming and estate management. With thirty thousand acres to oversee, I now understand that it was a sensible decision. Kit was always sensible, except when it came to riding his motorbike in the middle of winter through Trevethick's freezing lanes. I put my head in my hands as I remember his broken body lying in the mortuary.

Why, Kit, why? I ask for the thousandth time.

The worsening weather through the glass wall reflects my mood. I stand and walk over to look at the view. On the river there are a couple of barges heading in opposite directions, a police launch cruising east, and the river bus heading to Cadogan Pier. I scowl at the scene. During all the time I've lived this close to the pier, I've never taken the river bus. As a child I'd always hoped my mother would take me and Maryanne, but it never happened. She was always too busy. Always. And she never instructed our various nannies to take us. That's another grievance I have against Rowena. Of course, Kit wasn't with us then—he was already at boarding school.

Shaking my head, I walk around the piano and spy the sheet music I've been working on all weekend. The sight of the pages lifts my mood, and to take a break from my computer, I sit down to play.

O f the three kitchens Alessia cleans, this is her favorite. The wall, base cupboards and worktops are made of pale blue glass that is easy to wipe down. It's sleek and uncluttered—so different from the haphazard rural kitchen of her parents' home. She checks the oven, just in case the Mister has baked something, but she finds it's still pristine. Alessia suspects it has never been used.

She is drying the last plate when the music begins. She stops, recognizing the melody immediately. It's from the manuscript she's seen so many times on his piano, but the melody goes further than she's read, the notes soft and sad, falling in mournful blues and grays around her.

This she has to see.

With quiet care she places the plate on the worktop and sneaks out of the kitchen toward the living room. She peers in and sees him at the piano. Eyes closed, he's feeling the music, every note expressed on his face. As she watches him—his brow furrowed, head tilted, lips parted—he takes her breath away.

She's captivated.

By him.

By the music.

He's talented.

The piece is sad, full of longing and grief, and the notes echo through her head in subtler tones of blue and gray now that she's watching him. He really is the most handsome man she's ever seen. He's even more handsome than—*No!*

Ice-blue eyes stare at me. Furious.

No. Stop thinking about that monstrous man!

She halts the memory. It's too painful. And she concentrates on the Mister as the melancholic melody draws to its end. Before he spots her, Alessia tiptoes back to the kitchen—she doesn't want to make him cross again by being caught peeking and not working.

As she finishes washing the worktop, she replays his composition in her head. And now the only room she has left to clean is the living room—where he is.

Plucking up her courage, she grabs some polish and a cloth, ready to face him. She hovers at the entrance while he stares at his computer. He glances up and sees her, his face registering pleased surprise.

"It is okay, Mister?" she asks, and waves the can of polish in the direction of the room.

"Sure. Come in. Do what you need to do, Alessia. And my name's Maxim."

She gives him a quick smile and starts with the sofa, plumping the cushions and sweeping the odd crumb onto the floor with her hand.

W ell, this is distracting. . . .

How can I possibly concentrate with her moving about in such close proximity? I pretend to read the revised cost-to-complete for the remodeling of the Mayfair mansion blocks, but really I'm watching her. She moves with such easy, sensuous grace; bending over the sofa, lithe, toned arms reaching out and delicate, long-fingered hands cupping the crumbs from the seat cushions and brushing them off. A frisson runs through me, and my whole body is suddenly humming with a delicious tension, attuned to her presence in the room.

Could this be any more illicit? She's so close but so unattainable. She moves to plump the black scatter cushions on the couch, and her housecoat swings forward and stretches out across her backside, betraying the pink underwear beneath.

My breathing shallows, and I have to suppress a groan.

I'm a fucking pervert.

She finishes with the sofa, and her eyes stray toward me. I endeavor to look engrossed in the spreadsheet in my hand while the hairs on the back of my neck rise to attention. Taking the can of polish, she sprays some onto the cloth she's holding and heads to the piano. With another quick, anxious glance at me, she begins the slow process of buffing it to a brilliant shine. She stretches across it, the housecoat rising to above the backs of her knees.

Oh, God!

With a deliberate and even pace, she works her way around the piano, buffing and polishing, her breathing becoming faster and harder with the exertion. It's agonizing. I close my eyes and imagine how I could elicit the same response from her.

Shit. I cross my legs to hide my body's natural reaction. This is getting farcical. She's just cleaning my fucking piano.

She continues to dust the keyboard, though the keys make no sound. Her eyes shoot to me again, and I quickly look at the figures on the spreadsheet, which swim on the page, making no sense. When I dare to peer up at her, she's bending down, her face pensive, and she seems to be appraising the manuscript that sits on the music rest. She's looking at my composition, and her brow creases as if she's concentrating hard.

Can she read music?

Is she reading my score?

She looks up and meets my gaze. Her eyes widen with embarrassment, and her tongue escapes from her mouth to lick her upper lip as a rosy flush stains her cheeks.

Fuck.

Averting her eyes, she bobs down behind the piano, presumably to dust the legs or the stool.

I cannot bear it.

My phone rings, startling me. It's Oliver.

"Hi," I say into the phone, my voice hoarse, and I've never been so grateful for the interruption. I have to get out of the drawing room.

Hell, I promised myself that I wouldn't let her chase me out again.

"Trevethick?"

"Yes. Oliver. What is it?"

"We have a planning issue which I think is going to need your attention."

I stalk into the hallway as Oliver drones on about soffits and load-bearing walls within the Mayfair development.

When he leaves the room, it's as if a storm has passed overhead to wreak havoc elsewhere—in the hallway, perhaps. Alessia breathes a sigh of relief, grateful that he's gone. She hears him on the phone, his voice deep but melodious. She doesn't think she's ever been so acutely aware of someone else before.

She must stop thinking about him and concentrate on cleaning! She finishes dusting the piano, though she can't shake the uncanny feeling that he'd been watching her while she cleaned.

No. That's impossible.

Why would he be watching me?

Maybe he's checking on her cleaning capabilities like Mrs. Kingsbury. Alessia smiles at the silly idea and realizes she feels a great deal warmer than she did when she arrived. She isn't sure if the heat is within the room or within herself.

Warmed by his presence.

Her ludicrous train of thought elicits another smile. As he's out of the room, she seizes the opportunity to run and fetch the vacuum cleaner. The Mister is at the end of the hall leaning against the wall, all long legs and restless foot-tapping. He is talking into the phone in a low tone, but he watches her as she goes into the kitchen. She carries the vacuum cleaner into the living room to find him back at his desk but still talking on the phone. He rises when he sees her. "Hold on a minute, Oliver. Go ahead," he says to her, and he waves in the direction of the room, granting Alessia permission to vacuum as he leaves once more. He's undone the black hoodie he's wearing. Underneath she sees a gray V-neck T-shirt that has a black winged coronet and LA 1781 written on it. She flushes as she notices a little chest hair peeking through the top of the V. In her mind she hears her mother's voice scolding her in that tone she has: *Alessia! What are you doing?*

I am looking at a man, Mama.

A man I find attractive.

A man who makes my blood run hotter.

She imagines her mother's scandalized expression, and it makes her smile.

Oh, Mama, it's so different here in England. Men. Women. How they behave. Their interaction.

Alessia's mind goes to a darker place. To *him*.

No. Do not think of that man.

She's safe now, here in London with the Mister. And she must concentrate on keeping her job.

The vacuum cleaner is a make called Henry. Painted on his red cylinder are two big eyes and a smile. Whenever she sees Henry, she can't help but smile. She plugs him into the wall and begins to vacuum the rug and the wooden floor. Fifteen minutes later she's finished.

The Mister is not in the hallway as she pulls Henry back to his sleeping place in the laundry room cupboard. Alessia gives him a friendly pat before shutting the cupboard door and heading into the kitchen.

"Hi," the Mister says as he comes into the kitchen. "I have to go out. Your money is on the console table. You can lock up and set the alarm?"

She nods, so blinded by his broad smile that she has to stare down at the floor. But inside her, joy unfurls like a morning glory because he's leaving and she'll be able to play the piano.

He hesitates for a moment before holding out a large black umbrella.

"You're welcome to borrow this. It's still raining cats and dogs outside."

Cats and dogs?

Alessia is stunned. She glances quickly at his face, and her heart skips a beat at his warm smile and this generous gesture. She takes it from him. "Thank you," she whispers.

"You're welcome. Until Wednesday, Alessia," he says, and he leaves her alone in the kitchen. A few moments later, she hears the front door close.

Alessia stares at the umbrella. It's old-fashioned, with a wooden handle and a gold collar. It is exactly what she needs. Marveling at the Mister's generosity, she wanders into the living room and sits down at the piano. She props the umbrella up against the end of the keyboard and in honor of the terrible weather begins to play Chopin's "Raindrop" Prelude.

I bask and glow in the wake of Alessia's whispered "Thank you." I am ridiculously pleased with myself. I'm finally able to help her with this small gesture. I'm not accustomed to doing good deeds—though I probably have an ulterior motive for my kindness, a motive I don't want to analyze too deeply right now, as it might confirm I'm the shallow fucking bastard I think I am. Still, I feel good about this gesture, and it's a novel feeling.

With renewed energy I bypass the lift and fly down the main staircase to the ground floor. I'm reluctant to leave, but I have a meeting with Oliver and various contractors at the Mayfair development. Glancing down at my clothes, I hope they don't expect me to arrive in a suit. That's just not my style.

No. That was Kit's thing, and he had a wardrobe full of bespoke Savile Row suits to prove it.

Outside, I dodge the raindrops and hail a cab.

• • •

"I think that went well," says Oliver. I nod as we walk through the new limestone atrium of one of the rebuilt mansion blocks. Workmen in high-vis jackets and yellow hard hats go about their business around us as we make our way to the boarded front of the building. The dust in the air claws at my throat. I need a drink.

"You've got a flair for this, Trevethick. I think the contractor liked your suggestions."

"Oliver. It's Maxim. Please use my name. You used to. Before."

"Very good, my lord."

"For fuck's sake."

"Maxim." Oliver gives me a brief smile. "We'll need to get an interior designer to source everything for the show apartment, probably within the next month. I've compiled a list of three that Kit liked to use."

Kit? Kit was Kit. Why can't I be Maxim?

"Caroline might be a good idea," I say.

"Oh? Lady Trevethick?"

"My mother suggested her."

Oliver bristles.

Oh? What does Oliver have against Caroline? Or is he bridling against Rowena? She often has that effect on people.

"I'll talk to Caroline, but send me the names of the others and some examples of their work," I respond.

Oliver nods, and I remove my hard hat and hand it to him.

"Until tomorrow," he says, and pushes open the rickety door of the temporary wooden hoarding that hides the façade of the building.

The rain has finally stopped, but it's dark. I pull up the collar of my coat and wait for a cab while I decide whether to go to my club or go home.

Walking around the baby grand piano, I think about Alessia stretched across it while she was buffing the ebony to a glossy shine. It gleams under the chandelier. Who would have thought I'd be so attracted to a woman in a nylon housecoat and large pink panties?

How could she have worked her way under my skin in such a short time? I know nothing about her, except she's unlike any woman I've ever met. The women in my life are bold and confident and know what they want and how to ask for it. She's not like that. Demure and totally focused on her job, Alessia seems reluctant to engage with me . . . almost as if she wants to be invisible. She confounds me. Her shy acceptance of the umbrella comes to mind and makes me smile. She was so surprised and appreciative, and I wonder what her life must be like that she's so grateful for such a simple gesture.

I sit on the piano stool and read through my first manuscript, recalling her face as she pored over the score. Perhaps she reads music. Maybe she even plays. And part of me wants to know what she thinks of my composition. But I realize I'm just speculating. My only certainty right now is the dull ache in my groin.

Fuck it. Go out and get laid.

But instead I stay at the piano, playing each song over and over in turn.

Alessia lies on the small folding cot that serves as her bed in a tiny room in Magda's house. Her mind is churning, she has so much to do—but her thoughts return once again to the green-eyed Mister. She sees him at the piano. His eyes closed, his brow furrowed, and his mouth slack as he feels the music—and later his warm expression as he hands her the umbrella. His hair rumpled and his full lips curved in an inviting smile. She wonders what they would be like to kiss.

Her hand moves down her body, over her breast.

He could kiss her here.

She gasps, embracing her fantasy, and her hand moves farther down, and she imagines that it's his hand on her.

Touching her.

Here.

She starts to caress herself, stifling her moans, mindful of the thin walls of her room.

She thinks of him as her body builds.

Climbing.

Higher.

His face.

His back.

His long legs.

She climbs further.

His taut behind.

His flat stomach.

She groans as she comes, and, exhausted, she falls asleep.

Only to dream of him.

I toss and turn in my sleep.

> *She stands in the doorway. A vision in blue.*
> *Come in. Lie with me. I want you.*
> *But she turns, and she's in my drawing room. Polishing*
> *   the piano.*
> *She's wearing nothing but pink panties.*
> *I reach over to touch her, but she disappears.*

And I wake.

Fuck.

I'm hard. Painfully so.

Hell. I need to get out more.

I take quick care of myself.

When was the last time I did this? I need to get laid. Tomorrow. That's what I'll do. I turn over and fall into a fitful sleep.

· · ·

The following afternoon Oliver is taking me through the accounts for each of the estates. Our offices are just off Berkeley Square in a Georgian house that was converted into offices during the 1980s by my father. The building is owned by the Trevethick estate and houses two other companies on the upper floors.

I'm trying to concentrate on the numbers we're discussing, but I'm conscious that the door to Kit's office is ajar. It's distracting. I cannot bring myself to work in there yet. I can almost hear him talking on the phone or laughing at one of my poor jokes or berating Oliver about some transgression. I half expect him to bound in off the street. He was so at ease in this world and in charge of his domain. He made it look effortless.

But I know he envied my freedom.

It's okay for you fucking your way through London, Spare. Some of us have to work for a living.

I stand over Kit's lifeless, fractured body with the A&E doctor.

Yes. This is him, I confirm.

Thank you, Lord Trevethick, she murmurs.

It was the first time anyone had used the title. . . .

"So I think we can leave things as they are for the next quarter and then review," Oliver says, dragging me back into the present. "Though you should really go and visit the estates."

"Yes. I should."

At some point . . .

I am only vaguely aware of the recent history of the three estates, but I know that through the good stewardship of my grandfather, my father, and my brother all of them are profitable. Unlike many of our peers, the Trevelyans are not struggling for money.

Angwin House, set in the Cotswolds in Oxfordshire, is thriving. Open to the public, it has a vast garden center, a children's jungle gym and petting zoo, a tearoom, and open pastures for the general public to enjoy. Tyok in Northumberland is rented out lock, stock, and barrel to a rich American who fancies himself a lord. Kit and Oliver often speculated as to why he hadn't bought his own stately home, and now I'm wondering the same. Tresyllian Hall in Cornwall, on the other hand, is one of the largest organic farms in the United Kingdom. John, my father, the eleventh Earl of Trevethick, had pioneered organic farming while all his contemporaries had sneered at his initiative. More recently, to diversify the Trevethick portfolio and increase revenues, Kit had conceived and built a development of luxury holiday houses on the edge of the estate. They are in demand, especially in the summer.

"Now, we need to discuss how *you* intend to use the estates going forward and the level of staffing you'll need."

"Oh?"

My heart sinks, and I struggle to remain engaged as Oliver drones on. My mind wanders. Tomorrow Alessia will be back. She's the only staff member I'm interested in at the moment, and for all the wrong reasons. This morning's punishing workout in the gym has done little to lessen my fascination with her.

I'm enthralled, and I don't even know the girl.

My phone buzzes, and I have a text from Caroline. As I read her words, my scalp tingles and my throat tightens.

> **I'm not pregnant. :'(**
> **I have nothing of Kit's.**
> **Not even his child.**

Shit! My grief rises from nowhere, ambushing me.

"Oliver, we're going to have to call it a day. Something's come up."

"Yes, sir," Oliver responds. "Tomorrow?"

"Yeah. Why don't you come to the flat tomorrow, midmorning?"

"Will do, my—Maxim."

"Good. Thank you."

I type out a reply to Caroline.

I'm coming over.

No. I want to go out.
Let's get drunk.

OK. Where?

Are you home?

No. At the office.

Okay. I'll join you in town.

Loulou's?

No. Soho House.
Greek Street.
I'll know fewer people.

I'll see you there.

The private members' club is crowded, but I manage to find a table on the second floor near the blazing fire. I prefer the intimacy of 5 Hertford Street, which I consider my club—but I'm a member of Soho House, too—as is Caroline. I take a seat, and I don't have to wait long before she appears. She looks tired, and sad, and thin. Her mouth is turned down and her eyes clouded and puffy. Her blond bob is dull and unkempt, and she's dressed in jeans and a sweater. Kit's sweater. This is not the effervescent Caroline I know. My heart aches as she approaches. I see my own grief engraved on her face.

I stand but say nothing as she walks into my arms, and I hold her close.

She sniffles.

"Hey," I whisper against her hair.

"Life's shit," she murmurs.

"I know." I hope my tone is soothing. "Do you want to sit? If you sit facing me, no one will see that you're upset."

"Do I look that bad?" She sounds offended, though a little amused. It's a glimpse of the Caroline I know. I kiss her forehead.

"Never, darling Caro."

She shrugs out of my hold. "You charmer," she grumbles, though I can tell she isn't angry. She sits down in the velvet chair facing me.

"What would you like to drink?"

"A Soho Mule."

"Good choice."

I signal the waiter and order.

"You've been a recluse this weekend," Caroline says.

"I've been busy."

"On your own."

"Yes," I say, and it feels good not to lie.

"What is it, Maxim?"

"What do you mean?" I give her a level I-don't-know-what-you're-talking-about stare.

"Have you met someone?" she asks.

What the hell!

I blink as an image of Alessia stretching over my piano and wearing nothing but pink panties comes to mind.

"You have!" Caroline says, startled.

I shift in my seat and shake my head. "No." My denial is emphatic.

Caroline raises a brow. "You're lying."

Fuck. Not emphatic enough.

"How can you tell?" I ask, as ever daunted by her ability to cut through my bullshit.

"I couldn't, but you always cave so easily. Tell me."

Damn!

"There's nothing to tell. I spent the weekend alone."

"That speaks volumes in itself."

"Caro, we're each dealing with Kit's absence in our own way."

"And . . . what are you not telling me?"

I sigh. "Do you really want me to talk about this?"

"Yes," she says, and I notice the wicked gleam in her eye, reminding me that the real Caroline is not far away.

"There is someone. But she doesn't know I exist."

"Seriously?"

"Yes. Seriously. It's nothing. Just a flight of fancy."

Caroline frowns. "This is not like you. You're never distracted by one of your, um . . . conquests."

I can't help my hollow laugh. "She's not a conquest—not by any stretch of my imagination."

She can barely look at me!

The waiter arrives with our drinks.

"When did you last eat?" I ask.

Caroline shrugs, and I shake my head. "You must be driving Mrs. Blake crazy. Let's eat. May we have the menu?" I ask the waiter, who nods and scuttles away.

I raise my glass to hers. "To absent loved ones." I hope we can change the subject.

"To Kit," she whispers, and we smile sadly at each other, bonded by our love for the same man.

It is two o'clock in the morning when we return, inebriated, to my flat. Caroline is reluctant to go home. *I don't* want *to go. It's not home without Kit.*

I cannot argue with her.

We both stagger into the hallway, and I enter the code into the alarm, silencing the incessant beeping.

"Do you have any blow?" Caroline slurs.

"No. Not today."

"What have you got to drink?"

"I think you've had enough."

She gives me a crooked, drunken smile. "Are you taking care of me?"

"I'll always take care of you, Caro. You know that."

"Then take me to bed, Maxim." She throws her arms around my neck, her face raised with blurry expectation and her unfocused eyes intent on my mouth.

Fuck. I grab her shoulders to hold her back. "No. I'll put you to bed."

"What do you mean?" Caroline scowls.

"You're intoxicated."

"And?"

"Caroline. This has to stop." I kiss her forehead.

"Why?"

"You know why."

Her face crumples, and tears well in her eyes as she staggers out of my hold.

I groan. "Don't. Please don't cry." I pull her back into my embrace. "We can't do this anymore."

Since when have scruples stopped me fucking?

I was supposed to go out tonight and find a willing hot woman.

"Is this because you've met someone?"

"No."

Yes.

Maybe.

I don't know.

"Come on, I'll put you to bed." I curl my arm around her shoulders and lead her into my seldom-used spare bedroom.

At some point in the night, the mattress dips as Caroline climbs in beside me. Relieved that I remembered to put on pajama bottoms, I pull her into my arms.

"Maxim," she whispers, and I hear the invitation in her voice.

"Go to sleep," I grumble, and close my eyes.

It doesn't matter to me that she was my brother's wife. She's my best friend and the woman who knows me best. She's also a warm body and a comfort, and I'm grieving, too—but I'm not going to fuck her again.

No. That's done.

She rests her head on my chest, and I kiss her hair and promptly fall asleep.

Chapter Six

Alessia cannot contain her excitement. She clutches the umbrella and enters *his* apartment. Today she's pleased to note that the alarm doesn't sound.

He's here!

Last night in her narrow bed, she'd dreamed of him again—malachite-green eyes, shining smile, and that expressive face—engrossed in his music as he played the piano. She'd woken breathless and full of desire. And the last time she'd seen him, he'd been kind enough to lend her his umbrella, and it had kept her dry on the way home and all day yesterday. She'd not received much kindness since she came to London, except from Magda, of course, so his gesture meant that much more. Pulling off her boots and leaving the umbrella in the hall, she hurries through to the kitchen. She is excited to see him.

She stops on the threshold.

Oh, no!

A blond woman wearing nothing but a man's shirt, *his* shirt, is standing in the kitchen making coffee. She looks up and gives Alessia a polite but warm smile. Alessia recovers her capacity to move and walks through the kitchen toward the laundry room with her head bowed, in shock.

"Good morning," the woman says. She looks as though she's just climbed out of bed.

His bed?

"Good morning, missus," Alessia mumbles as she walks past her. Once in the laundry room, she stands for a moment to process this crushing turn of events.

Who is this woman with big blue eyes?

Why is she wearing his shirt? A shirt Alessia had ironed for him only last week.

This woman is *with* him. She must be. Why else is she wandering around wearing *his* shirt? She must know *him* intimately.

Intimately.

Of course he has someone. Someone beautiful.

Like him.

Alessia's dreams lie in shards at her feet. Her face clouds as disappointment constricts her heart. Sighing, she removes her hat, gloves, and anorak and slips on her housecoat.

What did she expect? He will never be interested in her—she is just his cleaner. Why would he want her?

The small bubble of joy she'd felt this morning—the first in a long time—has burst. She puts on her sneakers and sets up the ironing board. Her earlier excitement is a distant memory as she's forced to face reality. From the dryer she fishes out his clean laundry, transferring it into the ironing basket. This is her place. This is what she was raised to do: keep house and look after a man.

She can still admire him from afar as she's done since she saw him naked on his bed. There is nothing to stop her from doing that.

Feeling discouraged, she exhales as she fills the iron with more water.

A lessia stands in the doorway. A vision in blue.
  Slowly she removes her scarf and lets her plait
  swing free.
Shake your hair out for me.
She smiles.
Come in. Lie with me. I want you.
But she turns, and she's in my drawing room. Polishing
  the piano. Studying my score.
She's wearing nothing but pink panties.
I reach over to touch her, but she disappears.
She's standing in the hall. Eyes wide. Clutching a broom.
Naked.
She has long legs. I want them wrapped around my
  waist.

"I made you some coffee," Caroline whispers.

I groan, reluctant to wake. A large part of my anatomy is also enjoying my dream. Fortunately, I'm on my front, so my erection is pressing against the mattress, hidden from my sister-in-law.

"You have no food. Shall we go out for breakfast, or shall I have Blake bring us something?"

I groan again, which is my way of saying fuck off and leave me alone. But Caroline is persistent.

"I met your new daily. She's very young. What happened to Krystyna?"

Shit! Alessia is here?

I roll over to find Caroline sitting on the side of the bed. "Do you want me to get back in?" she asks with a coy smile, her head nodding toward the pillow.

"No," I answer, gazing at her lovely but disheveled state. "You made coffee dressed like that?"

"Yes." She frowns. "Why? Does my body offend you? Or are you pissed off I'm wearing one of your shirts?"

I have the grace to laugh, and I reach out and squeeze her

hand. "Your body would never offend anyone, Caro. You know that."

But Alessia will get the wrong idea. . . .

Fuck. Why do I care?

Caroline twists her mouth in an ironic smile.

"But you don't want it," she says, her voice suddenly quiet. "Is this because you've met someone?"

"Caro. Please. Let's not go over that again. We can't. Besides, you said you were on."

"Surfing the crimson tide has never been an issue for you," she scoffs.

"Good God, when did I tell you that?" I put my hands on my head and stare in horror up at the ceiling.

"Years ago."

"Well, I apologize for oversharing."

Women! They fucking remember everything.

"And why the hell did you have to remind me?" Her face loses all semblance of humor as her sorrow resurfaces. She stares unseeing out the windows, and her voice is soft and raw and anguished. "We tried for two years for a child. Two whole years. It's what we both wanted." Her tears begin to slip down her cheeks. "And now he's gone, and I've lost everything. I have nothing." She puts her head in her hands and begins to weep.

Fuck. I'm an idiot. Sitting up, I pull her into my arms and let her cry. I grab a tissue from the box on the bedside table.

"Here." I hand it to her. She clutches it as if it holds the meaning of life, and I continue, my voice low, tender, and sad, "We can't keep doing this while we're both grieving. It's not fair on either of us, or to Kit. And you haven't lost everything. You have your own money. And you still have the house. We'll sort out a stipend for you from the estate if you need it. In fact, Rowena thinks you should do the interior design for the Mayfair apartments." I kiss her hair. "You'll always have me, but not as a diversion, Caro—as a friend and brother-in-law."

Caroline sniffs and wipes her nose. She leans back and gazes at me with heartbreaking, watery blue eyes.

"It's because I chose him, isn't it?"

My heart sinks. "Let's not go through that again."

"Is it because you've found someone else? Who is she?"

I do not want to have this conversation. "Let's go out for breakfast."

I shower and dress in record time, and I'm relieved to find that Caroline is still in the spare room en suite when I take my empty coffee cup into the kitchen. My heartbeat rockets at the thought of seeing Alessia.

Why am I nervous? Or am I excited?

Much to my disappointment, she isn't in the kitchen, so I venture to the scullery, where she's ironing one of my shirts. Unobserved, I watch her. She irons with the same sensuous grace I noticed the other day, in long, easy strokes, her brow furrowed in concentration. She finishes the shirt and suddenly looks up. Her eyes widen when she sees me, her cheeks flushing with a rosy glow.

Man, she is lovely.

"Good morning," I say. "I didn't mean to startle you."

She places the iron on the rest and stares at it, rather than at me, her brow more furrowed than before.

What? Why won't she look at me?

"I'm just taking my sister-in-law out for breakfast." *Why am I telling her this?*

But her eyelashes flutter as she blinks, and I know she's processing this information. In a rush I continue, "If you could change the sheets in the spare room, that would be great."

She stills, then nods, avoiding my gaze, while her teeth worry her upper lip.

Oh . . . I want to feel those teeth on me.

"I'll leave the money as usual—"

Her face tilts up, and she gives me a dark glance with her expressive beautiful eyes, and my words dry in my throat.

"Thank you, Mister," she whispers.

"My name's Maxim." I want to hear her say my name in her seductive accent, but she stands mute in her awful housecoat and gives me a tight smile.

"Maxim!" Caroline calls, then walks into the now-cramped scullery. "Hello again," she says to Alessia.

"Alessia, this is my friend and sister-in-law...um...Caroline. Caroline, Alessia."

This is awkward. I'm surprised how self-conscious I feel making the introductions.

Caroline gives me a puzzled look, which I ignore, but she directs a kind smile at Alessia.

"Alessia, lovely name. Is it Polish?" Caroline asks.

"No, missus. It is from Italy."

"Oh, you're Italian."

"No, I am from Albania." She takes a step back and begins to fiddle with a stray thread on her housecoat.

Albania?

She doesn't want to talk about this, but I'm so curious that I press on. "You're a long way from home. Are you studying here?"

She shakes her head and starts to pull at the thread, more evasive than ever. It's clear she isn't going to elaborate.

"Maxim. Let's go," Caroline says, tugging at my arm while maintaining her quizzical look. "Lovely to meet you, Alessia," she adds.

I hesitate. "Bye," I say, reluctant to leave her.

B ye," Alessia whispers, and she watches him follow Caroline out of the kitchen.

Sister-in-law?

She hears the front door close.

Sister-in-law.

Kunata.

As she returns to the ironing, she says the words out loud in English and Albanian, and the sound and meaning make her smile. But it's odd that his sister-in-law should be here, wearing his clothes. Alessia shrugs. She's seen enough American TV shows to know that relationships between men and women are different in the West.

Later she strips the bed in the spare room. It's modern and chic and white like the rest of the apartment, but the most pleasing aspect of it is that it's been used. With a relieved grin, she collects more white bedding from the linen closet and remakes the bed.

Since meeting Caroline, one thought has plagued Alessia. In the Mister's bedroom, she has the chance to satisfy her curiosity. She wraps her arms around herself and approaches the wastebasket with caution. Taking a deep breath, she peeks in.

She grins.

No condoms.

Alessia goes about cleaning and tidying his bedroom with a little of the joy she'd felt earlier that morning.

I s it her?" Caroline asks.

"What?" I scoff as we sit in a cab on the way to the King's Road.

"Your daily."

Shit.

"What about my daily?"

"Is it her?"

"Don't be ridiculous."

Caroline crosses her arms. "That's not a no."

"I'm not going to dignify that with a response." I stare out at the drab Chelsea streets through the cab's steamed-up window as I feel a flush creep up my neck, betraying me.

How did I give myself away?

"I've never seen you so solicitous with your staff."

I scowl at her. "Speaking of staff," I say, "was it Mrs. Blake who organized Krystyna for me?"

"I think it was. Why?"

"Well, I was a little surprised that she upped and left without so much as a good-bye and Miss Albania took her place. No one told me."

"Maxim, if you don't like the girl, get rid of her."

"That's not what I'm saying."

"Well, you're acting pretty bloody weird about her."

"No I'm not."

"Whatever, Maxim." Caroline's mouth presses into a hard line as she folds her arms and stares out the misting cab window, leaving me to my own thoughts.

What I really want is information about Alessia Demachi. I process what I know. Fact one, she's Albanian, not Polish. I know very little about Albania. What brings her to the UK? How old is she? Where does she live? Does she travel far each morning? Does she live alone?

I could follow her home.

Stalker!

I could ask her.

Fact two, Alessia is reluctant to talk. Or is she reluctant to talk to *me*? The thought is depressing, and I stare at the rain-lashed streets, sulking like a needy adolescent.

Why does this woman confound me?

Is it that she's so mysterious?

That she's from a completely different background to me?

The fact that she works for me?

That makes her off-limits.

Fuck.

The truth is, I want to bed her. There. I admit it to myself. That's what I want, and I have a severe case of blue balls to prove it. What's more, I don't know how to make that happen, especially as she won't talk to me. She won't even look at me.

Does she find me repellent?

Maybe that's it. She just doesn't like me.

Hell, I don't know *what* she thinks of me. I'm very much at a disadvantage. For all I know, she could be rummaging through my belongings right now, learning more about me. Figuring me out. I grimace. Maybe that's why she dislikes me.

"She seems terrified of you," Caroline observes.

"Who?" I ask, though I know full well who she's talking about.

"Alessia."

"I'm her boss."

"You're awfully touchy about her. I think she's terrified because she's crazy about you."

"What? Now you're hallucinating. She can barely stand to be in the same room as me."

"QED." Caroline shrugs.

I frown at her.

She sighs. "She can't be in the same room as you because she likes you and doesn't want to give herself away."

"Caro, she's my daily. That's all." I'm emphatic, and it's an effort to throw Caroline off the scent, though this gives me hope. She smirks as the cab pulls up outside Bluebird. I hand the cab-driver a twenty, ignoring Caroline's look.

"Keep the change," I tell him as we climb out of the cab.

"That's an excessive tip," Caroline grumbles. I say nothing, too lost in thoughts of Alessia Demachi, and hold the door of the café open for her.

"So your mother thinks I should pick myself up by my boot-straps and get back to work?" Caroline says as we're led to our table.

"She thinks you're very talented and that working on the May-fair development will be a welcome diversion."

Caroline presses her lips together. "I think I need time," she whispers, and her eyes dim with sadness.

"I understand."

"We only buried him two weeks ago." She pulls Kit's sweater up to her nose and inhales.

"I know, I know," I say, and wonder if his scent is still on the sweater.

I miss him, too. And actually, it's thirteen days since his burial. Twenty-two days since he died.

I swallow the harsh, hard knot that forms in my throat.

I missed my workout this morning, so I vault up the stairs to my flat. Breakfast has taken longer than I intended, and I'm expecting Oliver at any minute. Part of me also hopes that Alessia will still be there. As I approach my front door, I hear music coming from the flat.

Music? What's going on?

I slide my key into the lock and cautiously open the door. It's Bach, one of his preludes in G Major. Perhaps Alessia is playing music through my computer. But how can she? She doesn't know the password. Does she? Maybe she's playing her phone through the sound system, though from the look of her tatty anorak she doesn't strike me as someone who has a smartphone. I've never seen her with one. The music rings through my flat, lighting up its darkest corners.

Who knew that my daily likes classical?

This is a tiny piece of the Alessia Demachi puzzle. Quietly I close the door, but as I stand in the hallway, it becomes apparent that the music is not coming from the sound system. It's from my piano. Bach. Fluid and light, played with a deftness and understanding I've only heard from concert-standard performers.

Alessia?

I've never managed to make my piano sing like this. Taking off my shoes, I creep down the hallway and peer around the door into the drawing room.

She is seated at the piano in her housecoat and scarf, swaying a little, completely lost in the music, her eyes closed in concentration as her hands move with graceful dexterity across the keys. The music flows through her, echoing off the walls and ceiling in a flawless performance worthy of any concert pianist. I watch her in awe as she plays, her head bowed.

She is brilliant.

In every way.

And I'm completely spellbound.

She finishes the prelude, and I step back into the hall, flattening myself against the wall in case she looks up, not daring to breathe. However, without missing a beat she goes straight into the fugue. I lean against the wall and close my eyes, marveling at her artistry and the feeling that she puts into each phrase. I'm carried away by the music, and as I listen, I realize that she wasn't reading the music. She's playing from memory.

Good God. She's a fucking virtuoso.

And I remember her intense focus when she examined my score while she was dusting the piano. Clearly she was reading the music.

Shit. She plays at this standard and she was reading *my* composition?

The fugue ends, and seamlessly she launches into another piece. Again Bach, Prelude in C-sharp Major, I think.

What the fuck is she doing cleaning when she plays like this?

The front doorbell sounds, and suddenly the music ceases.

Shit.

I hear the loud scrape of the piano stool on the floor and, not wanting to be caught eavesdropping, I barrel down the hallway in my socks and open the door.

"Good afternoon, sir." It's Oliver.

"Come in," I say, a little breathless.

"I let myself in downstairs. I hope you don't mind. Are you okay?" Oliver asks as he enters. He stops and stares at Alessia, who is now standing in the hall silhouetted against the light from the drawing-room doorway. As I open my mouth to say something to her, she scoots into the kitchen.

"Yes. I'm fine. Go on through. I just need a word with my daily."

Oliver frowns in confusion but makes his way to the drawing room.

I take a deep breath and run both my hands through my hair, trying to contain my . . . wonder.

What the hell?

I stride into the kitchen, where I find a panicked Alessia struggling into her anorak.

"So sorry. So sorry. I am so sorry," she mumbles, unable to look at me. Her face is pale and strained, as if she's fighting back tears.

Shit.

"Hey, it's okay. Here, let me help you with that." My tone is gentle as I take hold of her coat. It's every bit as cheap, thin, and nasty as it looks. The name MICHAL JANECZEK is sewn into the collar. Michal Janeczek? Her boyfriend? My scalp prickles as all the little hairs on the back of my neck rise. Maybe this is why she doesn't want to talk to me. She has a boyfriend.

Fuck. The disappointment is real.

I slip her jacket over her arms and shoulders.

Or maybe she simply doesn't like me.

Pulling the anorak more tightly around her body, she steps out of my reach while she fumbles with her housecoat and stuffs it into a plastic shopping bag.

"I am sorry, Mister," she says once more. "I will not do it again. I will not." And her voice cracks.

"Alessia, for heaven's sake. It was a pleasure to hear you play. You can play anytime."

Even if you do have a boyfriend.

She stares at the floor, and I can't resist. Stepping forward, I reach out and gently tilt her chin so that I can see her face.

"I mean it," I say. "Anytime. You play so well." And before I can stop myself, I let my thumb trace her full bottom lip.

Oh, God. So soft.

Touching her is a mistake.

My body responds immediately. *Fuck.*

She draws in a sharp breath, and her eyes grow impossibly large.

I drop my hand. "I'm sorry," I whisper, appalled that I'm pawing the girl. Though Caroline's words come back to me.

She likes you and doesn't want to give herself away.

"I must go," Alessia says, and not bothering to remove the scarf from her head, she scoots around me and bolts for the front door. As I hear it close, I notice that she's left her boots. I reach for them and rush to the front door and open it. But she's disappeared. Looking at her boots in my hand I turn them over and I'm distressed to see that they're so old that the soles are worn thin.

Hence the wet footprints.

She must be penniless if this is what she's wearing. Scowling, I take them back to the kitchen and glance through the glass door that leads out onto the fire escape. The weather is fine today, so even in her trainers her feet won't get wet.

What on earth possessed me to touch her? That was a mistake. I rub my thumb and forefinger together, recalling the softness of her lip. Groaning, I shake my head. I'm shocked and embarrassed that I've overstepped the mark with her. Taking a deep breath, I go to join Oliver in the drawing room.

"Who was that?" Oliver asks.

"My daily."

"I don't have her on the roster of employees."

"Is that a problem?"

"Yes. How do you pay her? With cash?"

What the fuck is he implying?

"Yes. Cash," I snap.

Oliver shakes his head. "You're the Earl of Trevethick now. She'll need to go on the payroll."

"Why?"

"Because Her Majesty's Revenue and Customs will take a dim view of you paying cash to anyone. Trust me, they're all over our accounts."

"I don't understand."

"All employees have to go through the books. Did you organize her?"

"No. Mrs. Blake did."

"I'm sure it won't be a problem. I just need her details. She's from the UK, yes?"

"Well, no. She says she's Albanian."

"Oh. Then she may need a work permit to be here—unless she's studying, of course."

Oh, shit.

"I'll get the details for you. Shall we discuss the rest of the staff?" I ask.

"By all means. Shall we start with those who work at Trevelyan House?"

A lessia runs to the bus stop, unsure why she's running or from whom. How could she have been stupid enough to get caught? He said he didn't mind her playing the piano, but she doesn't know whether to believe him. He may be calling Magda's friend right now to have her fired! Her heart pounding, feeling confused, she sits on the bench to wait for the bus that will take her to Queenstown Road station. She isn't sure if her increased heart rate is from her mad dash along Chelsea Embankment or from what happened in the Mister's apartment.

She caresses her lower lip with her fingertips. Closing her eyes, she recalls the delicious jolt that went through her when he touched her. Her heart somersaults once more, making her gasp.

He touched her.

Like he does in her dreams.

Like he does in her imagination.

So gentle.

And tender.

Isn't that what she wants?

Perhaps he likes her. . . .

She gasps once more.

No. She cannot think like this.

It's impossible.

How could he like her? She's just his cleaner.

But he helped her into her coat. No one has ever done that before. She stares down at her feet.

Zot!

She realizes that she's left her boots in the apartment. Should she go back and retrieve them? She has no shoes except the pair she's wearing and her boots, one of the few possessions she retains from home.

She can't go back. He's meeting with someone. If she angered him by playing the piano, he is sure to be angrier still if she interrupts him. She sees the bus in the distance and resolves to collect her boots on Friday—if she still has a job.

Her teeth toy with her upper lip. She needs this job. If she gets fired, Magda might turn her out on the street.

No, that will not happen.

Magda wouldn't be that cruel, and Alessia still has Mrs. Kingsbury's and Mrs. Goode's houses to clean, though neither of them has a piano. However, it's not just the piano that Alessia needs—she needs the money. Magda and her son, Michal, are emigrating to Canada soon. They will join Magda's fiancé, Logan, who lives and works in Toronto. Alessia will have to find somewhere to live. Magda charges her a pittance of a hundred pounds a week for the tiny bedroom, and from her research on Michal's computer she knows this is a bargain. Finding other lodgings in London for so little is going to be a challenge.

Her heart warms when she thinks about Michal. He is generous with his time and his computer. Alessia's knowledge of the cyber world is limited, as her father was strict with the use of the old computer at home. But Michal is not. He is all over social media. Facebook, Instagram, Tumblr, Snapchat—Michal loves them all. She smiles thinking of the selfie he took yesterday of the two of them. He likes to take the selfies.

The bus arrives, and still feeling giddy from the Mister's touch, she climbs aboard.

"Well, that's a run-through of all the staff. I need your daily's details so I can add her to the payroll," Oliver says. We're seated at the small dining table in my drawing room, and I had hoped we'd concluded our meeting.

"Now I have a proposition for you," he continues.

"What?"

"I think it's best if you take a thorough tour and inspect both the estates that are in your direct control. Tyok we can do when the tenant vacates."

"Oliver, I've lived on these estates at various points in my life. Why do I need to inspect them?"

"Because you're the boss now, Maxim. It will show the staff you care and that you're committed to them and to the estates' longevity."

What? My mother would have my head on a plate if I felt anything less. For her it's always been about the earldom, the bloodline, and the family—which is ironic, considering *she* abandoned them. But not before she'd imparted to Kit her passion for our family's history and legacy. She'd schooled him well. He knew his duties. And like the good man he was, he rose to the challenge.

As did Maryanne. She knew our history, too.

Me. Not so much.

Maryanne had learned by osmosis; she was a curious child.

I was always too distracted and lost in my own world.

"Of course I'm committed to the staff and the estates," I growl.

"They don't know that, sir," Oliver says calmly. "And . . . well, your behavior there the last time . . ." His voice trails off. I know he's referring to the night before Kit's funeral, when I'd drunk my way through a portion of Kit's cellar at Tresyllian Hall. I was angry. I knew what his death signified for me. And I didn't want the responsibility.

And I was in shock.

I missed him.

I still miss him.

"I was in fucking mourning," I mutter, feeling defensive. "I still am. I didn't ask for all this."

I'm not ready for this huge obligation.

Why didn't my parents foresee this?

My mother never made me feel as though I was going to be good at anything. She concentrated on my brother. She had tolerated her two younger children. Loved us, even, in her own way.

But she adored Kit.

Everyone adored Kit. My blond, blue-eyed, smart, confident, overindulged elder brother.

The heir.

Oliver holds up his hands in a conciliatory gesture. "I know. I know. But you have some bridges to mend."

"Well, maybe we should schedule a trip in the next few weeks."

"I think sooner rather than later."

I don't want to leave London. I've made a little headway with Alessia, and the thought of not seeing her for a few days is . . . displeasing.

"When, then?" I snap.

"No time like the present."

"You're kidding."

Oliver shakes his head.

Fuck.

"Let me think about it," I mutter, and I know I'm pouting like a spoiled child.

I am the definition of a spoiled child.

Gone are the days when I could do what the hell I wanted.

And I shouldn't take my anger out on Oliver.

"Very good, sir. I've cleared my diary for the next few days to come with you."

Oh, great.

"Fine," I grumble.

"Tomorrow, then?"

"Sure. Why not. We'll make it a royal progress." I grit my teeth.

"Maxim, I know there's a great deal to take on board, but having all your staff well motivated will make a significant difference. They only know a certain side of you." He pauses, and I understand that he's referring to my less-than-spotless reputation. "Just talking to the estate managers on their home turf will mean so much to them. Your meeting with them last week was too brief."

"Okay, okay, you've made your point. I've agreed, haven't I?" I know I'm being petulant, but deep down I don't want to leave.

Well, I don't want to leave Alessia.

My daily.

Chapter Seven

It's a cold and gloomy Tuesday afternoon. Exhausted, I lean against the chimney stack of the old tin mine and stare out toward the sea. The sky is dark and ominous, and a bitter Cornish wind slices through me. A storm is brewing, and the sea rages and crashes against the cliffs beneath, the sound booming and echoing through the ruined building. The first freezing spots of sleet from the coming storm spatter on my face.

As children, Kit, Maryanne, and I used to play in and around the ruin of this tin mine that stands on the edge of the Trevethick estate. Kit and Maryanne had always played the heroes, and I was always the villain. *How apt.* It was typecasting, even then. I smile at the memory.

A considerable fortune had been made from these mines, and the profits swelled the Trevelyan coffers over the centuries. But they were closed in the late 1800s as they became less profitable, and the workers emigrated to places like Australia and South

Africa, where the mining industry was flourishing. I spread my hand over the worn stone of the chimney stack, cold and rough to the touch but still standing after all these centuries.

Like the earls of Trevethick . . .

My visit has been a success. Oliver had made a good call insisting I visit both estates. And I'm beginning to reevaluate my doubts about him. He's done nothing but steer me in the right direction. Perhaps he does have the Trevethick earldom and its continuing prosperity in his heart. The staff now know I'm behind them and that I don't want to make radical changes. I've discovered that I'm very much an "if it ain't broke, don't fix it" devotee. My smile is rueful. . . . I'm also too lazy to be anything else, for now. But truth is, under Kit's authority and shrewd management the Trevelyan estates have been thriving. I hope I can keep them that way.

I'm weary from being encouraging and upbeat for the past few days and from listening to everyone. I'm not used to expending such positive energy. I've met so many people here and at Angwin in Oxfordshire, people I'd never met before who work on each estate. I've been coming to both of these places since I was a child, and I never had an inkling how many people work behind the scenes. Meeting everyone has been draining. All that talking, listening, reassuring, smiling—especially when I don't feel like smiling.

I gaze at the path that leads down to the sea and think of Kit and me as two young boys racing to the soft, sandy beach below. Kit always won . . . always. But then he was four years older than me. And then in late August, armed with bowls and buckets and anything else that would hold them, we three children would pick blackberries from the brambles that lined the path, and our cook, Jessie, would make blackberry-and-apple crumble for supper, Kit's favorite.

Kit. Kit. Kit.

It was always Kit.

The heir. Not the spare.

Fuck.

Why race through the icy lanes on a freezing night?

Why? Why? Why?

And now he lies beneath cold, hard slate in the Trevelyan family crypt.

Grief tightens my throat.

Kit.

Enough.

I whistle for Kit's gundogs. On command, Jensen and Healey, two Irish setters, return from their romp along the path and come bounding toward me. They are named after cars. Kit was obsessed with all four-wheeled vehicles, especially fast ones. From an early age, he could strip an engine and put it back together in no time.

He was a true all-rounder.

The dogs jump up at me, and I rumple both sets of ears. They live at Tresyllian Hall on the Trevethick estate, cared for by Danny, Kit's housekeeper. No. *My* housekeeper, for fuck's sake. I've contemplated taking them back to London, but my apartment is no place for two working dogs used to roaming the Cornish countryside and the thrill of game shoots. Kit adored them, even though they are useless gundogs. And Kit loved a shoot, too.

I wrinkle my nose in distaste. Shooting is big business, which means the holiday homes are booked out year-round. Bankers and hedge-fund managers seek their thrills at the wrong end of a gun during the open season. Affluent surfers and their families rent from spring through to autumn. Surfing I enjoy. Clay shooting I enjoy. But I am not a fan of killing helpless birds. My father, on the other hand, like my brother, loved the sport. He taught me how to shoot, and I do understand that the sport helps to keep the estate profitable.

I pull up my collar, push my hands deeper into the pockets of my overcoat, and turn to trek back up to the great house. Feeling glum and restless, I trudge through the wet grass, the dogs following close behind.

I want to be back in London.

I want to be back near *her*.

My thoughts keep returning to my sweet daily, with her dark eyes, her beautiful face, and her extraordinary musical talent.

Friday, I'll see her Friday, provided I haven't scared her away.

A lessia shakes the umbrella free of the snowflakes that had started falling fast and furious on her way to the Mister's apartment. She is not expecting him to be at home—after all, he'd left money for her last week that included payment for today. But she is ever hopeful. She has missed his brooding presence. She's missed his smile. She has thought of him constantly.

Taking a deep breath, she opens the door. The silence that greets her is nearly her undoing.

No alarm *noise.*

He is here.

He is back.

Early.

The abandoned leather duffel bag in the hallway also confirms his presence, and so do muddy footprints in the hall. Her heart rockets into overdrive. She is thrilled; she is going to see him again.

Carefully she places his umbrella in the stand by the door so it won't drop and wake him if he's asleep. She'd borrowed it on Monday night. She hadn't asked, but she didn't think he would mind, and it had kept her dry from the freezing rain as she'd made her way home.

Home?

Yes . . . Magda's house is home now. Not Kukës. She tries not to think of her old home.

She removes her boots and tiptoes along the hallway, through the kitchen, and into the laundry room. Changing into her sneakers and housecoat, she dons her scarf and decides what to clean first. He has been absent since Friday, so everything is clean. The ironing and washing are up to date, and his closet is finally neat and organized, but it's packed. The kitchen still looks as spotless and tidy as she had left it on Monday afternoon; nothing has been touched. She has to mop up the hall, but first she will dust the shelves with all the records, then wash the windows in the living room. The balcony has a glass wall that looks out over the Thames and to Battersea Park beyond. Grabbing the window-cleaning spray and a cloth from the cupboard, Alessia heads into the living room.

She halts in her tracks.

The Mister is here. Propped up on the L-shaped couch. Eyes closed, lips parted, hair mussed and standing on end, he's fast asleep. He is fully dressed and still wearing his overcoat, though it's open, revealing his sweater and jeans. His filthy boots are planted firmly on the rug. In the white light that swirls through the glass wall, Alessia spies the telltale trail of dried mud all the way back to the door.

She stares at him, enthralled, and moves closer, drinking him in. His face is relaxed but a little pale, his jaw is rough with stubble, and his full lips quiver with each breath. He looks younger and not quite as unattainable as he sleeps. If she dared, she could reach down and stroke the stubble on his cheek. Would it be soft or prickly? She smiles at her silliness. She isn't that brave, and though it's tempting, she doesn't want to anger him by waking him.

What concerns her most is that he looks uncomfortable. Briefly she wonders whether she should wake him so that he can go to bed, but at that moment he stirs and his eyelids open and bleary eyes meet hers. Alessia's breath hitches.

His dark lashes flutter over drowsy eyes, and he smiles and holds out his hand. "There you are," he mumbles, and his sleepy smile galvanizes her into action. She thinks he wants help to come to his feet, so she steps forward and takes his hand. All at once he tugs her down onto the sofa, kissing her quickly and curling his arm around her so that she's resting on top of him, her head on his chest. He mutters something unintelligible, and she realizes he must still be asleep. "I missed you," he murmurs, and his hand grazes her waist, then rests on her hip, holding her to him.

Is he asleep?

She lies paralyzed on top of him, her legs between his, her heart beating an insane rhythm, one hand still clutching the window-cleaning fluid and the cloth.

"You smell so good." His voice is barely audible. He takes a deep breath, his body relaxing beneath her, and his breathing mellows into the rhythm of sleep.

He's dreaming!

Zot! What should she do? She lies stiff and unyielding on top of him, terrified and fascinated at the same time. But what if . . . ? What if he . . . ? All manner of horrible scenarios suddenly run through her mind, and she closes her eyes to bring her anxiety under control. Isn't this what she wants? What she has been longing for in her dreams? What she secretly desires in her private moments? She listens to his breathing. In. Out. In. Out. It's steady. It's slow. He really is asleep. She rests against him, gathering her thoughts, and as time ticks by, she relaxes a little. She spies a smattering of his chest hair in the V of his T-shirt and sweater. It's provocative. She lays her cheek on his chest and closes her eyes and inhales his familiar scent.

It's soothing.

He smells of sandalwood and the fir trees in Kukës. He smells of wind and rain and exhaustion.

Poor man.

He is so tired.

She purses her lips and leaves a shadow of a kiss against his skin.

And her heartbeat spikes.

I've kissed him!

She wants nothing more than to remain where she is, to enjoy this new and thrilling experience. But she cannot. She knows it's wrong. She knows he's dreaming.

Closing her eyes for one more minute, she delights in the rise and fall of his chest beneath her. She yearns to wrap her arms around him and curl up on top of him. But she can't. She lets go of the cleaning fluid and the cloth, depositing them on the sofa, then reaches for his shoulders and shakes him gently.

"Please, Mister," she whispers.

"Hmm," he grunts.

She pushes a little harder. "Please. Mister. Move."

He raises his head and opens his tired eyes, confused. His expression turns from confusion to horror.

"Please. Move," she says again.

His hands fall away, releasing her. "Shit!" He sits up immediately and gapes at her in utter dismay as she scrambles off him. But before she can run, he grabs her hand.

"Alessia!"

"No!" she shouts.

And he lets go immediately.

"I'm so sorry," he says. "I thought . . . I thought . . . I was . . . I must have been dreaming." Slowly he stands, his face full of remorse, holding his hands up in submission. "I'm sorry. I didn't mean to frighten you." He drags his hands through his hair and rubs his face as if trying to rouse himself. Alessia stays out of his reach but scrutinizes him and sees how strained and tired he looks.

He shakes his head to clear it. "I'm so sorry," he says again. "I've been driving all night. I got in at four this morning. I must have fallen asleep when I sat down to undo my laces." They both look at his boots and at the clumps of dried mud he's left in his wake.

"Oops. Sorry," he says with a sheepish shrug.

From deep inside, her compassion for this man blossoms. He's exhausted, and he's apologizing for making a mess in his own home? That's not right. He has shown her nothing but kindness, giving her his umbrella, helping her into her coat, and when he caught her at the piano, he was complimentary and generous in his offer to let her play.

"Sit," she says, spurred on by her compassion.

"What?"

"Sit down," she says more forcefully, and he does as he's told. She kneels at his feet and begins to untie his bootlaces.

"No," he says. "You don't have to do that." Alessia bats his hand away, ignoring him, and undoes his boots, pulling each off in turn. Then she stands, feeling more confident that this is the right thing to do.

"You sleep now," she says, and grasping his boots in one hand, she holds out the other to help him up.

He glances from her eyes to her fingers, his hesitation unmistakable. After a beat he takes her hand, and she hauls him off the sofa. Gently she leads him down the hallway and into his bedroom. There she releases him, draws back the duvet from his bed, and points. "You sleep," she says, and walks around him to the door.

"Alessia," he calls before she leaves his room. He looks despondent and uncertain. "Thank you," he says.

She nods and exits, still holding his filthy boots. She closes the door behind her and leans against it, her hand at her throat in an effort to contain her emotions. She takes a deep cleansing breath. She's gone from uncertainty and confusion to delight and wonder to compassion and assertiveness in the space of a few minutes.

And he kissed her.

And she kissed him.

She touches her fingers to her lips. It was brief but not unpleasant.

Not unpleasant at all.

I missed you.

She takes another deep breath to calm her pounding heart. She

has to get a grip on reality. He'd been asleep. He'd been dreaming.
He hadn't known what he was saying or what he was doing. She
could have been anybody. She shakes off her disappointment. She
is just his cleaner. What could he possibly see in her? Feeling a
little deflated, but with her equilibrium restored, she picks up the
Mister's leather duffel bag and heads back to the laundry room to
clean his boots and sort his clothes for washing.

I stare at the closed bedroom door, feeling every shade of stupid
known to man. How could I have been so fucking idiotic? I
frightened her.

Shit.

I have no hope with her.

She'd appeared in my dream, a vision in blue—even in that
ugly housecoat—and I'd welcomed her.

I rub my face in frustration. I'd left Cornwall at eleven the
previous night, and the five-hour drive had been exhausting. It
was a stupid thing to do. I nearly fell asleep several times. I had to
open my car windows even though it was freezing and sing along
to the radio to stay awake. And the real irony is that I drove home
to see her. The weather forecast threatened a rare blizzard, and I
didn't want to be stuck in Cornwall for a week . . . so I came home
early.

Fuck.

I've blown it.

But she knelt at my feet and undid my shoes and led me to
bed as if I were a child. Led me to bed to sleep. I snort. To sleep!

When was the last time anyone did that for me?

I don't remember any woman putting me to bed and leaving
me. . . .

And I frightened her.

Shaking my head in self-disgust, I peel off my clothes and
leave them on the floor where they fall. I'm too tired to do any-

thing but crawl into bed. As I shut my eyes, I find myself wishing she had undressed me completely and joined me ... here. I groan as I recall her sweet, wholesome scent, roses and lavender, and how soft she felt in my arms. Feeling simultaneously morose and aroused, I fall fast asleep and surrender to her in my dreams.

I wake with a start and an odd feeling of guilt. My phone is buzzing on my bedside table. I didn't leave it there. I pick it up, but I'm too late. It's a missed call from Caroline. I place it back on my bedside table, noting that my wallet, spare change, and a condom are also there. I frown, and then I remember.

Oh, God. Alessia.

I jumped her.

Bugger.

I screw my eyes shut to escape the embarrassment that washes over me.

Fuck. A. Duck.

I sit up, and sure enough my clothes have been tidied away. She must have emptied my jeans pockets. It seems such an intimate thing to do, rummaging through my possessions, her fingers on my clothes, my stuff.

I'd like her fingers on me.

That's not going to happen, you idiot. You frightened the poor girl.

How many houses does she clean anyway? How many pockets does she rummage through? I dislike the thought. Perhaps I should hire her full-time. Then the dull ache in my gut would never go ... unless ... unless ... There's only one way I'll be rid of this ache.

Shit. That's not going to happen.

I wonder what the time is. There are no shimmers on the ceiling. Glancing out the window, I see nothing but a wall of white.

Snow.

The predicted blizzard has arrived. A glance at my alarm clock confirms it's 1:45 P.M. She should still be here. I leap out of bed and in my dressing room pull on a pair of jeans and a long-sleeved T-shirt.

Alessia is in the drawing room, where she's cleaning the windows. All evidence of my muddy walk through the flat has disappeared.

"Hi," I say, and wait to see how she reacts. My heart is thundering. I feel like I'm fifteen years old again.

"Hi. You sleep well?" She gives me a brief but unreadable look, then studies the cloth she's holding.

"Yes, thank you, and sorry about earlier." Feeling ridiculous and self-conscious, I wave in the direction of the sofa where my misdemeanor took place. She nods and rewards me with a small, tight smile, and her cheeks turn a lovely shade of pink.

I look beyond her through the windows, where the view is obscured by swirling snowflakes. The snowstorm is in full force, and outside is a turbulent torrent of white.

"It doesn't often snow like this in London," I say, moving to stand beside her at the window.

We're talking about the weather?

She steps beyond my reach, but she stares out of the windows. The snow is so dense I can hardly see the river below.

She shivers and wraps her arms around her body.

"Do you have far to go?" I ask, worried about her making her way home in this storm.

"West London."

"How do you get home normally?"

She blinks a couple of times while she processes my words. "Train," she answers.

"Train? From where?"

"Um . . . Queenstown Road."

"I'll be surprised if the trains are still running."

I head over to my desk in the corner of the room, shuffle the mouse, and my iMac springs to life. A picture of Kit, Caroline, Maryanne, and me with Kit's two Irish setters appears on my desktop, and with it I feel a wave of nostalgia and sadness. Shaking my head, I check online for the latest on local transport. "Um . . . South Western Trains?"

She nods.

"They've suspended all services."

"Sus-pen-ded?" Her brow creases.

Oh, she doesn't understand.

"The trains aren't running."

"Oh." She frowns again, and I think I hear her say "suspended" several times under her breath, her lips forming the word.

"You can stay here," I offer, trying not to focus on her mouth and knowing full well that she won't stay, especially given how I behaved earlier. I flinch and add, "I promise to keep my hands off you."

She shakes her head rather too quickly for my liking. "No. I must go." She twists the cloth in her hands.

"How will you get home?"

She shrugs. "I shall walk."

"Don't be ridiculous. You'll get hypothermia."

Especially in those boots and that horrid excuse for a coat.

"I must return home." She's adamant.

"I'll take you."

What? Did that just pop out of my mouth?

"No," she says with another emphatic shake of her head, her eyes growing wide.

"I'm not taking no for an answer. As your . . . um, employer, I insist."

She pales.

"Yep. I'll just finish getting dressed"—I glance down at my feet—"and then we'll go. Please." I gesture to the piano. "If you want to play, do." And I turn and head back to my bedroom, wondering why I've volunteered to take her home.

Because it's the right thing to do?

Because I want to spend more time with her.

A lessia watches him pad out of the room in his bare feet. She's stunned. He's going to drive her home? She will be alone in a car with him.

Is this okay?

What would her mother say?

A vision of her mother with her arms crossed and her face etched in meek disapproval comes to her mind.

And her father?

Instinctively she cups her cheek.

No. Her father would not approve.

Her father had approved of only one man.

A cruel man.

No. Do not think of him.

The Mister is taking her home. She's glad she's memorized the address to Magda's house. She can still see her mother's untidy handwriting scrawled on the scrap of paper that had been her lifeline. She shivers and glances outside once more. It will be cold, but if she's quick, she can leave while the Mister is changing and not inconvenience him. Yet the thought of walking all that distance does not appeal. She has done it before from much farther away. Then it had taken her six or seven days with a stolen map. She shivers once more. A week she'd like to forget. Besides, he said she could play his piano. She gives the Steinway a fervent look, claps her hands with excitement, and dashes to the laundry room, where she changes in seconds. Grabbing her coat, scarf, and hat, she hurries back to the piano.

Leaving her coat on a chair, she sits down on the stool and takes a steadying breath. She places her hands on the keys, enjoying the cool, familiar feel of the ivory. For her the piano is grounding. It's home. Her safe place. Glancing once more out the window, she begins "Les jeux d'eaux à la Villa d'Este," her favorite piece by Liszt, the music swirling up and around the piano, dancing in brilliant shades of white like the snowflakes outside. Her memories of her father, her six days of homelessness, and her mother's disapproval are lost in the whirling, icy colors of the music.

I lean against the doorframe and watch her, mesmerized. Her performance is phenomenal, each note measured and played with such precision and emotion. The music flows effortlessly through her . . . from her. Each and every nuance is there on her beautiful face and in the music as she feels her way through the piece. A piece I don't know.

She's taken off the headscarf. I've been wondering if she wears it for religious reasons, but maybe it's just for when she's cleaning. Her hair is thick and dark, almost black. As she plays, a strand comes loose from her plait and curls around her cheek. What would her hair look like loose and cascading over her bare shoulders? I close my eyes, imagining her naked as I do in my dreams, letting the music wash over me.

Would this ever get old? Listening to her?

I open my eyes.

Watching her. Her beauty. Her talent.

Playing such a complex piece from memory. The girl is a genius.

While I was away, I'd thought that I'd embellished her performance in my imagination. But no. Her technique is flawless.

She's flawless.

In every way.

She finishes the piece, her head lowered, eyes closed, and I applaud. "That was breathtaking. Where did you learn to play so well?"

Her cheeks flush as she opens her dark eyes, but a shy smile lights up her face, and she shrugs. "At home," she answers.

"You can tell me more about it in the car. Are you ready?"

She stands, and it's the first time I've seen her out of that hideous nylon housecoat. My mouth dries. She's slimmer than I'd thought, but her delicate curves are all woman. She's wearing a tight green V-neck sweater; the soft swell of her breasts strains against the wool and emphasizes her narrow waist, and her skin-tight jeans showcase the gentle flare of slender hips.

Fuck.

She's gorgeous.

She quickly slips out of her trainers, drops them into her plastic shopping bag, and tugs on her battered brown boots.

"Don't you wear socks?" I ask.

She shakes her head as she bends and laces each boot, but her cheeks pink once more.

Maybe no socks is an Albanian thing?

I glance out the window, glad to be taking her home. Not only will I get to spend more time with her, but I'll find out where she lives and stop her from catching frostbite in her feet.

I hold out my hand. "Give me your coat," I say, and she offers me a hesitant smile when I help her into it.

This rag will never keep her warm.

When she turns to face me, I notice a little gold cross around her neck and a badge on her sweater—for a school?

Shit.

"How old are you?" I ask in a sudden panic.

"I have twenty-three years."

Old enough. Good.

I shake my head, feeling relieved. "Shall we go?" I ask.

She nods and, clasping her plastic bag, follows me out of the flat.

We wait in silence for the lift to take us down to the basement garage.

Once in the lift, Alessia stands as far away from me as she can. She really doesn't trust me.

After my behavior this morning, am I surprised?

The thought depresses me, and I try to look as calm and nonchalant as possible, but I'm so acutely aware of her. All of her. Here in this small space.

Maybe it's not just me. Maybe she just doesn't like men. This thought is even more upsetting, so I brush it aside.

The basement garage is small, but because the family estate owns the building, I have parking spaces for two cars. I don't need two, but I keep them anyway, a Land Rover Discovery and an F-Type Jaguar. I'm not a petrolhead like Kit. He was an avid collector, and now his fleet of rare vintage cars is mine. I like a motor that's new and hassle-free. Christ knows what I'm going to do with Kit's collection. I'll have to ask Oliver. Maybe sell them? Give them to a museum in Kit's name?

Lost in these thoughts, I press the remote for the Discovery, and its lights flash in welcome and it unlocks. With its four-wheel drive, it'll easily tackle London's snowbound streets. Only now do I notice that the car is filthy, still covered in mud and grime from my journey to Cornwall, and when I open the passenger door for Alessia, I see the sorry mess of litter in the footwell. "Hang on," I say, and gather up the empty coffee cups, crisp packets, and sandwich wrappers. I stuff them into a plastic bag I find on the seat and dump it all in the back.

Why am I not tidier?

A lifetime of nannies and boarding school and staff to clean up after me has taken its toll.

With what I hope is a reassuring smile, I gesture for Alessia to climb in. I'm not certain, but she looks like she's stifling a smile. Maybe the mess is amusing her.

I hope so.

She snuggles down in the seat, her eyes wide as she looks over the dashboard.

"What's the address?" I ask as I push the ignition.

"Forty-three Church Walk, Brentford."

Brentford! Lord. In the sticks.

"Postcode?"

"TW8 8BV."

I program the destination into the navigation and ease the car out of its parking space. With the press of a button on the rearview-mirror console, the garage door gradually lifts, revealing the white maelstrom outside. The snow is already three or four inches deep, and it's still falling fast.

"Wow," I say, almost to myself. "I've never seen it like this." I turn to Alessia. "Does it snow in Albania?"

"Yes. There is much more snow where I am from."

"Where is that?" I drive onto the street and head to the end of the road.

"Kukës."

I've never heard of it.

"It is a small town. Not like London," Alessia clarifies.

A warning beep sounds. "Please put your seat belt on."

"Oh." She's surprised. "We don't wear these where I come from."

"Well, it's the law here, so buckle up."

She pulls the strap across her chest and looks down for the catch, then presses the belt home. "There," she says, pleased with herself, and it's my turn to stifle a smile. Perhaps she doesn't travel by car very often.

"You learned to play the piano at home?" I ask.

"My mother teaches me."

"Does she play as well as you?"

Alessia shakes her head. "No." And she shivers. I don't know if she's cold or if something else is spooking her. I crank up the heat, and we turn onto Chelsea Embankment. The lights from Albert Bridge wink through the swirling snow.

"It is pretty," Alessia murmurs as we drive past.

"It is."

Like you.

"We'll take it slow," I add. "We're not used to snow like this in London." Fortunately, the roads are relatively quiet as we turn off the Embankment. "So what brought you to London, Alessia?"

She shoots me a wide-eyed look, then frowns and looks down at her lap.

"Work?" I prompt.

She nods but seems to deflate like a balloon, withdrawing into herself.

Shit. A tingle runs down my spine. Something is off. *Way off.*

I try to reassure her. "It's okay. We don't have to talk about that." Hurriedly I continue, "I wanted to ask you, how do you remember each piece so well?"

She raises her head, and it's obvious that she's more comfortable with this topic of conversation. She taps her temple. "I see the music. Like a painting."

"You have a photographic memory?"

"Photographic memory? I don't know. I see the music in colors. It is the colors that help me to remember."

"Wow." I've heard of this. "Synesthesia."

"Syn-a-thee—" She stops, unable to pronounce the word.

"Synesthesia."

She tries again, with a little more success. "What is this?" she asks.

"You see musical notes as colors."

"Yes. Like that." She nods enthusiastically.

"Well, that makes sense. I've heard that many accomplished musicians are synesthetes. Do you see anything else in color?"

She looks puzzled.

"Letters? Numbers?"

"No. Just music."

"Wow. That's really something." I give her a smile. "I meant what I said the other day. You can use my piano anytime. I love hearing you play."

She gives me a glorious smile that I feel in my groin. "Okay," she whispers. "I like to play your piano."

"I like to listen." I grin back, and we fall into an easy silence.

Forty minutes later I turn in to a cul-de-sac in Brentford and we arrive outside a modest semidetached house. Night has fallen, but I see a curtain pull back in the front room and a young man's face clearly visible in the light from the streetlamp.

Her boyfriend?

Fuck. I have to know.

"Is that your boyfriend?" I ask, and my heart kick-starts, thumping in my ears as I wait for her answer.

She laughs, a soft, musical laugh that makes me grin. It's the first time I've heard her laugh, and I want to hear it again . . . and again.

"No. That's Michal, Magda's son. He's fourteen."

"Oh. He's tall!"

"He is." Her face lights up, and I feel a momentary pang of jealousy. She's obviously fond of him. "This is Magda's house."

"I see. Is she a friend?"

"Yes. She is a friend of my mother. They are . . . how do you say? Pen friends."

"I didn't know those still existed. Do they visit each other?"

"No." She presses her lips together and examines her fingernails. "Thank you for taking me to my home," she whispers, shutting down that conversation.

"It was a pleasure, Alessia. I'm sorry about this morning. I didn't mean to pounce on you."

"Pounce?"

"Um . . . jump. Like a cat."

She laughs again, her face shining and beautiful.

I could get used to that sound.

"You were dreaming," she says.

Of you.

"Do you want to come in and drink a cup of tea?"

It's my turn to laugh. "No. I'll spare you that. And I'm more of a coffee person."

She frowns for a moment. "We have some coffee," she says.

"I'd better get back. It will take a while with the roads like this."

"Thank you again for driving me here."

"I'll see you on Friday."

"Yes. Friday." She gives me a radiant smile that illuminates her lovely face, and I'm smitten.

She climbs out of the car and heads to the front door. It cracks open, shedding a soft glow onto the snowy path, and the tall young man stands on the doorstep. Michal. He scowls at me as I start the car.

I laugh.

Not her boyfriend, then, and I turn the Discovery around, crank the music up, and with a ridiculous smile plastered on my face drive back into London.

Chapter Eight

"Who was that?" Michal asks, his voice clipped and frosty, as he glares at the vehicle outside. He's only fourteen, but he towers over Alessia, all shaggy black hair and skinny loose limbs.

"My boss," she answers as she peeks through the front door to watch the car drive away. She shuts the door behind her and, unable to contain her glee, gives Michal a quick, spontaneous hug.

"All right." Michal shrugs out of her embrace, his face flushed but his brown eyes bright with embarrassed delight. Alessia beams at him, and his answering shy smile hints at his adolescent crush on her. She steps back, careful not to be overly affectionate. She doesn't want to hurt his feelings. After all, he and his mother have been good to her.

"Where's Magda?" she asks.

"In the kitchen." His face falls, and so does his voice. "Something's not right. She's smoking a lot."

"Oh, no." Alessia's pulse quickens with a sense of foreboding.

Taking off her coat, she hangs it on one of the pegs in the small hallway and goes into the kitchen. Magda is holding a cigarette, sitting at the tiny Formica table. The smoke curls above her in a hazy cloud. Though small, the kitchen is neat and tidy as usual, and the radio is burbling in Polish in the background. Magda looks up, relieved to see her.

"You got home through the snow. I was worried. Good day?" Magda asks, but Alessia notices her strained smile and the tension in her lips as she takes a long drag from her cigarette.

"Yes. Are you okay? Is your fiancé okay?"

Magda is a few years younger than Alessia's mother, though usually she looks at least ten years younger. Blond and curvy, with hazel eyes that sparkle with her wicked sense of humor, she rescued Alessia from the streets. Today, though, she looks tired, her skin pallid and her lips pinched. The kitchen stinks of cigarette smoke, which Magda normally hates—even as a smoker herself.

She blows smoke into the room. "Yes. He's fine. It's nothing to do with him. Shut the door and sit down," she says. A tremor runs up Alessia's spine. Perhaps Magda is going to ask her to leave. She shuts the kitchen door, pulls out the plastic chair, and sits.

"Some men from the immigration department were here today looking for you."

Oh, no.

Alessia pales, and she hears the blood hammering in her ears.

"It was after you left for work," Magda adds.

"Wh-wh-what . . . what did you tell them?" she stutters as she tries to still the trembling in her hands.

"I didn't speak with them. Mr. Forrester from next door did. They knocked on his door because we were not here. He did not like the look of them and told them he had never heard of you. He said that Michal and I were away in Poland."

"Did they believe him?"

"Yes. Mr. Forrester thinks so. They left."

"How did they find me?"

"I don't know." Magda makes a face. "Who knows how these

things work?" She takes another drag from her cigarette. "I have to write to your mother."

"No!" Alessia grasps Magda's hand. "Please."

"I've already written and told her that you arrived safely. That was a lie."

Alessia flushes. Magda does not know the full story of her journey to Brentford. "Please," she says. "I don't want to worry her."

"Alessia, if they catch you, you'll be deported to Albania—" Magda stops.

"I know," Alessia whispers, and a trickle of sweat runs down her spine as fear tightens her throat. "I cannot go back," she mouths.

"You realize that Michal and I are leaving in two weeks. You have to find somewhere else to stay."

"I know. I know. I'll find something." Anxiety flutters in Alessia's stomach. Every night she lies in bed going through her options. So far she has saved three hundred pounds from her cleaning work. She will need the money for a deposit on a room. With Michal's help and the use of his laptop, she will try to find a place to live.

"I'll get supper started," Magda says with a sigh as she stubs out her cigarette. The smoke swirls out of the ashtray, blending with the tension in the room.

"Let me help," Alessia responds.

Later Alessia is huddled on her cot, staring at the ceiling. With her fingers she worries the gold cross she wears around her neck. The light from the streetlamp shines through the sheer curtains across the old, peeling wallpaper. Her mind races as she tries not to panic. Earlier, after an hour searching online, she'd found a room in a house that is near Kew Bridge station. Magda says that it's not far from here. Alessia has an appointment to see it on Friday evening when she's back from cleaning the Mister's apartment. She can barely afford it, but she needs to move, especially if the immigration department is catching up with her. She cannot be deported. She cannot go back to Albania.

She cannot.

She turns over to escape the shaft of light and snuggles up in the thin duvet to preserve as much warmth as she can. Thoughts swirl in her head, overwhelming her. She wants them to stop.

Don't think about Albania.

Don't think about this journey.

Don't think about the other girls . . . about Bleriana.

She closes her eyes, and immediately she sees the Mister asleep on the sofa, his hair a mess, his lips parted. She remembers lying on him. She remembers his swift kiss. She imagines that she's lying on him again, inhaling his scent and kissing his skin and feeling the steady beat of his heart against her breast.

I missed you.

She groans.

Every night he occupies her thoughts. He is handsome. More than handsome—he is beautiful and kind.

I love hearing you play.

He drove her home. He didn't have to do that.

You could stay here.

Stay with him?

Perhaps she could ask him for help.

No. Her situation is her problem. It's not of her making, but it's one she must deal with. She has made it this far on nothing but her ingenuity. And there's no way in hell she's going back to Kukës. Not to *him.*

He's shaking me hard. Stop this. Stop this now.

No. Don't think of him!

He's the reason she's in England. She has put as many miles as she can between them.

Think of the Mister. Only the Mister.

Her hand travels down her body.

Think only of him. . . .

What had he called her? What is it called?

Synesthesia . . . She repeats the name over and over and over while her hand moves and takes her higher and higher.

· · ·

The following morning she wakes to a white wonderland. It's so quiet. Even the distant hum of traffic is muffled by the blanket of sparkling snow. As she looks out her bedroom window, still huddled under her covers, she feels the same rush of delight she always experienced as a child when it snowed in Kukës. Then she remembers that today she is cleaning Mrs. Kingsbury's house. On the plus side, it's in Brentford and only a short walk away. On the minus, it's Mrs. Kingsbury, who follows her through the house criticizing her cleaning methods. But Alessia suspects that Mrs. Kingsbury grouses because she's a lonely old lady, and in spite of her complaining she always offers Alessia tea and biscuits when she's finished. They sit and chat, and Mrs. Kingsbury tries to keep her there for as long as possible. Alessia doesn't understand why Mrs. Kingsbury lives on her own. She's seen photographs of her family on her mantelpiece. Why aren't they taking care of her? After all, Nana lived with her parents after her grandfather died . . . Perhaps Mrs. Kingsbury needs a lodger? Someone to look after her. She certainly has the room, and after all, Alessia is lonely, too.

Dressed only in Michal's tatty SpongeBob SquarePants pj bottoms and his old Arsenal football shirt, she gathers her clothes for the day and bolts down the stairs and through the kitchen into the bathroom.

Magda has been generous with Michal's old clothing. She often complains he's growing too fast, but it's been to Alessia's advantage. Most of the clothes she owns were once his. Except socks. Michal wears huge holes in them, so he can't hand them down. She has two pairs of her own, but that's all.

Don't you wear socks?

Alessia flushes, remembering the Mister's comment from yesterday. She couldn't bring herself to tell him she can't afford new ones. Not while she's saving for a deposit on a room.

She switches on the electric shower that is mounted over the bath and waits a few moments for the water to heat up. She strips off her clothes, climbs into the bathtub, and washes as quickly as possible beneath the trickle of water.

My hands are braced on the shower wall. I'm panting while steaming hot water cascades over me. I've been reduced to jerking off in the shower . . . again.

Fuck. What has become of my life?

Why don't I just go out and get laid?

Her eyes, the color of a rich espresso, peek up at me through long lashes.

I groan.

This has to stop.

She's my fucking daily. Last night I tossed and turned alone in my bed again. Her laugh echoed over and over in my dreams. She was carefree and happy, playing the piano for me, wearing nothing but those pink panties, her hair falling long and lush past her breasts.

Ah . . .

Even my grueling workout this morning had done little to get her out of my system.

There is only one way.

That's not going to happen.

But the smile she gave me when she stepped out of the car, it gives me hope, and I'll see her tomorrow. With that positive thought, I turn off the shower and grab a towel. As I shave, I check my phone. Oliver has messaged me. He's stuck in Cornwall because of the weather, which means I can spend the morning replying to condolence e-mails and then have lunch with Caroline and Maryanne. And this evening I'm going out with the lads.

"Finally got you out of your lair. Should I address you as 'Lord Trevethick' or 'milord' now, bro?" Joe says as he holds up his pint of Fuller's in salute.

"Yes. I don't know whether to address you as 'Trevethick' or 'Trevelyan' now," Tom grumbles.

"I'll answer to either," I reply with a shrug. "Or my name—you know, Maxim."

"I should call you Trevethick from now on . . . though it will be hard to get used to. It is your title, after all, and I know my father is bloody touchy about his!"

"Thank fuck I'm not your father." I raise a brow.

Tom rolls his eyes.

"Won't be the same without Kit around," Joe mutters, his ebony eyes glinting in the firelight and serious for once.

"Yes, rest in peace, Kit," Tom adds.

Joseph Diallo and Thomas Alexander are my oldest and closest friends. After I'd been expelled from Eton, my father sent me to Bedales. There I met Joe, Tom, and Caroline. We boys bonded over our love of music and, at the time, our lust for Caroline. We formed a band, and Caroline . . . well, she'd eventually chosen my brother.

"Rest in peace, Kit," I murmur, and add under my breath, "I miss you, you fucker."

The three of us are ensconced in the snug at the Coopers Arms, a warm and welcoming public house not far from my flat. Nursing our pints by the blazing fire, we're two rounds in, and I'm beginning to feel the beer buzz.

"How are you holding up, mate?" Joe asks, tossing his shoulder-length dreads to one side. Joe, as well as being an excellent swordsman, has a promising career as a men's fashion designer. His father, an émigré from Senegal, is one of the most successful hedge-fund managers in the UK.

"Good, I guess. But I'm not sure I'm ready for all the responsibility."

"I get it," Tom says. Red-haired and amber-eyed, Tom is the third son of a baronet, who followed family tradition by joining the army. As a lieutenant in the Coldstream Guards, he did a couple of tours of duty in Afghanistan and saw too many of his comrades fall. Two years ago he was invalided out of the army from wounds inflicted two years prior by an IED in Kabul. His left leg is held together by titanium, his temper not so much. Both Joe and I have come to recognize that pugnacious gleam in Tom's eyes, and we know when it's prudent to change the subject or get him out of the room. At his request we never mention The Incident.

"When is the memorial service?" Tom inquires.

"I was discussing that at lunchtime with Caroline and Mary-anne. We thought after Easter."

"How's Caroline?"

I shift in my seat. "Grieving." I shrug, giving Tom a level gaze.

Tom regards me, eyes narrowed, his interest piqued. "Something you not telling us?"

Shit.

Following The Incident, not only is Tom belligerent but he's become irritatingly insightful. "Come on, Trevelyan, you're not playing with a straight bat. What is it?"

"No. Nothing you need to know. How's Henrietta?"

"Henry? She's great, thanks, but she keeps dropping bloody almighty hints that I need to buck up and pop the fucking question," Tom replies with a doleful look.

Joe and I both grin. "You're a doomed man, bro," Joe says, and claps him on the back.

Of the three of us, Tom is the only one in a long-term relationship. Henrietta is a saint. She nursed Tom through the trauma of his injuries, and she puts up with all of his bullshit, his PTSD, his temper. He could do a lot worse.

Both Joe and I like to play the field. Well, I used to. Unbidden, a vision of the raven-haired Alessia Demachi comes to my mind.

When did I last have sex?

I frown because I can't remember. *Shit.*

"And Maryanne?" Joe asks, distracting me.

"She's okay. Grieving, too."

"Does she need comforting?"

Comforting like I comforted Caroline?

"Mate!" I scoff in warning.

House rules. Sisters are off-limits. I shake my head. Joseph still has a not-so-soft spot for my sister. She could do a lot worse, he's a good guy, but I decide to burst his bubble. "She met some bloke while she was skiing in Whistler. He lives in Seattle. He's a clinical psychologist or something. She plans to see him soon, I think."

Joe gives me a quizzical look. "Really?" He rubs his rakish goatee, his eyes full of speculation. "Well, if he makes it over here, we'll have to see if this geezer measures up."

"He may be coming over next month. She's pretty excited about it."

"You know, now that you're the earl, you'll need to provide an heir and a spare," Tom says.

"Yeah, yeah. Time enough for that yet."

That's what I've always been. The Spare . . . Kit's nickname for me. It turns out the title and lands needed the spare.

"Yeah. There's no way you're ready to settle down, mate. You're as much of a serial shagger as I am. And I need a wingman," Joe says with a broad grin.

"Come on, Trevelyan, you've shagged your way through most of London," Tom taunts, and I don't know if he's disgusted or impressed.

"Fuck off, Tom," I say, and we all laugh.

The pub's landlady rings the bell above the bar. "Time, gentlemen, please," she calls.

"Back to mine?" I ask. Both Tom and Joe agree, and the three of us sink our pints. "You okay to walk back?" I ask Tom.

"Fuck off. I got myself here, didn't I?"

"I'll take that as a yes."

"I'm running a fucking 5K in April, you wanker."

I hold my hands up in surrender. I keep forgetting that physically he's mended. . . .

It is clear and sunny but bitterly cold, a day where her breath precedes her in a cloud of vapor as she hurries along Chelsea Embankment. There are still large patches of snow welded in icy clumps to the sidewalks, but the roads have been sanded. Traffic has returned to normal, and London is up and running again. Alessia's train was delayed this morning, and now she's a little late. But she would have happily walked from Brentford just to see *him*.

Alessia grins. She is finally at the front door to the Mister's apartment, her favorite place in the world. She slips her key in the lock and braces herself for the sound of the alarm but is relieved at the silence. Closing the door, she's surprised by the smell. The apartment reeks of stale alcohol.

Crinkling her nose at the unexpected odor, she removes her boots and pads barefoot into the kitchen. The worktops are littered with empty bottles of beer and greasy pizza boxes.

She jumps when she sees an athletic, attractive young man standing at the open fridge drinking orange juice directly from the carton. His skin is dark, he has long, knotted hair, and he's dressed only in his boxer shorts. Alessia gapes at him. He turns toward her, and his face erupts in a broad grin of perfect white teeth.

"Well, hi there," he says, his dark eyes widening in appreciation.

Alessia blushes and mumbles, "Hi," then scurries into the laundry room.

Who is this man?

She scrambles out of her coat, and from her plastic bag slips on her cleaning uniform: housecoat and headscarf. Lastly she slides her feet into her sneakers.

Alessia peeks around the laundry room door into the kitchen. The Mister, wearing a black T-shirt and his ripped jeans, is standing beside the fridge sharing the carton of orange juice with the stranger.

"I just frightened your barefoot help. You tapped that yet? She's hot."

"Fuck off, Joe. And I'm not surprised you frightened her. Put some clothes on, you fucking exhibitionist."

"Sorry, your lordship." The stranger tugs at his hair and bows his head.

"Fuck off again," the Mister says mildly, and he takes another swig of orange juice. "You can use my bathroom."

The dark-haired man laughs and, turning to go, spies Alessia watching the banter. He grins again and waves at her, causing the Mister to look in her direction. His eyes light up, and a slow smile spreads across his face, and Alessia has no choice but to come out of hiding.

"Joe, this is Alessia. Alessia, Joe." There is a warning tone to his voice, but Alessia doesn't know if it is directed at her or at Joe.

"Good morning, Alessia. Please excuse my state of undress." Joe gives her a theatrical bow, and when he's upright, he has a wicked, amused glint in his dark eyes. His body is toned and lean—like the Mister's. Each muscle of his abdomen is clearly defined.

"Good morning," she whispers.

The Mister gives Joe a brooding glare. But Joe ignores him and winks at Alessia before he strolls out of the kitchen, whistling.

"Sorry about that," the Mister says as he turns emerald eyes on her. "How are you today?" His slow smile returns.

Her flush deepens as her heart somersaults. Any inquiry he makes about her well-being, even one so commonplace, lifts her spirits.

"I am good. Thank you."

"I'm glad you made it here. The trains running okay?"

"They are a little late."

"Good morning." A man with fiery red hair limps into the kitchen wearing only his boxer shorts and a scowl.

"Good God," the Mister mumbles under his breath, and he scrapes his hand through his tousled hair.

Alessia regards this new friend who has joined them. Tall and handsome, his limbs are fair, with shockingly livid scars that crisscross his left leg and his left side like the tracks at a railway junction.

He notices Alessia staring at his scars.

"War wound," he growls.

"I'm sorry," she whispers, and she lowers her gaze to the floor, wishing it would open and swallow her whole.

"Tom, do you want some coffee?" the Mister asks, and it seems to Alessia he's trying to defuse the sudden tension in the room.

"Bloody right. I need something for this god-awful hangover."

Alessia scuttles back into the laundry room to start on the ironing. At least she's out of sight and won't offend any of the Mister's friends from in there.

I watch Alessia's hasty retreat into the scullery, her plait bouncing from side to side and brushing her waist.

"Who's the pretty girl?"

"My daily."

Tom nods with lascivious approval. I'm glad she's gone back into her lair, away from Tom's and Joe's prying eyes. Their reaction makes me uneasy. Suddenly, surprisingly, I feel proprietary. It's an unfamiliar emotion. I don't want my friends ogling her. She's mine. Well, she's my employee.

You're the Earl of Trevethick now. She'll need to go on the payroll. Shit.

She's *almost* my employee. I need to sort out her employment status sooner rather than later. I don't want Oliver or the Revenue breathing down my neck.

"What happened to Krystyna? I liked the old bird," Tom says as he rubs his face.

"Krystyna's gone back to Poland. Now, will you go and put some fucking clothes on? There is a lady present, for fuck's sake," I growl.

"Lady?"

Tom pales at the look I give him, and for once he doesn't rise to the bait. "Sorry, old chap. I'll go and get dressed. Milk, no sugar for me." He shuffles out of the kitchen and back to the guest room. I chide myself for inviting my friends to stay when Alessia is working here. I'm not going to make that mistake again.

A lessia has managed to avoid the men for most of the morning, and she's glad when they finally leave. She even contemplated hiding in the forbidden room, but Krystyna had been adamant. She is not to enter.

She's cleared the blankets off the sofa in the living room and has stripped and remade the bed in the spare room. *His* bedroom is now tidy, and she was surprised and delighted to note there were still no used condoms in the wastebasket. Perhaps he's disposing of them a different way. She doesn't dwell on this thought, because it depresses her. She enters his walk-in closet to put away the ironing and gather up his dirty clothes. It's only been a couple of days, but it's a mess again.

The Mister is sitting at his computer and working, doing whatever it is that he does. She still has no idea how he makes his living. She recalls the smile that lit up his face when he first saw her this morning. His dazzling smile is contagious. Grinning like an idiot, she examines the pile of clothing on the floor of his closet. Kneeling down, she picks up one shirt, then glances quickly at the half-open door. Satisfied that she's alone, she holds the shirt to her face, closes her eyes, and inhales his scent.

So good.

"There you are," he says.

Alessia jumps and bolts upright rather too quickly, so that she stumbles backward. Two strong hands grab her arms and save her from falling.

"Easy," he says, and gently holds her while she finds her balance. As soon as she does, to her regret, he releases her, but his touch still echoes through her body. "I was looking for a sweater. It's a bright day, but cold. Are you warm enough?" he asks.

She nods vigorously, trying to catch her breath. Right now, in this small space with him, she's too warm.

He surveys the pile of clothes on the floor and frowns. "It's a mess, I know," he mumbles with a sheepish expression on his face. "I'm pathologically untidy."

"Path-o-log—"

"Pathological."

"I do not know this word."

"Oh . . . um . . . it refers to an extreme behavior."

"I see," Alessia responds, and she looks down at the clothes again and nods. "Yes. Pathological." She gives him a wry expression, and he laughs.

"I'll sort this out," he says.

"No. No. I do it." Alessia waves him away.

"You shouldn't have to."

"It is my job."

He grins and reaches across her for a chunky cream sweater on one of the shelves. His arm brushes her shoulder, and she freezes as her heart goes into overdrive.

"Sorry," he says, looking a little disheartened as he leaves the closet.

Once he's gone, Alessia recovers her equilibrium.

Can he not tell the effect he has on me?

And he caught her sniffing his shirt. She covers her face. He must think she's a complete idiot. Feeling mortified and angry with herself, she sinks to her knees and sorts through the pile of clothing, folding the clothes that don't need washing and putting all his dirty stuff into the laundry basket.

I can't keep my hands off her. Any excuse.

Leave her alone, dude.

And if I touch her, she freezes. I amble back to the drawing room, feeling glum. She just doesn't like me.

Is this a first?

I think so. I've never struggled with women before. They've always been an easy diversion for me. With a healthy bank account, a flat in Chelsea, a pretty face, and an aristocratic family, I've never had a problem.

Ever.

Except now.

I should ask her out for a meal.

She looks like she could do with a decent meal.

Suppose she says no?

Then at least I'll know.

I pace the length of the windowed wall in the drawing room, stopping to gaze out at the Peace Pagoda for a few minutes and trying to summon the nerve.

Why is this so difficult? Why her?

She's beautiful. She's talented.

She's not interested.

Perhaps it's as simple as that.

The first woman who's ever said no.

She's not said no. She might give me a chance.

Ask. Her. Out.

I take a deep breath and wander back into the hallway. She is standing outside my darkroom looking at the door and holding a laundry basket.

"It's a darkroom," I say as I stride toward her.

Her lovely brown eyes meet mine. She's curious. And I remember that I'd asked Krystyna not to clean it sometime ago. It's been a while since I've been in it myself.

"I'll show you." I'm grateful that she doesn't back away like she normally does. "Do you want to see?"

She nods, and as I grab the laundry basket, my fingers brush hers. My heart slams against my ribs. "Let me have this." My voice is gruff as I try to calm the pounding in my chest. Placing the basket on the floor behind me, I open the door, switch on the light, and stand aside to let her enter.

Alessia enters the small room. It glows with red light and smells of mysterious chemicals and the stale air of inactivity. There's a bank of dark counter cabinets lining one wall, with large plastic trays on top. High above the cabinets are shelves crowded with bottles and stacks of paper and photographs. Beneath the shelves is an empty washing line from which a few pegs hang.

"It's just a darkroom," he says, and flicks on the dim overhead light so the red glow vanishes.

"Photography?" Alessia asks.

He nods. "It's a hobby. I thought at one time I would take it up professionally."

"The photographs in the apartment—you take them?"

"Yes. All of them. I had a few assignments, but . . ." His voice trails off.

The landscapes and the nudes.

"My father was a photographer." He turns to a glass cabinet filled with cameras that's behind him. He opens one of the doors and takes out a camera. Alessia catches the name "Leica" on the front.

Holding the camera up to my eye, I study Alessia through the lens. She is all dark eyes, long lashes, high cheekbones, and full, parted lips. My groin tightens.

"You're beautiful," I whisper, and press the shutter.

Alessia's mouth drops open, but she shakes her head and covers her face with her hands, though they don't conceal her smile. I take another shot.

"You are," I say. "Look." And I hold the back of the camera out to her so that she can see the image. She stares down at her face that's been captured digitally in fine detail and then looks up at me—and I'm lost. Lost in the magic of her dark, dark gaze. "See," I murmur. "You're stunning." Reaching forward, I tip up her chin and, leaning down, inching closer and closer so she has a chance to move away, I brush my lips against hers. She gasps, and as I pull back, she touches her fingers to her mouth, her eyes growing rounder.

"That's how I feel," I whisper, my heart pounding.

Will she slap me? Will she flee?

She stares at me. An ethereal vision in the muted light, she tentatively raises her hand and traces my lips with her fingertips. I freeze, closing my eyes as her tender touch reverberates through my body.

I daren't breathe.

I don't want to frighten her away.

I feel her feather-light touch, everywhere.

Everywhere.

Fuck.

And before I can stop myself, I pull her into my embrace and wrap my arms around her. She melts against the length of my body, her warmth leaching into me.

Oh, man, the feel of her.

I slide my fingers under her scarf and gently slip it off her head. Clasping her plait at the base of her neck, I tug lightly, bringing her lips up to mine. "Alessia," I breathe, and kiss her again, softly, slowly, so as not to frighten her. She stills in my arms, then brings her hands up to clutch my biceps, closing her eyes as she accepts me.

I deepen the kiss, my tongue teasing her lips, and she opens her mouth.

Fuck.

She tastes of warmth and grace and sweet seduction. Her tongue hesitant and faltering against mine. It's captivating. It's arousing.

I have to hold myself back. I want nothing more than to bury

myself in this girl—but I don't think she'll let me. I draw back.
"What's my name?" I murmur against her lips.

"Mister," she whispers as I run my thumb down her cheek.

"Maxim. Say Maxim."

"Maxim," she breathes.

"Yes." I love the sound of my name in her accent.

See, that wasn't so hard.

Suddenly there's a loud, insistent banging on the front door.

Who the hell is that? How did they get into the building?

Reluctantly I step back. "Don't go anywhere." I hold up my
finger in warning.

"Open the door, Mr. Trev ... an!" a disembodied voice bellows
from outside. "Immigration!"

"Oh, no," Alessia whispers, and she clutches her throat, her
eyes wide with fear.

"Don't be afraid."

The knock rattles the door once more. "Mr. Trev ... yan!" The
voice is perceptibly louder.

"I'll deal with this," I mutter, pissed off that we've been interrupted. Leaving Alessia in the darkroom, I head down the hallway.

Through the peephole in the front door, I assess the two men
outside. One is short, the other is tall, and both are dressed in
cheap gray suits and black parkas. They don't look particularly
official. I pause, debating whether or not to answer. But I should
find out why they're here and if it's anything to do with Alessia.

I thread the sturdy security chain through the catch and open
the door.

One of the men tries to burst in, but with my body pressed
against the door, the chain holds. He's the short one. Thickset
and balding, he oozes aggression from every pore in his body and
from his sly, shrewd eyes. "Where is she, mister?" he barks.

I recoil.

Who are these lowlifes?

Baldy's partner looms behind him: thin, silent, and menacing.
The hairs on the back of my neck stand to attention.

"Can I see some ID?" My voice is equally menacing.

"Open the door. We're from immigration, and we believe you have a failed asylum seeker in your apartment." The stocky guy speaks again as his nostrils flare in anger. He has a distinct Eastern European accent.

"You need a warrant to search these premises. Where is it?" I hiss with the authority that comes from a life of privilege and several years at one of the best public schools in Britain.

The large man hesitates for a moment, and I smell a rat.

Who the fuck are these men?

"Your warrant, where is it?" I snarl.

Baldy looks uncertainly at his cohort.

"Where is the girl?" The tall, thin bloke speaks.

"There is no one here but me. Who are you looking for?"

"A girl—"

"Aren't we all?" I sneer. "Now, can I suggest you fuck off and come back with a warrant or I'll call the police." Taking my phone out of my back pocket, I hold it up in front of them. "But just so we're clear. There are no girls here, let alone illegal immigrants." I lie easily, a skill that's also a product of several years at one of the best public schools in Britain. "Shall I call the police?"

Both of them take a step back.

At that moment Mrs. Beckstrom, who lives in the neighboring flat, opens her front door, holding Heracles, her yappy lapdog.

"Hello, Maxim," she calls.

Bless you, Mrs. Beckstrom.

"Very well, Mr. Trev . . . Trev." He can't pronounce my name.

It's Lord Trevethick to you, fucker!

"We shall be back with a warrant." He turns on his heel, jerks his head at his colleague, and they brush past Mrs. Beckstrom on their way toward the stairs. She glares at them, then smiles at me.

"Good afternoon, Mrs. B.," I say with a wave, and close the door.

How the hell did those thugs find out that Alessia was here? Why are they chasing her? What has she done? There's no "immigration" department. It's called Border Force and has been for years. I take a deep breath in an effort to damp down my anxiety and head back into the darkroom, where I suspect Alessia will be trembling in a corner.

She's not there.

She's not in the kitchen.

My concern mushrooms into full-scale panic as I race through the flat calling her name. She's not in the bedrooms or the drawing room. Finally I search the scullery. The fire-escape door is ajar, and her coat and boots are missing.

Alessia has fled.

Chapter Nine

Alessia flies down the fire escape, her heart racing as adrenaline and fear fuel her body. Once she reaches the bottom, she's in the side alley. She should be safe here. The gate to the street at the rear of the building is locked from the inside. But to be sure, she ducks between two of the dumpsters, where the residents of Mister Maxim's block dispose of their trash. She leans against the brick wall and drags air into her lungs, trying to catch her breath.

How have they found her? *How?*

She had recognized Dante's voice immediately, and all her suppressed memories had surfaced in a terrifying rush.

The dark.

The smell.

The fear.

The cold.

The smell. Ugh. The smell.

Tears well in her eyes, and she tries to blink them away. She has led them to *him*! She knows how ruthless they are and what they are capable of doing. She lets out a loud sob and puts her fist in her mouth as she cowers on the cold ground.

He could be hurt.

No.

She has to check. She can't flee if he's hurt.

Think, Alessia. Think.

The only person who knows she is here is Magda.

Magda!

No. Did they find Magda and Michal?

What have they done to them?

Magda.

Michal.

Mister . . . *Maxim.*

Her breath comes in short, sharp bursts as panic closes her throat. She thinks she's going to faint, but suddenly her stomach roils, bile rises in her throat, and before she knows it, she's doubled over and vomiting her breakfast onto the ground. As she retches and retches, she splays her hands on the brick wall until there's nothing left in her stomach. The physical effort of throwing up leaves her wrung out but a little calmer. Wiping her mouth on the back of her hand, she stands, feeling dizzy, and peeks into the alley to see if anyone has heard her. She's still alone.

Thank God.

Think, Alessia, think.

The first thing she has to do is check that the Mister is okay. Taking a deep breath, she leaves her refuge between the dumpsters and makes her way back up the fire escape. She moves cautiously as a sense of self-preservation kicks in. She needs to know the coast is clear, but she cannot be seen by them. It's six stories high, so by the time she reaches the fifth story, she's winded. She inches her way up the next staircase and peeps through the metal railings into the penthouse apartment. The laundry door is closed, but she can see into the living room. There's no sign of life at first, but then, all of a sudden, the Mister barges into the living room, and she can tell he's fetching something from his desk. He's there for a moment before he bolts back out of the room.

Her body slumps against the metal balustrade. He's safe.

Thank God.

With her curiosity appeased and her conscience reassured, she staggers back down the fire escape, knowing she has to check that Magda and Michal are okay.

At ground level in the alley once more, she changes into her boots and makes her way to the gate at the rear entrance of the apartment block. It opens onto the backstreet, not onto Chelsea Embankment. She pauses for a moment. Perhaps Dante and Ylli will be there waiting for her? They will be out front, surely? With her heart beating a frantic tempo, she opens the gate and peers into the street. The only sign of life is a dark green sports car speeding to the end of the road; there's no sign of Dante and his sidekick, Ylli. Taking her woolly hat out of her bag, she tugs it on, tucks her hair inside, and sets off for the bus stop.

She walks briskly along the street, fighting the urge to run, knowing that might attract unwanted attention. She keeps her head down and her hands in her pockets, and with each step she prays to her grandmother's God to keep Magda and Michal safe. She says it over and over again, alternating between her native tongue and English.

Ruaji, Zot.

Ruaji, Zot.

God keep them safe.

I've stood paralyzed in the hallway for what seems like an age. I'm filled with dread, and my blood is thundering in my ears.

Where the fuck is she?

What the hell is she mixed up in?

What do I do?

How can she face those guys on her own?

Fuck it. I have to find her.

Where will she go?

Home.

Brentford.

Yes.

I dash down the hall to the drawing room and snatch the car keys from my desk, then run to the front door, stopping only to grab my coat.

I feel sick, my stomach churning.

There is no way those guys were from "immigration."

When I reach the garage, I press the electronic key, expecting the Discovery to open, but instead the Jag beeps to life.

Shit. In my haste I've picked up the wrong key.

Fuck it.

I don't have time to go back upstairs for the correct key. I clamber into the F-Type Jag and press the ignition. The engine roars to life, and I ease the car forward out of its parking space. The garage doors rise gradually, and I exit to the left onto the street and race to the end of the road, turning left again toward Chelsea Embankment. But that's as far as I get. Traffic is slow because it's Friday afternoon and the beginning of rush hour. The crowded roads exacerbate my anxiety and do nothing for my temper. I run through my interaction with the thugs repeatedly, looking for any clues as to what might have happened to Alessia. They sounded Eastern European. They looked rough. Alessia bolted—so she either knows them or believes they're from the "immigration" department, which means she must be in the UK illegally. This doesn't surprise me. She's brought every conversation we've had about what she's doing in London to an abrupt end.

Oh, Alessia. What are you up to?

And where the hell are you?

I hope that she's gone back to Brentford, because that's where I'm headed.

Alessia sits on the train nervously fingering the small gold cross that hangs around her neck. It was her grandmother's, and it's the only possession she has that belonged to her dear nana. She treasures it. In times of stress, it brings her comfort. Though her mother and father are not religious, her grandmother was. . . . She fiddles with it now and keeps repeating her mantra.

Please keep them safe.

Please keep them safe.

Her anxiety is overwhelming. They found her. How? How do they know about Magda? She needs to know that Magda and Michal are okay. Normally she likes traveling by train, but today it's too slow. As the train reaches Putney, Alessia knows that it will be another twenty minutes before it reaches Brentford.

Please hurry.

Her thoughts turn to Mister Maxim. At least he is safe, for now. Her heart stutters.

Maxim.

He kissed me.

Twice.

Twice!

He said lovely words. About her.

You're beautiful.

You're stunning.

And he kissed her!

That's how I feel.

If circumstances were different, she would be ecstatic. She touches her fingers to her lips. It was a bittersweet moment. Her dreams were finally realized, only to be shattered by Dante—again.

There's no way she can be involved with the Mister. *No.* Maxim. His name is Maxim.

She has brought such terrible danger to his home. She has to
protect him.

Zot! Her job.

She will be out of a job. Nobody wants trouble coming to their
front door and criminals like Dante threatening them.

What will she do?

She needs to be careful when she returns to Magda's. She cannot let Dante find her there.

She cannot.

She must protect herself, too.

Fear grips her throat, and she shudders. She hugs herself, trying to contain her distress. All her vague hopes and dreams are
lost. And in a rare moment of self-pity, she rocks to and fro, trying
to find some comfort and alleviate her fear.

Why does the train have to take so long?

It pulls in to Barnes station, and the doors open.

"Please. Please hurry," Alessia whispers, and her fingers find
her gold cross once more.

I speed down the A4, my mind hopping from Alessia to those
men and then to Kit as I dodge through the traffic.

Kit? What would you do?

He would have known. He always knew.

I remember our Christmas holiday. Kit had been in such good
form. Maryanne and I had joined him and Caroline at a jazz festi-
val in Havana. A couple days later, we'd all flown down to St. Vin-
cent and taken a boat to Bequia to spend Christmas together in
a private villa. Maryanne had gone on to Whistler to ski and to
spend New Year's Eve with friends, and Caroline, Kit, and I had
returned to the UK for Hogmanay.

It had been an amazing week.

And the day after New Year's Day, Kit died.

Or killed himself.

There. I thought it.

My unspoken suspicion.

Damn it, Kit. You fucker.

The A4 becomes the M4, and I spy the high-rise towers that dominate the Brentford landscape and signal that I'm near. I come off the motorway hitting the slip road at fifty miles per hour. I slow down, but fortunately, the lights at the junction are green, and I cruise through them thankful that I'd brought her home earlier in the week and know where she lives.

Six minutes later I pull up in front of her house, leap out of the car, and dash up the short pathway. There are still clumps of snow on the grass and the sad remains of a snowman. The doorbell trills somewhere inside, but there's no response. The house is empty.

Fuck.

Where is she?

Apprehension overwhelms me. *Where could she be?*

Of course! She'll be coming here by train.

I'd seen the sign for the station as I'd turned in to Church Walk. I sprint back down the path and turn right on to the main road. The station is less than two hundred meters on my left.

Thank God it's so close.

As I dash down the station stairs, I see a train waiting on the far platform, but it's heading into London. I stop and focus my attention. There are only two platforms, and the one I'm on is for trains traveling out of London. All I have to do is wait. An electronic display hanging overhead announces that the next train arrives at 15:07. I check my watch; it's 15:03 now.

I lean against one of the white iron pillars that support the station roof and wait. There are a few other commuters waiting for the train, too. Most of them, like me, are seeking shelter from the elements. I watch as the frigid wind blows a discarded crisp packet in gusts along the station platform and across the train tracks. But it doesn't hold my attention for long. Every few seconds I glance at the empty track, praying for the London train to materialize.

Come on. Come on. I will it to arrive.

Finally the train appears around the bend, and it slowly—oh, so fucking slowly—pulls in to the station and stops. I stand up straight, my stomach churning with anxiety as the doors open and a few people alight from the train.

Twelve of them.

But not Alessia.

Fucking hell.

As the train leaves the station, I check the electronic sign again. The next train is due in fifteen minutes.

That's not too long.

It's a fucking age!

Hell.

I'm glad that even in my haste to leave the flat, I remembered my coat. It's bloody cold. I cup and blow on my hands, stamp my feet, and pull up my coat collar in an effort to keep warm. Thrusting my hands into the pockets, I pace up and down the platform while I wait.

My phone buzzes, and for some insane reason I think it might be Alessia, but of course she doesn't have my number. It's Caroline. Whatever she wants can wait. I ignore the call.

After an intolerable fifteen minutes, the 15:22 from London Waterloo comes into view around the bend. It slows as it approaches the station, and after an agonizing minute it stops.

Time suspends.

The doors open, and Alessia is first off the train.

Oh, thank fuck.

Relief nearly brings me to my knees, but just the sight of her calms me down.

When Alessia sees him, she stops short in complete astonishment. The other disembarking passengers stream past them as she and Maxim stare at each other, drinking each other in. The doors close with a hiss of compressed air, and the train gradually pulls out of the station, leaving them on their own.

"Hello," he says, breaking the silence between them as he approaches her. "You left without saying good-bye."

Her face falls, and her eyes fill with tears that spill down her cheeks.

H er anguish rips through me.

"Oh, baby," I whisper, and open my arms. She puts her face in her hands and begins to weep. Feeling at a loss, I fold her into my embrace and hold her. "I've got you. I've got you," I whisper against her green woolly hat. She sniffles, and I lift her chin and plant a tender kiss on her forehead. "I mean it. I've got you."

Alessia's eyes widen, and she pulls away. "Magda?" she whispers, alarmed.

"Let's go." I take her hand, and together we hurry up the metal staircase and out onto the road. Her hand is cold in mine, and I want nothing more than to whisk her away to somewhere safe. But first of all I have to know what's going on. What trouble she's in. I only hope that she'll open up and tell me.

We walk quickly but in silence across the road and back to 43 Church Walk. At the front door, Alessia fishes out a key from her pocket, unlocks the door, and we both step inside.

The front hallway is tiny and made more crowded by the two packing boxes that stand in the corner. Alessia removes her hat and anorak, and I take them from her and hang them on one of the pegs on the wall.

"Magda," she calls up the stairs while I shed my coat and hang it beside hers, but there's no answer. The house is empty. I follow her into the tiny kitchen.

Jesus, the place is a shoebox!

From the threshold of the dated but tidy 1980s kitchen, I watch Alessia fill the kettle. She's in her tight jeans and the green sweater that she wore the other day.

"Coffee?" she asks.

"Please."

"Would you like milk and sugar?"

I shake my head. "No, thank you." I loathe instant coffee and can only tolerate it black, but now isn't the right time to tell her.

"Sit," she says, and points to the little white table. I do as I'm told and wait, watching her while she prepares our drinks. I am not going to rush her.

She makes tea for herself—strong, with sugar and milk—and eventually hands me a mug inscribed BRENTFORD FC that bears the team logo. Taking the seat opposite me, she gazes down at the contents of her mug, which is emblazoned with the Arsenal shield, and an uncomfortable silence settles between us.

Finally I can bear it no longer. "Are you planning to tell me what's going on? Or do I have to guess?"

She doesn't respond, but her teeth worry her upper lip. Under any normal circumstance, this would drive me crazy, but seeing her this distraught is sobering.

"Look at me."

At last her big brown eyes meet mine.

"Tell me. I want to help."

Her eyes widen with what I assume is fear, and she shakes her head.

I sigh. "Okay. Let's play twenty questions."

She looks puzzled.

"You answer each question yes or no."

Her frown deepens, and she clutches the little gold cross that hangs at her neck.

"Are you a failed asylum seeker?"

Alessia gazes at me, then gives me the briefest shake of her head.

"Okay. Are you here legally?"

She blanches, and I have my answer. "Not legally, then?"

After a beat she shakes her head again.

"Have you lost the power of speech?" I hope she notices the trace of humor in my voice.

Her face brightens, and she half smiles. "No," she says, and her cheeks color a little.

"That's better."

She takes a sip of her tea.

"Talk to me. Please."

"You will tell the police?" she asks.

"No. Of course not. Is that what you're worried about?"

She nods.

"Alessia, I won't. You have my word."

Placing her elbows on the table, she clasps her hands together and rests her chin on them. A range of conflicting emotions crosses her face as the silence expands and fills the room. I hold my tongue, silently begging her to talk. At last her dark eyes meet mine. They're full of determination. She sits up straight and places her hands in her lap. "The man who came to your apartment, his name is Dante." Her voice is a pained whisper. "He brought me and some other girls from Albania to England." She looks down at her mug of tea.

A shiver runs up my spine to my scalp, and I have a horrible sinking feeling in my stomach. Somehow I think I know what she's about to say.

"We thought we were coming here to work. For a better life. Life in Kukës is hard for some women. The men who brought us here . . . We were betrayed—" Her soft voice halts over the word, and I close my eyes as revulsion and bile rise in my throat. It's as bad as it could possibly be.

"Human trafficking?" I whisper, and I watch her reaction.

She nods once, her eyes tightly closed. "For sex." Her words are barely audible, but in them I hear her shame and her horror.

Fury like nothing I've felt before ignites inside me. I clench my fists trying to control my anger.

Alessia is pale.

And everything about her falls into place.

Her reticence.

Her fear.

Of me.

Of men.

Fuck. Fuck. Fuck.

"How did you escape?" I ask, trying to keep my voice even.

We're both startled by the rattle of a key in the front door. Alarmed, Alessia leaps to her feet, and I jump up, knocking my chair to the floor.

"Stay here," I growl, pulling open the kitchen door.

A blond woman in her forties stands in the hallway. She gasps in alarm when she sees me.

"Magda!" Alessia cries. Dodging around me, she runs to embrace Magda.

"Alessia!" Magda exclaims, and hugs her. "You're here. I thought . . . I thought . . . I'm sorry. I'm sorry," Magda babbles, anguish in her voice, as she begins to cry. "They were here again. Those men."

Alessia takes Magda by the shoulders. "Tell me. Tell me what happened."

"Who is this?" Magda turns her tearstained face to me with suspicion.

"This is . . . Mister Maxim. It is his apartment that I clean."

"Did they come to his apartment?"

"Yes."

Magda gulps and holds her hands up to her mouth. "I'm so sorry," she whispers.

"Perhaps Magda would like some tea, and she can tell us what happened," I say gently.

The three of us are sitting at the table while Magda puffs on a brand of cigarette that is unfamiliar to me. I've declined her offer to try one. The last time I smoked a cigarette, it set off a chain of events that led to my expulsion from school. I was thirteen and with a local girl in the grounds at Eton.

"I don't think they were from the immigration department. They had a photograph of Michal and you," Magda says to Alessia.

"What? How?" I ask.

"Yes. They found it on Facebook."

"No!" Alessia exclaims, and clamps her hand over her mouth in horror. She looks at me. "Michal has taken the selfies with me."

"The selfies?" I ask.

"Yes. For the Facebook," Alessia says, frowning. I quickly mask my amused expression.

Magda continues, "They said they knew where Michal went to school. They knew all about him. All his personal information is on his Facebook page." She takes a long drag of her cigarette, her hand trembling.

"They threatened Michal?" Alessia's face is ashen.

Magda nods. "I had no choice. I was scared. I'm sorry." Her voice is little more than a whisper. "There was no way I could contact you. I gave them the address where you were working."

Well, that clears that mystery up.

"What do they want with you, Alessia?" she asks.

Alessia gives me a brief, imploring look, and I realize that Magda doesn't know the full details of how Alessia came to London. I run my hand through my hair.

What to do? This is far more than I bargained for. . . .

"Have you contacted the police?" I ask.

Magda and Alessia both speak at once: "No police." They are emphatic.

"Are you sure?" I can understand Alessia's reaction, but not Magda's. Perhaps she's here illegally, too.

"No police," Magda says, banging her hand on the table, startling both Alessia and me.

"Okay," I say, raising my palm to placate her. I've never met people who don't trust the police.

It's obvious that Alessia can't stay in Brentford, and neither can

Magda and her son. The thugs who turned up on my doorstep
were bristling with barely contained violence. "Is it just the three
of you living here?" I ask.

They both nod.

"Where is your son now?"

"At a friend's house. He's safe. I called him before I got home."

"I don't think it's safe for Alessia to stay here, or you for that
matter. These men are dangerous."

Alessia nods. "Very dangerous," she whispers.

Magda's face whitens. "But my job. My son's school. We are
only here for another two weeks before I leave—"

"Magda, no!" Alessia tries to silence her.

"For Canada," Magda continues, disregarding Alessia's
objection.

"Canada?" I look to Alessia and back at Magda.

"Yes. Michal and I are emigrating. I'm getting remarried. My
fiancé lives and works in Toronto." Her brief smile is a fond one.
I offer her my congratulations, then turn my attention to Alessia.

"And what are you going to do?"

She shrugs as if she's got everything under control. "I will find
another place to stay. *Zot!* I am to see a place this evening." She
glances at the kitchen clock. "Now!" She stands up, panicked.

"I don't think that's a good idea," I interject. "And frankly,
that's the least of your worries right now." She's illegally in the
country—how is she going to find somewhere to stay?

She sits back down.

"Those men could come back at any time. They could easily
snatch you off the street." I shudder. They want her.

Evil fuckers.

What can I do?

Think. Think.

We could all hole up in Trevelyan House in Cheyne Walk,
but Caroline would ask questions, and I don't want that—it's too
complicated. I could take Alessia back to my flat—but they've
already been there. One of the other properties? Maryanne's

place? No. Perhaps I could take her to Cornwall. No one would find us there.

And as I contemplate my options, I realize I don't want to let her out of my sight.

Ever.

The thought surprises me.

"I want you to come with me," I say to her.

"What?" Alessia exclaims. "But—"

"I can find you somewhere to live. Don't worry about that." *Jesus, I have enough property at my disposal.* "But you're not safe here. You can come with me."

"Oh."

I turn my attention to Magda. "Magda, as far as I can see, you have three options since you don't want to involve the police. We can move you to a local hotel for now, or we can put you up in a house in town. Or I can organize some close-protection security for you and your son, and you can stay here."

"I cannot afford a hotel." Magda's voice fades while she gapes at me.

"Don't worry about the money," I reply.

I do the calculations in my head. It's not much in the scheme of things. And Alessia will be safe.

Worth every penny.

And maybe Tom will give me a discount. He's a mate, after all.

Magda scrutinizes me, her fixed stare intense. "Why are you doing this?" she asks, bewildered. I clear my throat and wonder why myself.

Because it's the right thing to do?

No. I'm not that altruistic.

Because I want to be alone with Alessia? *Yes. That's the real reason.* But given what she's been through, she's not going to want to be alone with me. *Is she?*

I run my hand through my hair, uncomfortable with my thoughts. I don't want to examine my motives too closely. "Because Alessia is a valued employee," I answer.

Yes. That sounds convincing.

Magda eyes me with suspicion.

"Will you come with me?" I ask Alessia, ignoring Magda's doubtful expression. "You'll be safe."

A lessia is overwhelmed. His level gaze is sincere. He's offering her a way out. This man she barely knows. Yet he came all the way from Chelsea to check that she was okay. He waited for her at the station. He held her while she cried. She can only remember her grandmother and her mother doing that for her. Apart from Magda, no one else in England has treated her with such kindness. It's a generous offer. Too generous. And Dante and Ylli are her problem, not his. She doesn't want to drag him into this mess. She wants to protect him from them. But she is illegally in England. She has no passport. Dante has it and all her belongings, so she's stuck.

And Magda is leaving soon, bound for Toronto.

Mister Maxim is waiting for her answer.

What will he want in return for his help?

Alessia knows so little about him. She doesn't even know what he does for a living. All she knows is that the life he leads is very different from hers.

"This is just to keep you safe. No strings attached," he says.

Strings attached?

"I don't want anything from you," he clarifies, as if he can read her mind.

No strings attached.

She likes him. She more than likes him. She's a little in love with him—but she understands it's a crush. And yet he's the only person she's told about how she came to England.

"Alessia, please answer me," he persists. His expression is anxious, his eyes wide and open and honest. He radiates concern. Can she trust him?

Not all men are monsters, are they?

"Yes," she whispers before she can change her mind.

"Great," he says, and he sounds relieved.

"What?" Magda snaps, looking at Alessia in surprise. "Do you know him?"

"She'll be safe with me," he says. "I'll take good care of her."

"I want to go, Magda," Alessia whispers.

If she goes, Magda and Michal will be safe.

Magda lights another cigarette.

"What do you want to do?" Mister Maxim turns his attention to Magda, who looks from Alessia to him, confounded.

"You haven't told me what those men want, Alessia," Magda says. Alessia had been vague about how she came to England. She had to be. Her mother and Magda are the best of friends, and she didn't want Magda e-mailing her mother to tell her what had happened. Her mother would have been devastated.

Alessia shakes her head. "I cannot. Please," she pleads.

Magda huffs. "Your mother?" she says, pulling at her cigarette.

"She cannot find out."

"I don't know."

"Please," Alessia begs.

Magda sighs with resignation and turns to Maxim. "I don't want to leave my house," she says.

"Okay. Close protection it is." He stands up, long, lean, and impossibly handsome, and fishes his iPhone out of his jeans pocket. "I need to make some calls." He leaves them staring after him as he closes the kitchen door.

When Tom Alexander was invalided out of the army, he set up a security company based in central London. He deals with high-profile, high-net-worth clients. And now me. "What have you got yourself into, Trevelyan?"

"I don't know, Tom. All I know is I need 24/7 security for a woman and her son who live in Brentford."

"Brentford? This evening?"

"Yes."

"You're bloody lucky I can help you."

"I know, Tom. I know."

"I'll come down myself and bring my best man. Dene Hamilton. I think you've met him. Served with me in Afghanistan."

"Yes. I remember him."

"See you in an hour."

Alessia stands in the hallway wearing Magda's son's anorak and holding two plastic shopping bags.

"Is that everything?" I sound as bewildered as I feel.

I can't believe this is all she has.

Alessia pales and lowers her eyes.

I frown.

The girl has nothing.

"Okay," I offer. "I'll take those, and let's go." She hands me both bags and still won't look me in the eye. I'm astonished at how little they weigh.

"Where are you going?" asks Magda.

"I have a place in the West Country. We'll go there for a few days while we work out what's to be done."

"Will I see Alessia again?"

"I hope so." *But there's no way on earth she's coming back here while those bastards are on the loose.*

Magda turns to Alessia. "Good-bye, sweet girl," she whispers.

Alessia hugs Magda and clings to her. "Thank you," she says as tears begin to trickle down her face. "For saving me."

"Hush, dear girl," Magda murmurs. "I would do anything for your mother. You know that." She releases Alessia and holds her at arm's length. "You are so strong and brave. You will make your mother proud." She cups Alessia's face and kisses her cheek.

"Say good-bye to Michal for me." Alessia's voice is strained and soft and full of sorrow. And my heart constricts.

Am I doing the right thing?

"We will both miss you. Maybe one day you'll come to Canada and meet my wonderful man?"

Alessia nods, but she's too choked up to say anything else, and she leaves through the front door while trying to wipe away her tears. I follow her, holding all that she has in the world.

Outside on the path, Dene Hamilton surveys the street. Tall, broad-shouldered, with close-cropped black hair, he's more menacing than his refined gray suit suggests. He's ex-army, like Tom, and it shows in his alert stance. He'll work in a shift pattern with another bodyguard who'll be arriving in the morning. Tom's people will safeguard Magda and Michal around the clock, and they'll remain until the two of them leave for Canada.

I stop to shake Hamilton's hand.

"We've got this, Lord Trevethick," he says, his dark eyes gleaming beneath the streetlamp as he scans the road and misses nothing.

"Thank you," I reply. It still catches me off guard when I'm addressed by my title. "You have my number. Contact me if they need anything."

"Will do, sir." Hamilton gives me a gracious nod, and I follow Alessia. She averts her face when I put my arm around her, perhaps to hide the fact that she's still crying.

Am I doing the right thing?

With a brisk wave to Magda, who's standing on the doorstep, and to Hamilton, I lead Alessia to the F-Type. I unlock it and hold the passenger door open for her. She hesitates, her expression strained. I reach up to stroke her jaw with the back of my hand. "I've got you." My tone is gentle, to reassure her. "You're safe."

Alessia throws her arms around my neck and hugs me hard, totally taking me by surprise. "Thank you," she whispers, and before I can respond, she releases me and climbs into the car. I ignore the knot in my throat and put both her bags in the boot and climb in beside her.

"This will be an adventure," I say, trying to lighten the mood. But Alessia gazes at me, her eyes brimming with sorrow.

I swallow.

I'm doing the right thing.

Yes.

I am.

But maybe not for the right reasons.

I exhale, push the ignition, and the engine growls into life.

Chapter Ten

I turn the Jaguar left onto the A4 and speed along the three-lane highway. Alessia is hunched down in the passenger seat with her arms wrapped around herself, but at least she's remembered to put on her seat belt. She's staring out at the passing industrial buildings and car showrooms, but occasionally she wipes a sleeve across her face, and I know she's still crying.

How can women cry so quietly?

"Do you want me to stop for tissues?" I ask. "I'm sorry I don't have any."

She shakes her head but doesn't look at me.

I understand why she's emotional. *What a day.* If I'm astounded by today's events, she must be overwhelmed. Completely overwhelmed. I think it's best if I leave her alone to gather her thoughts. Besides, it's late, and I have to make some calls.

I press the phone icon on the touch screen and find Danny's number. The sound of its ringtone echoes through the car via the hands-free system. Within two rings she answers.

"Tresyllian Hall," she says in her familiar Scottish brogue.

"Danny, it's Maxim."

"Master Maxim . . . I mean—"

"It's okay, Danny, don't worry," I interrupt her, with a quick glance at Alessia, who's now looking at me. "Is the Hideout or the Lookout available this weekend?"

"I think they're both available, my—"

"And next week?"

"The Lookout is booked for a weekend clay shoot."

"I'll take the Hideout, then."

Appropriate.

"I need"—I glance at Alessia's pale face—"I need two of the rooms made up and some of my clothes and toiletries brought over from the Hall."

"You'll not be staying at the Hall?"

"Not at the moment, no."

"Two rooms, you say?"

I had hoped for one. . . .

"Yes, please. And could you ask Jessie to stock the fridge for breakfast and maybe a snack tonight. And some wine and some beer. Tell her to improvise."

"Of course, milord. When will you be arriving?"

"Late tonight."

"Of course. Is everything all right, sir?"

"Everything's fine. Oh, and, Danny, can we get the piano tuned?"

"I had all of them tuned yesterday. You mentioned you wanted them all done when you were here."

"That's great. Thanks, Danny."

"You're welcome, my—" I press the OFF button before she finishes.

"Would you like to listen to some music?" I ask Alessia. She turns red-rimmed eyes to me, and my chest tightens. "Okay," I say, not waiting for her answer. On the media screen, I find what

I hope will be a soothing album and press PLAY. The sound of acoustic guitars fills the car, and I relax a little. We have a long drive ahead.

"Who is this?" Alessia asks.

"A singer-songwriter called Ben Howard."

She stares at the screen for a moment, then goes back to gazing out the window.

I reflect on all my past interactions with Alessia in light of what she's told me today. Now I understand why she's been so reticent around me, and my heart is leaden. In my fantasies I'd imagined that when I was finally alone with her, she would be laughing and carefree, gazing at me with adoring doe eyes. The reality is very different.

Very. Different.

And yet . . . I don't mind. I want to be with her.

I want her safe.

I want her. . . .

That's the truth.

I've never felt like this before.

Everything has happened so fast. And I still don't know if I'm doing the right thing. But I know I can't abandon her to those lowlifes. I want to protect her.

How chivalrous.

My thoughts take a darker turn as I dwell on morbid fantasies of what she might have had to endure and of what she might have seen. This young woman in the hands of those monsters.

Fuck. I grip the steering wheel tighter as anger surges like sulfuric acid in my gut.

If I ever get hold of those men . . .

My rage is murderous.

What have they done to her? I want to know.

No. I don't want to know.

I do.

I don't.

I glance at the dashboard.

Shit. I'm speeding.

Slow the fuck down, mate.

I ease my foot off the accelerator.

Steady.

I take a deep, cleansing breath.

Calm down.

I want to ask her what she's endured. What she's seen. But now is not the right time. All my plans, all my fantasies will be for nothing if she can't bear to be with a man . . . any man.

And I realize that I can't touch her.

Fuck.

Alessia tries but fails to stem her tears. She's dazed, drowning in her emotions.

Her fear.

Her hope.

Her despair.

Can she trust the man sitting beside her? She has placed herself in his hands. Willingly. And she's done that before—with Dante—and that didn't turn out so well.

She doesn't know Mister Maxim. Not really. He's shown her nothing but kindness since she met him—and what he's done for Magda is beyond what any reasonable man could be expected to do. Until she met Maxim, Magda had been the only person in England whom Alessia trusted. She had saved Alessia's life. She had taken her in, fed and clothed her, and found her work, through a network of Polish women who live in West London and help each other.

And now Alessia is traveling miles and miles from that place of refuge. Magda has reassured her that Mrs. Kingsbury's and Mrs. Goode's houses would be covered by one of the other girls while Alessia is away.

How long will she be gone?

And where is the Mister taking her?

She tenses. Perhaps Dante is following them?

She tightens her arms around her body. Thinking of Dante reminds her of her nightmare journey to England. She doesn't want to think about that. She never wants to think about it again. But it haunts her in moments of quiet and in her nightmares. What's become of Bleriana, Vlora, Dorina, and the other girls?

Please let them have escaped, too.

Bleriana was only seventeen, the youngest of the girls.

Alessia shudders. The song on the car stereo is about living in the confines of fear. Alessia squeezes her eyes shut. Her stomach constricts with fear, the fear she's been living with for so long, and her tears continue to fall.

W e pull in to the Gordano Services on the M5 just after 10:00 P.M. I'm hungry in spite of the cheese sandwich Magda made for me back in Brentford. Alessia is asleep. I wait for a moment to see if she'll wake now that the car has come to a standstill. Under the glow from the halogen lights in the car park, she looks serene and ethereal—the curve of her translucent cheeks, her dark lashes splayed out above them, and the stray lock of hair from her plait that curls beneath her chin. I contemplate letting her sleep but decide I can't leave her alone in the car.

"Alessia," I whisper, and her name is a prayer. I'm tempted to stroke her cheek, but I resist and whisper her name once more. She wakes with a gasp and a wide-eyed start, looking frantically around her. When her eyes meet mine, she stills.

"Hey. It's me. You've been asleep. I want something to eat, and I need the loo. Do you want to come with me?"

She blinks several times, her long lashes fluttering over expressive but unfocused eyes.

She is gorgeous.

Rubbing her face, she looks around the car park, and her whole body suddenly tenses and radiates anxiety. "Please, Mister, don't leave me here," she says quietly.

"I've no intention of leaving you here. What's wrong?"

She shakes her head, paler now.

"Let's go," I say.

Outside, I stretch as she clambers out of the car and almost runs to my side, her eyes scanning the surroundings.

What's happened?

I offer her my hand, and she grabs it, holding tight. Then to my delight and surprise, she curls her other hand around my biceps and clings to me.

"You know, I was Maxim earlier," I say, trying to make her smile. "I much prefer it to Mister."

She flashes me an anxious look. "Maxim," she whispers, but her eyes dart all over the car park.

"Alessia, you're safe."

She looks doubtful.

This will never do.

Releasing her hand, I grasp her shoulders. "Alessia, what's wrong? Please tell me."

Her expression changes, her wide eyes haunted and bleak.

"Please," I beg, watching the vapor from our breath mingle between us in the frosty air.

"I escaped," she whispers.

Shit! The rest of her story—I'm going to hear it here in a service station off the M5. "Go on," I encourage her.

"It was a place like this." She looks around again.

"What? A motorway services?"

She nods. "They stopped. They wanted us to wash. To be clean. They were being . . . um . . . kind. Or so some of the girls thought. They made it seem like it was for our . . . um . . . What is the word? Our . . . um . . . good. Benefit. Our benefit. But if we were cleaner, we would bring a higher price."

Fuck. This is going to make me angry again.

"Before. On the journey. I heard them talking. In English.

About why we were going to England. They didn't know I understood. And I knew what they were going to do."

"Shit!"

"I told the other girls. Some of them did not believe me. But
three of the girls did believe me."

Bloody hell! There are more women!

"It was night, like now. One of the men, Dante, took three of
us to the restrooms. We ran. All of us. He could not catch us all.
It was dark. I ran into the woods. I ran and ran. . . . I ran away. I
don't know about the other girls." Her voice is tinged with guilt.

Oh, God.

I can bear no more. Overcome by what this young woman has
braved, I fold her into my arms and hold her tightly. "I've got you,"
I whisper, feeling raw and exposed and enraged on her behalf. We
stand for seconds, minutes—I don't know how long—in the cold
car park, and finally, tentatively, she wraps her arms around me
and relaxes into my hold, hugging me back. She fits perfectly in
my arms. I can rest my chin on her head, should I so choose. She
looks up at me, and it's as if she's seeing me for the first time. Her
dark eyes are intense. Full of questions. Full of promise.

My breath catches in my throat.

What is she thinking?

Her eyes move to my lips, and she raises her head, her objec-
tive clear.

"You want me to kiss you?" I ask.

She nods.

Fuck.

I hesitate. I've vowed not to touch her. She closes her eyes,
offering herself to me. And I can't resist. I plant a soft, chaste kiss
on her lips, and she melts against me with a moan.

It's a wake-up call to my libido. I groan, staring down at her
parted lips.

No.

Not now.

Not here.

Not after what she's been through.

Not in a service area on the M5.

I kiss her forehead. "Come on. Let's eat." Surprised by my restraint and taking her hand, I lead her into the building.

A lessia trails beside Maxim, clinging to him while they cross the asphalt. She focuses on his comforting embrace and tender kiss, not what happened the last time she was in a service station. She tightens her hold on him. He makes her forget, and for that she's grateful. The doors to the concourse open, and they step into the building, but she halts, bringing them both to a stop.

The smell. *Zot.* The smell.

Fried food.

Sweet food.

Coffee.

Disinfectant.

Alessia winces as she recalls being hustled to the restrooms. Not one bystander noticed her plight.

"You okay?" Maxim asks.

"I have the memories," she says.

He squeezes her hand. "I've got you," he says. "Come on. I really need the lavatory." He gives her a rueful smile.

Alessia swallows. "I do, too," she says shyly, and follows him to the restrooms.

"Unfortunately, I can't take you in there with me." Maxim tilts his head at the entrance. "I'll be right outside here when you come out, okay?" he says. "You go."

Alessia, reassured, takes a deep breath and walks into the bathroom, giving him a last glance before she turns the corner. There is no line for the stalls. Only two women, one older, one younger, are there, washing their hands at the basins. Neither of them looks as if she's been trafficked from Eastern Europe.

Alessia chides herself.

What was she expecting?

The older lady, who must be at least fifty, turns to use the hand dryer, catches Alessia's eye, and smiles. Feeling encouraged and more confident, Alessia heads into a cubicle.

When she exits, Maxim is there, leaning against the opposite wall, tall and muscular, one thumb hooked in the belt loop of his jeans. His hair is ruffled and messy, his vivid green eyes intense. He grins when he sees her, his face lighting up like a child's at New Year's, and he holds out his hand. Gladly, she takes it.

The coffee shop is a Starbucks; Alessia recognizes it from the many she's seen in London. Maxim orders a double espresso for himself and, at her request, a hot chocolate.

"And what would you like to eat?" he asks.

"I am not hungry," she replies.

He raises his eyebrows. "You didn't have anything at Magda's. I know you didn't eat anything in my flat."

Alessia frowns. She threw up her breakfast as well, but she isn't about to tell him that. She shakes her head. She's too upset by the day's events to eat.

Maxim huffs in frustration and orders a panini.

"Actually, make that two," he says to the barista, giving Alessia a sideways look.

"I'll bring them over," the barista replies, directing a coquettish smile at Maxim.

"We'd like them to go." Maxim hands her a twenty-pound note.

"Of course." The barista bats her eyelashes at him.

"Great, thanks." He doesn't return her smile but turns his attention to Alessia.

"I have money," Alessia says.

Maxim rolls his eyes. "I've got this."

They move to the end of the counter to wait for their order. Alessia wonders what she will do about money. She has a little, but she needs what she has for a deposit on a room. Though he did say that he could find her a room.

Did he mean a room in his apartment? Or somewhere else?

She doesn't know. And she has no idea how long they will stay or where they're going or when she'll be able to earn more cash. She'd like to ask him, but it's not her place to question a man.

"Hey, don't worry about money," Maxim says.

"I—"

"Don't. Please." His expression is serious.

He's generous. Once again Alessia wonders what he does for a living. He has the big apartment, two cars. He organized the security for Magda. Is he a composer? Do composers make a lot of money in England? She doesn't know.

"I can see your brain working from here. What is it? Ask me? I don't bite," Maxim says.

"I want to know what is your job."

"What I do for a living?" Maxim smiles.

"Are you a composer?"

He laughs. "Sometimes."

"I thought that's what you did. I liked your pieces."

"You did?" His smile broadens, but he looks a little embarrassed. "You speak very good English," he says.

"Do you think so?" Alessia flushes at the unexpected compliment.

"Yes, I do."

"My grandmother was English."

"Oh. Well, that explains it. What was she doing in Albania?"

"She visited in the 1960s with her friend Joan, who is Magda's mother. As children Magda and my mother sent letters and became friends. They live in different countries but have remained very good friends, though they have never met."

"Never?"

"No. Though my mother would like to, one day."

"Two ham-and-cheese paninis," the barista says, interrupting them.

"Thanks." Maxim accepts the bag. "Let's go. You can tell me

more in the car," he says to Alessia as he picks up his coffee. "Bring your drink." Alessia follows him out of the Starbucks, sticking close.

In the car Maxim downs his espresso, puts the empty cup in the cup holder, and, removing half of his panini from its paper wrapper, takes an enormous bite.

Its appetizing aroma fills the car.

"Hmm," Maxim murmurs in exaggerated appreciation. As he chews, he throws Alessia a sideways look. She stares at his mouth and licks her lips.

"Want some?" he asks.

She nods.

"Here, help yourself." He passes her the second panini, then starts the car, a smirk on his face. Alessia allows herself a cautious bite of the sandwich. A string of melted cheese sticks to her lips. She uses her fingers to scoop it into her mouth and licks her fingers. Realizing how ravenous she is, she takes another bite. It's delicious.

"Better?" Maxim asks, his voice low.

Alessia grins. "You are cunning like the wolf."

"Cunning is my middle name," he says, looking pleased with himself, and Alessia can't help but laugh.

B oy, that's a good sound.

At the petrol station, I pull up beside the high-octane pump. "This won't take a minute. Eat." I grin and get out of the car. But Alessia scrambles out after me, clutching her panini, and comes to stand beside me at the pump.

"Miss me already?" I quip, trying to lighten the mood. Her lips curl in the semblance of a smile, but her eyes scour our surroundings. She's apprehensive, and this place is making her more anxious. I fill the tank.

"It is expensive!" Alessia exclaims when she sees the cost.

"Yes, I suppose it is." And I realize I've never paid attention to how much fuel costs. I've never had to. "Come on, let's go pay."

In the queue for the register, Alessia stands beside me, taking the occasional bite of her sandwich and gazing at the shelves in what looks like wonder.

"Do you want anything? Magazine? A snack? Something sweet?" I ask.

She shakes her head. "There is so much to buy here."

I look around. Everything seems so commonplace to me. "Don't you have shops in Albania?" I tease.

She purses her lips. "Of course. In Kukës there are many shops, but not like this."

"Oh?"

"This is tidy and ordered. Very neat. Pathological."

I grin. "Pathologically tidy?"

"Yes. The opposite of you."

I laugh. "The shops aren't tidy in Albania?"

"Not in Kukës. Not like this."

At the register I slide my credit card into the chip and PIN machine, conscious that she's watching my every move.

"Your card is magic," Alessia says.

"Magic?" And I have to agree with her. It is magic. I've done nothing to earn the money that's paying for the petrol. My wealth is merely an accident of birth.

"Yes," I murmur. "Magic."

Back at the car, we climb in, and I wait before pressing the ignition.

"What?" Alessia asks.

"Seat belt."

"I forget. It's like the nodding and the shaking."

What is this?

"In Albania we shake our head to say yes, and we nod to say no," she explains.

"Wow. That must be confusing."

"Your way is confusing. Magda and Michal had to teach me."

Clutching the other half of my panini, I start the car and cruise down the slip road back onto the M5.

So she mixes up yes and no? I wonder if I should review any of our previous conversations, given this new information.

"Where are we going?" Alessia asks, staring ahead into the dark night.

"My family has a place in Cornwall. It's another three hours or so."

"It is a long way."

"From London? Yes."

She takes a sip of her hot chocolate.

"Tell me about your home," I say.

"Kukës? It's a small town. Nothing much happens. . . . It's . . . um . . . what is the word? Alone?"

"Isolated?"

"Yes. Isolated. And . . . rural." She shrugs and seems reluctant to say more.

"Cornwall is rural. You'll see. Earlier you were telling me about your grandmother."

She smiles. She seems happier to talk about her grandmother. This is what I'd envisaged when I hatched our escape plan this afternoon, an easy and relaxed conversation where I find out more about her. I settle back in my seat and give her an expectant look.

"My grandmother and her friend Joan came to Albania as missionaries."

"Missionaries? In Europe?"

"Yes. The Communists banned religion. Albania was the first atheist nation."

"Oh. I had no idea."

"She came to help the Catholics. She smuggled books into Albania from Kosovo. Bibles. You know. What she did, it was dangerous. She met an Albanian man and—" She pauses, and her face softens. "They fell in love. And . . . how do you say it? The rest is history."

"Dangerous?" I asked.

"Yes. She has many hair-stand-up stories."

"Hair-stand-up?" I smile. "I think you mean hair-raising."

She grins. "Hair-raising."

"And Magda's mother?"

"She moved on to Poland as a missionary and married a Polish man," she says, as if this is obvious. "They were the best of friends. And their daughters became the best of friends."

"And that's why you came to Magda's when you escaped."

"Yes. She has been a good friend to me."

"I'm glad you've had someone."

And now you have me.

"Do you want the other half of your panini?"

"No thank you."

"Will you share it with me?"

Alessia eyes me for a moment. "Okay," she says, and fishing it out of the bag, she offers it to me.

"You take first bite."

She smiles and does exactly that, then hands it to me.

"Thank you." I flash her a quick grin. I'm relieved that she seems happier. "More music?"

She nods while chewing.

"Your choice. Just press that button and scroll through the tracks."

Alessia squints at the screen and starts exploring my playlists. She's diligently absorbed in the task. Illuminated by the screen, her face is serious and earnest. "I do not know any of this music," she murmurs.

I hand her back the panini. "Choose one."

Her finger taps the display, and I smile when I see what she's chosen.

Bhangra. Why not?

A man starts singing a cappella. "What language is this?" Alessia asks, and takes another bite. A melted piece of mozzarella escapes out of the corner of her mouth. With her index finger, she pushes it back into her mouth and sucks her finger clean. My body comes to attention.

I grip the steering wheel. "Punjabi. I think."

The band kicks in on the track, and Alessia passes the panini back to me. She sways in her seat to the rhythm. "I have not heard anything like this."

"I sometimes use this as part of a set when I'm DJing. More?" I ask, offering her what's left of the sandwich.

She shakes her head. "No. Thank you."

I pop the remainder into my mouth, pleased that I managed to get her to eat more.

"DJing?" she asks.

"You know, in a club. For people to dance to. I DJ a couple of nights a month in Hoxton."

I glance at Alessia, who is staring blankly at me.

She has no idea what I'm talking about.

"Okay, I'll have to take you to a club."

Alessia's look is still blank, but she continues to tap her feet to the beat. I shake my head. How sheltered was this girl's upbringing?

Given what she's experienced, not so sheltered. What horror has she endured? My mind races, my thoughts depressing me.

But then I recall her confession in the car park.

She escaped.

Escaped!

"They wanted us to be clean . . . we would bring a higher price."

I exhale.

I hope, for her sake, that she managed to avoid any horror. But somehow I doubt it. The journey alone must have been a nightmare. I try to grasp the magnitude of what she's been through and what she's achieved. She escaped. Found a place to live. A job. And she escaped again this afternoon from my flat. While she has nothing, she's one resourceful young woman: ingenious, talented, courageous, and beautiful. My heart swells with unexpected pride.

"You really are something, Alessia," I whisper, but she's lost in the music and doesn't hear me.

It's after midnight when I pull up the gravel drive and park outside the garage of the Hideout, one of the luxury holiday homes on the Trevethick estate. I don't want to overwhelm Alessia with the Hall—maybe that can happen later. The truth is, I want her to myself. There are too many staff in the great house, and I haven't figured out what I'll say about her or *to* her about the estate. Right now she doesn't know who I am, what I have, and what my birthright entails. And I like that . . . I like that a lot.

She's asleep. She must be exhausted. I study her face. Even in the harsh glare of the garage's security light, her features are soft and delicate in repose.

Sleeping beauty.

I could look at her for hours. She grimaces briefly, and I wonder what she's dreaming about.

Me?

I consider carrying her into the house but dismiss the idea. The steps down to the front door are steep and can be slippery. I could kiss her awake. She should be woken with a kiss, like a princess. I'm being ridiculous, and I remember that I've vowed not to touch her.

"Alessia," I whisper. "We're here."

Opening her eyes, she regards me sleepily. "Hello," she says.

"Hello, beautiful. We've arrived."

Chapter Eleven

Alessia blinks the sleep from her eyes and peers through the windshield. All she sees is a piercing light above a large steel door and a smaller wooden door to the side. The rest of the view is shrouded in darkness, though in the distance she hears a faint rumble. With the heater off, the frigid winter air infiltrates the car. Alessia shivers.

She is here. *Alone with him.*

She shoots him an anxious glance. Now that she's sitting in the dark, with this man she hardly knows, she wonders at the wisdom of her decision. The only people who saw her leave with him were Magda and the security guard.

"Come on," Maxim says, and, climbing out of the car, he goes to the trunk to retrieve her bags, his shoes crunching on the gravel.

Dismissing her unease, she opens the car door and steps onto the gravel.

Outside, it's cold. She huddles into her anorak as the icy wind whistles in her ears. The rumble in the distance is louder. She wonders what it is. Maxim puts his arm around her, in a gesture that she suspects is to protect her from the cold. Together they walk to the gray wooden door. He unlocks it and pushes it open, ushering her ahead of him. He flips a switch inside the gatepost, and small lights embedded in the side of the flagstone steps light the path down to a stone courtyard.

"This way," he says, and she follows him down the steep steps. An imposing contemporary house lit by uplighters in the ground stands before them. Alessia marvels at its modernity—all glass and white walls, bathed in light. Maxim unlocks the front door and guides her inside. He flips another light switch, and subtle downlighters illuminate the alabaster space with a soft glow. "Let me have your coat," he says, and she shrugs out of her anorak.

They are standing in an open hallway beside an impressive cloud-gray galley kitchen that's part of a vast wood-floored room. To the rear there are two turquoise sofas with a coffee table between them, and beyond that shelving stacked with books.

Books! She admires them and notices another door beside the shelves.

This house is so big.

The staircase next to her is enclosed in glass. The wooden steps appear to be suspended in the air, but they are anchored in a massive concrete block that runs down the center of the stairwell and extends to upper and lower floors.

It's the most contemporary house she's ever been in. And yet in spite of its modern design, it has a welcoming, warm feel.

Alessia begins to undo her bootlaces as Maxim marches into the kitchen and places her bags and their coats on the worktop. As she removes her boots, she's surprised by the warmth of the floor underfoot.

"This is it," he says, gesturing at their surroundings. "Welcome to the Hideout."

"The Hideout?"

"It's the name of this house."

On the other side of the kitchen is the main living area, with a white dining table that seats twelve people and two large dove-colored sofas that stand in front of a sleek steel fireplace.

"It looks bigger than from outside," Alessia says, intimidated by the scale and elegance of the house.

"Deceptive. I know."

Who cleans this place? It must take hours!

"And this house, it belongs to you?"

"Yes. It's a holiday home that we rent out to the public. It's late and you must be exhausted. But would you like something to eat or a drink before bed?"

Alessia hasn't moved from her spot in the hallway.

He owns this, too? He must be a very successful composer.

She nods at his offer.

"Do you mean yes?" he asks with a grin.

She smiles.

"Wine? Beer? Something stronger?" he asks, and she steps closer. Where she's from, women generally don't drink alcohol, though she's sneaked a raki or two, but only in the last couple of years, on New Year's Eve. Her father doesn't approve of her drinking.

Her father doesn't approve of many things . . .

Her grandmother had given her wine. But Alessia had not cared for it. "Beer," she says, because she's only ever seen men drink it—and to spite her father.

"Good choice." Maxim grins, and from the fridge he removes two brown bottles. "Pale ale okay?"

She doesn't know what that means, so she nods.

"Glass?" he asks, as he pops off both tops.

"Yes. Please."

From another cupboard he takes out a tall glass and deftly pours one of the bottles into it. "Cheers," he says as he hands

Alessia her drink. He clinks her glass with his beer bottle and takes a swig, his lips circling the bottle's neck. He closes his eyes, savoring the taste, and for some reason she has to look away.

His lips.

"*Gëzuar*," she whispers. He raises his eyebrows, surprised to hear her speaking her native tongue. It's a toast, mainly made by men, but he doesn't know that. She takes a sip, and the chilled amber liquid runs down her throat.

"Mmm." She closes her eyes in appreciation and takes another, longer draft.

"Are you hungry?" His voice is husky.

"No."

The sight of her enjoying the simple pleasure of a beer is a thrill. But now, probably for the first time ever, I'm a little lost for words. I don't know what she expects. It's strange. We have nothing in common, and the intimacy we shared in the car seems to have vanished.

"Come, I'll give you a quick tour." I offer her my hand and show her into the larger living space. "Drawing room. Um . . . living area, I suppose. It's all open-plan." I wave my hand in the general direction of the room.

Now that she's farther into the room, Alessia notices the gleaming white upright piano against the wall beside her.

A piano!

"You can play to your heart's content while you're here," Maxim says.

Her heart skips a beat, and she beams at him as he releases her hand. She lifts the lid. Written on the inside is the word:

KAWAI

She doesn't recognize the name, but that doesn't bother her. She presses middle C, and it echoes in a golden yellow hue through the big room.

"*E përkryer*," she breathes.

Perfect.

"Balcony over there." Maxim points to the wall of glass at the far end of the room. "The sea is beyond."

"The sea?" she exclaims, and whips her head to his, wanting confirmation.

"Yes," he says, puzzled and amused by her response.

She races to the glass. "I've never seen the sea!" she whispers, squinting through the murky dark and flattening her nose against the cold glass in her desperation to catch a glimpse. To her disappointment there is nothing but a jet-black night beyond the balcony.

"Never?" Maxim sounds incredulous as he steps up beside her.

"No," she says. She notices the little smudge marks her nose and breath have made on the window. Pulling her sleeve over her hand, she rubs them away.

"We'll take a walk on the beach tomorrow," he says.

Alessia's smile becomes a yawn.

"You're tired." Maxim glances at his watch. "It's half past midnight. Do you want to go to bed?"

Alessia stills, gazing at him as her heartbeat soars, and his question hangs between them full of possibility.

Bed? Your bed?

"I'll show you to your room," he murmurs, but neither of them moves. They stare at each other, and Alessia can't decide whether she's relieved or disappointed. Perhaps more disappointed than relieved—she doesn't know.

"You're frowning," he whispers. "Why?"

She remains mute, unable or unwilling to articulate what she's thinking or feeling. She is curious. She likes him. But she knows nothing about sex.

"No," he utters, as if talking to himself. "Come on, I'll take you to your room." He collects her plastic bags from the kitchen counter, and she follows him up the staircase. At the top of the stairs is a brightly lit landing with two doors. Maxim opens the second one and switches on the light.

The off-white room is spacious and airy, with a king-size bed against the far wall and a large window to one side. The linen is off-white, too, but the bed is scattered with cushions that match the colors in the dramatic seascape that hangs above the bed.

Maxim waves her inside and places her bags on a colorful embroidered bench. As she approaches the bed, she stares at her reflection in the dark window. Maxim moves to stand behind her. Mirrored in the glass, he's tall, lean, and more than handsome, and she looks wan and scruffy beside him. In every way, they are not equals, and that's never been more apparent than at this moment.

What does he see in me? I am only his cleaner.

Her mind casts back to his sister-in-law in the kitchen. She had looked elegant and stylish wearing only his oversize shirt. Alessia turns her head so she's no longer taunted by her own image while Maxim draws down the pale green blind and continues to show her around the room.

"There's an en suite here for you," he says gently, pointing to the bathroom door and diverting her from her discouraging thoughts.

My own bathroom!

"Thank you," she says, but the words seem woefully inadequate for the debt she owes him.

"Hey," he says, standing in front of her, his bright eyes brimming with compassion. "I realize that this is all very sudden, Alessia. And we hardly know each other. But I couldn't leave you at the mercy of those men. You have to understand that." He catches a loose strand of hair that's worked its way free from her braid and gently tucks it behind her ear. "Don't worry. You're safe here. I'm not going to touch you. Well, not unless you want me to." Alessia catches a trace of his scent, evergreen and sandalwood.

She closes her eyes, trying to keep a tight rein on her emotions. "This is my family's holiday home," he continues. "Think of our time here as a holiday. A place to think, reflect, get to know each other, and get some distance from all the recent dreadful events in your life."

A lump forms in Alessia's throat, and she bites her upper lip. *Don't cry. Don't cry. Mos qaj.*

"My room's next door, if you need anything. But right now, it's really late and what we both need is some sleep." He plants a tender kiss on her forehead. "Good night."

"Good night." Her voice is hoarse and almost inaudible.

He turns and leaves the room, and she's finally alone, standing in the confines of the most glorious bedroom she has ever been invited to sleep in. She looks from the painting to the bathroom door to the magnificent bed, and slowly she sinks to the floor. Wrapping her arms around herself, she begins to weep.

I hang our coats in the cloakroom, then collect my beer from the kitchen counter and enjoy a long draft.

What a day!

That first sweet kiss, I groan thinking about it—interrupted by those fucking thugs—and then her sudden disappearance and my mad drive to that godforsaken corner of West London.

And her revelation. *Sex-trafficked.*

Fuck—that was one hell of a shock.

And now we're here. Alone.

I rub my face, trying to process everything that's happened. I should be tired after the long drive and the trials and tribulations of the day, but instead I'm wired. Glancing up at the ceiling, I pinpoint where Alessia should, I hope, be sleeping peacefully. She's the real reason I'm restless. It took every shred of self-control not to pull her into my arms and . . . And what? Even after all she's told me, I can't keep my thoughts above my waist. I'm like a fucking horny schoolboy.

Leave the woman alone.

But the truth is, I still want her and don't my blue balls know it.

Hell. After all Alessia's been through, she deserves a break.

She doesn't need my lascivious attention.

She needs a friend.

Bugger. What the hell is wrong with me?

I grab my beer and drain the bottle, then reach for Alessia's glass. She's hardly touched her drink. I take a swig and run a hand through my hair. I know damn well what's wrong with me.

I want her. Badly.

I'm infatuated.

There, I've admitted it to myself. She's invaded my thoughts and my dreams since I laid eyes on her.

I fucking burn for her.

But in all my fantasies, she shares my desire. I want her, yes. But I want her wet and willing—I want her to want me, too. I know I could seduce her, but right now if she were to say yes, she'd be doing so for all the wrong reasons.

Besides, I promised her that I wouldn't touch her unless she wanted me.

I close my eyes.

When did I acquire a conscience?

Deep down I know the answer. I am hamstrung by our inequality.

She has nothing.

I have everything.

And if I take advantage of her, what would that make me? No better than those fuckers with the Eastern European accents. I've brought her to Cornwall because I want to protect her from them—and now I have to protect her from myself.

Fuck.

This is uncharted territory.

While I down the remaining beer, I wonder what's happening at the Hall. I decide that I can find out tomorrow, and I'll also let

Oliver know where I am. I doubt there's anything urgent to deal with and I'm sure he'll be in touch if there is. I can work down here. I have my phone, though I wish I'd brought my laptop.

Right now I need some sleep.

Leaving the empty glass and the beer bottle on the counter, I switch off the lights and head upstairs. I pause outside her bedroom door and listen.

Shit!

She's crying.

I've had my fill of wailing women over the last four weeks: Maryanne, Caroline, Danny, Jessie. An image of Kit's lifeless body comes to mind, and my own grief rises raw and unexpected.

Kit. Fuck. Why?

Suddenly I'm bone tired. I contemplate leaving her to cry but hesitate outside her door as the sound pierces my mourning heart. I can't leave her sobbing. Sighing, I steel myself, then knock gently on the door and let myself in.

She's crumpled on the floor, her head in her hands, right where I left her. Her grief is a reflection of my own.

"Alessia. Oh, no!" I exclaim, and scoop her into my arms. "Hush, now," I murmur, my voice cracking. I sit down on the bed, cradle her in my lap, and bury my face in her hair. Closing my eyes, I inhale her sweet scent and tighten my arms, holding her and rocking gently.

"I've got you," I whisper past the knot that constricts my throat. I couldn't rescue my brother from the demons that drove him out on his motorbike into an icy night, but I can help this beautiful girl, this beautiful, brave girl. Her sobbing ceases, and she splays her hand over my racing heart and holds it there, I don't know for how long. Finally she quiets and relaxes against me.

She's fallen asleep.

In my arms.

In the safety of my arms.

What a privilege this is—to hold a sleeping beauty.

I press a soft kiss in her hair and shift her onto the bed, then cover her with the throw. Her plait snakes across the pillow, and for a moment I consider untying it and freeing her hair, but she mumbles something unintelligible in her own language, and I don't want to wake her. I wonder once more if I haunt her dreams like she haunts mine. "Sleep, beautiful," I whisper, and switch off the light before I step onto the landing. I close her door, anxious that the glare shouldn't wake her, then turn out the hall light and stride into my bedroom, leaving my door ajar.

Just in case she needs me . . .

I press the electronic closer for the blinds, which descend over the French windows facing the sea. In the walk-in wardrobe, I strip off my clothes and find a pair of pajamas that Danny has brought over from the main house and slip on the bottoms. In London I rarely wear pajamas, but in Cornwall, with all the staff present, I have no choice. Leaving my clothes in a heap on the floor, I head into the bedroom and climb into bed. I turn off the bedside lamp and stare into the inky darkness.

Tomorrow will be a better day. Tomorrow I'll have the lovely Alessia Demachi to myself. I lie in bed questioning my judgment. I've taken Alessia away from all that she knows. She's destitute, friendless, and totally alone. Well, she has me, and I have to behave myself. "You're going soft in your old age," I mutter, and fall into an exhausted, dreamless sleep.

It's the shrill sound of her scream that wakes me.

Chapter Twelve

It takes me a couple of seconds to orient myself, and she screams again.

Fuck.

Alessia.

I fly out of bed as adrenaline fuels my body, bringing all my senses to attention. Punching the lights on in the hall, I burst into her room. Alessia is sitting up in her bed. Her head whips around at the sound and light from the hallway, her eyes wild with terror.

She opens her mouth to scream again.

"Alessia, it's me, Maxim."

Her words rush out in a torrent: "*Ndihmë. Errësirë. Shumë errësirë. Shumë errësirë!*"

What?

I sit down beside her on the bed, and she launches herself at me, nearly knocking me over and wrapping her arms around my neck.

"Hey," I soothe her once I've regained my balance, and I hold her, stroking her hair.

"*Errësirë. Shumë errësirë. Shumë errësirë,*" she whispers over and over as she clings to me, trembling like a newborn foal.

"English. In English."

"The dark," she whispers against my neck. "I hate the dark. It is so dark here."

Oh, thank fuck.

I'd imagined all manner of horrors and was prepared to fight any number of monsters, but I relax at her words. Keeping one arm around her, I lean over and switch on the bedside light.

"That better?" I ask, but she doesn't let go. "It's okay. It's okay. I've got you," I repeat several times.

After a few minutes, her trembling ceases and her body relaxes. She sits back, and her eyes meet mine.

"I am sorry," she whispers.

"Hush. Don't worry. I'm here."

She glances down at my chest, and a slow flush pinks her cheeks.

"Yeah, I normally sleep naked. Count yourself lucky I put these on," I quip.

Her mouth softens. "I know," she says, and peeks up at me through her long lashes.

"You know?"

"Yes. You sleep naked."

"You've seen me?"

"Yes." Her smile is unexpected.

"Well, I'm not sure how I feel about that." I'm grateful that she's back from whatever terror she was facing in the dark, but she continues to glance around the room anxiously.

"I am sorry. I did not mean to wake you," she says. "I was frightened."

"Was it a nightmare?"

She nods. "And when I open my eyes and it is … it is so dark—" She shivers. "I did not know if I was dreaming or awake."

"I think that would make anyone scream. It's not like London here. There's no light pollution in Trevethick. The dark here is . . . dark."

"Yes. Like the—" She stops and cringes in revulsion.

"Like?" I whisper. The teasing amusement in her eyes has vanished, replaced by a harrowed, strained expression. Turning her face away, she stares down at her lap.

I rub her back when I'm met with her silence. "Tell me," I prompt.

"In the—how do you say—*kamion* . . . Truck. In the truck," she says, suddenly inspired.

I swallow. "Truck?"

"Yes. That brought us to England. It was metal. Like a box. And dark. And cold. And the smell . . ." Her words are barely audible.

"Fuck," I say under my breath, and fold her in my arms again. She seems a little more reluctant to hug me this time, probably because I'm shirtless but I'm not going to leave her to face these gruesome nightmares on her own. In one swift movement, I stand, cradling her against my chest.

She gasps in surprise.

"I think you should sleep with me." And without waiting for a response, I carry her into my room, flick on the lights, and deposit her on the floor beside the walk-in wardrobe. Inside I find the pajama shirt and hand it to her. I point to the en suite. "You can go and change in there. You can't be comfortable sleeping in your jeans and that school sweater." I grimace at her green woolen pullover.

She blinks rapidly.

Shit. Perhaps I've really overstepped the mark.

And suddenly I feel a little self-conscious. "Unless of course you'd rather sleep alone."

"I have never slept with a man," she whispers.

Oh.

"I won't touch you. This is just sleep—so the next time you scream, I'll be right there."

Of course, I'd like to make her scream in a different way.

Alessia hesitates, looking from me to the bed, and her lips purse with what I think is resolve. "I want to sleep here, with you," she whispers and she marches into the en suite, not shutting the door until she's found the light switch.

Feeling relieved, I stare at the closed bathroom door.

At twenty-three she's never slept with a man?

I'm not going to think about that right now. It's after three in the morning, and I'm tired.

Alessia gazes at her pale face in the mirror. Wide eyes with dark circles beneath them reflect back at her. Taking a deep breath, she shakes off the remnants of her nightmare: she'd been back in the container, but this time without the other girls.

She was alone.

In the dark.

In the cold.

With that smell.

She shivers and strips off her clothes. She'd forgotten where she was until *he* appeared.

Mister Maxim. Saving her again.

Her own Skënderbeu . . . Albania's hero.

He's making a habit of this.

And she's going to sleep with him.

He'll keep her nightmares at bay.

If her father found out, he would kill her. And her mother . . . she visualizes her mother fainting at the news that Alessia is sleeping with a man. A man who is not her husband.

Don't think about Baba and Mama.

Her dear, dear mother had sent Alessia to England thinking she was saving her.

She was wrong. So wrong.

Oh, Mama.

For now she is safe with Mister Maxim. She struggles into the pj top, which is too big. She undoes her braid, shakes out her hair, then tries to tame it with her fingers but gives up. Gathering her clothes under one arm, she opens the door.

Mister Maxim's room is larger and airier than the other bedroom. It's also off-white, but here the furniture is polished wood, matching the sleigh bed that dominates the room. He is standing on the far side of the bed, and his eyes widen as he studies her. "There you are," he says, his voice husky. "I was wondering if I should send a search party."

Her gaze drifts from his startling green eyes to the tattoo on his arm. She has only glimpsed parts of it before, but even from across the room she can see the design.

A two-headed eagle.

Albania.

"What?" He follows her stare and looks down at his tattoo. "Oh. This," he says. "It's a folly of youth." He sounds a little embarrassed, and he frowns, seemingly puzzled by her keen interest. She can't take her eyes off the ink as she walks toward him. He raises his elbow so she can have a better look.

Inscribed across his biceps is a black shield bearing the image of an ivory two-headed eagle hovering over five yellow circles that are in the shape of an inverted V. Alessia places her clothes on the footstool at the end of the bed and raises her hand to touch his arm, glancing at Maxim for permission.

I hold my breath as she traces the outline of my tattoo, her finger skirting across my skin, her light touch echoing through my body, toward my groin, and I suppress a groan.

"This is the symbol for my country," she whispers. "The two-headed eagle is on the Albanian flag."

What are the odds?

I grit my teeth. I'm not sure how long I can bear her touch without reciprocating.

"But not these yellow circles," she adds.

"There're called bezants." I sound really hoarse.

"Bezant."

"Yes. It represents a coin."

"In Albanian, we have the same word. Why do you have this tattoo? What does it mean?" Alluring eyes peer up at me.

What can I say?

This is the shield from my family's coat of arms.

I don't want to explain my family's heraldry at three o'clock in the morning. And the truth is, I had the tattoo done to piss off my mother. She hates them . . . but of the family coat of arms? How could she complain?

"Like I said, a youthful folly." My eyes stray from her eyes to her lips. I swallow. "It's too late to discuss this now. Let's sleep." I toss back the quilt on the bed and step aside so that she can climb in. She obliges, revealing long, slender legs beneath the pajama shirt that is way too big for her.

This is torture.

"What is this word 'folly'?" she asks as I walk around the bed. She's propped herself up on her elbow, and her glorious dark hair falls in a riot of loose waves over her shoulders, past the contour of her breasts, and onto the bedding. She looks gorgeous, and I'm going to have to keep my hands off her.

"'Folly' in this case means a foolish action," I say as I join her in bed. I almost snort at the irony of my word definition.

If sleeping next to this beautiful girl isn't folly, I don't know what is.

"Folly," she whispers as she lays her head on the pillow. I dim the bedside light so it glows in the darkness, but I don't switch it off, just in case she wakes again.

"Yes. Folly." I lie down and close my eyes. "Go to sleep."

"Good night," she whispers, her voice soft and sweet. "And thank you."

I groan. This is going to be torture. I turn on my side, away from her, and start counting sheep.

*I'm lying on the lawn near the towering stone wall that
    surrounds the kitchen garden at Tresyllian Hall.*

The summer sun warms my skin.

*The scent from the lavender that rings the lawn and the
    sweet fragrance of the roses that climb the wall waft
    over me.*

I'm warm.

I'm happy.

I'm home.

A girlish laugh catches my attention.

*I turn my head, drawn to the sound, but I'm blinded
    by the sun and can see her only in outline. Her long,
    raven hair blows in the breeze, and she's swathed in a
    translucent blue housecoat. It billows out around her
    slim silhouetted figure.*

Alessia.

*The scent of the flowers intensifies, and I close my eyes to
    inhale their sweet, intoxicating perfume.*

When I open them, she's gone.

I wake with a start. Morning is bleeding through the cracks
between the blinds. Alessia has trespassed onto my side of the
bed, and she's nestled under my arm, her hand balled in a fist on
my abdomen, her head on my chest. Her leg intertwined with
mine.

She is all over me.

And fast asleep.

And my cock is wide awake and rock hard.

"Oh, God," I whisper, and brush my nose against her hair.

Lavender and roses.

Intoxicating.

My heart rate flips into overdrive as I make a mental list of all
the possibilities this scenario presents: Alessia in my arms. Ready.

Waiting. She is so tantalizing, so close . . . too close. If I roll over, she'll be on her back, and I can finally bury myself in her. I stare up at the ceiling, praying for self-control. I know if I move, she'll wake, so I torture myself some more and lie still, enjoying the sweet, sweet agony of having her sprawled all over me. I gather a lock of her hair between my fingers, surprised by how soft and silky it feels. She stirs, her fisted hand flexes, and her fingers splay out on my belly, tickling the beginning of my pubic hair.

Fuck!

I'm so hard and want nothing more than to grab her hand and wrap it around my erection. I'll probably explode if I do.

"Mmm," she murmurs. Her eyelids flicker open, and she looks dreamily up at me.

"Good morning, Alessia." I'm breathless.

She gasps and scrambles to put some space between us.

"I was enjoying your visit to my side of the bed," I tease.

She pulls the covers up to her chin, her cheeks rosy, her smile shy. "Good morning," she says.

"Sleep well?" I ask as I roll onto my side to face her.

"Yes. Thank you."

"Hungry?" *I know I am. And not for food.*

She nods.

"Do you really mean yes?"

She frowns.

"You said in the car yesterday that in Albania it's the opposite."

"You remembered." She sounds pleased and surprised.

"I remember everything you say." I want to tell her that she looks very lovely this morning. But I refrain. I'm behaving.

"I like sleeping with you," she says, confounding me.

"Well, that makes two of us."

"I did not have bad dreams."

"Good. Me neither."

She laughs, and I try to recall the dream that woke me. All I know is that she was part of it. As usual. "I dreamt about you."

"Me?"

"Yes."

"Are you sure it was not a nightmare?" she teases.

I grin. "Quite sure."

She smiles. She has a bewitching smile. Perfect white teeth. Pink lips that are parted possibly in invitation. "You look very desirable." The words come out of my mouth in an unguarded moment. Her deep brown eyes dilate, captivating me.

"Desirable?" Her breath catches.

"Yes."

The silence stretches between us as we gaze at each other.

"I don't know what to do," she whispers.

I close my eyes and swallow while her words from last night echo in my head.

I have never slept with a man.

"You're a virgin?" I whisper, and open my eyes to study her face.

She blushes. "Yes."

Her simple affirmation is like an ice bath to my libido. I've only slept with one virgin, and that was Caroline. It was my first time, too, and it was a disaster that nearly got us expelled from school. After that my father took me to a high-class brothel in Bloomsbury.

If you're going to start fucking girls, Maxim, you'd better learn how to fuck.

I was fifteen, and Caroline moved on. . . .

Until Kit's death.

Bloody hell.

Alessia's a virgin at twenty-three? Of course she is. What did I expect? She's different from every woman I've ever known. And she's looking at me all big eyes and expectation. I wonder again at the folly of bringing her here.

Alessia frowns, anxiety etched on her face.

Shit.

Reaching forward, I brush my thumb against her pouty bottom lip. She inhales sharply. "I want you, Alessia. Very much. But I want you to want me, too. I think we need to get to know each other before we take whatever this is any further."

There. That was the grown-up response. Yes?

"Okay," she whispers, but she looks uncertain, and possibly a little disappointed.

What does she expect of me?

And I know I need to put some distance between us to think about this. Here in my bed she's a distraction, a pouting, soft-lipped, and beautiful distraction. I sit up and cup her face in my hands. "Let's just enjoy this holiday," I murmur, and kiss her, and clamber out of bed.

Now is not the time.

It's not fair to her.

And it's not fair to me.

"Are you leaving?" Alessia asks as she sits up in bed. Her hair tumbles down around her small frame like a veil. Her eyes are round with concern; she looks effortlessly sexy, swamped in my pajama shirt.

"I'm going to grab a shower, then cook us breakfast."

"You can cook?"

I laugh at her shock. "Yeah. Well, I can cook bacon and eggs." I give her a sheepish smile and stride into the bathroom.

Bugger.

More self-abuse in the shower.

Water streams over my body, and with one hand spread on the marble tiles supporting me, I come quickly, thinking of her hand on my stomach and her hand wrapped around my dick.

A virgin.

I frown. Why am I making such a big deal of this? At least she hasn't been brutalized by those fuckers. Anger flares in my gut as I think of the men coming after her. She's safe here in Cornwall. So that's something.

Perhaps she's religious. She did say her grandmother was a

missionary, and she wears a gold cross around her neck. Or maybe premarital sex is a taboo in Albania. I have no idea. I wash my hair and my body with the soap Danny left for me.

This is not what I had in mind when I brought her down here. Her inexperience is an issue. I like sexually adventurous women who know what they're doing, know what they want, and know their limits. Breaking in a virgin is a big responsibility. I towel-dry my hair.

It's a tough job, but someone has to do it.

Might as well be me.

I stare at the cad in the mirror.

Dude. Grow up.

Maybe she wants a long-term relationship.

I've had two relationships, but neither of them for longer than eight months. So not that long. Charlotte was socially ambitious, and she moved on to a baronet from Essex. Arabella was too into drugs for my liking. I mean, who doesn't like a bump now and then, but every day? No way. I think she's in rehab again.

A relationship with Alessia. What would that entail?

I am getting way ahead of myself here. Wrapping a towel around my waist, I head back into the bedroom. She's gone.

Fuck. My heart rate doubles.

Has she fled? Again?

I knock on the door of her room. No reply. I enter, and I'm relieved to hear the shower.

For fuck's sake, get a grip.

I leave her and go to get dressed.

Alessia doesn't think she'll ever leave this shower. At home in Kukës, the bathroom had a rudimentary shower and the floor had to be mopped after each use. At Magda's the shower was over the bath. This shower has its own enclosed space, and the hot water cascades over her from the biggest showerhead she's ever seen. Even bigger than the one in Mister Maxim's bathroom at his apartment. It's blissful and like nothing she's experienced before. She washes her hair and carefully shaves her body with the disposable razor Magda gave her.

She scrubs herself with the body wash she's brought from home. Her soapy hand moves over her breasts, and she closes her eyes.

I want you, Alessia. Very much.

He wants her.

Her hand moves down.

And in her mind it's *his* hand on her body. Touching her. Intimately.

She wants him, too.

She recalls waking up in his arms and feeling the warmth and strength of his body against her skin. Her belly flutters at the memory as her hand moves. Faster. Faster. And faster. She leans against the warmed tiles. And raises her head. Her mouth open as she gulps in air.

Maxim.

Maxim.

Ah.

Her muscles clench deep inside as she comes.

Catching her breath, she opens her eyes.

This is what she wants . . . isn't it?

Can she trust him?

Yes.

He's done nothing to shake the trust she's placed in him. Last night he rescued her from her night terrors, he was kind and gentle. He let her sleep with him to keep her nightmares away.

She feels safe with him.

She hasn't felt safe for so long. It's a novel feeling, even though she knows that Dante and Ylli are still out there somewhere looking for her.

No. Do not think about them.

She wishes she knew more about men. Men and women in Kukës don't interact like they do in England. At home men socialize with men, women with women. It has always been this way. Not having brothers and kept separate from her male cousins in social situations, her experience was limited to the few male students she met at university—and her father, of course.

She runs her hands through her hair.

Mister Maxim is not like any man she's ever known.

With the water pouring onto her face, she resolves to put all her problems out of her mind. Today, as Maxim says, it's a holiday. Her first.

Wrapping her hair in a towel and her body in a bath sheet, she pads into the bedroom. A pounding beat is coming from downstairs. She listens. The music seems at odds with what she knows about him. His compositions suggest a quieter, more introspective man than the one blasting this loud music through the house.

She lays out her clothes on the bed. All of them, with the exception of her jeans and bra, had been given to her by Magda and Michal. She frowns, wishing she had something more attractive to wear. She slips on an off-white, long-sleeved T-shirt to wear over her jeans. It's a little shapeless, but it will have to do. It's all she has.

Towel-drying, then brushing out her hair, she leaves it loose and heads downstairs. Through the glass wall surrounding the staircase, she watches Maxim in the kitchen. He's wearing a pale gray sweater and the ripped black jeans and has a tea towel draped over his shoulder while he stands at the stove. He's frying bacon—the aroma is delicious—and he's shuffling to the beat of the dance music that is thumping through the room. Alessia cannot help but grin. While cleaning his apartment, she had never seen any evidence that he could cook.

Men, where she is from, don't cook.

Or dance while cooking.

The flex of his broad shoulders, the swivel of his slim hips, and his bare feet tapping in perfect time to the music are mesmerizing. She feels a delicious tightening in her belly. He rakes his fingers through his damp hair and then flips the bacon. Her mouth waters.

Mmm . . . the smell.

Mmm . . . the sight of him.

He turns suddenly, and his face lights up when he sees her on the stairs. His enormous smile mirrors hers.

"One egg or two?" he shouts above the music.

"One," she mouths as she comes down the stairs and into the big room. She turns and gasps as she looks out through the floor-to-ceiling windows.

The sea!

"*Deti! Deti!* The sea!" she shouts, sprinting to the glass wall of doors that lead onto the balcony.

I lower the heat under the bacon and hurry to the balcony doors to join Alessia, who's jumping from foot to foot, incandescent with excitement.

"Can we go down to the sea?" Her eyes are alive with delight as she bounces up and down like a child.

"Of course. Here." I unlock the balcony door and slide it open so that she can go outside. A gust of glacial air catches us both by surprise. It's freezing, but she rushes out, not caring about her wet hair, bare feet, or thin T-shirt.

Doesn't this woman have any decent clothes?

I pick up a gray throw that's draped over the back of the sofa and walk out after her. I wrap my arms and the blanket around her, holding her as she admires the view. Her face is lit up with wonder.

The Hideout and our three other holiday homes are built along a rocky promontory. A small winding path at the end of the garden leads down to the beach. It's a bright, clear day. The sun is shining, but it's bitterly cold in the howling wind. The sea is a chilly blue, flecked with white surf, and we hear the boom of the waves as they crash against the cliffs on each side of the cove. The air smells fresh and salty. Alessia turns to me, her expression one of complete awe.

"Come on, let's eat." I'm conscious that breakfast is on the stove. "You'll catch your death out here. We'll go down to the beach after breakfast." We head back inside and close the door. "I just have to do the eggs!" I shout above the music.

"Let me help!" Alessia shouts back, following me into the kitchen area, still draped in the blanket.

I turn the Sonos volume down via the app on my phone. "That's better."

"Interesting music," Alessia says in a tone that tells me that perhaps it's not her thing.

"It's Korean house. I use a few tracks when I DJ." I retrieve the eggs from the fridge. "Two eggs?"

"No, one."

"You sure?"

"Yes."

"Okay. Just one. I'm having two. You can make some toast. Bread is in the fridge, and the toaster is over there."

Together we work in the kitchen, and I'm able to watch her. Using her long, nimble fingers, she fishes the toast out of the toaster and butters each slice.

"Here." I take the two plates out of the warming drawer and place them on the counter, ready for toast.

She grins as I serve up the rest of our breakfast.

"I don't know about you, but I'm famished." I abandon the frying pan in the sink, collect both plates, and usher her toward the dining table, where I've laid two places.

Alessia looks impressed.

Why does this make me feel like I've finally achieved something?

"Sit here. You can enjoy the view."

H ow was that?" Maxim asks.

They are seated at the large dining table, Alessia at the head, where she's never sat before, and she's enjoying the view, the seascape.

"Delicious. You are a man with many accomplishments."

"You'd be amazed," he says dryly, his voice a little husky. And for some reason his tone and the way he looks at her make her breath catch.

"Do you still want to go for a walk?"

"Yes."

"Okay." Taking his phone, he dials a number. Alessia wonders who he's calling.

"Danny," he says. "No. We're fine. Can you bring a hair dryer over . . . oh, there are? Okay. Then I need a pair of Wellingtons or walking boots. . . ." He looks directly at Alessia. "What size?" he asks.

She has no idea what he's talking about.

"Shoe size," he clarifies.

"Thirty-eight."

"That's, um . . . size five, and some socks if you have any. Yes. For a woman . . . It doesn't matter. And a decent bloody warm coat . . . Yes. For a woman . . . Slim. Small. As soon as possible." He listens for a moment. "Fantastic," he says, and hangs up.

"I have a coat."

"You won't be warm enough. And I don't know about the Albanian sock thing, but it's cold out there."

She flushes. She has only two pairs of socks because she can't afford more—and she couldn't ask Magda for another pair. Magda had done enough for her.

Dante and Ylli had confiscated her luggage, and when she'd arrived in Brentford, Magda had burned most of the clothes she'd been wearing. They were no longer fit to be worn.

"Who is Danny?"

"She lives not far from here," Maxim says, directing his attention to the empty plates as he stands to clear the table.

"Let me," she says, shocked that he's clearing up. "I will wash them, too." She takes the plates from him and places them in the sink.

"No. I'll do this. There should be a hair dryer in the chest of drawers in the wardrobe in your room. Go dry your hair."

"But—" *Surely he's not going to wash up! No man does that!*

"No buts. I'll do it. You've cleaned up after me often enough."

"But it is my job."

"Today it isn't. You're my guest. Go." His tone is clipped. Stern. A frisson of apprehension runs up her spine. "Please," he adds.

"Okay," she whispers, and hurries out of the kitchen, confused and wondering if he's angry with her.

Please don't be angry.

"Alessia," he calls. She stops at the foot of the stairs and studies her feet. "Are you okay?" She nods before she dashes up the stairs.

W hat the fuck?

What did I say? I watch her retreating figure noting that she deliberately avoids eye contact with me.

Shit.

I've upset her, but I don't know how or why. I'm tempted to go after her but decide against it and begin to load the dishwasher and clean up.

Twenty minutes later, as I'm putting away the frying pan, the entry phone rings.

Danny.

I glance up at the stairs, hoping that Alessia will appear, but she doesn't. I press the buzzer to let Danny in and turn off the music, knowing she will not approve.

The hair dryer's high-pitched wheeze rings in her ears as Alessia brushes and brushes her hair beneath its heat. With each stroke her heartbeat settles to a more even pace.

He had sounded like her father.

And she'd reacted the way she'd always reacted to her father, by getting out of his way. Baba has never forgiven her or her mother that his only child is a girl. Though it's her poor mother who bears the brunt of his anger.

But Mister Maxim is nothing like her father.

Nothing.

She finishes her hair and knows that the only way to restore her equilibrium and forget about her family for a while is to play the piano. Music is her escape. It's been her only escape.

When she comes back downstairs, Mister Maxim has disappeared. She wonders where, but her fingers are itching to play. She sits down at the little white upright, lifts the lid, and with no preamble launches into her angry Bach Prelude in C Minor. The music blazes through the room in hues of brilliant orange and red, burning away any thoughts of her father and setting her free.

When she opens her eyes, Maxim is watching her.

"That was incredible," he whispers.

"Thank you," she says.

He takes a step closer and strokes her cheek with the back of his finger, then tilts her chin up so she's lost in his magnetic gaze. His eyes are the most spectacular color. Up close she notices that the irises are a darker green around the edge—the color of a Kukës fir—while toward the dilating pupil they're lighter, like a fern in the spring. When he leans down, she thinks he's going to kiss her. But he doesn't.

"I don't know what I did to upset you," he says.

She puts her fingers over his mouth, silencing him.

"You did nothing wrong," she whispers. His lips purse into a kiss against her fingertips, and she removes her hand.

"Well, if I did, I'm sorry. Now, do you want to go for a walk on the beach?"

She beams at him. "Yes."

"Okay. You need to wrap up warm."

Alessia is impatient. She practically pulls me down the stony path. At the bottom we step onto the beach, and Alessia can contain herself no more. She releases my hand and runs toward the raging sea, her hat flying off and her hair whipping in the wind.

"The sea, the sea!" she cries, and twirls around, her arms in the air. Her earlier pique is forgotten, her smile is wide and her face bright, lit from within by her joy. I stride across the coarse sand and rescue her discarded woolly hat. "The sea!" she shouts again above the roar of the water, and she gesticulates wildly, her arms like a crazy windmill, welcoming each wave as it crashes to the shore.

It's impossible not to smile. Her unbridled enthusiasm for this first-time event is too appealing and too affecting. I grin as she squeals and dances back to avoid the breakers on the shoreline. She looks ridiculous, dressed in oversize Wellingtons and an oversize coat. Her face is flushed, her nose pink, and she is utterly breathtaking. My heart clenches.

She runs toward me with childish abandon and grabs my hand. "The sea!" she cries once more, and drags me to the crashing waves. And I go willingly, surrendering myself to her joy.

Chapter Thirteen

They walk hand in hand along the coastal path and stop by an old ruin.

"What is this place?" Alessia asks.

"It's an abandoned tin mine."

Alessia and Maxim lean against the chimney stack, staring out at a choppy sea that's crested with white surf as the chill wind whistles between them. "It is so beautiful here," she says. "It is wild. It reminds me of my home."

Except I'm happier here. I feel . . . safe.

That's because I am with Mister Maxim.

"I love this place, too. It's where I grew up."

"In the house where we are staying?"

He looks away. "No. My brother built that quite recently." Maxim's mouth turns down, and he seems lost.

"You have a brother?"

"I did," he whispers. "He died." He digs his hands deep into his coat pockets and stares out at the sea, his face bleak, carved like stone.

"I am sorry," she says, and from his pained, raw expression she suspects that his brother's death is a recent event.

Reaching out, she places a hand on his arm. "You miss him," she says.

"Yes," Maxim whispers, turning his face toward her. "I do. I loved him."

She is surprised by his candor. "Do you have other family?"

"A sister. Maryanne." His fond smile is brief. "And then there's my mother." His tone becomes dismissive.

"Your father?"

"My father died when I was sixteen."

"Oh. I am sorry. Your sister and mother, do they live here?"

"They used to. They visit sometimes," he says. "Maryanne works and lives in London. She's a doctor." He flashes her a proud smile.

"*Ua.*" Alessia is impressed. "And your mother?"

"She's mostly in New York." His answer is curt. He doesn't want to discuss his mother.

And she doesn't want to discuss her father.

"There are mines near Kukës," she says to change the subject, and she gazes up at the gray-stoned chimney stack. It's like the chimney on the road to Kosovo.

"Really?"

"Yes."

"What do they mine?"

"*Krom.* I don't know the word."

"Chromium?"

She shrugs. "I don't know the English."

"I think I'd better invest in an English-Albanian dictionary," Maxim mutters. "Come on, let's walk into the village. We can have lunch."

"Village?" Alessia has seen no sign of any dwellings on their walk.

"Trevethick. It's a small village just over the hill. Popular with tourists."

Alessia falls into step beside him.

"The photographs in your apartment, are they from here?" she asks.

"The landscapes. Yes. Yes, they are." Maxim beams. "You're observant," he adds, and from his raised brows Alessia can tell he's impressed. She gives him a shy smile, and he takes her gloved hand.

They emerge from the path onto a lane too narrow to have sidewalks. The hedgerows on either side are high but cut back from the road. The brambles and bare-twigged bushes are orderly and trimmed, and here and there they are covered in clumps of snow. They walk down and around a sweeping corner, and the village of Trevethick appears at the bottom of the lane. The stone and whitewashed houses are like nothing Alessia's seen before. They look small and old, but charming nonetheless. The place is quaint—pristine—with no trash anywhere. Where she comes from, there is garbage and construction debris in the streets, and most of the buildings are built from concrete.

At the waterfront two stone quays stretch out to embrace the harbor where three large fishing boats are moored. Around the waterfront are a few shops—a couple of boutiques, a convenience store, a small art gallery—and two pubs. One called The Watering Hole, the other, The Two-Headed Eagle. A sign hangs outside, bearing a shield Alessia recognizes. "Look!" She points at the emblem. "Your tattoo."

Maxim winks at her. "You hungry?"

"Yes," she replies. "That was a long walk."

"Good day, milord." An elderly man in a black scarf, a green waxed coat, and a flat cap is leaving The Two-Headed Eagle. He is followed by a shaggy dog of indeterminate breed wearing a red coat with the name BORIS embroidered in gold across the back.

"Father Trewin." Maxim shakes his hand.

"How are you bearing up, young man?" He pats Maxim on the arm.

"Good, thank you."

"I'm pleased to hear it. And who is this fine young lady?"

"Father Trewin, our vicar, may I introduce Alessia Demachi, my . . . friend, visiting from overseas."

"Good afternoon, my dear." Trewin holds out his hand.

"Good afternoon," she says, shaking his hand, surprised and pleased that he would address her directly.

"And how are you enjoying Cornwall?"

"It is lovely here."

Trewin gives her a benign smile and turns to Maxim. "I suppose it's too much to hope that we'll see you at Sunday service tomorrow?"

"We'll see, Father."

"We lead by example, my son. Remember that."

"I know. I know." Maxim sounds resigned.

"Brisk day!" Father Trewin exclaims, moving on from that subject.

"Indeed."

Trewin whistles to Boris, who has sat patiently waiting for their pleasantries to cease. "In case you've forgotten, service starts at ten sharp." He gives them both a nod and heads on up the lane.

"Vicar is the priest, yes?" Alessia asks as Maxim opens the door to the pub and ushers her into the warmth.

"Yes. Are you religious?" he asks, surprising her.

"N—"

"Good afternoon, milord," says a large man with red hair and a complexion to match, interrupting their conversation. He stands behind an impressive bar that is hung with decorative jugs and pint glasses. There's a burning log fire at one end of the pub and several wooden high-backed benches on either side of a line of tables, most of which are occupied by men and women who could be locals or tourists, Alessia doesn't know. From the ceiling hang fishermen's ropes, nets, and tackle. The atmosphere is warm and friendly. There's even a young couple kissing at the back. Embarrassed, Alessia looks away and sticks close to Mister Maxim.

H i, Jago," I say to the barman. "Table for two for lunch?"
    "Megan will sort you out." Jago points to the far corner.
"Megan?"
Shit.
"Yeah, she's working here now."
Fuck.
I give Alessia a sideways glance and she looks puzzled. "Are you sure you're hungry?"
"Yes," Alessia replies.
"Doom Bar?" Jago asks, staring with overt appreciation at Alessia.
"Yes, please." I try not to glare at him.
"And for the lady?" Jago's voice softens, his eyes still on Alessia.
"What would you like to drink?" I ask.
She peels off her hat, releasing her hair. Her cheeks are flushed from the cold. "The beer I had yesterday?" she says. With her loose, dark curls falling almost to her waist, her shining eyes, and her radiant smile, she is an exotic beauty. I'm beguiled. Totally and utterly beguiled. I can't blame Jago for staring. "Half a pale ale for the lady," I say without looking at him.
"What is it?" Alessia asks as she begins to unzip Maryanne's quilted Barbour jacket. And I know I've been gawking at her. I shake my head, and she gives me a shy smile.
"Hello, Maxim. Or should I say 'milord' now?"
Shit.
I turn around, and Megan is standing in front of me, her expression as dark as her clothes. "Table for two?" she says with a saccharine tone and a smile to match.
"Please. And how are you?"

"Fine," she snaps, and my heart sinks, my father's voice ringing in my head.

Don't fuck the local girls, boy.

I stand aside for Alessia to precede me, and we follow in Megan's dour wake. She leads us to a table in the corner by a window that overlooks the quays. It's the best table in the establishment. So that's something.

"This okay for you?" I ask Alessia, deliberately ignoring Megan.

"Yes. It is good," Alessia responds, with a confused look at a moody Megan. I hold out her chair, and she sits. Jago arrives with our drinks, and Megan saunters off, presumably to fetch menus . . . or a cricket bat.

"Cheers." I hold up my pint.

"Cheers," Alessia replies. After a sip she says, "I do not think Megan is happy with you."

"No, I don't think so either." I shrug, brushing off the subject. I really don't want to discuss Megan with Alessia. "Anyway, you were saying about religion?"

She eyes me dubiously, as if pondering the Megan Situation, and then she continues, "The Communists banned religion in my country."

"You mentioned that in the car yesterday."

"Yes."

"But you wear a gold cross."

"Menus," Megan interrupts us, and hands us both a laminated card. "I'll be back to take your order in a minute." She turns abruptly and heads for the bar.

I ignore her. "You were saying?"

Alessia watches Megan's exit through suspicious eyes but says nothing about her. She continues, "It was my grandmother's. She was Catholic. She used to pray in secret." Alessia fondles her gold cross.

"So there's no religion in your country?"

"There is now. Since we became a republic when the Communists fell, but in Albania we don't make so much of it."

"Oh, I thought religion was everything in the Balkans?"

"Not in Albania. We are a . . . what is the word? Secular state. Religion is very personal. You know, just between a person and their God. At home we are Catholics. Most people in my town are Muslim. But we do not give it much thought," she responds with a quizzical look at me. "And you?"

"Me? Well, I suppose I'm Church of England. But I'm not religious at all." Father Trewin's words come back to me.

We lead by example, my son.

Bloody hell.

Maybe I should go to church tomorrow. Kit always managed to go at least one or two Sundays a month when he was down here.

Me, not so much.

That's another damn duty I have to fulfill.

"Are the English like you?" Alessia asks, pulling me back into the conversation.

"With regard to religion? Some are. Some aren't. The UK is multicultural."

"This I know." She smiles. "When I traveled on the train in London, there were so many different languages spoken."

"Do you like it? London?"

"It is noisy and crowded and very expensive. But it is exciting. I had never been to a big city before."

"Not even Tirana?" Thanks to my expensive education, I know the capital of Albania.

"No. I have never traveled. I had never seen the sea until you brought me here." Her glance out the window is wistful, but it gives me an opportunity to study her profile: long lashes, pert nose, pouting lips. I shift in my seat, my blood thickening.

Steady.

Megan appears with her pinched, angry face and scraped-back hair, and my problem subsides.

Boy, she is still bitter. It was one summer seven years ago. One fucking summer.

"Are you ready to order?" she asks, glaring at me. "Catch of the day is cod." She makes it sound like an insult.

Alessia frowns and glances quickly at the menu.

"I'll have the fish pie, please." And, irritated, I cock my head, daring Megan to say anything.

"For me also," says Alessia.

"Two fish pies. Any wine?"

"I'm fine with the beer. Alessia?"

Megan turns to the lovely Alessia Demachi. "For you?" she snaps.

"The beer is good for me, too."

"Thank you, Megan," I grunt in warning, and she shoots me a look.

She'll probably spit in my food—or, worse, in Alessia's.

"Shit," I murmur under my breath as I watch her march back to the kitchen.

Alessia studies my reaction.

"That goes back several years," I say, and tug at my sweater collar, embarrassed.

"What does?"

"Megan and I."

"Oh," Alessia says, her tone flat.

"She's ancient history. Tell me about your family. Do you have any siblings?" I ask, desperately trying to move on.

"No," she says abruptly, and it's obvious she's still considering Megan and me.

"Parents?"

"I have a mother and a father. Like all people." She raises a beautiful, arched eyebrow.

Oh. The delectable Demachi has teeth.

"And what are they like?" I ask, stifling my amusement.

"My mother is . . . brave." Her voice becomes soft and wistful.

"Brave?"

"Yes." Her expression turns somber, and she glances out the window once more.

Okay. This subject is definitely off-limits.

"And your father?"

She shakes her head and shrugs. "He is an Albanian man."

"And that means?"

"Well, my father is old-fashioned, and I do not . . . how do you say? We do not see eye for eye." Her face falls a little, and her troubled expression tells me this, too, is off-limits.

"Eye to eye," I correct her. "Tell me about Albania, then."

Her face brightens. "What do you want to know?" She looks up at me through those long dark lashes, and my groin tightens again.

"Everything," I whisper.

I watch and listen to her, enthralled. She is passionate and eloquent, painting a vivid picture of her country and her home. She tells me Albania is a special place where family is at the center of everything. It's an ancient country, influenced over the centuries by several cultures with differing ideologies. She explains that it's both Western and Eastern-facing, but more and more her country looks to Europe for inspiration. She's proud of her hometown. Kukës is a small place in the north near the border with Kosovo, and she enthuses about its spectacular lakes, rivers, and gorges, but most of all the mountains that surround it. She comes alive talking about the landscape, and it's clear this is what she misses about her homeland.

"And that is why I like it here," she says. "From what I have seen, the landscape in Cornwall is also beautiful."

We are interrupted by Megan and fish pie. Megan plunks the plates down on the table and leaves without a word. Her face is sour, but the fish pie is warming and delicious, and there's no sign that anyone spat in it.

"What does your father do?" I ask cautiously.

"He has a garage."

"Does he sell petrol?"

"No. He fixes cars. Tires. Mechanical things."

"And your mother?"

"She is at home."

I want to ask Alessia why she left Albania, but I know it will remind her of her harrowing journey to the UK.

"And what did you do in Kukës?"

"Well, I was studying, but my university closed, and so sometimes I work in a school with the little children. And sometimes I play the piano. . . ." Her voice tails off, and I don't know if it's because she's feeling nostalgic or if it's for another reason. "Tell me about your work." It's clear she wants to change the subject, and because I don't want to tell her what I do yet, I fill her in on my DJing career.

"And I've done a couple of summers in San Antonio in Ibiza. Now, that's a real party place."

"This is why you have so many records?"

"Yes," I answer.

"And what is your favorite music?"

"All music. I don't have a favorite genre. What about you? How old were you when you started playing?"

"I was four."

Wow. Early.

"Did you study music? I mean, music theory?"

"No."

That's even more impressive.

It's gratifying to see Alessia eat. Her cheeks are rosy, her eyes aglow, and I suspect that after two beers she's a little tipsy.

"Would you like anything else?" I ask.

She shakes her head.

"Let's go."

It's Jago who brings over our bill. I suspect Megan has refused or she's on a break. I settle up and take Alessia's hand as we leave the pub.

"I just want to make a quick detour to the shop," I say.

"Okay." Alessia's lopsided smile makes me grin.

The shops in Trevethick are owned by the estate and leased

to the locals. They do good business from Easter right through to the New Year. The only one that's actually useful is the general store. We're miles from the nearest big town, and it carries a huge range of items. A dulcet bell rings as we enter.

"If there's anything you need, let me know," I tell Alessia, who is looking at the magazine display, swaying slightly. I head to the counter.

"Can I help you?" asks the sales assistant, a tall young woman I don't recognize.

"Do you stock night-lights? For kids?"

She leaves the counter and searches the shelves in a nearby aisle. "These are the only night-lights we have." She holds up a box with a small plastic dragon inside.

"I'll take one."

"It'll need batteries," the assistant informs me.

"I'll take batteries, too."

She takes the package and returns to the counter, where I spy condoms.

Well, I might get lucky.

I glance around at Alessia, who is leafing through one of the magazines.

"I'll have a packet of condoms, too."

The young woman blushes, and I'm glad I don't know her.

"Which would you prefer?" she asks.

"Those." I point to my brand of choice. Hastily she puts the packet into a plastic bag with the night-light.

Once I've paid, I join Alessia at the front of the shop, where she's now checking out the small display of lipsticks.

"Is there anything you want?" I ask.

"No. Thank you."

Her refusal doesn't surprise me. I've never seen her wear makeup.

"Shall we go?"

She takes my hand, and we walk back to the lane.

"What is that place?" Alessia points at a distant chimney only partly visible as we walk up the lane toward the old mine. I know it, of course; it stands atop of the west wing of the great house that is Tresyllian Hall. My ancestral home.

Bugger.

"That place? It belongs to the Earl of Trevethick."

"Oh." Her brow creases for a moment, and we continue on in silence while I wage an inner war with myself.

Tell her you're the fucking Earl of Trevethick.

No.

Why not?

I will. Not yet.

Why not?

I want her to know me first.

Know you?

Spend time with me.

"Can we go down to the beach again?" Alessia's eyes are alight with excitement once more.

"Of course."

Alessia is entranced by the sea. She runs with the same uninhibited joy into the shallow surf. The Wellingtons keep her feet dry from the crashing waves.

She is . . . effervescent.

Mister Maxim has given her the sea.

Overcome with giddy delight, she closes her eyes, stretches out her arms, and breathes in the chilly, salted air. She can't remember ever feeling this . . . full. For the first time in a long time, she's enjoying a small slice of happiness. She has a keen sense of connection to the cold, wild landscape that somehow reminds her of her homeland.

She feels like she belongs.

She is complete.

Turning around, she regards Maxim as he stands on the shoreline with his hands deep in his coat pockets, watching her. The wind ripples his hair, the traces of gold glinting in the sun. His eyes are full of mirth and shine a burning emerald green.

He is breathtaking.

And her heart is full. Full to the brim.

She loves him.

Yes. She loves him.

She is giddy. Excited. And in love. This is what it should feel like. Joyful. Filling. Free. The realization surges through her like the bracing Cornish wind that whips her hair across her face.

She is in love with Mister Maxim.

All her unarticulated feelings bubble to the surface, and her face erupts into a megawatt smile. His answering smile is dazzling, and for a moment she dares to hope.

Perhaps one day he will feel the same way, too?

She dances over to him and in an unguarded moment launches herself at him, flinging her arms around his neck.

"Thank you for bringing me here," she exclaims, breathless.

He grins down at her as he holds her close. "It's my pleasure," he says.

"It will be!" she quips, and laughs as his eyes widen and his mouth drops open.

She wants him. All of him.

She whirls out of his arms and back into the shallows.

G ood God, she's tipsy, maybe even a little drunk. And beautiful. I'm infatuated.

Suddenly she slips and falls as a wave crashes over her.

Shit.

Panicked, I race to help. She tries to scramble to her feet and slips again, but when I reach her, she's laughing. And soaked. I help her up. "I think that's enough swimming for one day," I mutter. "It's freezing. Let's get you home." And I take her hand. Alessia gives me a crooked grin and trails after me across the sand toward the path back to the house. Pausing every few steps, she seems reluctant to leave the beach, but she's still giggling and appears happy enough. I don't want her catching a chill.

Back in the warmth of the Hideout, I pull her into my arms. "Your giggling is irresistible." I kiss her quickly, and slip off her soaking coat. Her jeans are sodden, but thankfully the rest of her clothes underneath seem dry. I rub her arms briskly to warm her. "You should go and change."

"Okay." Alessia grins and heads toward the stairs. Taking her coat—well, Maryanne's coat—I hang it up in the hallway over the radiator, where it will dry. I remove my boots and socks, which are also wet, then head into the guest cloakroom.

When I come out, she's disappeared and I assume she's gone upstairs to find a dry pair of jeans. I sit down on one of the kitchen barstools and call Danny to arrange supper.

Next I call Tom Alexander.

"Trevethick. How the devil are you?"

"Good, thanks. Anything to report from Brentford?"

"No. It's all quiet on the western front. How's Cornwall?"

"Cold."

"You know, old boy, I've been thinking. This is an awful lot of trouble to go to for your daily. She's a pretty girl and all that, but I hope she's worth it."

"She is."

"I've never known you to be a sucker for a damsel in distress."

"She's not a dam—"

"I hope you've sealed the deal."

"Tom, that's none of your fucking business."

"Okay. Okay. I'll take that as a no." He laughs.

"Tom," I warn.

"Yes. Yes. Trevethick. Keep your bloody hair on. It's all good here. That's all you need to know."

"Thank you. Keep me updated."

"Will do. Farewell." He hangs up.

I stare down at the phone.

Fucker.

I email Oliver.

To: Oliver Macmillan
Date: 2 February 2019
From: Maxim Trevelyan
Re: Whereabouts

Oliver

I'm in Cornwall attending to a private matter and staying at the Hideout. I'm not sure how long I'm going to be here.

Tom Alexander will be invoicing me for his services via his security company, payment for which should come out of my personal allowances.

If you need to reach me, email is better, as phone reception down here, as you know, is spotty.

Thanks.
MT

Then I text Caroline.

> In Cornwall. Will be here a while.
> Hope all well with you. Mx

She texts back immediately.

> **Do you want me to come down?**

No. Things to do.
Thanks for the offer.

Are you avoiding me?

Don't be silly.

☹ **I don't believe you.**
I'll call you at the Hall.

I'm not at the Hall.

Where are you, then?
And what the fuck are you doing
down there?

Caro. Leave it.
I'll call next week.

What are you up to?
I'm intrigued and I miss you.
I have to see the
Stepsow again this
evening. Cxxxx

Good luck. Mx

How the fuck am I going to explain to Caroline what's happening down here? I run my hands through my hair, hoping to find inspiration. Nothing comes to me, so I go looking for Alessia. She isn't in either of the upstairs bedrooms.

"Alessia!" I call as I come back into the main living area, but she doesn't reply. I dash down to the lower floor and quickly check the three ground-level guest bedrooms, the games and cinema room.

No Alessia.

Fuck.

I try to quell my rising panic and run back upstairs and through to the spa to see if she's in the Jacuzzi or the sauna.

No sign.

Where the fuck is she?

I check the scullery.

And there she is, sitting bare-legged on the floor, reading a book while the tumble dryer rumbles away.

"Here you are." I conceal my exasperation, feeling ridiculous for my concern. She stares up at me with warm brown eyes as I sink down onto the floor beside her.

"What are you doing?" I'm breathless as I lean against the wall. She draws her knees up and stretches her white top over them, concealing her legs. She rests her chin on her knees, her face an endearing shade of embarrassed pink.

"I'm reading, and I am waiting for my jeans to dry."

"I can see that. Why didn't you change?"

"Change?"

"Into another pair."

She blushes a deeper shade of pink. "I do not have another pair." Her tone is hushed and tinged with shame.

Bloody hell.

And I recall the two pathetic plastic bags that I packed into the boot of my car. They held everything she owns.

Closing my eyes, I lean my head back against the wall, feeling utterly stupid.

She has nothing.

Not even clothes. Or socks.

Shit.

Checking my watch, I realize it's too late to go shopping. And I've had two pints, so I can't—I don't drink and drive. "It's late now. Tomorrow I'll take you to Padstow, and we can get you some new clothes."

"I cannot afford new clothes. My jeans will be dry soon."

Without acknowledging her comment, I glance down at her book. "What are you reading?"

"I found this on the bookshelves." She holds up *Jamaica Inn* by Daphne du Maurier.

"Do you like it? It's set in Cornwall."

"I've just started it."

"From what I remember, I enjoyed it. Look, I'm sure I have something you can wear." I rise and hold out my hand. Clutching the book, she's a little wobbly as she stands, and the hem of her top is wet.

Shit. She'll catch a cold.

I try not to look at her long, naked legs. I try not to imagine them wrapped around my waist. I fail.

And she's wearing the Pink Panties.

Torture.

My need is a slow, dull ache.

I'll have to shower. Again.

"Come on." My voice is thick with desire, but fortunately she doesn't seem to notice. We head upstairs, and she ducks into the guest room while I explore the walk-in wardrobe to see what other clothes Danny has brought to the house.

Alessia appears by the door a few moments later wearing SpongeBob pajama bottoms and an Arsenal FC shirt.

"I have these," she says with an apologetic and still half-tipsy smile.

I stop rummaging.

Even in ridiculous, faded pajamas and a football shirt, she is stunning. "They'll do." I smirk as I imagine slipping those trousers off her hips and down her legs.

"These were Michal's," she says.

"I guessed."

"They were too small for him."

"They look a little big for you. We'll get you some clothes tomorrow."

She opens her mouth to protest, but I raise my finger to her lips. "Hush." Her lips are soft to my touch.

I want this woman.

She pouts and forms a kiss against my skin, and her eyes stray to my mouth and darken. My breath catches in my throat. "Please don't look at me like that," I whisper, taking my finger off her lips.

"Like . . . what?" Her voice is barely audible.

"You know. Like you want me."

She flushes and stares down at her feet.

"I am sorry," she whispers.

Shit. I've upset her. "Alessia." I close the space between us so I'm almost touching her. The enchanting scent of lavender and roses mixed with the salty air of the sea invades and intoxicates my senses. I stroke her cheek, and she leans her lovely face into my palm.

"I do want you," she murmurs, raising alluring eyes to mine. "But I don't know what to do."

I brush her bottom lip with my thumb. "I think you've had too much to drink, beautiful."

She blinks, and her eyes cloud with a look I don't understand. And with a lift of her chin she turns and walks out of the room.

What the hell?

"Alessia!" I call, and follow her, but she ignores me and descends the stairs.

I sigh and sit down on the top step and rub my face. I'm confused. I am trying—really fucking trying—to be noble here.

I snort at the irony.

I know the look she was giving me.

Hell. I've seen it often enough.

A fuck-me, fuck-me-now look.

Isn't that why I brought her here?

But she's tipsy, and she has no one, and she has nothing. Nothing at all.

She has me.

Hook. Line. And sinker.

If I fuck her, I'll be taking advantage.

Simple.

So I can't.

But I've offended her.

Shit.

The mournful strains of the piano suddenly fill the house. It's a melancholic Bach Prelude in E-flat Minor. I know it well because I studied it for my grade four or five music examination as a teen. She plays exquisitely, teasing out all the emotion and revealing the depths of the piece. Her skill is phenomenal. And she's articulating everything she feels through the music. She's pissed off. At me.

Bloody hell.

Maybe I should take her up on her offer—fuck her and take her back to London. But even as the thought enters my head, I know I can't do that.

I have to find somewhere for her to live.

I rub my face again.

She could live with me.

What? No.

I've never lived with anyone.

Would it be so bad?

The truth is, I don't want any harm coming to Alessia Demachi. I want to protect her.

I sigh.

What's happening to me?

Alessia pours her confusion into the Bach prelude she's playing. She wants to forget everything. His look. His doubt. His rejection. The music slowly moves through her and out into the room, filling it with the somber colors of regret. And as she plays, she surrenders herself to the melody and forgets. Everything.

When the final notes die, she opens her eyes, and Mister Maxim is standing by the kitchen counter, watching her.

"Hey," he says.

"Hey," she responds.

"I'm sorry. I didn't mean to upset you. That's twice today."

"You are very contrary," Alessia says, trying to voice her confusion. As an afterthought she adds, "Is it my clothes?"

"What?"

"That you do not like." After all, he's insisted he wants to buy her new clothes. She stands, and in an uncharacteristic, brave moment she gives him a quick twirl. She hopes she will make him smile.

Walking toward her, he eyes her football shirt and her cartoon pj's and rubs his chin as if considering her hypothesis. "I love that you're dressed like a thirteen-year-old boy." His tone is dry, but amused, too.

Alessia giggles. Loudly. Infectiously. And he laughs with her.

"That's better," he whispers. He grasps her chin and kisses her. "You are a very desirable woman, Alessia, whatever you're wearing. Don't let me or anyone else make you feel otherwise. You're also very, very talented. Play something else. For me. Please."

"Okay," she says, mollified by his kind words, and she sits down at the piano once more. She gives him a quick, knowing smile and starts to play.

It's my song.

The song I finished after I met her.

She knows it. By heart. And she plays it a damned sight better than I do. I started this song when Kit was alive . . . and now I hear my own sorrow and regret in the harmonies that fill the room. Grief hits me like a tidal wave, crashing over me. Drowning me. A knot forms in my throat, and I try to contain my emotion, but it expands, constricting my ability to breathe. I watch her, spellbound but aching as the music punctures my heart and touches the yawning void that is Kit's absence. Her eyes are closed. She's concentrating and losing herself in the sad, solemn melody.

I've tried to ignore my grief. But it's there. It's been there since the day he died. I told Alessia that I loved him. I did. I really did love him. My big brother.

But I never told him.

Not once.

And now I miss him more than he'll ever know.

Kit.

Why?

Tears burn behind my eyes as I lean against the wall, trying to fight my anguish and loss. I cover my face with my hands.

I hear her gasp, and she stops. "I'm sorry," she whispers. I shake my head, unable to speak or look at her. Hearing the scrape of the stool, I know that she's stepped away from the piano. Then I feel her near me, and she touches my arm. It's a compassionate gesture. And it's my undoing.

"That reminded me of my brother." I squeeze the words past the lump in my throat. "We buried him here, three weeks ago."

"Oh, no." She sounds crestfallen, and she wraps her arms around me, surprising me, and whispers, "I am so sorry."

I bury my face in her hair and inhale her soothing scent. And I cannot stop the tears sliding down my face.

Shit.

She's unmanned me.

I didn't cry at the hospital. I didn't cry at the funeral. I haven't cried since my father died when I was sixteen years old. Yet here. Now. With her I let go. And I sob in her arms.

Chapter Fourteen

Alessia's heart rate accelerates as she panics. Confused, she holds him, her mind in a whirl.

What has she done?

Mister Maxim. Mister Maxim. Maxim.

She thought he'd find it amusing that she knew his piece.

But no, she's reminded him of his grief. Her remorse is swift and merciless and flutters staccato in her belly. How could she have been so insensitive? He tightens his hold on her as he weeps, making no sound. Three weeks is no time. No wonder he's still grieving. She draws him closer and strokes his back. She remembers how she felt when her grandmother passed away. Nana had been the only one who understood her. The only person she could really talk to. She's been gone a year.

She swallows the burning sensation in her throat. Maxim is vulnerable and sad, and she wants nothing but to make him smile again. He has done so much for her. She runs her hands up his shoulders and to the nape of his neck and, clasping his head, turns his face to hers. His gaze holds no expectations; all she sees in his luminous green eyes is his sorrow. Slowly she pulls his mouth to hers and kisses him.

I groan when her lips brush mine. Her kiss is timid but so unexpected and oh, so sweet. I screw my eyes shut as I fight the outpouring of my grief. "Alessia." Her name is a blessing. My hands cradle her head, my fingers threading through her soft, silky hair as I accept her hesitant, unschooled kiss. She kisses me once, twice, three times.

"I've got you," she whispers.

And her words draw all the air from my lungs. I want to crush her to me and never let her go. I can't remember the last person who consoled me in my hour of need.

Alessia kisses my neck. My jaw. And my lips once more.

And I let her.

Gradually, my grief recedes, leaving only hunger in its wake. My hunger for her. I've been fighting my attraction to her since I saw her standing in my hallway holding that broom. But she's broken through all my defenses. She's exposed my grief. My need. My lust. And I'm powerless to resist.

She moves to hold and stroke my face, which is still damp with tears, and her caress spirals like a tornado through my body. I'm lost. Lost to her compassion, her courage, and her innocence. I'm lost to her touch.

My body responds.

Fuck.

I want her. I want her now. I've wanted her forever.

I tilt her head back and move one hand to hold the nape of her neck, my fingers still in her hair. With the other hand, I circle her waist and pull her against the length of my body. I deepen the kiss, my lips more insistent. Alessia lets out a little gasp, and I seize the moment and tease her tongue with the tip of mine. She tastes as sweet as she looks, and she moans.

I light up like Piccadilly Circus.

She pushes at my chest, suddenly breaking our kiss, and stares up at me with a dazed, astonished look.

Shit. What's this?

She's breathless, flushed, and her pupils are dilated. . . .

Man, she's exquisite. I don't want to let her go. "You okay?"

A shy smile pulls at the corners of her mouth, and she nods.

Does she mean yes or no?

"Yes?" I want clarification.

"Yes," she whispers.

"Have you ever been kissed?"

"Only by you."

I don't know what to say to this.

"Again," she beseeches me, and I need no further prompting. My grief is a distant memory. I'm firmly in the now with this beautiful, innocent young woman. My fingers tighten in her hair, and I ease her head back so that her mouth is once more raised to mine. I kiss her again, tempting her lips apart with my tongue, and this time I'm met with the tip of hers.

I growl deep in my throat, my arousal complete, straining against black denim.

Her hands slide up my biceps, and she clings to me as our tongues stroke and tease and taste each other. Over and over.

I could kiss her all day.

Every day.

I slide my hand down her back to her perfect behind.

Oh. God.

Placing my palm on her backside, I push her against my erection.

She gasps and frees her lips from our kiss but doesn't let me go. She's breathing hard, eyes the color of night, wide and shocked.

Fuck.

I hold her startled gaze and, summoning every ounce of my self-control, I ask, "Do you want to stop?"

"No," she says quickly.

Thank fuck.

"What's wrong?" I ask.

She shakes her head.

"This?" I ask, and press my hips against her.

She gasps.

"Yes, beautiful. I want you."

Her lips part as she inhales.

"I want to touch you. Everywhere," I whisper. "With my hands. With my fingers. With my lips. And with my tongue."

Her eyes darken.

"And I want you to touch me," I add in a husky tone.

Her mouth forms a perfect, soundless O. But her gaze shifts from my eyes to my mouth to my chest and back to my eyes.

"Too fast?" I ask.

She shakes her head. And fists her fingers in my hair and tugs, drawing my lips back to hers.

"Ah," I murmur against the corner of her mouth as pleasure rushes down my spine to my groin. "That's right, Alessia. Touch me. I want you to touch me." I crave her touch.

She kisses me and hesitantly pushes her tongue between my lips. And I take all that she's got to give.

Oh, Alessia.

We kiss. And kiss until I think I'm going to burst. I skirt the waistband of her pajamas and slip my hand inside against the warm, soft skin of her behind. She stills for a second, then grips my hair firmly, tugging hard, and kisses me with ardor—greedy and feverish.

"Easy," I breathe. "Let's take this slow."

She swallows and places her hands on my arms, looking a little abashed.

"I like your hands in my hair," I reassure her, and to make amends I run my teeth along her jawline up to her ear. Her moan is soft and husky as her head falls into the palm of my hand.

It's music to my dick.

"You're so beautiful," I whisper, and my fingers clench in her hair, tugging gently. Her chin lifts, and I anoint the underside of her throat with feather-light kisses until I reach her ear. With my other hand, I squeeze her behind, as my lips seek hers once more, my tongue teasing and exploring her mouth, giving and taking as her lips learn mine and I learn hers. I trail kisses down her neck to where her pulse beats fast and furious beneath her skin.

"I want to make love to you," I whisper.

Alessia stills.

I cradle her face with both hands and brush her lips with my thumb. "Talk to me. Do you want to stop?" She bites her top lip, and her eyes dart toward the window, where the sky is color-washed with a splash of pink from the coming dusk. "No one can see us," I assure her.

Her smile is hesitant, but she whispers, "Do not stop."

I stroke her cheek with the backs of my fingers and lose myself in her dark, dark gaze. "Are you sure you want to do this?"

She nods.

"Tell me, Alessia. I need to hear you say it." I kiss the corner of her mouth once more, and she closes her eyes.

"Yes," she breathes.

"Oh, baby," I murmur. "Wrap your legs around me." I clasp her waist and lift her, easily. She puts her hands on my shoulders. "Legs. Round me." Face shining with what I hope is lust and excitement, she hooks her legs around my waist, and her arms circle my neck.

"Hold on."

I take the stairs while she kisses my throat.

"You smell good," she says, as if to herself.

"Oh, sweetheart, so do you."

I set her down beside the bed and kiss her again.

"I want to see you." My hands find the hem of her football shirt. Gently I pull it up and over her head. Even though she's wearing a bra, she crosses her arms in front of her breasts as her hair falls in a dusky, curling cascade to her waist.

She's shy.

She's innocent.

She's stunning.

I'm aroused and touched at once, but I want her to feel comfortable.

"Do you want to do this in the dark?"

"No," she says immediately. "Not the dark."

Of course. She hates the dark.

"Okay. Okay. I get it," I reassure her. "You're gorgeous." My voice is filled with breathless wonder as I discard her shirt on the floor. I smooth her hair off her face, my hands finding her chin. I gently kiss her again and again until she relaxes, splaying her hands on my chest and kissing me back. Her fingers bunch in my sweater, and she tugs.

I peer down at her. "You want me to take this off?"

She nods with enthusiasm.

"For you, beautiful, anything." I drag my sweater and T-shirt off and drop them beside her Arsenal FC top. She glances from my eyes to my naked chest, and I stay still . . . letting her look. "Touch me," I whisper.

She gasps.

"I want you to. I don't bite."

Not unless you ask me to . . .

Her eyes light up, and carefully she places her hand over my heart.

Fuck.

I'm sure it somersaults beneath her fingers.

I close my eyes, enjoying the searing sensation.

She leans forward and kisses my skin where my heart is thundering.

Yes.

I sweep her hair off her neck and skim my lips down her throat and across her shoulder to her bra strap. I smile against her fragrant skin. Her bra is pink. With my thumb and finger, I ease her strap off her shoulder as her ragged breathing fills my ears.

"Turn around," I murmur. Alessia raises heated eyes to mine and turns so her back is against my front. She crosses her arms, covering herself once more. I scoop her hair from her other shoulder and kiss her neck while slipping my other arm around her and across her belly and grasping her hip. I pull her against me so my erection is cradled at the top of her behind.

I groan in her ear and she squirms against me.

Fuck. Me.

With great care I ease down her remaining strap, skimming my fingers across her shoulder and pressing tender, wet kisses in their wake on her skin.

Her skin is soft. And fair. And almost flawless.

She has a little mole at the base of her neck beneath the chain that holds her gold cross. I kiss it. Her scent is clean and wholesome. "You smell wonderful," I murmur between kisses as I undo her bra. Moving my arm up her body, I feel the weight of her breasts on my forearm. She sucks in a breath and holds her bra against her body with crossed arms.

"Easy," I murmur, and while I hold her close, I skim my fingers down her stomach and between her hips. Then dip my thumb into the waistband of her pajamas and glide it along her belly as I tease her earlobe with my teeth.

"*Zot*," she moans.

"I want you," I whisper, and nip her again. "And I do bite."

"*Edhe unë të dëshiroj.*"

"English." I kiss that spot behind her ear and slip my hand inside her pajamas and slide my fingers over her sex.

She's shaved!

She stiffens against me, but I graze my thumb over her clitoris. Once. Twice. Three times. Four, and she throws her head back against my shoulder and whimpers.

"Yes," I whisper, and continue stroking her. Teasing her. Arousing her. With my fingers.

She drops her arms, her bra sliding to the floor, and she grabs my legs, pulling at my jeans and clenching her hands around the material. Her mouth drops open, her eyes are screwed shut, and she's panting.

"Yes, baby. Feel it." I tease her ear with my teeth. And she bites her upper lip as my fingers continues to tantalize her.

"*Të lutem, të lutem, të lutem.*"

"English."

"Please. Please," she rasps.

And I continue to give her what she wants. What she needs.

Her legs start to tremble. And I tighten my arm around her. She's close.

Does she know?

"I've got you," I whisper, and her grasp on me tightens so she's almost cutting off the circulation to my legs. She whimpers and suddenly cries out as her body slowly convulses, and she comes apart in my arms.

I hold her through her orgasm, and she sags against me.

"Oh, Alessia," I whisper at her ear, and, lifting her into my arms, I draw back the quilt and lay her down on the bed. Her hair fans out like a wild mane over the pillows and down over her breasts, concealing all but her dark pink nipples from me.

Fuck.

Bathed in the soft, rosy light from the gathering dusk, she's exquisite—even in SpongeBob pajama trousers. "Do you have any idea how beautiful you look right now?" I ask, and she turns astonished eyes to mine.

"*Ua,*" she whispers. "No. English. Wow."

"Wow. Yes." My jeans feel several sizes too small, and I want to rip off her pajamas and bury myself in her. But she needs time. I know this. I wish my cock understood. Not taking my eyes off hers, I undo the top button and unzip the fly of my jeans to give my erection some much-needed room.

Maybe I should remove them.

Leaving on my underwear, I slip my jeans off and drop them on the floor. I take a deep breath and try to bring my breathing under control.

"May I join you?" I ask.

Eyes wide, she nods, and I need no further encouragement. I lie down beside her, propped up on my elbow. I take a strand of her hair, marveling at its softness, and wind and unwind it around my fingers.

"You like?" I ask.

She smiles, a shy but carnal smile. "Yes. I like." And her tongue quickly skims her top lip. I stifle my groan, and, reaching up, I run the back of my index finger down her cheek, along her chin and down her neck. My fingers stop at her little gold cross.

The sight of it makes me pause.

"Are you sure you want to do this?" I ask.

Her fathomless eyes stare into mine, and I feel exposed, like she's scrutinizing my soul. It's sobering. I feel far more naked than I am.

She swallows. "Yes."

"If there's anything you don't like. Or you don't want to do. Tell me. Yes?"

She nods and reaches up to caress my face. "Maxim," she whispers, and I lean down and brush her lips with mine. She groans, and she threads her hands through my hair, and her tongue tentatively touches and moistens my top lip. Desire scorches through me like wildfire. I hold her chin and deepen our first horizontal kiss. I want her. All of her. Now. Here.

I revel in her response and her kiss. Exploring. Tasting. Wanting.

Abandoning her mouth, I trail my lips down her chin, down her throat, and along her sternum. With my hand I sweep her hair aside, revealing my goal. She gasps, her fingers pressed to my scalp as I gently lave her nipple and pull it into my mouth. And suck. Hard.

"Ah," she cries.

I blow gently on it, and she writhes beside me. I skim my hand over her hip and up to her other breast. Cupping it gently, I fondle and squeeze and marvel at how responsive she is when I brush the peak with my thumb. In a split second, her nipple is tall and rigid, matching its twin. She moans, and her hips start to move to a rhythm I know so well. I skate my hand down her body, caressing her as I go and continuing to tease her breasts with my lips.

My fingers slip under her waistband and she pushes her sex into my hand. I have her. In the palm of my hand. I groan. She's wet.

She's ready.

Fuck.

Slowly, slowly, I ease my finger inside her.

She's tight. And wet.

Yes.

I withdraw my finger and ease it into her once more. "Ah," she mewls, and she tenses and fists the sheets.

"Oh, baby, I want you so much." My lips are between her breasts. "I've burned for you since I first saw you."

Her body rises to meet my hand, and she tips her head back against the pillow. I kiss her stomach and leave a wet trail of possession down her skin, to her navel. I circle it with my nose while my fingers move in and out of her. I kiss her belly and run my tongue from hip to hip.

"*Zot . . .*"

"Time to say good-bye to these," I murmur against her belly. Removing my hand from inside her, I sit up.

"I never thought . . ." she says, but her voice fades as I ease her pajamas down her legs, then toss them on top of my jeans.

"Wow," I whisper. She's finally naked in my bed and she's sexy as hell. "You've seen me naked before."

"Yes," she whispers. "But you were lying down on your front."

"Okay." *Well, this might be an education.*

I yank my underwear off, finally freeing my straining cock. And before the sight of my erection can shock or alarm her, I lean over and kiss her. Really kiss her, pouring all my want and need into her first fully naked kiss. She responds, her lips greedy, kissing me back. I caress her waist, and my hand slides down to her hip, pulling her soft, sweet body against me. With my knee I ease her legs apart. Her body rises to meet mine as her hands grasp my head once more. Tasting her skin, I skim my lips down her throat to her gold cross. I twirl it with my tongue, enjoying the taste, while my hand moves once more to capture her perfect, shapely breast.

She moans when my thumb brushes over her nipple and it rises to a sweet bud beneath my touch. My lips follow, kissing and tugging gently.

"Oh *Zot*," she whines, tightening her fingers in my hair.

I don't stop. Restless and eager, my mouth moves from one nipple to the other, tugging, licking, kissing . . . sucking. She squirms and whimpers beneath me, and my hand travels south to my ultimate goal. Alessia stills as my fingers brush over her sex, her breathing broken and rapid.

Yes.

She's wet. Still.

My thumb finds the ultimate prize, and I circle her clitoris, again and again, and gradually I ease one finger inside her once more. Her hands stray from my head, stroking my back, and then she runs her fingernails over my shoulders and digs in. But I persist, moving my finger in and out, building the rhythm while my thumb grazes and circles her clitoris over and over.

Her hips are flexing in that age-old beat, and her legs stiffen beneath me. She's close. Abandoning her breasts, I kiss her mouth and tug her lower lip with my teeth. She clenches her fists against my shoulders as her head rolls back.

"Alessia," I whisper as she cries out, her orgasm ripping through her. I hold her close as her body quivers with aftershocks, and then I kneel between her legs. She opens dark eyes that gaze up at me in clouded wonder.

Reaching for a condom, trying to keep my body in check, I whisper, "Are you ready? It'll be quick."

Might as well be truthful.

She nods.

I reach for her chin. "Tell me."

"Yes," she breathes.

Thank. Fuck.

I rip the packet with my teeth and roll on the condom, and for a horrible moment I think I'm going to come here and now.

Fuck.

I bring my cock under control and cover her body with mine, keeping my weight on my elbows.

She closes her eyes and tenses beneath me.

"Hey," I whisper, and kiss her eyelids in turn. Her arms circle my neck, and she whimpers.

"Alessia." Her lips find mine, and she kisses me hungrily. Feverishly. Desperately. And I can hold off no more.

Slowly. Slowly. Slowly, I sink into her.

Oh. Good. God.

Tight. Wet. Heaven.

She cries out, and I still. "Okay?" I rasp as I let her adjust to my intrusion.

"Yes," she breathes after a beat.

I'm not sure whether or not to believe her, but I take her at her word and begin to move. Into her. Once. Twice. Thrice. Again. And again. I rock against her.

Don't come. Don't come. Don't come.

I want to prolong this forever.

She groans, and her hips begin to move in a fitful, fledgling counterpoint.

"Yes, move with me, beautiful," I encourage her as her short, breathy gasps of pleasure spur me on.

"Please," she whispers, begging for more, and I willingly oblige. Sweat beads on my back as my body fights my restraint. I push and push until finally she stiffens beneath me and her fingernails dig into my flesh.

I move once, twice . . . a third time, and she screams as she lets go, her cry and her climax my undoing.

I come. Forcefully. Loudly. And calling out her name.

Chapter Fifteen

Maxim is heavy on top of her, his breathing forced and urgent, while Alessia lies panting beneath him. She's overwhelmed with sensation and a bone-deep fatigue, but most of all by his . . . invasion. She feels consumed. He shakes his head, leans up on his elbows, taking his weight off her, and clear, concerned eyes burn into hers. "Are you okay?" he says.

She makes a mental inventory of her body. In truth she's a little sore. She had no idea that the act of love was so physical. Her mother had told her it would hurt the first time.

And she was right.

But then, once her body got used to his presence, she'd enjoyed it. More than enjoyed it. At the end she'd lost all sense of self and shattered into tiny little pieces, exploding inside—and it had been . . . incredible.

He eases out of her, the alien feeling making her wince. He covers them both with the duvet and, leaning on his elbow, stares down at her with concern. "You haven't answered me. Are you okay?"

She nods, but the narrowing of his eyes tells her that he's not convinced.

"Did I hurt you?"

She bites her lip, still unsure what to say, and he flops down on the bed beside her and closes his eyes.

*S*hit. I hurt her.

I'd been transported from the depths of despair to an earth-shattering climax, but my rosy, postcoital, best-fuck-ever glow vanishes like a magician's rabbit. I reach down and yank the condom off my dick, disgusted with myself. When I drop it on the floor, I'm shocked to see my hand smeared with blood.

Her blood.

Fuck.

I rub my hand on my thigh and turn back to face the recrimination in her lovely face. But she stares at me, looking apprehensive and vulnerable.

Bloody hell.

"I'm sorry I hurt you." I kiss her forehead.

"My mother said to me it would hurt. But only the first time." She pulls the quilt up to her chin.

"Only the first time?"

She nods, and hope blossoms in my chest. I caress her cheek. "So you'd be willing to give it a second try?"

"Yes, I think so," she says, giving me a coy smile, and my cock thickens in approval.

Again? Already?

"Only . . . only if you want to," she adds.

"Only if I want to?" I can't keep the incredulity out of my voice. I laugh and swoop down and kiss her. Hard. "Sweet, sweet Alessia," I whisper against her lips. She grins up at me, and suddenly my heart thunders. I need to know. "Was it good . . . for you?"

She blushes her not-so-innocent shade of pink. "Yes," she whispers. "Especially at the end when I—"

When you came!

I grin, and elation radiates through my chest.

Thank fuck!

Her attention turns to her hands, which are still clutching the quilt, and her brow creases.

"What is it?" I ask.

"For you," she says quietly. "Was it good for you?"

I laugh. "Good?" I laugh again, head held back, and I'm deliriously happy, and it's been a while since I felt that way. "Alessia, it was exceptional. That was the best fuck . . . um . . . sex I've had in years."

Why is that?

Her eyes widen, and she gasps in horror. "That is a bad word, Mister Maxim." She tries to feign disapproval, but her eyes twinkle with mirth. I beam down at her and run my thumb over her bottom lip.

"Say 'Maxim.'" I want to hear my name in her provocative accent again.

Her cheeks redden once more.

"Say it. Say my name."

"Maxim," she whispers.

"Again."

"Maxim."

"That's better. I think we should get you cleaned up, beautiful. I'll run us a bath."

I throw off the covers and climb out of bed, and, collecting the condom from the floor, I stride into the bathroom.

Fuck.

I feel . . .

Giddy.

I'm a grown man, and I'm giddy!

Sex with her is better than being amped on coke . . . any drug. Any day.

I dispose of the contraceptive and turn on the taps over the bath, then add some bubble bath and watch the water turn to sweet-smelling foam. Taking one of the facecloths, I put it on the side.

Gushing water fills the tub, and I marvel at the day's events. I've finally laid my daily. Normally, once I've bedded a woman, I can't wait to be alone. But that's not how I feel today. Not with Alessia. I'm still enchanted by whatever spell she's cast over me. And, what's more, I get to spend this week and maybe next week with her. . . . The prospect is exciting.

My cock stirs in agreement.

I glance at myself in the mirror and catch my euphoric grin, and for a moment I don't recognize myself.

What the fuck is happening to me?

I run my hand through my hair in an effort to tame it and remember her blood on my hand.

A virgin.

I'll have to marry her now. I snort at my ridiculous thought as I wash my hands, but I wonder if any of my ancestors found themselves in that position. Two of my forebears were involved in well-documented, scandalous liaisons, but my knowledge of my family history is sketchy at best. Kit was thoroughly versed in the family's history and lineage. He paid attention. My father made sure of that. My mother made sure of that. It was all part of Kit's duties as heir. He knew that keeping the earldom intact meant everything to our family.

But he's no longer here.

Fuck. Why didn't I pay attention?

The bath is full, and I wander back into the bedroom, feeling a little despondent. But the sight of Alessia staring at the ceiling lifts my spirits.

My daily.

Her expression is completely unreadable. She turns and sees me and immediately shuts her eyes.

What?

Oh, I'm naked.

I want to laugh but decide that it's probably not a good idea, so I lean against the doorframe, cross my arms, and patiently wait for her to open her eyes again.

After a few moments, she pulls the bedding over her nose and peeps above it, with only one eye open.

I grin. "Take a good look." I spread my arms wide.

She blinks, and her eyes shine with a combination of embarrassment, amusement, curiosity, and, I think, a little admiration. She giggles and pulls the covers over her head. "You are teasing me." Her voice is muffled.

"Yes, I am." Unable to contain myself, I saunter to the bed, and her knuckles whiten as she tightens her hold on the quilt. I lean over and brush her fingers with my lips. "Let go," I whisper, and I'm surprised when she does. I whisk off the bedding, and she squeals, but I scoop her up into my arms and stand tall. "Now we're both naked," I say as I nuzzle her ear. She folds her arms around my neck, and I carry her, giggling, into the bathroom and set her down beside the tub. Immediately she covers her breasts.

"You don't have to be shy." I tease a strand of her hair and wind it around my index finger. "You have great hair. And a great body, too."

Her half smile and timid glance tell me this is what she needs to hear. I tug gently on the strand, and she leans toward me so that I'm able to kiss her forehead. "Besides, look." With my chin I point to the picture window behind the bath. She turns, and her sharp intake of breath lets me know she loves the view. The window looks out over the cove, and at the horizon the sun is kissing the sea in a spectacular symphony of color: gold, opal, pink, and orange burst through the purple cloudscape and over the darkening water. It's splendid.

"*Sa bukur.*" Her voice is full of wonder. "So beautiful." And she loosens her arms.

"Like you," I say, and kiss her hair. Her delicious fragrance—lavender and roses mixed with the scent of fresh sex—fills my nostrils. I close my eyes. She's more than beautiful. She's the whole package. Bright. Talented. Funny. And courageous. Yes, above all, courageous. My heart stutters, and suddenly I'm overwhelmed with emotion.

Fuck.

Swallowing hard to contain my feelings, I offer her my hand and bring her fingers to my lips. I kiss each in turn before she steps into the bath.

"Sit."

She quickly twists her hair into a gravity-defying knot that perches on her head and sinks beneath the bubbles. She winces, and I feel a stab of guilt, but her face relaxes as she looks out at the mesmerizing sunset.

I have an idea. "I'll just be a minute." I duck out of the bathroom.

The water is deep, hot, and soothing, and the bubbles have an exotic fragrance that Alessia doesn't recognize. She examines the bottle of bath gel. It reads:

JO MALONE

LONDON

ENGLISH PEAR & FREESIA

It smells expensive.

She leans back and stares out the window, and her body gradually unwinds.

The view.

Ua!

It's a picturesque scene. The sunset in Kukës is spectacular, but it sets behind the mountains. Here the sun is sinking languidly into the sea, illuminating a golden path on the water.

Remembering how she stumbled in the waves earlier, she smiles. How foolish she'd been. Foolish and free for a few hours at least, and now here she is in Mister Maxim's bathroom. It's bigger than the en suite in the guest room—and has two sinks beneath ornate mirrors. She feels a momentary pang that Maxim's brother, who had built the property, could no longer enjoy it. It's a fine house.

Catching sight of the washcloth, Alessia grabs it and gently washes between her thighs. The area is a little tender.

She'd done it.

It.

On her own terms, with someone of her own choosing, someone she desires. Her mother would be shocked. Her father . . . She shudders to think what he might do if he knew. And she'd done it with Mister Maxim, an Englishman, he of the startling green eyes and the face of an angel. She hugs herself, recalling how gentle and considerate he'd been, and her heart beats a little faster. He'd made her body come alive. She closes her eyes and remembers his clean scent, his fingers on her skin, the softness of his hair . . . his kiss. His blazing eyes, full of desire. She sucks in a breath. . . . And he wants to do it again. Her muscles tighten deep in her belly. "Ah," she whispers. It's a delicious feeling.

Yes. She wants to do it again, too.

She chuckles and hugs herself harder, trying to contain her dizzying elation. She feels no shame. This is how she's supposed to feel. This is love, isn't it? She grins and feels a little smug.

Maxim reappears carrying a bottle and two glasses. He's still naked.

"Champagne?" he offers.

Champagne!

She has read about champagne. But never thought she'd experience the taste.

"Yes, please," she says, as she sets the washcloth aside and tries to look anywhere but at his penis.

She's fascinated and embarrassed at the same time.

Large. Hooded. Flexible. Not how it was earlier.

Her experience of male genitalia has been limited to works of art. It's the first time she's ever seen one in the flesh.

"Here, hold these." Maxim interrupts her thoughts, and a blush steals across her face. He hands her the champagne glasses and smiles down at her. "You'll get used to it," he says, and his eyes sparkle with humor. Alessia wonders if he was referring to the champagne . . . or his penis, which makes her blush even more. Tearing off the copper-colored foil, he twists the wire cage and pops off the cork with ease. He pours the bubbling liquid into the glasses. Alessia is surprised and delighted to see that it's pink. Putting the bottle down on the windowsill, he clambers into the opposite end of the bath and carefully sinks into the water. The foam rises to the brim. He grins, waiting for the water to spill over the side of the bath—but it doesn't. She draws up her knees as he slides his feet on either side of her.

He takes a glass from her and clinks the one she holds. "To the bravest, most beautiful woman I know. Thank you, Alessia Demachi," he says, and he's no longer playful but deadly serious, gazing intently at her, his eyes darker, no longer sparkling.

Alessia swallows in response to the pulsing deep in her belly.

"*Gëzuar*, Maxim." Her voice is husky as she raises the glass to her lips and takes a sip of the chilled liquid. It's light and bubbly and tastes of fine summers and rich harvests. It's delicious. "Mmm," she murmurs in appreciation.

"Better than beer?"

"Yes. Much better."

"I thought we should celebrate. To first times." He holds up his glass, and she does the same.

"First times," she says, and turns to stare out the window at the setting sun. "The champagne is the same color as the sky," she says in wonder, and she knows that Maxim is watching her, but he, too, turns to enjoy the magnificent view.

"So decadent," she says, almost to herself. She's bathing with a man, a man who is not her husband, a man she's just had sex with for the first time ever, and she's drinking pink champagne.

She doesn't even know his full name.

A shocked giggle bubbles up from her happy place.

"What?" he asks.

"Your family name, is it Milord?"

Maxim's mouth drops open, and then he chuckles. Alessia pales a little and takes another sip.

"I'm sorry." He seems chastened. "That's just a . . . um . . . No. My surname is Trevelyan."

"Trev-el-ee-an." Alessia repeats it a couple of times. It's a complicated name, for a complicated man? Alessia doesn't know. He doesn't seem complicated—just very different from any man she knows.

"Hey," Maxim says. Placing his glass on the windowsill, he grabs the soap and lathers it between his hands. "Let me wash your feet." He holds out his hand.

Wash my feet!

"Let me," he whispers when she hesitates. Setting her glass on the sill, she tentatively places her foot in his hand, and he begins to massage the soap into her skin.

Oh.

She closes her eyes as his strong fingers work methodically over her instep, up her heel, and around her ankle. He rubs the sole with just the right amount of pressure.

"Ah . . ." she moans.

When he reaches her toes, he washes each individually, then rinses them off, gently tugging and twisting each one. She squirms beneath the water and opens her eyes. His steady gaze holds hers and leaves her breathless.

"Good?" he asks.

"Yes. More than good." She sounds hoarse.

"Where do you feel it?"

"Everywhere."

When he squeezes her little toe, all her muscles clench deep inside her. She gasps, and he raises her foot and, with a wicked smile, kisses her big toe.

"Now the other one," he orders in a soft voice. This time she doesn't hesitate. His fingers work their magic once more, and by the time he's finished, her entire body has turned to liquid. He kisses each toe in turn, except the smallest, which he puts into his mouth and sucks. Hard.

"Ah!" Her belly flutters. She opens her eyes to the same intense look, though now his lips are curled in a private smile. He kisses the ball of her foot.

"Better?"

"Mmm . . ." She can manage only an incoherent mumble.

A strange need claws at her belly.

"Good. I think we should get out before the water goes cold." He stands and with long legs steps out of the bath. Alessia shuts her eyes. She doesn't think she'll ever get used to seeing him naked or get used to the aching, hungry sensation lingering deep, deep within her.

"Come on," he says. He has wrapped a towel around his waist and is offering her a navy robe. Feeling a little less shy, she stands and takes his hand as he helps her out of the bath. He envelops her in the robe, which is soft but far too big for her. She turns to face him, and he kisses her, properly, fully, his tongue exploring her mouth. His fingers at her nape, holding her, guiding her. When he releases her, she's breathless.

"I could kiss you all day," he murmurs. Tiny drops of water cling to his body like dew. In her dazed state, Alessia wonders what they would taste like if she licked them off.

What!

She inhales sharply at her wayward thoughts.

How wanton.

She smiles. Perhaps she'll get used to seeing him naked.

"Okay?" he asks. She nods, and, taking her hand, he walks her back into the bedroom, where he releases her. He picks up his jeans from the floor and drags them on. She watches wide-eyed while he towel-dries his back.

"Enjoying the view?" He's smirking at her.

Her face is suddenly warm, but she holds his gaze. "I like looking at you," she whispers.

His smirk transforms into a charming, sincere smile. "Well, I like looking at you, too, and I'm all yours," he says, but his brow creases with uncertainty and he looks away. He recovers quickly and pulls on his T-shirt and sweater, then swaggers toward her and caresses her cheek, his thumb brushing the line of her jaw. "You don't have to get dressed if you don't want to. I'm expecting Danny with our supper."

"Oh?"

Danny again? Who is she? Why won't he talk about her?

Leaning down, he kisses Alessia. "More champagne?"

"No thank you. I will get dressed."

*O*h. From her tone I think she wants me to leave her alone while she dresses. "You okay?" I ask. Her small smile and nod confirm that she's fine. "Good," I mumble, and return to the bathroom to collect our glasses and the Laurent-Perrier.

The sun has finally disappeared, shrouding the horizon in darkness. Downstairs in the kitchen, I switch on the lights and put the champagne in the fridge while I consider Alessia Demachi.

Man, she's unexpected.

She seems happier and more relaxed, but I'm not sure if it was the foot massage, the bath, the champagne, or the sex. Watching her response in the bath had been a carnal treat. When she closed her eyes and moaned as I massaged her feet, she was breathtaking, her sexuality innate.

The possibilities . . .

For fuck's sake.

I shake my head at my lascivious thoughts.

I was determined to leave her alone.

Determined.

But when I finally surrendered to my grief, she distracted and comforted me. And I succumbed . . . to a woman wearing Sponge-Bob pajamas and an old Arsenal FC shirt. I can scarcely believe it.

I wonder what Kit would have made of Alessia.

You're not fucking the staff, are you, Spare?

No. Kit probably would not have approved of what I've done, though he would have liked Alessia. He always had an eye for a pretty girl.

"This house is so warm," Alessia says, interrupting my thoughts. She stands in front of the kitchen counter wearing those pajama bottoms and the white top.

"Too warm?" I ask.

"No."

"Good. More fizz?"

"Fizz?"

"Champagne?"

"Yes. Please."

I retrieve the bottle from the fridge and charge our glasses once more.

"What would you like to do?" I ask once she's taken a sip. I know what I want to do, but given she's sore, it's probably not a good idea.

Maybe later tonight.

Taking her glass, Alessia sits down on one of the sofas in the reading area and eyes the chess set on the coffee table. The entry phone buzzes.

"That will be Danny," I say, and release the latch at the entry phone.

Alessia leaps up from the sofa.

"It's okay. There's nothing to worry about," I reassure her.

Through the glass wall, I watch Danny take hesitant steps

down the steep, illuminated stone stairway carrying a white plastic crate. It looks heavy.

I open the door and trot out in my bare feet to meet her halfway up the steps.

Fuck. The ground's freezing.

"Danny. Let me take that."

"I've got it. Maxim, you'll catch your death of cold out here," she scolds, her expression disapproving. "I mean, my lord," she adds as an afterthought.

"Danny. Give me the crate." I'm not taking no for an answer.

Pursing her lips, she hands it to me, and I grin at her. "Thank you for this."

"I'll come and put it on for you."

"It's fine. I'm sure I can work it out."

"It would be much easier if you were up at the house, sir."

"I know. I'm sorry. And thank Jessie for me."

"It's your favorite. Oh, and Jessie put a spud jack in the crate for the potatoes. They've already been in the microwave, so they shouldn't take long to crisp up. Now, get inside with you. You're not wearing shoes." She scowls while shooing me into the house. And because it's freezing, I do as I'm told. Through the full-height windows, she spies Alessia on the sofa and gives her a wave, which Alessia returns.

"Thank you," I call from the shelter of the doorway with its cozy underfloor heating. I don't introduce her to Alessia. I know it's rude. But I really want to remain in our bubble for a little longer. Introductions can happen later.

Danny shakes her head, her white hair ruffled by the chilly wind, and turns to go back up the steps. I watch her ascend. She hasn't changed in all the years I've known her. This woman has tended my grazed knees, bandaged my cuts and scrapes, and iced my bruises since I was old enough to walk—always in her plaid skirt and stout shoes, never in trousers. No. I smile; it's Jessie, her partner for twelve years, who wears the trousers in that relationship. Briefly I wonder if they're ever going to marry. It's been legal for long enough. They have no excuse.

"Who is that?" Alessia asks, and peeks into the crate.

"That's Danny. I told you, she lives near here, and she's brought our supper." I retrieve the casserole dish from inside the crate. There are four large potatoes, and my mouth waters when I spot the banoffee pie.

Man, Jessie can cook.

"The stew needs heating, and we can have it with baked potatoes. Sound okay?"

"Yes. It is very okay."

"Very okay?"

"Yes." She blinks. "My English?"

"Is great," I answer, and, grinning, I brandish the spiked potato baker from the crate.

"I can do that," she says, though she looks a little doubtful.

"No. I'll do it." I rub my hands together. "I'm feeling domestic this evening, and trust me—it doesn't happen often. So take advantage."

Alessia arches a brow, amused, as if she's seeing me in an entirely new light. I hope it's a good thing.

"Here." In one of the cupboards, I find an ice bucket. "You can fill this with ice. The fridge in the scullery dispenses ice. It's for the champagne."

A glass or two later, Alessia is curled up on one of the turquoise sofas, her feet tucked beneath her, watching me while I finish putting the stew in the oven.

"Do you play?" I ask, as I come and sit beside her. Alessia's eyes flick to the marble chess set and back to me, her expression unreadable.

"A little," she says, and takes a sip of her drink.

"A little, eh?" It's my turn to raise an eyebrow. *What does she mean?* Without taking my eyes off her, I grab a white pawn and a gray one and shuffle them between my cupped hands and offer them to her in my fists. She licks her top lip and deliberately traces her index finger over the back of one hand. A tremor runs from my hand up my arm and directly to my dick.

Wow.

"This one," she says, looking up at me through inky lashes. I shift in my seat, trying to bring my body under control, and turn up my palm. It's the gray pawn. "Black." I turn the board so that the gray chess pieces are in front of her. "Okay. I'll start."

Four moves in and I'm dragging my hands through my hair. "As usual, you've been holding out on me, haven't you?" My tone is wry. Alessia bites her top lip in an effort to suppress her smile and look serious. But her eyes are alive with amusement as she watches me struggle to outmaneuver her.

Of course she can play like an ace.

Man, she is full of surprises.

I scowl in the hope that it'll intimidate her into making a mistake. Her smile broadens, lighting up her beautiful face, and I can't help my answering grin.

She is stunning.

"You're rather good at this," I observe.

She shrugs. "There is not much to do in Kukës. At home we have an old computer but no games consoles and clever phones. Piano, chess, and books, and some TV, that is what we have." She glances at the bookshelf at the end of the room, her eyes full of appreciation.

"Books?"

"Oh, yes. Many, many books. In Albanian and English. I wanted to be an English teacher." She studies the board for a moment, all humor gone.

Now she's a cleaner on the run from sex-trafficking thugs.

"But you enjoy reading?"

"Yes." She brightens. "Especially in English. My grandmother smuggled books into the country."

"You mentioned that. Sounds risky."

"Yes. It was dangerous for her. Books in English were banned by the Communists."

Banned!

Once again I realize that I know very little about her homeland.

Dude, concentrate.

I take her knight, feeling smug. But one glance at her face tells me she's hiding her smirk. She slides her rook left three squares and chuckles. "*Schah* . . . no. Check."

Shit!

"Okay, our first and last game of chess," I grumble as I shake my head in self-disgust.

This is like playing Maryanne. She always beats me.

Alessia tucks her hair behind her ear, takes another sip of champagne, and twirls her gold cross with her fingers. She's thoroughly enjoying herself—thrashing me.

It's a humbling moment.

Concentrate.

Three moves later she has me.

"Checkmate," she says, assessing me intently, and her solemn expression steals my breath away.

"Well played, Alessia Demachi," I whisper as desire heats my blood. "You're very good at this."

She glances at the board, breaking the spell. When she raises her head, she gives me a coy smile. "I played chess with my grandfather since I am six years. He was—how do you say?—a demon player. And he wanted to win. Even against a child."

"He taught you well," I murmur, recovering my equilibrium. What I really want to do is take her right here on the sofa. I consider pouncing on her—but concede that we should eat first.

"Is he still alive?" I ask.

"No, he died when I am twelve years."

"I'm sorry."

"He had a good life."

"You say you wanted to be an English teacher. What happened?"

"My university closed. They had no money. And my courses stopped."

"Well, that sucks."

She giggles. "Yes. It sucks. But I like working with little children. And I teach them music and read English to them. But only for two days each week, as I am not . . . what is the word? Qualified. And I help my mother at home. Another game?" she asks.

I shake my head. "I think my ego might need some time to recover before we do that again. Are you hungry?"

She nods.

"Good. That stew smells amazing, and I'm starving." Beef stew with prunes is my favorite of all Jessie's dishes. She used to cook it for winter shoots on the estate when Kit, Maryanne, and I were pressed into service as beaters, driving the birds toward the guns. The aroma is tantalizing. After all our activities today, I'm famished.

Alessia insists on dishing up, and I let her do that while I set the table. Surreptitiously I watch her as she busies herself in the kitchen. Her movements are neat and elegant. She has an intrinsic, sensuous grace, and I wonder if she's ever been a dancer. When she turns, her glorious hair spills down around her elfin face, and with a delicate flick of her wrist she flips it out of the way. Her long, slender fingers hold the knife as she slices open the baked potatoes, releasing wisps of steam. With her brow fixed in concentration, she spreads butter on them, and she stops to lick some melted butter from her index finger.

My groin tightens.

Oh, sweet Lord.

She glances up and catches me watching her.

"What is it?" she asks.

"Nothing." My voice is gruff. I clear my throat. "I just like looking at you. You're quite lovely." I move quickly and fold her in my arms, taking her by surprise. "I'm glad you're here with me." My lips meet hers in a quick, loving kiss.

"I am glad, too," she says with a shy smile. "Maxim." My face splits in two. I love hearing my name in her accent. I grab our plates.

"Let's eat."

The beef-and-prune stew is aromatic, sweet, and tender. "Mmm," Alessia murmurs, closing her eyes in appreciation. "*I shijshëm.*"

"Is that Albanian for 'I hate this'?" Maxim asks.

She giggles. "No. It's delicious. Tomorrow I will cook for you."

"Do you?" he asks.

"Cook?" Alessia places her hand on her heart, affronted. "Of course. I am an Albanian woman. All Albanian women cook."

"Okay. We'll go shopping tomorrow for ingredients." His grin is infectious, but as he regards her, his face grows more serious.

"One day," he says, "will you tell me the whole story?"

"Story?" Her heart begins to thud.

"Of how and why you came to England."

"Yes. One day," she says.

One day. One day! ONE DAY!

Her heart skips a beat. Those two words imply a tangible future with this man.

Don't they?

But as what?

Alessia is confused about how men and women interact in England. It's different in Kukës. She's seen enough American TV shows—when her mother wasn't monitoring what she was watching—and in London she's seen how free and easy men and women are in public together. Kissing. Talking. Holding hands. And she knows that these couples are not married. They are lovers.

Maxim holds her hand.

They talk.

He makes love to her. . . .

Lovers.

Surely that's what she and Mister Maxim are now.

Lovers.

Hope stirs in her heart, and it's a rousing but scary sensation. She loves him. She should tell him. But she's too shy to declare herself. And she doesn't know how he feels about her. But she knows she would walk to the end of the earth for him.

"Would you like dessert?" he asks.

Alessia pats her stomach. "I am full."

"It's banoffee pie."

"Banoffee?"

"Bananas, toffee, and cream."

She shakes her head. "No thank you."

He takes their empty plates to the kitchen counter and returns with a slice of banoffee pie. Sitting down, he places the plate on the table and takes a bite. "Mmm . . ." he says with exaggerated appreciation.

"You are teasing me. You want me to want your dessert?" she says.

"I want you to want a great many things. Right now it's dessert." Maxim smirks and licks his lips. With his fork he scoops up a small piece smothered in cream and offers it to her. "Eat," he whispers, his voice seductive and his heated stare mesmerizing. In response, she parts her lips and accepts the mouthful.

Oh, Zot i madh!

She closes her eyes and savors the confection as it dissolves. It's a sweet slice of heaven. When she focuses on him again, he's smiling with an I-told-you-so grin. He presents her with another, larger piece. This time she opens her mouth without hesitating. But he pops it into his own mouth, grinning with mischief as he chews. She laughs. He is so playful. She pouts, and he rewards her with a wicked grin and another bite of pie. His eyes stray to her lips as he gently wipes the corner of her mouth with his index finger.

"You missed this," he murmurs, holding up his cream-smeared finger. Gone is his humor. It's replaced by a darker, simmering look. Alessia's pulse thrums faster. And she doesn't know if it's the champagne that's making her bolder or his scorching gaze, but she surrenders to her instincts. Leaning in toward his finger and with her eyes on his, she licks the cream off with the tip of her tongue. Maxim closes his eyes, and a low hum of appreciation rumbles in his throat. Emboldened by his reaction, she licks again, then kisses the tip before gently teasing it with her teeth. Maxim's eyes fly open, and she closes her lips around his finger and sucks. Hard.

Mmm . . . He tastes clean. Male.

Maxim's mouth drops open. Alessia continues to suck, watching his pupils dilate as his eyes linger on her mouth. His response is arousing. Who knew she had the power to stir him? It's a revelation. She scrapes her teeth against the pad of his finger, and he groans.

"Screw the pie," he says, almost to himself and he withdraws his finger slowly from her mouth. He clasps her head and kisses her, his tongue going the way of his finger. Wet. Hot. Exploring and claiming her. Alessia responds immediately, her fingers twisting in his hair and hungrily kissing him back. He tastes of banoffee pie and Maxim. It's a heady mix.

"Bed or chess?" he murmurs against her lips.

Again? Yes! A thrill travels at light speed through her body.

"Bed."

"Good answer." He caresses her cheek, brushing his thumb across her bottom lip, and smiles, his eyes alight with sensual promise. Taking each other's hand, they walk upstairs. On the threshold of the bedroom, he flips the wall switch so that only the bedside lamps illuminate the room. He turns unexpectedly and kisses her, his hands on each side of her face as he backs her against the wall. Her heart begins to pound as he presses his body along the length of hers. He wants her. She can feel him.

"Touch me," he breathes. "Everywhere." And his lips are on hers again, possessive and needy, coaxing a moan from deep in her throat. "Yes. Let me hear you." His hands slide down to her waist. She splays her hands on his chest while his lips continue to savor her mouth. When he releases her, they are both panting. He rests his forehead against hers, their breath mingling, both of them straining for air.

"What you do to me." His voice is as soft as a spring breeze. He looks down at her, the longing in his eyes burning into her soul. He grips the hem of her top and pulls it over her head. She's naked beneath, and her natural inclination is to cover her breasts. But he catches her hands and grips them, keeping his eyes on hers. "You're stunning. Don't hide." He kisses her again while interlacing his fingers with hers so they are palm to palm. Holding her still, he continues the sweet invasion of her mouth. When she pulls away for air, he kisses her throat, her jaw, and his teeth skim her chin before he plants large wet kisses on the pulse point at her neck.

Her blood drums through her body with a reckless beat. Inside, she's melting. Everywhere. She flexes her fingers, but he doesn't let them go.

"Do you want to touch me?" he asks against her throat.

She groans.

"Tell me."

"Yes," she whispers, and he tugs her earlobe gently with his teeth. Squirming against him, she moans and flexes her fingers again. This time he releases her and his hands grab her hips and tug her against his erection.

"Feel me," he murmurs.

She does. All of him.

Ready. Waiting. For her.

Her heart stutters, and she gasps.

He wants her. And she wants him.

"Undress me," he coaxes, and her fingers find the hem of his T-shirt. Hesitating for only a moment, she drags it up and over his head. Once she's dropped his clothes on the floor, he puts his hands on his head.

"Now what are you going to do with me?" he asks, and a pleased, sexy smile curls his lips.

Alessia inhales, overwhelmed by his bold invitation as her eyes flit over his body. Her fingers are itching to touch him. To feel his skin beneath hers.

"Go on," he whispers, a seductive challenge in his voice. She wants to touch his chest, his stomach, his belly. She wants to kiss him there, too. The thought elicits a strange, delicious tightening deep inside her. Hesitantly, she raises her hand, and with her index finger she traces a line from his chest down between his abdominal muscles to his navel. His eyes never leave hers, his breath hitches, and she continues skating her finger down over his belly through the hair to the top button of his jeans. Her courage deserts her, and she hesitates.

Maxim grins and grabs her hand, raising it to his lips and kissing her fingertips. He turns it over and places his lips and the tip of his tongue on the inside of her wrist where her blood is pumping. He circles his tongue deliberately over her pulse, and Alessia gasps. With a smile he releases her and clasps her head. His lips find hers once more, and he explores her mouth.

She's panting when he lets her go. "My turn," he says. And with infinite care and a feather-light touch, he trails his index finger between her breasts, down her stomach, to her navel, which he rings twice before proceeding to the waistband of her pj's. Alessia's heart starts thumping, echoing in an insane rhythm in her head.

Suddenly he kneels down in front of her.

What?

She grabs his shoulders to stay upright. His hands move around to her behind as he kisses the underside of each breast and trails soft, sweet kisses to her navel.

"Ah," she groans as his tongue rims and dips into her belly button. She runs her fingers through his hair, and he looks up at her and gives her a wicked grin. With his hands on her behind, he sits back on his haunches and pulls her forward, holding her in place, and runs his nose up her sex.

"Wha—!" Alessia exclaims in shock. She tightens her fingers in his hair, and he groans.

"You smell good," he whispers, and she gasps. His hands slip into the waistband of her pj's and cup her bare backside, kneading her flesh as he rubs his nose over her clitoris, on and on.

This is not what she was expecting. The sight of him on his knees at her feet, doing what he's doing to her body, is too stimulating. She closes her eyes, tips her head back, and moans. His hands shift, and she feels her pj's gliding down her legs.

Zot.

His nose stays at the apex of her legs.

"Maxim!" she cries, scandalized, and she tries to pull his head away.

"Hush," he murmurs. "It's okay." And his tongue replaces his nose as he resists her feeble attempts to stop him.

"Ah," Alessia moans as he continues to tease her, his tongue circling around and around and around. She stops fighting him. Losing herself to the sensation and reveling in the carnal delight of his touch. Her legs begin to tremble, and Maxim grasps her hips and persists in his delicious torment.

"Please," she begs, and he stands in one fluid movement. She clutches his hips, and he kisses her again, his hands in her hair pulling her head back, and she opens up for him, relishing his tongue. He tastes different—salty, slick, and she realizes he tastes of her!

O perëndi!

His mouth on hers, his hand skims down her body, his thumb brushing over her nipple, tracing the line of her waist, then down to the junction of her thighs. His fingers tease her where moments before his tongue had been, and he slips a finger inside her. Quivering and driven by instinct, she presses her hips toward him, trying to find relief against his hand.

"Yes," he hisses with obvious pleasure as he circles his finger inside her, pushing in and out. When she tips her head back and closes her eyes, he withdraws his hand and tugs at his jeans. The zipper obliges, and out of his back pocket he produces a condom. He makes short work of removing his jeans, and Alessia watches dazed but fascinated as he rips open the packet and rolls the condom over his erection. She's breathing hard and fast . . . but she wants to touch him. There. Except she doesn't have the nerve. Yet.

And they're not even in bed. . . . What is he going to do? He kisses her again and puts his hands around her waist.

"Hold on," he whispers, and he lifts her. "Wrap your legs and arms around me."

What? Again?

She does as he asks, surprised once more by her own agility while he puts his hands under her behind and leans her back against the wall.

He's panting. "You okay?" he asks.

She nods, wide-eyed and needy. Her body aches for him. She wants him . . . badly. He kisses her and eases his hips forward and slowly sinks into her.

She groans and winces as he stretches and fills her.

He stops. "Too much?" he asks, and she hears his concern. "Tell me." His voice is urgent. "If you want to stop. Just say."

She flexes her thighs. This is okay. She can do this. She wants this. She lays her forehead against his. "More. Please."

He groans, and he begins to move, flexing his hips. Slow at first, but as Alessia pants and moans, he increases his rhythm. She tightens her hold around his neck as he picks up speed. The feeling is intense as the sensation spirals through her body. And she starts to build as he moves and moves.

Oh. No. This is too much. It's too overwhelming. She digs her nails into his shoulders.

"Maxim, Maxim," she whimpers. "I can't."

Immediately he stops moving, his breathing ragged. He kisses her and takes a deep breath, and without breaking their intimate contact he turns and walks to the bed. He sits down on the bed, then eases her gently onto her back and gazes at her with eyes the color of a forest in spring, his pupils large, betraying his need. Reaching up, she caresses his cheek, marveling at his athleticism.

"Better?" he asks as he nestles between her legs and holds his weight on his forearms.

"Yes," she whispers, and her fingers thread through his soft hair. His teeth nip at her lips, and he begins to move again. Gradually at first, but increasing his speed. This is easier, not quite as deep, and before she's aware of it, her body is no longer her own but moving to Maxim's rhythm, matching his pace as he moves back and forth into her time and again. She's lost in him, with him . . . building and building, stiffening and stiffening.

"Yes," Maxim hisses, and he pushes once more and suddenly stills with a growl. Alessia cries out as she explodes around him once, twice, again, spiraling out of control beneath his tense body.

When she opens her eyes, his forehead is against hers, his eyes screwed shut.

"Oh, Alessia," he breathes.

After a moment he opens his eyes, and she strokes his cheek as they gaze at each other. He is so dear. So, so dear.

"*Të dua,*" she whispers.

"What does that mean?"

She smiles, and he responds in kind, his face full of wonder and . . . reverence, maybe. He bends and kisses her lips, her eyelids, her cheeks, her jaw, and slowly eases himself out of her. Alessia whimpers feeling the loss, then she drifts, replete but exhausted, and falls asleep in his arms.

She lies curled up beside me, swaddled in the quilt.

Small. Vulnerable. Beautiful.

This young woman who has been through so much is now here beside me, where I can protect her. I stretch out, watching the steady rise and fall of her chest: her lips parted as she breathes, her dark lashes fanned out over her cheeks. Her skin is fair, her lips rosy. She's gorgeous, and I know that I will never tire of looking at her. I'm enthralled and spellbound by her. She's magical, in every way.

I've had sex too many times to count, but I've never felt this connected. It's a foreign and unsettling feeling, as is my yearning for more.

I brush a stray lock of hair off her forehead simply as an excuse to touch her. Alessia stirs and mumbles something in Albanian, and I freeze, afraid that I've woken her. But she settles once more into a peaceful sleep and I remember that she'll fear the dark should she wake. Careful not to disturb her, I climb out of bed and hurry downstairs to retrieve the night-light I purchased earlier. I fit the batteries, switch it on, and place it on the bedside table next to Alessia. Should she wake, she won't be in darkness.

Slipping back under the covers, I lie down and study her. She's lovely—the curve of her cheek, of her chin, the way that tiny gold cross nestles in the hollow at the base of her throat—she's exquisite. She looks young but serene as she sleeps. Taking a strand of her hair, I wind it around my finger. I hope to God she's feeling safer now. And that her dreams aren't the nightmares she endured yesterday. She sighs, and her lips curl in a smile. Her expression is encouraging. I gaze at her until I can no longer keep my eyes open. And before I drift off to sleep, I murmur her name.

Alessia.

Chapter Sixteen

I sense her before I'm fully awake. The warmth of her body seeps into mine. Enjoying the feel of her skin on my skin, I open my eyes to greet the misty morning and the lovely Alessia. She's fast asleep and curled around me like a fern, her hand on my belly, her head on my chest. My arm is wrapped possessively around her shoulders, holding her close, and she's naked. I grin as my body rouses.

What a difference a day makes.

I lie for a moment cherishing her heat and the fragrance of her hair. She shifts and mumbles something unintelligible, and her eyelids flutter open.

"Good morning, beautiful," I whisper. "This is your early-morning wake-up call." And I ease her onto her back. She blinks a couple of times as I kiss the tip of her nose and nuzzle the pulse point beneath her ear, and she beams and throws her arms around my neck as my hand travels down to her breast.

• • •

The sun is shining. The air is crisp and cold. "No Diggity" blares over the sound system as I drive up the A39 toward Padstow. I've ruled out going to Sunday service. There'll be too many people at the local parish church who know me. Once I've told Alessia who I am and what I do . . . then maybe. I glance at her as her heels bounce in time to the music. She flashes me a quick crotch-tightening grin.

Man, she is captivating.

Her smile lights up the Jag's interior—and me.

I give her a wicked smile in return, remembering this morning. And last night. She tucks her wild hair behind her ear, and an innocent blush steals across her cheeks. Perhaps she's thinking about this morning, too. I hope so. I see her, a vision in my bed, head tipped back in ecstasy, her mouth open as she cries out and comes, her hair spilling over the edge of the bed. My blood heads south at the thought. *Yeah.* She seemed to enjoy it. She seemed to enjoy it very much. Shifting in my seat at the memory, I reach across to squeeze her knee.

"You okay?" I ask.

She nods, her deep brown eyes sparkling.

"Me, too." I take her hand, bring it to my lips, and give her a grateful kiss on her palm.

I feel buoyant—more than buoyant, I'm elated. I'm happier than I've been . . . since . . . since Kit died. No. Since before Kit's death. And I know it's because I'm with Alessia.

I'm intoxicated with her.

But I don't dwell on my feelings. I don't want to. They are new and raw and a little unsettling. I've never felt like this. Truth is, I'm excited. I'm going shopping with a woman, and I'm looking forward to it—is this a first?

But I suspect it will be a battle with Alessia. She's proud. Maybe it's an Albanian characteristic. At breakfast she was adamant that I couldn't buy her any new clothes. But she's sitting beside me in her only pair of jeans, the thin, graying white top, her leaky boots, and my sister's old jacket. This is a fight she's not going to win.

I park in the spacious car park by the quay. She's curious, peering through the windscreen at our surroundings.

"Want to look around?" I ask, and we climb out of the car.

It's a picture-postcard scene: antiquated houses and cottages built of gray Cornish stone line the small harbor where a few fishing boats are moored up, idle, because it's a Sunday.

"This is a good view," Alessia says. She's huddled in her coat, and I stretch my arm around her shoulders and hold her to me.

"Let's go and get you some warm clothes," I offer with a smile, but she immediately steps out of my embrace.

"Maxim, I cannot pay for new clothes."

"It's my treat."

"Treat?" She frowns.

"Alessia, you have nothing. This is very easy for me to put right. Please. Let me. I want to."

"It is not right."

"Says who?"

She taps her finger to her lips, and it appears that this is not an argument she's considered. "Me. *I* say," she answers eventually.

I sigh. "They are a gift for all your hard work—"

"They are a gift because I have sexual intercourse with you."

"What? No!" I laugh, appalled and amused in equal measure. I quickly scan the quay to check no one can hear us. "I offered to buy you clothes before the sex, Alessia. Come on. Look at you. You're freezing. And I know your boots leak. I've seen your wet footprints in my hallway."

She opens her mouth to speak.

I hold up my hand to stop her. "Please," I insist. "It would give me great pleasure."

She purses her lips, unimpressed. I try a different tack. "I'm going to buy them for you anyway, whether you're there or not. So you can come with me and choose something you like or leave it to me."

She folds her arms.

Fuck. Alessia Demachi has a stubborn streak.

"Please. For me," I beseech her, holding out my hand. She glares at me, and I give her my very best smile. Then she sighs—resigned, I think—and puts her hand in mine.

Yes.

Mister Maxim is right. She needs clothes. Why is she being so obstinate about his generous offer? It's because he's done so much for her already. She trots beside him along the quay, trying to ignore the scandalized voice of her mother that rings in her head.

He is not your husband. He is not your husband.

She shakes her head.

Enough!

She's not going to let her absent mother make her feel guilty. She is in England now. She is free. Like an English girl. Like her grandmother. And Mister Maxim said that she is on holiday, and if it gives him pleasure . . . After the pleasure he's given her, how can she refuse? She blushes recalling his . . . what did he call it?

Early-morning wake-up call.

Alessia fights back her smile. He could wake her up like that any day.

And he cooked her breakfast again.

He is spoiling her.

She hasn't been spoiled in a very long time.

Ever?

She glances up at him as they walk into the center of Padstow, and her heart lurches. He looks down at her, his eyes lively, and his handsome face erupts into a wide grin. He looks roguish this morning. It must be the stubble on his face. She likes the feel of it beneath her tongue. She loves the feel of it against her skin.

Alessia!

She had no idea she could be so wanton. Mister Maxim has woken a monster. She laughs to herself.

Who knew?

Her thoughts take a somber turn. What is she going to do when they go back to London and the holiday comes to an end? She wraps one hand around his biceps and squeezes his hand with the other. She doesn't want to think about that. Not now. Not today.

This is a holiday.

As they walk, the words became her mantra.

This is a holiday.

Ky është pushim.

Padstow is bigger than Trevethick, but the old, cramped houses and narrow lanes are the same. It's a picturesque little town. The place is bustling with people, tourists and locals out enjoying the sunshine in spite of the cold. There are children eating ice cream. Young people holding hands, like Maxim and her. And older people happily arm in arm. Alessia is amazed that people can express their affection so freely on the streets. It is not the same in Kukës.

I turn into the first shop that sells women's clothing. It's a local chain store, and I stand in the middle of the shop staring at all that's on offer. Everything looks pleasant enough, but frankly I'm a little overwhelmed. Alessia is hanging on my arm like a limpet. And I have no idea where to start. I'd had the vague idea that I'd have her cooperation, her enthusiasm, even—but she doesn't seem interested in the merchandise.

A young sales assistant approaches us. Blond and breezy, with a bright, girl-next-door smile and a bouncing ponytail to match, she asks, "Can I help you, sir?"

"My . . . um, girlfriend needs everything. She's left all her stuff in London, and we're here for a week."

Girlfriend? Yes. That works.

Alessia looks up at me, surprised.

"Sure. What do you need?" the assistant asks with a cheery glance at Alessia.

Alessia shrugs.

"Let's start with jeans," I interject.

"What size?"

"I do not know," Alessia replies.

The assistant looks puzzled, and then stands back appraising her. "You're not from around here, are you?" she says pleasantly.

"No." Alessia flushes.

"I think you're a small, either a UK size eight or ten." She gives us an expectant look, waiting for confirmation.

Alessia nods, though I think it's because she doesn't want to be rude.

"Why don't you go into the changing room, and I'll find some jeans in those sizes, and we'll go from there?"

"Okay," Alessia mumbles, and with an inscrutable look at me, she follows the assistant to the changing rooms.

I hear the assistant inform Alessia, "My name's Sarah, by the way." I breathe a sigh of relief and watch Sarah retrieve a couple of pairs of jeans from the shelves.

"Dark and light denim and a pair in black," I prompt. Her ponytail bobs merrily as she flashes me a smile and gathers several pairs.

Wandering around the shop, I rifle through some clothes racks trying to decide what would look good on Alessia. I've been shopping with women before, but they've always known what they wanted. I am dragged along on these trips either to pay or to give an opinion that will be ignored. The women I know all have confidence in their own style. I wonder if I should send her shopping with Caroline.

What?

Back in London?

No. That's probably not a good idea.

Not yet.

I frown. *What am I doing?*

I'm fucking my daily. That's what I'm doing.

In my mind I hear her cry as she orgasms. My dick hardens at the memory.

Bugger.

Yes. I'm fucking her, and I want to do it again.

That's why I'm here.

I like her. Really like her. And I want to protect her from all the shit she's endured. . . . And I have so much, and she has nothing.

I snort. It's a redistribution of wealth. Yes. How altruistic and socialist of me. My mother would not be thrilled. That thought makes me smile.

I find a couple of dresses I like, one in black and one in emerald green, and hand them to the assistant.

Will Alessia like these?

I sit down in a convenient chair outside the dressing-room area and wait, trying to put aside my disquieting thoughts.

Alessia appears wearing the green dress.

Wow.

I feel a little light-headed.

I've never seen her in a dress.

Her hair cascades down below her breasts, which are swathed in a soft fabric that clings.

Everywhere.

Breasts. Flat stomach. Hips. The dress stops short at her knees, and she's barefoot. She looks sensational—a little older, maybe, but more womanly and sophisticated.

"It is not too low?" Alessia asks, tugging at the neckline.

"No." My voice is hoarse, and I cough to clear it. "No, it's fine."

"Do you like it?"

"Yes. Yes. I like it a lot. You look lovely."

She gives me a shy smile. I hold up my finger and motion for her to turn around. She does quickly and giggles.

The fabric clings to her arse, too.

Yep. She's gorgeous.

"I approve," I say, and she heads back into the dressing room.

Forty-five minutes later, Alessia has a new wardrobe: three pairs of jeans, four long-sleeved tops in various colors, two skirts, two plain shirts, two cardigans, two dresses, two sweaters, a coat, socks, tights, and underwear.

"That's one thousand three hundred and fifty-five pounds, please." Sarah beams at Maxim.

"What!" Alessia squeaks.

Maxim hands over his credit card, pulls Alessia into his arms, and kisses her long and hard. She is breathless when he releases her, and she stares down at the floor, mortified. She cannot face Sarah. In Alessia's town, holding hands in public is considered forward. Kissing. No. Never. Never in public.

"Hey," Maxim murmurs, putting his hand beneath her chin to pull her face up.

"You spend too much," she whispers.

"Not for you. Please. Don't be angry with me."

Her gaze lingers on my face, but I have no idea what she's thinking.

"Thank you," she says finally.

"You are most welcome," I reply, relieved. "Now we're going to get you some decent shoes."

Alessia's face lights up like a summer's day.

Ah. Shoes . . . the way to every woman's heart.

In a nearby shoe shop, she chooses a pair of stout ankle boots in black.

"You'll need more than one pair of shoes," I say.

"These are all I need."

"Here, these are nice." I hold up a pair of ballet flats. I wish they stocked high-heeled fuck-me shoes, but alas—everything in the store is practical.

Alessia hesitates.

"I like these," I say, hoping my opinion will influence her decision.

"Okay. If you like them. They are nice."

I grin. "And I like these." I hold up a brown leather knee-high boot with a heel.

"Maxim," Alessia objects.

"Please."

She gives me a reluctant smile. "Okay."

We can leave your boots for recycling here," Maxim says as they stand at the sales counter. Alessia looks down at the new boots she's wearing and then at her old pair. They are all she has left of her clothes from home.

"I would like to keep them," she says.

"Why?"

"They are from Albania."

"Oh." He looks surprised. "Well, perhaps we can get them resoled."

"Resoled? What is this?"

"Repaired. The bottom of the shoe replaced. Understand?"

"Yes. Yes," she replies, excited. "Resoled."

She watches as Maxim hands over his credit card once more. How can she ever repay him?

One day she'll earn enough money to pay him back. In the meantime she has to think of something she could do for him. "Remember, I want to cook," she says.

This is one way.

"Today?" Maxim asks as he picks up her bags.

"Yes. I want to cook for you. To say thank you. Tonight."

"Okay. Let's take these bags back to the car, and we can shop for food after we've had some lunch."

They dump the bags in the small trunk of the car, and as they walk hand in hand to a restaurant, Alessia tries not to dwell on

Maxim's generosity. It is rude in her culture to reject a gift, but she knows what her father would call her if he knew what she was doing. He would either kill her or have a heart attack. Probably both. She's already dishonored him, and until recently she had the bruises to prove it. Once again she wishes he were more open-minded—and less violent.

Baba.

Her mood nosedives.

W e lunch at Rick Stein's Café. Alessia's quiet, and when we order our food, she's a little subdued. I wonder if it's because I've spent money on her clothes. Once the waitress has taken our order, I reach over and take Alessia's hand, giving it a reassuring squeeze. "Alessia, don't worry about the money. For the clothes. Please." She gives me a tight smile and takes a sip of her sparkling water.

"What's wrong?"

She shakes her head.

"Tell me," I insist.

She shakes her head again, turning away to stare out the window.

Something is off.

Shit. Have I upset her?

"Alessia?"

She turns back to face me, and she looks distraught.

Fuck.

"What is it?"

She gazes at me, dark eyes clouded with misery, and it's like a knife to my gut.

"Tell me."

"I cannot pretend I am on holiday," she says softly. "You buy me all these things, and I can never pay you the money. And I don't know what will happen to me when we go back to London. And I am thinking about my father and what he would do to me"—she pauses and swallows—"and to you, if he knew what we had done. I know what he would call me. And I'm tired. I'm tired of being afraid." Her voice is a raw whisper, and tears shine in her eyes. She looks directly at me. "That is what I am thinking."

I stare back. Paralyzed, but empty and aching. For her.

"That's a lot to think about," I murmur.

The waitress returns with our food and cheerily places my Californian chicken sandwich in front of me and the butternut squash soup in front of Alessia. "Everything okay?" she asks.

"Yes. Fine. Thanks," I say, dismissing her.

Alessia picks up her spoon and stirs her soup while I'm helpless and floundering for something to say. Her voice barely audible, she says, "I am not your problem, Maxim."

"I never said you were."

"That is not what I mean."

"I know what you mean, Alessia. Whatever happens between us, I want to be sure you're okay."

She gives me a sad smile. "I am grateful. Thank you."

Her response angers me. I don't want her gratitude. I think she's got some old-fashioned notion about being my mistress. And what her father has to do with us, I don't know. It's 2019. Not 1819.

What the hell does she want?

Fuck. What do I want?

I watch as she lifts her soup spoon to her lips, her face pale and sad.

At least she's eating.

What do I want? From her?

I've had her beautiful body.

And it's not enough.

It hits me. Like a sledgehammer. Right between the eyes.

I want her heart.

Fuck.

Chapter Seventeen

Love. Confusing. Irrational. Frustrating . . . Exhilarating. This is what it feels like. I am madly, crazily, ridiculously in love with the woman sitting opposite me.

My daily. Alessia Demachi.

I've felt like this since I first laid eyes on her standing in my hallway clutching a broom. I remember how disconcerted I was. . . . How angry. How the walls closed in on me and I had to escape because I didn't understand the depth of my feelings. This is what I was running from. I thought I was just wildly attracted to her. But no. It's not just her body I crave. It's never been just that. I'm drawn to her in a way I've never been to any other woman. I love her. That's why I went after her when she fled to Brentford. That's why I brought her here. I want to protect her. I want her happy. I want her with me.

Fuck.

It's a revelation.

And she has no idea who I am or what I do. And I know so

little about her. In fact, I have no idea how she feels about me. Yet she's here with me, so surely that means something. I think she likes me. But then again what choice does she have? I'm her only option. She was afraid, and she had nowhere to run. And on some level I knew that, and I tried to stay away from her, but I couldn't, because she's carved her way into my heart.

I've fallen in love with my cleaner.

Well, this is a fine fucking mess.

And now she's finally opening up to me—but in spite of all I've done, she's still afraid. I've not done enough. My appetite evaporates.

"I am sorry. I did not want to be the kill buzz," she says, interrupting my thoughts.

"Kill buzz?"

She frowns. "My English?"

"I think you mean buzzkill."

Her smile is halfhearted.

"You're not," I reassure her. "We'll figure this out, Alessia. You'll see."

She nods, but she doesn't look convinced. "You are not hungry?"

I eye my chicken sandwich, and my stomach rumbles. She giggles, and it's the most wonderful sound in the world.

"That's better." I delight in her amusement, relieved that she's recovered her sense of humor, and I turn my attention back to my meal.

A lessia relaxes. She can't remember talking about her feelings to him before, and he doesn't seem angry with her. When he glances at her, his eyes are warm, his expression reassuring.

We'll figure this out, Alessia. You'll see.

She looks down at her butternut squash soup, her appetite returning. She marvels at the chain of events that has brought her here. When her mother put her into the minibus on the freezing back road in Kukës, she knew that her life would change beyond all recognition. She had such hope for a new life in England. She didn't expect the journey to be so hard, or so dangerous. And the irony was that she had been trying to run from danger.

And yet it brought her to him.

Mister Maxim.

He of the handsome face and easy laugh and brilliant smile. She watches him as he eats. He has impeccable table manners. He's neat and tidy and chews with his mouth closed. Her English grandmother, who was a stickler for manners, would have approved.

When he looks across at her, his eyes are a luminous green. The most extraordinary color. The color of the Drin. The color of her home.

She could watch him all day.

He gives her a reassuring smile. "Okay?" he asks.

Alessia nods. She loves the warmth of his smile when he looks at her, and she loves the heat in his eyes . . . when he wants her. She blushes and looks down at her soup. She never expected to fall in love.

Love is for fools, her mother used to say.

Maybe she is a fool, but she loves him. And she's told him. But of course he doesn't understand her native tongue.

"Hey," he says.

She looks up. He's eaten his food.

"How's your soup?"

"It is good."

"Well, eat up. I'd like to get you home."

"Okay," she says, and she likes the idea of "home." She'd like to make her home with him. Permanently. But she knows it's not possible.

A girl can dream.

The drive back to Trevethick is more muted than their earlier journey. Maxim is preoccupied and listening to strange music playing over the sound system. Their stop at a supermarket called Tesco on the way out of Padstow has yielded all the ingredients Alessia needs to make *tavë kosi*, her father's favorite dish. She hopes Maxim will like it. She gazes out at the passing countryside. Still cloaked in winter, the landscape reminds her of home. Though here the trees are cropped short and warped by the bitter Cornish wind.

She wonders how Magda and Michal are getting on in Brentford. It's Sunday, so Michal will probably be doing his school homework or online gaming, and Magda will be cooking or talking to her fiancé, Logan, via Skype, or maybe she's packing for their move to Canada. Alessia hopes they are safe. She glances at Maxim, who seems lost in his own thoughts; he would know how Magda and Michal are if he's been in touch with his friend. Maybe he'll let her use his phone later, and she can catch up with the news from home.

No, Brentford is not her home.

She doesn't know where her next home will be.

Determined to keep her spirits up, she lets go of that thought and listens once more to the extraordinary sounds coming from the sound system. The colors are clashing: purples, reds, turquoise . . . it's like nothing she's heard before.

"What is this music?" she asks.

"It's from the soundtrack of *Arrival*."

"Arrival?"

"The film."

"Oh."

"Have you seen it?"

"No."

"It's great. A real headfuck. About time and language and the difficulties of communication. We can watch it at home. Do you like the music?"

"Yes. It's strange. Expressive. And colorful."

His smile is brief. Too brief. He has been brooding. She won-

ders if he's dwelling on their earlier conversation. She has to
know. "Are you angry with me?"

"No. Of course not! Why would I be angry with you?"

She shrugs. "I don't know. You are quiet."

"You've given me a lot to think about."

"I am sorry."

"There's no need to apologize. You haven't done anything
wrong. If anything . . ." He trails off.

"You have not done anything wrong," she says.

"I'm glad you think that." He gives her a quick, sincere smile
that dispels her doubts.

"Is there any food you don't eat?" she asks, and wishes she'd
found out before they went shopping.

"No. I eat pretty much anything. I went to boarding school," he
answers, as if this explains his entire ethos on food. But Alessia's
knowledge of boarding schools is limited to Enid Blyton's Malory
Towers, a favorite book series of her grandmother.

"Did you like it?" she asks.

"First one no. I was expelled. The second one yes. It's a good
school. I made good friends there. You met them."

"Oh, yes." Alessia blushes as she remembers the two men in
their underwear.

They settle into an easier conversation, and by the time they
arrive home, she's more cheerful.

We carry the bags into the house, and while Alessia unpacks
the groceries, I take her clothes upstairs. I put them in the
spare bedroom, then change my mind and place the bags in the
walk-in wardrobe in my room. I want her in here with me.

It's presumptuous.

Fuck.

I'm tangling myself in knots. I don't know how to behave with
her.

Sitting down on the bed, I put my head in my hands. Did I have a game plan before we got here?

No.

I was thinking with my dick. And now . . . well, I hope I'm thinking with my head and following my heart. During the drive home, I contemplated what to do. Should I tell her that I love her? Should I not? She's given me no indication of how she feels about me, but then she's reticent about most things.

She's here with me.

That means something, surely?

She could have stayed with her friend, but that would have meant those gangsters returning and finding her. My blood turns to ice. I shudder to think what they would do to her if they did. No. I was her only option. She has nothing. How could she go on the run?

Yet she arrived in the UK with nothing, and she survived. She's resourceful, but at what cost to herself? The thought weighs heavily on me. What did she do during the time between her arrival and finding Magda?

The anguish in her eyes in the restaurant. It was . . . affecting.

I'm tired of being afraid.

I wonder how long she's felt this way. Since she got here? I don't even know how long she's been in the UK. There's so much I don't know about her.

But I want her to be happy.

Think. What to do?

First. We have to make her legal here. And I have no idea how to do that. My solicitors should know the answer. I can only imagine Rajah's face when I tell him I'm harboring an illegal immigrant.

Her grandmother was English. Maybe that will help.

Fuck. I don't know.

What else could I do?

I could marry her.

What?

Marriage?

I laugh out loud, because the idea is so absurd.

Why not?

It would freak my mother out. For that reason alone, it's worth popping the question. Tom's words from our night at the pub come back to me: *You know, now that you're the earl, you'll need to provide an heir and a spare.*

I could make Alessia my countess.

My heart starts hammering. That would be a bold move.

And maybe a little sudden.

I don't even know if she has feelings for me.

I could ask her.

I roll my eyes. I am going round and round in circles. The truth is, I need to find out more about her. How could I ask her to be my wife? I know where Albania is on the map, but that's about it. Well, I can put that right, now.

I drag my phone out of my pocket and open Google.

It's dark when my phone starts to complain about its remaining battery life. I'm sprawled across the bed, reading everything I can about Albania. It's a fascinating place, part modern, part ancient, with a turbulent history. I've found Alessia's hometown. It's in the northeast, nestled among mountain ranges and a few hours' drive from the capital. From all I've read, it does appear that life is more traditional in that region.

This explains a great deal.

Alessia is cooking downstairs. Whatever she's making, its savory aroma is enticing. I get up and stretch and head downstairs to see her.

She's still dressed in her white top and jeans, and she has her back to me at the stove, mixing something in a pan. My mouth waters; it smells delicious.

"Hi," I greet her, and sit down on one of the barstools at the counter.

"Hi." She gives me a quick smile, and I notice she's plaited her hair. I plug my phone into one of the charging sockets beneath the counter and fire up the Sonos.

"Is there any music you'd like to hear?" I ask.

"You choose."

I select a mellow playlist and hit PLAY. RY X blasts out of the speakers overhead, making us both jump. I turn it down. "Sorry about that. What are you cooking?"

"A surprise," she says with a coquettish glance over her shoulder.

"I love surprises. It smells good. Can I do anything to help?"

"No. This is my thank-you. Would you like to drink?"

I laugh. "Yes. I would like a drink. Do you mind that I'm correcting your English?"

"No. I want to learn."

" 'Would you like *a* drink?' is what we say."

"Okay." She flashes me another smile.

"And yes, I would. Thank you."

She sets the pan aside and from the counter takes an open bottle of red wine and pours me a glass.

"I've been reading about Albania."

She whips her eyes to mine, her face lighting up like the early dawn. "Home," she whispers.

"Tell me more about life in Kukës."

Maybe it's because she's distracted while cooking supper, but she finally opens up and starts to describe the house she lived in with her father and mother. It's beside a vast lake, surrounded by fir trees. . . . And while she's telling me, I watch and marvel at how she moves about behind the counter with such ease and grace, as if she's been cooking in this kitchen for years. Whether it's grating nutmeg or adjusting the timing on the oven. She's like a professional. And as she cooks, she tops up my wine, washes dishes, and gives me insights into her claustrophobic life in Kukës.

"So you don't drive?"

"No," she answers as she lays the table for us.

"Does your mother drive?"

"Yes. But not often." She smiles when she sees my consternation. "You know that most Albanians did not drive until the mid-1990s. Before the fall of the Communists. We had no cars."

"Wow. I had no idea."

"I would like to learn."

"To drive? I'll teach you."

She's taken aback. "In your fast car? I do not think so!" She laughs as if I've suggested flying to the moon for lunch.

"I could teach you." We have enough land here, we don't need to be on the public highway. We'll be safe. A vision of her driving one of Kit's cars, maybe his Morgan, comes to mind. Yes. That would be suitable for a countess.

Countess?

"This will take another fifteen minutes or so to cook," she says, and she taps her lips with her finger. There's something on her mind.

"What would you like to do?"

Alessia chews her bottom lip.

"What is it?" I ask.

"I'd like to talk to Magda."

Of course she wants to talk to her. Magda's probably her *only* bloody friend. Why didn't I think of that?

"Sure. Here." I unplug my phone and find Magda's contact details. When the call connects, I hand the phone to Alessia, who gives me a grateful smile.

"Magda . . . Yes, it's me." Alessia moves to sit down on the sofa while I try and fail not to eavesdrop. I imagine that Magda is relieved to hear that Alessia is still in one piece. "No. Fine." Alessia glances up at me, her eyes shining. "Very fine," she says with a wide grin, and I find myself reciprocating.

I'll take "very fine" any day.

She laughs at something Magda says, and my heart swells. It's so good to hear her laugh; she doesn't do it often enough.

As she talks, I try not to watch her, but I can't resist. Unconsciously she winds a lock of hair that's escaped from her plait around her fingers as she tells Magda about the sea and her impromptu dip in it yesterday.

"No. It's beautiful here. It reminds me of home." She looks up at me again, and I'm caught in her all-consuming gaze.

Home.

I could make this her home. . . .

My mouth dries.

Mate! You are getting way ahead of yourself!

I look away, breaking the spell of Alessia's stare. I'm troubled by where my thoughts are heading and take a sip of wine. My reaction is all too new and too presumptuous.

"How is Michal? And Logan?" she asks, hungry for news, and she's soon lost in a lively conversation about packing and Canada—and weddings.

Alessia laughs again, and her voice changes, becoming softer . . . sweeter. She's talking to Michal, and I know from her tone that she's exceptionally fond of him. I shouldn't be jealous—he's a kid—but maybe I am? I'm not sure I appreciate this new and unwelcome feeling.

"Be good, Michal. . . . I miss you. . . . Bye."

She glances at me once more. "Okay. I will. . . . Good-bye, Magda." She hangs up and wanders back to me to hand me my phone. She looks happy. I'm glad she made the call.

"All good?" I ask.

"Yes. Thank you."

"And with Magda?"

"She is packing. She's happy and sad to be leaving England. And she is relieved to have the security man near."

"Great. She must be excited to start a new life."

"She is. Her fiancé is a good man."

"What does he do?"

"Something to do with computers."

"I should get you a phone, and then you can speak to her when you want."

She looks appalled. "No. No. That is too much. You cannot do that."

I raise a brow, knowing full well that I can.

She arches a brow in return, displeased, but I'm saved by the ping of the oven timer.

"Dinner is cooked."

A lessia places the casserole dish on the table beside the salad she's made. She's pleased that the yogurt crust has risen into a crisp, golden brown dome. Maxim is impressed. "It looks good," he says, and Alessia suspects he's being overeffusive.

She serves him a portion and sits down. "It is lamb, rice, and yogurt with a few secret . . . um . . . ingredients. We say *tavë kosi*."

"We don't bake our yogurt here. We put it on our muesli."

She laughs.

He takes a bite and closes his eyes as he savors the food. "Mmm." He opens his eyes and nods enthusiastically. He swallows. "This is delicious. You weren't lying when you said you could cook!"

Alessia blushes under his warm gaze.

"You can cook for me anytime."

"I would like that," she murmurs. She would like that very much.

W e talk and drink and eat. I ply her with wine and questions. Many questions. About her childhood. School. Friends. Family. Reading about Albania has inspired me. Sitting across from Alessia is inspiring, too; she's so full of life. Her eyes are shining and expressive as she talks. And she's animated, using her hands to demonstrate a point.

She's captivating.

Occasionally she will tuck that stray strand of hair away, her fingers skimming around the shell of her ear.

I'd like her fingers on me.

I anticipate unraveling her plait later and running my fingers through her soft, luscious hair. It's heartwarming to see her so carefree and talkative for a change. From the sweet flush on her cheeks, I suspect it might be the wine. I take a sip of the tasty Italian Barolo that's working its magic.

Replete, I push my plate away and refill her glass. "Tell me about a typical day in Albania."

"For me?"

"Yes."

"There is not much to tell. If I am working, my father will drive me to the school. And when I am home, I help my mother. Washing. Cleaning. Like I do for you." Espresso eyes peek up, unmasking me with her knowing look. It's sexy as hell. "And that is all I do," she adds.

"Sounds rather dull." Too dull for bright Alessia. And I suspect a little lonely.

"It is." She laughs.

"From what I've read, northern Albania is quite conservative."

"Conservative." She frowns and takes a quick sip of her wine. "Do you mean traditional?"

"Yes."

"Where I am from, we are traditional." She stands to clear the crockery from the table. "But Albania is changing. In Tiranë—"

"Tirana?"

"Yes. It's a modern city. It is not so traditional or conservative there." She puts the plates in the sink.

"Have you been?"

"No."

"Would you like to go?"

She takes her seat once more and tilts her head to the side, brushing her index finger across her lips. Her look is wistful for a brief moment. "Yes. One day."

"Have you traveled at all?"

"No. Only in books." Her smile brightens the room. "I have

traveled all over the world in books. And I've been to America watching TV."

"American TV?"

"Yes. Netflix. HBO."

"In Albania?"

She grins at my surprise. "Yes. We have television!"

"So, back home, what did you do for kicks?" I ask.

"Kicks?"

"Fun. You know. Fun."

She looks a little puzzled. "I read. Watch TV. Practice my music. Sometimes I listen to the radio with my mother. The BBC World Service."

"Do you go out?"

"No."

"Never?"

"Sometimes. In the summer we will walk in the town in the evening. But it is with my family. And sometimes I play the piano."

"A recital? For the public?"

"Yes. At the school and weddings."

"Your parents must be proud."

A shadow crosses her face. "Yes. They were. Are," she corrects herself, and her voice falters and dips, becoming soft and sad. "My father, he likes the attention." Her demeanor changes, and she seems to fold in on herself.

Shit. "You must miss them."

"My mother. I miss my mother," she answers quietly, and takes another sip of wine.

Not her dad? I don't push her on that. Her mood has shifted. I should change the subject, but if she misses her mother so much, perhaps she wants to return. I remember what she told me:

We thought we were coming here to work. For a better life. Life in Kukës is hard for some women. We were betrayed—

Maybe that's what she wants. To go home. And though I dread what her answer might be, I ask her anyway. "Would you like to go back?"

"Back?"

"Home."

Her eyes widen with fear. "No. I cannot. I cannot." Her tone is a hushed, rushed whisper, and the fine hairs on my neck stand on end.

"Why?"

She remains mute, but I want to know. I press her. "Is it because you don't have a passport?"

"No."

"Then why? Was it that bad?"

She screws her eyes shut and bows her head as if ashamed. "No," she whispers. "It's because . . . it's because I am betrothed."

Chapter Eighteen

My chest constricts as if I've been kicked in the solar plexus.

Betrothed?

What medieval claptrap is this?

She looks up at me. Her eyes wide, exposing her distress. Adrenaline pumps through my body; I'm ready for a fight. "Betrothed?" I whisper, knowing full well what it means.

She's fucking promised to another.

She bows her head again. "Yes." Her voice is barely audible.

I have a rival. *Shit.*

"And you were going to tell me this . . . when?"

Her eyes are scrunched shut as if she's in pain.

"Alessia, look at me."

She lifts her hand to her mouth—to suppress a sob? I don't know. She swallows, then raises her eyes to meet mine. Her expression is raw, her despair palpable. My anger dissolves in a second, leaving me in turmoil.

"I am telling you now," she says.

She's unavailable.

The pain is instant. Visceral. Shocking. I'm in free fall.

What the hell?

My world has shifted. My ideas. My vague plans. Being with her . . . marrying her . . .

I can't.

"Do you love him?"

She draws back and gapes at me in shock. "No!" It's a breathless, passionate denial. "I do not want to marry him. That is why I left Albania."

"To get away from him?"

"Yes. I was to be married in January. After my birthday."

It was her birthday?

I stare blankly at her. And suddenly the walls are closing in on me. I need space. Like when I first met her. I'm suffocating in a whirlwind of doubt and confusion. I need to think. I stand, and in one deliberate move, raise my hand to sweep my hair aside and gather my thoughts. Alessia recoils beside me. She cowers and clasps her head in her hands as if she's waiting—

What?

"Fuck. Alessia! Did you think I was going to hit you?" I exclaim, and step back, horrified by her reaction. Another piece of the puzzle that is Alessia Demachi falls into place. No wonder she always stood out of my reach. And I'm ready to kill the motherfucker. "Did he hit you? Did he?"

She looks down at her lap. Ashamed, I think.

Or maybe she has some misplaced loyalty to the fucking arsehole from Buttfuck, Nowhere, who has a spurious claim on my girl.

Fucking hell.

I clench my fists, my rage murderous. She's so still. Head bowed. Folding in on herself.

Calm down, mate. Calm yourself.

I take a deep cleansing breath, my hands on my hips. "I'm sorry."

Her head whips up. Her look direct and earnest. "You have done nothing wrong."

Even now she's trying to pour oil on my troubled waters.

The few steps between us are too great a distance. She watches me warily as I approach, and cautiously I crouch down beside her. "I'm sorry. I didn't mean to frighten you. I'm just shocked that somewhere out there you have a . . . suitor, and I have a rival for your affections."

She blinks rapidly, and her face softens as a rosy tinge marks her cheeks.

"You have no rivals," she whispers.

My breath catches, and warmth spreads in my chest, chasing the last of the adrenaline away. These are the sweetest words that she has said to me.

There's hope.

"This man, he's not your choice?"

"No. He is my father's choice."

I reach for her hand and bring it to my lips, planting one soft kiss on her knuckles.

"I cannot go back," she whispers. "I have dishonored my father. And if I return, I will be forced into marriage."

"Your . . . betrothed. Do you know him?"

"Yes."

"You don't love him?"

"No." Her vehement, monosyllabic response tells me all I need to know. Perhaps he's old. Or unattractive. Or both.

Or he hits her.

Fuck.

Standing, I pull her into my arms, and she comes willingly, putting her hands on my chest. I fold her against my body and hold her. And I don't know if I'm comforting her or myself. The thought of her with someone else, someone who mistreats her, is horrifying. I bury my face in her fragrant hair, grateful that she's here. With me. "I'm sorry that you've had to put up with so much shit," I murmur.

Looking up at me, she brushes her index finger over my lips. "That is a bad word."

"It is. It's a bad word for a bad situation. But you're safe now. I've got you." Leaning down, I brush my lips against hers and it's like a spark to dry kindling, my body comes alive. It takes my breath away. She closes her eyes and tilts her head back, offering her mouth to me. I cannot resist. In the background, RY X is still singing in his husky, melancholy falsetto about only falling in love. It's soulful. And rousing. And relevant.

"Dance with me." My voice is hoarse. Alessia gasps as I tighten my hold on her and start to sway with her in my arms. She splays her hands on my chest and glides them over my shirt, feeling me. Touching me. Reassuring me. And curling her fingers around my upper arms as she moves with me.

Slowly.

We shuffle from side to side to the unhurried and seductive rhythm of the ethereal song. Her hands slide up my arms and over my shoulders and into my hair. She nuzzles my chest.

"I have never danced like this," she murmurs.

My hand skims down her body to the base of her spine, holding her to me. "I've never danced with you."

With my other hand, I gently tug on her plait, lifting her lips to mine. I kiss her. Long. Slow. Tasting her. Rediscovering her sweet mouth with my tongue while we sway together. I unfasten the elastic tethering her hair and slide it off. I groan as she shakes her head, and her hair falls wild and free down her back. Cradling her face, I kiss her again. I want more. So much more. I need to reclaim her. She's with me. Not with some violent bastard from a godforsaken town a world away.

"Come to bed," I whisper, my voice low.

"I have to wash the dishes."

What?

"Fuck the dishes, baby."

Her brow furrows. "But—"

"No, you don't. Leave them."

And the thought pops into my head. *If I married her—she'd never have to do another dish again.*

"Make love with me, Alessia."

She sucks in a breath, and an inviting, shy smile curls her lips.

We flow together. My hands cocoon her head as I move, slowly savoring every delectable inch of her. She is soft and strong and beautiful beneath me. I kiss her, pouring my heart and soul into her mouth. It's never felt like this. Each stroke is bringing me closer to her. Her legs hold me in place, and her hands run over my back. Her nails etching her passion on my skin. I lean up and study her dazed face. Her eyes are wide and her pupils the darkest, most carnal espresso. I want to see her. All of her. I stop and press my forehead against hers.

"I need to see you." I ease out of her and roll us over so that she's on top of me. She's breathless and unsure. With my arm under her behind, I slide her up my body so her legs are on either side of my hips. And I sit up so she's astride me, her arms on my shoulders. I clasp her face and kiss her. Moving my hand down to caress her breast, I deliberately tease her nipple between my thumb and finger as my lips skim from her mouth along her jaw to her throat. She tips her head back and lets out a husky moan of pure pleasure. My erection throbs in response.

Yes.

"Let's try this," I murmur against the fragrant skin of her shoulder. I wrap my arm around her waist and lift her, my eyes on hers as I lower her slowly onto me.

Fuck.

She's tight. And wet. And exquisite.

Her mouth drops open as she gasps, her eyes large with want. "Ah," she breathes, and my lips seize hers, my fingers in her hair as I claim her mouth again.

She's panting and gripping my shoulders when I pull back.

"Okay?" I ask.

She gives me a frantic shake of her head. "Yes," she breathes, and it takes me a moment to realize she's reverted to the Albanian form of yes. I take her hands and lean back until I'm lying on the bed, staring at the woman astride me. The woman I love.

Her hair spills down over her shoulders and breasts in a riotous, sensual tumble. She leans forward and spreads her hands on my chest.

Yes. Touch me.

She sweeps her fingers and palms over my skin. Feeling me. Through my chest hair and over my nipples, which pucker in delight.

"Ah," I breathe.

She bites her lower lip, stifling her wanton, victorious smile.

"That's right, beautiful, I love your touch."

I love you.

She leans down and kisses me. "I like touching you," she says softly. Shyly. And my cock strains for more.

"Take me," I murmur.

She pauses, not understanding, and I lift my hips to give her a clue. Alessia cries out, and it's a loud, guttural sound of pleasure that almost pushes me over the edge. She splays her hands on my chest, trying to keep her balance. I grasp her hips. "Move. Like this," I hiss through my teeth. I ease her up and back down. And she gasps, but, placing her hands on my arms, she rises up and back down.

"That's it." I close my eyes and enjoy the sensual feel of her.

"Ah," she calls out.

Shit.

Make this last.

She moves. Slowly and hesitantly at first. But as her confidence builds, she finds her rhythm. I open my eyes as she rises once more, and this time I flex my hips, meeting her. Her cry is visceral and wakes every sense in my body.

Fuck. I grab her hips, moving her faster and faster. She's panting. Short, sharp gasps for air. Gripping my arms. Her head lolling from side to side with each thrust of mine.

Head tipped back. Calling to the gods, she's every inch a goddess. Her hold on my arms tightens, and she cries out and stills
on top of me as she comes.

It's enough to trigger my release, and I cry out, holding her to
me as I come and come and come.

Alessia lies in the afterglow of their lovemaking. Maxim has
his head on her stomach, his arms around her, as she runs
her fingers idly through his hair. She loves the feel of his hair
beneath her fingers. Her mother never gave any indication that
the sexual act could be so pleasurable. Perhaps that is not the
relationship she has with Baba. Alessia frowns. She doesn't want
to think about her parents having sex, but her mind wanders,
and she remembers her grandmother, Virginia. Now, *she* married for love. They were happy. Even when they were older, her
grandparents would exchange looks that made Alessia blush. Her
nana's was a marriage that she hoped to emulate. Not her parents'
marriage. They were never demonstrative with each other.

Maxim never hesitates to hold her hand or kiss her in public.
And he talks to her. When has she ever sat for an evening and had
a proper conversation with a man? Where she comes from, if a
man talks to a woman for any length of time, it is considered by
some to be a sign of weakness.

She glances at the little light-up dragon on the nightstand, a
beacon in the darkness. He bought this for her because he knows
she's scared of the dark. He brought her here to protect her. He
cooked for her. He bought her clothes. He made love to her. . . .

Tears prick the corners of her eyes, and her heart overflows
with uncertainty and longing, burning her throat with unspoken
emotion. She loves him. Her fingers tighten in his hair as she's
overwhelmed by her feelings for him. He wasn't angry with her
when she told him she was betrothed. If anything, he was anxious
that her heart might belong to another.

No. My heart is yours, Maxim.

And he was shocked that she thought he might beat her. Her hand goes automatically and instinctively to her cheek; her father is less of a talker, more of a man of action. . . .

She runs her fingers over Maxim's shoulder and traces the outline of his tattoo. She wants to know him better. Perhaps she should ask him more questions. He is evasive about his job. Maybe he has many? She shakes her head. It is not her place to question him. What would her mother say if she did? For now she will enjoy the little bubble that they share together in Cornwall.

Maxim nuzzles her belly and kisses it, distracting Alessia from her unsettling thoughts of home. He looks up at her, his eyes a vibrant emerald in the soft glow from the little dragon. "Stay with me," he says.

She smooths his hair off his forehead and frowns. "I am staying with you."

"Good," he says, and he kisses her belly again, but his time his mouth moves lower . . . and lower.

I open my eyes as early-morning light seeps through the gaps in the blinds. I'm wrapped around Alessia. My head on her chest, my arm around her waist. The warmth and sweet smell of her skin invades my senses, and my body rises to greet her. Gently I nuzzle her neck, leaving drowsy kisses at her throat.

She rouses, her eyelids fluttering open.

"Good morning, princess," I whisper.

She smiles, a sleepy, sated look on her face. "Good morning . . . Maxim." Her tone is tender, and I think I hear her love in the way she says my name. Or maybe I'm imagining it because I want to hear it.

There. I want her love.

All of it.

I'm prepared to admit it to myself.

But can I admit it to her?

The whole day extends before us, open and free—and I'm with her. "Let's spend the day in bed." My voice is husky with sleep.

Her fingers skim my chin. "Are you tired?"

I grin. "No . . ."

"Oh," she says, and her smile mirrors mine.

His tongue. His mouth. What he does to her. Alessia is lost in a storm of sensation. Her hands tighten on his wrists as she hangs on a precipice. She's close. So close. He teases her again and again with his able tongue and gradually eases a finger inside her, and she falls, her orgasm ripping through her as she cries out.

Maxim kisses her belly, her breasts, as he inches up her body and stills above her.

"That is a fantastic sound," he whispers, and he rolls on a condom and oh, so slowly sinks into her.

When I return from the bathroom, her side of the bed is empty.

Oh.

The disappointment is real. I'm ready for more. I don't ever think I'll have enough of Alessia.

Judging by the gray light seeping into the room, it must be midmorning. And it's raining. I raise the blinds, and then I hear her, so I scramble back into bed. Crockery rattling, she enters the bedroom. She's wearing my pajama top and carrying breakfast on a tray. "Good morning again," she says with a radiant smile, her hair flowing down over her shoulders.

"Well, hello, coffee!" The aroma is mouthwatering. I love proper coffee. I sit up, and she places the tray on my lap. Eggs. Coffee. Toast. "This is a treat."

"You said you wanted to stay in bed." She climbs in beside me and steals a piece of buttered toast.

"Here." I scoop up some scrambled eggs on a fork and offer it to her. She opens her mouth, and I feed her.

"Mmm . . ." she says, and closes her eyes in appreciation.

My dick rouses at the sight.

Steady. Let's eat first.

The eggs are amazing. She's added feta cheese, I think.

"This is heaven on a plate, Alessia!"

Her cheeks pink, and she takes a sip of coffee.

"I wanted to play some music."

"On the piano?"

"No—I mean, to listen."

"Oh. You need a phone. Here." I reach over and grab my iPhone.

I really must get her a phone.

"This is the code." I punch in my security code to unlock it. "And I use this app. Sonos. You can have music anywhere in the house." I hand it to her.

She starts flicking through the app. "You have so much music."

"I like music."

She shoots me a quick smile. "Me, too."

I take a sip of coffee.

Ugh!

"How much sugar did you put in this?" I splutter.

"Oh, I'm sorry. I forget you don't have the sugar." And she screws up her face, and I think it's because she cannot contemplate coffee without sugar.

"Is this how you drink it?"

"In Albania? Yes."

"I'm amazed you have any teeth left."

She grins, showing me she has perfect teeth. "I have never tried coffee without sugar. I will make you some more." She hops out of bed, all long naked legs and flowing raven hair.

"It's okay. Don't go."

"I want to." And she disappears once more, taking my phone

with her. A few moments later, I hear Dua Lipa singing "One Kiss" over the sound system downstairs. Alessia doesn't just like classical music. I smile. . . . I think the artist is Albanian, too.

A lessia dances around the kitchen, preparing another coffee for Maxim. She cannot remember a time when she felt this content. She came close at times when she was dancing and singing with her mother in the kitchen in Kukës. But here there is more room to dance, and with the lights on she can see her image reflected in the glass wall that leads to the balcony. She grins; she looks so happy. It's such a contrast to when she arrived in Cornwall.

Outside, it's a cold and wet morning. She shimmies over to the window and stares out at the scene. The sky and sea are a dismal gray, and the wind is battering and sculpting the silvery trees that line the path to the beach, but it's still a sight she finds magical. The surf is crashing on the shore, white-whipped and foamy, yet she can only hear the faint roar of the waves and cannot feel a draft through the glass doors. She's impressed. The house is well built, and she's grateful that she's here, warm and cozy with Maxim.

The espresso machine burbles, and she sashays back across the room to make his coffee.

Maxim is still in bed, but he's finished his breakfast and placed the tray on the floor. "There you are. I missed you," he says when Alessia returns with fresh, unsweetened coffee. She hands him the cup, and he drains the entire contents as she gets back into bed.

"That's better," he says.

"You like it?"

"Very much." He puts the coffee cup aside. "But I like you more." He hooks his index finger over the first button of the oversize pj top that she's wearing and tugs. The button opens, revealing the soft swell of her breast, and with his eyes burning into hers he runs his finger gently over her skin and across her nipple. Her breath catches as her nipple peaks and hardens beneath his touch.

Her lips part in a silent gasp, and her gaze is intense and inviting. My dick stirs.

"Again?" I whisper.

Will I ever have my fill of this woman?

Alessia's coy smile is encouragement enough. Leaning forward, I press my lips against hers and undo the rest of her buttons, and slip the pajama shirt off her shoulders. "You're so beautiful." My words are an invocation.

Her eyes on mine, she raises her hand hesitantly, and her finger traces the line of my jaw, brushing my stubble. Through her parted lips, I watch as she runs her tongue across the underside of her top teeth. "Hmm . . ." Her voice rumbles in her throat.

"You like it, or do you want me to shave?" I whisper.

She shakes her head. "I like this." Her fingertips stroke my chin.

"You do?"

She nods and, leaning in, plants a soft kiss at the corner of my mouth and runs her tongue over my stubble, following the line her finger took earlier. I feel it in my groin.

"Oh, Alessia." I grasp her face and lower us both onto the bed, kissing her as we recline. My lips are on hers, my tongue is on hers, and she's as greedy as ever, taking all I have to give. My hand travels down her body, over her breast, her waist, and her hip, and I cup her backside and squeeze. My lips follow, worshipping her breasts in turn until she's squirming beneath me. And when I gaze at her to catch my breath, she's panting.

"I want to try something new," I murmur.

Her mouth forms the letter O.

"Okay?" I ask.

"Yes . . ." she says, but her wide-eyed look tells me she's uncertain.

"Don't worry. I think you'll like it. But if you don't, just tell me to stop."

She caresses my face. "Okay," she whispers.

I kiss her once more. "Turn over."

She looks puzzled.

"Onto your front."

"Oh." She giggles and does as she's told. I prop myself up on my elbow and sweep her hair aside and off her back. She has a beautiful back and an even lovelier backside. I glide my hand down the curve of her spine to her behind, enjoying the soft, smooth planes of her skin. Leaning over her, I kiss the little mole at the base of her neck.

"You're so lovely," I murmur in her ear, and plant soft kisses from there down her neck and along her shoulder as my hand continues to descend and move between her buttocks. She wiggles her arse beneath my palm as I slip my hand farther between her legs and begin to circle her clitoris with my fingers. Her head is lying on the bed, her cheek to the sheet so I can easily observe her. Alessia's eyes are closed, her mouth open as she inhales, absorbing the pleasure elicited by my fingers.

"That's right," I whisper, and slip my thumb into her. She whimpers. She's wet and warm and wonderful. She pushes her behind against my hand, and I circle my thumb inside her. She gasps, and it's a call to my bursting dick. I keep up the rhythm. Round and round. She tightens her hold on the sheets and screws up her eyes as she moans. She's close. So close. And I withdraw my thumb and reach for a condom.

She blinks up at me. Wanting. Ready.

"Don't move," I murmur, and shift between her legs, parting them with my knee. I pull her up onto my lap so she's sitting astride me facing the wall. My dick snuggles in the line between her buttocks.

One day . . .

"We're going to do this from behind," I murmur.

Her head whips around to me, her eyebrows raised in alarm.

I laugh. "No. Not like that. Like this." Lifting her, I ease her slowly down on my erection. Her fingernails dig into my thighs, and her head drops back on my shoulder while I graze her earlobe with my teeth. She's panting, but she tenses her legs and haltingly rises up and down again.

Fuck. Yes.

"That's right," I whisper, and I shift my hands to her breasts, cupping them both and teasing each nipple between my thumb and forefingers.

"Ah!" she cries, and it's a primeval, sexy sound.

Fuck.

"You okay?"

"Yes!"

Slowly I lift her up and over, and she places her hands on the bed. I ease back and then forward into her. She cries out and, bending down, places her head and shoulders on the bed.

She looks amazing. Her hair sprawled across the sheets, her eyes tight shut, her mouth open, and her arse in the air. The mere sight of her makes me want to come.

She also feels amazing.

Every. Single. Fucking. Inch of her.

I grasp her hips and move into and out of her again.

"Yeah . . ." she groans, and I start to move. Harder. Really move. Harder still.

This is heaven.

She cries out. And I stop.

"No!" Her voice is hoarse. "Please. Don't stop."

Oh, baby!

And I'm unleashed. I take her. Over and over, sweat beading on my brow and trickling down my body, as I hold back my release until, finally, she cries out and climaxes around me again and again and again. I thrust once more and join her, loving her, filling her, and collapsing on top of her while calling out her name.

Alessia lies on her front, breathless, spiraling down from her climax, as he lies on top of her. His weight is . . . agreeable. She never knew her body had such capacity for pleasure. She's sweaty and languid and satisfied, wrung out from her incredible orgasm.

But as she recovers her composure, truth be told, she feels a little guilty at this indolence. She has never spent the whole morning in bed.

He nuzzles her ear.

"You're incredible," he whispers as he moves to her side and gathers her in his arms.

She closes her eyes. "No, you are," she says. "I never knew . . . I mean . . ." She stops and looks up at him.

"That it could be so intense?"

"Yes."

His brow crinkles. "Yes. I know what you mean." He gazes through the window at the gray, rain-soaked vista. "Do you want to go out?"

She snuggles closer, filling her senses with him. The smell of his skin. His warmth. "No. I like being here with you."

"I like it, too." He kisses the top of her head and closes his eyes.

I wake alone from my doze only to hear the strains of Rachmaninoff—my favorite of his concertos—coming from downstairs. It sounds odd . . . and then I realize, it's just the piano. Of course there's no orchestra.

Oh, this I have to see.

I jump out of bed and drag on my jeans, but I can't find my sweater, so I grab the throw from the end of the bed, wrap it around my shoulders, and head downstairs.

Alessia is playing the piano wearing nothing but my cream sweater. She's found some earbuds and is listening to my iPhone with her eyes closed, and she's playing. Without the sheet music. Without an orchestra. Is she listening to the concerto?

She must be.

Her fingers fly over the keys, and the music surges through the room with so much feeling and finesse it leaves me breathless. She leaves me breathless. I can almost hear the orchestra in my imagination.

How does she do this?

She truly is a prodigy.

I watch her. Transfixed as the music soars.

It's . . . emotional.

She reaches the crescendo at the end of the movement, her head bobbing in time to the music, her hair rippling down her back . . . and she stops. She sits for a moment. Her hands in her lap as the notes fade into the ether. I feel I'm intruding, watching her like she's an exotic species in her own unique habitat. But I can't help it, I break the spell and raise my hands and applaud.

She opens her eyes, surprised, I think, to see me there.

"That was sensational."

She takes the earbuds out of her ears and gives me a shy smile. "I'm sorry. I didn't mean to wake you."

"You didn't."

"I've only played this a few times. I was learning it before I left . . ." She stops.

"Well, you play it very well. I could hear the orchestra."

"From the phone?"

"No. In my imagination. You were that good. Were you listening to the piece?"

She flushes. "Thank you. Yes. I was."

"You should be on the stage. I would pay to see you."

She grins.

"What colors did you see?" I ask.

"In the music?"

I nod.

"Oh . . . this is a rainbow," she says with such raw enthusiasm. "So many different colors." She opens up her arms to try to convey the complexity of what she sees . . . but it's something I'll never know.

"It's . . . it's . . ."

"Like a kaleidoscope?"

"Yes. Yes." She nods vigorously with a huge smile, and I realize that the word must be the same in Albanian.

"As it should be. I love this piece."

I love you.

I step toward her and kiss her on the lips. "I am in awe of your talent, Miss Demachi."

She stands and places her arms around my neck. I wrap us both in the throw that I'm wearing.

"I am in awe of yours, Mister Maxim," she says, and she laces her fingers around my neck and pulls my lips toward hers.

What? Again!

She moves up and down. More graceful this time. Tall and proud. She looks amazing as her breasts bounce with her. Her eyes are intent on me. She's embracing her power, and it's so fucking sexy. Her tempo is perfect, and she takes me higher and higher. She leans down and threads her fingers through mine, squeezing them, then kisses me. An openmouthed, wet, and warm, demanding kiss.

"Oh, beautiful," I moan . . . I'm close.

And she leans up and tilts her head back and cries out my name as she comes.

Fuck! I'm lost. And I let go and join her.

When I open my eyes, she's gazing down at me in wonder.

Alessia is sprawled on Maxim's chest, and they're lying on the floor of the living room, by the piano. Her heart is slowing and her breathing subsiding, but she shivers. She's a little cold.

"Here." Maxim drapes the throw over her. "You are going to

wear me out." He flinches as he pulls the condom off but smiles up at her.

"I like wearing you out. And I like looking down at you," she whispers.

"I like looking up at you."

Watching him come when she's on top of him gives her a sense of power. A power she never thought she'd have—it's heady. Now if she could just pluck up the courage to touch all of him . . .

His glowing green eyes burn into hers. "You really are something, Alessia," he says, and he smooths her hair from her face. For a moment she thinks he's going to say something else. But he smiles up at her, a glorious smile. Then he adds, "I'm hungry."

She gasps. "I must feed you." She tries to move, but he holds her in place. "Don't go. You're keeping me warm. I should light a fire." He kisses her jaw, and she snuggles into him, feeling a peace she didn't know was possible.

"We should go out to eat," Maxim says. "It must be after four o'clock." The rain is still hammering down outside.

"I want to cook for you."

"You do?"

"Yes. I like cooking," Alessia replies. "Especially for you."

"Okay."

Alessia winces as she sits up on me.

"What is it?" I ask, and I sit up in one swift move so we're nose to nose. The throw falls to her waist, and I pull it up to keep her warm.

She blushes. "I am a little sore."

Fuck! "Why didn't you tell me?"

"Because you probably wouldn't have done that . . ." she says, averting her eyes and her voice low.

"Damned right!" I close my eyes and place my forehead on hers. "I'm sorry," I whisper.

I'm an idiot.

She places her fingers on my lips. "No. No. Don't be sorry."

"We don't have to do this."

What am I saying?

"I want to do this. I mean it. I really like it," she insists.

"Alessia, you have to talk to me. Tell me. Frankly, I could do this all day with you. But enough. We're going out. First, though, let's have a shower and get cleaned up." I lift her off me, stand up, collect our clothes from the floor, and together we head back upstairs.

I turn on the water in the shower as Alessia watches me, huddled in the throw, her eyes dark and mysterious. The afternoon sun is beginning to fade. I switch on the lights and test the water. It's toasty.

"Ready?" I ask her.

She nods and lets the throw fall to her feet, and she dashes past me into the piping-hot stream of water. I join her, and we both stand under the cascading shower as it warms us. I grab the shower gel, pleased that she's becoming more comfortable about revealing her gorgeous body.

That's what happens when you spend the day fucking. . . .

I grin and begin to lather some soap in my hands.

She has never showered with anyone. She can feel him move about behind her, his body brushing against her . . . *that* part of his body brushing against her as she stands beneath the shower. The part she hasn't dared touch yet. She wants to—she just needs to find the self-confidence.

The water is deliciously hot. She closes her eyes and enjoys the soothing feel of it bouncing off her skin, making it a little pink.

He moves her hair from her back and places a wet kiss on her shoulder.

"You're so beautiful," he says.

She feels his hands at her neck, and with circular strokes he starts to massage the soap into her skin. His strong fingers knead her muscles.

"Ah," she groans.

"You like?"

"Yes, muchly."

"Muchly?"

"My English?"

Alessia senses Maxim's grin.

"Is much better than my Albanian."

She giggles. "This is true. It is funny—I say the wrong word, and it sounds right to me, but when you say it, it does sound wrong."

"It must be my accent. Do you want me to wash you all over?" His voice is husky.

"All over?" Alessia's breath hitches.

"Mmm-hmm," Maxim confirms, the sound a low, sexy rumble near her ear. He puts his arms around her and soaps his hands and begins to knead the soap into her skin. He washes her neck, her breasts, her belly, and gently between her thighs. Her head rolls back on his chest as she surrenders to his touch, feeling his excitement against the top of her backside. She moans, and his breathing deepens, becoming harsher in her ear.

Suddenly he stops. "There, you're done. And I think we should get out."

"What?" She feels bereft without his hands on her.

"Enough." He opens the shower door and exits the shower.

"But," she protests.

He grabs a towel and puts it around his waist, covering his erection. "I only have so much willpower, and, amazingly, my body is ready for action again."

She pouts, and he laughs. "Don't tempt me." He holds up the blue robe and waits for her. She shuts off the water and steps out of the shower, where he wraps her in the robe and holds her. "You are irresistible. But as much as I want you . . . enough. And

I'm hungry." He kisses the top of her head and releases her. She watches him leave the bathroom, feeling her heart swell with her love for him.

Should I tell him?

But as she follows him into the bedroom, her courage fails her. She likes how they are at the moment. She has no idea how he'll react, and she doesn't want to burst their bubble.

"I will get dressed and cook for you."

He cocks an eyebrow. "You don't have to get dressed."

She feels her cheeks pink. *He has no shame.* But he beams, his smile so dazzling that it takes her breath away.

I t's almost midnight, and I lie gazing at Alessia, who is fast asleep beside me.

What a wonderful, lazy, falling-in-love Monday.

It's been a perfect day.

Making love. Eating. Making love. Drinking. Making love. And listening to Alessia play the piano . . . and watching her cook.

She shifts and mumbles something in her sleep. Her skin is translucent in the light from the little dragon, her breathing soft and even. She must be exhausted after all we've done . . . yet she's still a little shy. One of these days, I want her to touch me. Everywhere.

I stiffen at the thought.

Enough!

She will. In her own time, I'm sure. We didn't even leave the house today. All day. And she cooked for me once more, another delicious and wholesome meal. Tomorrow I'd like to do something special with her—something outdoors, provided the weather improves.

Show her where you grew up.

No. Not yet. I shake my head.

Tell her.

An idea comes to mind, and if the weather is better tomorrow, it will be fun, and it may give me the opportunity to tell her who I am. . . . We'll see.

I plant a tender kiss on her temple, inhaling her sweet fragrance. She stirs and mumbles something unintelligible, but she settles and sleeps on.

I've fallen in love with you, Alessia.

I close my eyes.

Chapter Nineteen

Alessia wakes listening to the low rumble of Maxim's voice. She opens her eyes to see him sitting up next to her, on the phone. He smiles down at her and continues his conversation. "I'm glad Miss Chenoweth agreed," he says. "I think a twenty-bore for the lady. I'll have my Purdeys."

She wonders what he's talking about. Whatever it is, his eyes shine with excitement.

"Let's use the easy birds. The teals." Maxim winks at her. "About ten? Great. I'll see Jenkins then. Thanks, Michael." He ends the call and snuggles back down into bed, his head on the pillow facing her. "Good morning, Alessia." He leans across and gives her a swift kiss. "Sleep well?"

"Yes. Thank you."

"You look lovely. Hungry?"

She stretches out beside him, and his eyes darken. "Hmm . . ." she says.

"You look very tempting."

She smiles.

"But you said you were sore." He kisses her on her nose. "And I have a surprise for you today. After breakfast we're going out. Dress warm. And you might want to plait your hair."

He climbs out of bed.

Alessia pouts. She was sore yesterday. She feels fine this morning, but before she can cajole him into a little more time in bed, he waltzes naked into the bathroom. All she can do is admire his fine physique, the muscles in his back rippling as he walks, his long legs . . . his backside. He turns and gives her a wicked smile, then closes the door.

She grins.

What does he have planned?

W"here are we going?" Alessia asks. She's wearing her green hat, her new coat, and I know she's wearing layers beneath. I think she'll be warm enough.

"It's a surprise." I give her a sideways look, then ease the car into gear.

Before she woke this morning, I called the Hall and spoke to Michael, the estate manager. It's a crisp, bright day, perfect for what I've arranged. After all our rigorous activity yesterday, we need a break and some fresh air.

Rosperran Farm has been part of the Trevethick estate since Georgian times. The Chenoweth family has been tenant farmers there for more than a hundred years. The present incumbent, Abigail Chenoweth, has given us permission to set up in one of the fallow southerly fields. As we get nearer, I wish I were in the Discovery. My Jag isn't good with fields, but we can park on the road. When we pull up, the gate is already open, and inside I spy Jenkins and his Land Rover Defender. He gives me a cheery wave.

I flash an enthusiastic grin at Alessia. "We're going to shoot clays."

Alessia looks bemused. "Clays?"

"Clay pigeons?"

She appears to be none the wiser.

I'm now less certain that this is a good idea. "It'll be fun."

She gives me a worried smile, and I get out of the car. It's a cold day, but not so cold that I can see the condensation of my breath. Hopefully we'll be warm enough.

"Good morning, my lord," Jenkins says.

"Hi." I check to see if Alessia has overheard, but she's climbing out on her side of the car. "'Sir' will do, Jenkins," I mutter as she approaches us. "This is Alessia Demachi." She takes his outstretched hand.

"Good morning, miss."

"Good morning." She gives him a charming smile, and Jenkins flushes. His family has served the Trevelyans for three generations, though mainly at Angwin, our Oxfordshire estate. Jenkins flew the family coop four years ago and has been working at Tresyllian Hall as an assistant gamekeeper. He's a little younger than me and a keen surfer. I've seen him on a board—he put Kit and me to shame. He's also an excellent shot and an expert gamekeeper. He runs many of the shoots on the estate. Beneath his flat cap and shock of sun-bleached hair, he has a good brain and a cheerful, easy smile.

Alessia looks up at me with a puzzled expression. "We are hunting birds?"

"No. We're shooting clays."

She looks nonplussed.

"They're discs made of clay."

"Oh."

"I've brought a couple of shotgun choices for the lady. I have your Purdeys, and Ms. Campbell insisted I bring your shooting jacket, sir."

"Great."

"And coffee. And sausage rolls. And hand warmers." Jenkins smiles.

Trust Danny.

"The traps are set. Teals," he says.

"Excellent." I turn to Alessia. "Good surprise?" I ask her, feeling doubtful.

"Yes," she says, but she doesn't sound certain.

"Have you shot a gun before?"

She shakes her head. "My father has guns."

"He does?"

"He hunts."

"Hunts?"

She shrugs. "Well, he will go out with his gun. He will go out overnight. To shoot wolves."

"Wolves!"

She laughs at my expression. "Yes. We have wolves in Albania. But I have never seen one. I'm not sure my father has either." She smiles at me. "I would like to shoot."

Jenkins gives her a warm smile and directs her to the back of the Defender, where he has our guns and all the necessary equipment.

She listens intently to what he has to say. He takes her through a safety briefing and shows her how the gun works and what she needs to do. While he does, I change quickly into my waistcoat and jacket. It's chilly, but I'm warm enough in these old clothes. I open my gun case and remove one of the Purdey twelve-bore shotguns. It's a rare vintage piece that belonged to my grandfather. He commissioned a matching pair of Purdey Over-and-Under shotguns in 1948. The silver engravings are exquisite and bear the charges from the Trevethick coat of arms intricately interwoven, with Tresyllian Hall in the background; the stock is a rich, gleaming walnut. The pair of guns were handed down to my father on my grandfather's death, and when Kit turned eighteen, my father gave him one of the guns as a birthday gift. When my father died, Kit gave me this one—the one that belonged to my dad.

And now, with Kit gone, I own both of them.

I'm hit by a sudden wave of sadness. A vision of the three of us in the gun room, my father cleaning this gun, my brother cleaning his then twenty-bore, and me looking on, as an excited eight-year-old finally allowed in the gun room. My father calmly explained how to dismantle the gun, how to oil the stock, grease the steels, clean the barrel and the action. He was meticulous. And so was Kit. I remember watching them with wide-eyed fascination.

"All set, sir?" Jenkins pulls me out of my reverie.

"Yes. Great."

Alessia is wearing protective eyeglasses and ear defenders. She still manages to look lovely. She cocks her head to one side.

"What?" I ask.

"I like this jacket."

I laugh. "This old thing? It's just Harris tweed." I grab some cartridges, protective glasses, and some ear defenders and break open the barrel of my gun.

"Ready?" I ask Alessia.

She nods, and with her Browning shotgun open, we all walk over to the makeshift shooting area that Jenkins has set up with some hay bales.

"I have the traps set just beyond that ridge for a low driven target," Jenkins says.

"Can I see a bird?"

"Sure." Jenkins presses his remote, and a clay flies into the air about one hundred meters in front of us.

Alessia gasps. "I will never hit that!"

"Yes you will. Watch. Stand back."

And I feel like showing off. She's a better pianist than me, she can cook better than me, and she beat me at chess. . . .

"Give me two birds, Jenkins."

"Yes, sir."

I put on my glasses and ear protection. Then open and load the barrel with two cartridges and mount my gun. Ready. "Pull!"

Jenkins releases two clays that soar up in front of us. I squeeze the trigger and pop off the top barrel, then the second, hitting both clays so that they shatter, the shards falling to the ground like hail.

"Shot, sir," Jenkins says.

"You hit them!" Alessia exclaims.

"I did!" I can't help my smug grin. "Okay, your turn." I open the barrel and stand aside for her.

"Feet apart. Your weight on your back foot. Good. Look at the trap. You've seen the trajectory of the clay, you'll want to follow it up in a smooth movement." She nods vigorously. "Mount the stock as hard against your shoulder as you can. You don't want any recoil."

"Okay."

I'm amazed that she's following what I'm saying.

"Right foot back a bit, miss," Jenkins adds.

"Okay."

"Here are your cartridges." I hand her two, and she loads them into the chamber and charges the gun. I stand back.

"When you're ready, shout 'Pull.' Jenkins will send up one clay, and you have two chances to hit it."

She gives me an anxious glance and mounts her gun. She looks every bit the country woman, even in her woolly hat, her cheeks rosy and her plait hanging down her back.

"Pull!" she shouts, and Jenkins releases a bird.

It sails up before us, and she fires first one, then the second shot.

And misses.

Both times.

She pouts as the clay smashes on the ground several feet away from us.

"You'll get the hang of it. Have another go."

A steely glint appears in her eye, and Jenkins steps forward to give her some pointers.

On the fourth clay, she hits it.

"Yes!" I shout in encouragement. She dances over to me.

"Whoa! Whoa! Barrel down!" both Jenkins and I exclaim simultaneously.

"Sorry." She giggles and opens the gun. "Can I have another shoot?"

"Of course. We have all morning. And it's 'shot.'"

She beams at me. Her nose is pink, but her eyes are bright and lively with the thrill of a new experience. Her smile could melt the hardest of hearts, and mine fills with elation. It's so gratifying to see her enjoying herself after all she's been through.

A lessia and Maxim sit in the trunk of Mr. Jenkins's car, their legs hanging over the back, sipping coffee from a thermos and eating pastries with some kind of meat inside. Alessia thinks it's pork.

"You did well," Maxim says. "Twenty out of forty clays isn't bad going for a first time."

"You did much better."

"I've done this before. Many times." He takes a sip of coffee. "Did you enjoy it?"

"Yes. I'd like to do it again. Maybe when it is not so cold."

"I would like that."

She smiles as her heart skips a beat. He wants to do this again, too. That's a good sign, surely. She takes a sip of coffee.

"Ay!" She grimaces.

"What is it?"

"No sugar."

"Is it that bad?"

She takes another cautious sip and swallows. "No. It's not that bad."

"Your teeth will thank you. What would you like to do now?"

"Can we walk by the sea again?"

"Sure. And then we can go for lunch."

Jenkins returns. "The trap's all packed, sir."

"Great. Thanks for this morning, Jenkins."

"It's a pleasure, my—sir."

"I'd like to take my guns back to the Hideout and give them a clean there."

"Of course. You'll find all you need in the case."

"Excellent."

"Good day, sir." We shake hands. "Miss," he says, and he touches his fingers to his cap as a slow flush spreads across his cheeks.

"Thank you, Jenkins," Alessia says, and when she gives him a brilliant smile, his cheeks redden more. I think she has a new conquest.

"Shall we go?" I ask her.

"It is your gun?"

"Yes."

She frowns.

"Jenkins keeps it for me. By law, it has to be locked up. We have a gun cabinet at the Hideout."

"Oh," she says, her confusion obvious.

"Ready?" I ask to distract her.

She nods.

"I'll have to take this home." I hold up the gun case. "And we can go for a walk on the beach, then somewhere nice for lunch."

"Okay."

I open the car door for her, and she gives me a fleeting smile as she climbs in.

That was close.

Just tell her.

Every day I don't tell her who I am, I'm lying to her.

Fuck.

It's as simple as that. I open the boot and place the gun case inside.

Just fucking tell her.

I get in beside her, close the car door, and glance across at her.

"Alessia—"

"Look!" she exclaims, and points through the windscreen. Before us stands a magnificent buck deer, its coat gray and long, appropriate for the winter months, its usual white spots hidden in among its fur. Where the hell did it come from? It's less than four years old, judging by its size, but it sports an impressive set of antlers, which I know it'll shed over the next couple of months. I wonder if it's from the fallow deer herd we have at the Hall or if it's wild. If it's from the Hall, how did it get out? It peers down its imperious nose, fixing us with black eyes.

"*Ua*," Alessia whispers.

"Have you ever seen a deer?" I ask.

"No."

We stare at the beast as it flares its nostrils and sniffs the air.

"Maybe the wolves ate them all," I whisper.

She turns to me and laughs, head back and free. It's such an endearing sound.

I made her laugh!

In the nearby field, Jenkins starts his Land Rover, spooking the buck. It rears back, turns, and bolts over the drystone wall into some scrubland.

"I didn't know there were wild animals in this country," Alessia says.

"We have a few." I start the car, feeling that the moment to tell her is lost.

Bollocks.

I'll tell her later.

And deep down I know the longer I wait, the worse it's going to be when I finally spill the beans.

My phone buzzes in my jacket. It's a text, and I know it's from Caroline.

That's another issue I have to deal with at some point. But right now I'm going to take my lady for another walk on the beach.

Alessia holds up the little dragon, a lantern in the darkness as they lie in bed. "Thank you," she whispers. "For today. For yesterday. For this."

"It's my pleasure, Alessia," Maxim responds. "I've had a wonderful day."

"I did, too. I don't want it to end. This has been the very best day."

Maxim strokes her cheek with his index finger. "The very best day. I'm glad I got to spend it with you. You really are lovely."

She swallows, glad that the fading light will hide her blush. "I'm not sore anymore," she whispers.

Maxim stills, his eyes searching hers.

"Oh, baby," he says and suddenly his mouth swoops down on hers.

It's after midnight, and Alessia dozes beside me. I must tell her about who I am.

Earl of Trevethick.

Fuck.

She deserves to know. I rub my face.

Why am I so reluctant to come clean?

Because I don't know how she feels about me.

And also, apart from my title, there's the small matter of my wealth.

Bugger.

My mother's suspicious nature has left its mark.

Women will only want you for your wealth, Maxim. Remember that.

God. Rowena can be such a bitch.

Gently, in order not to wake her, I lift a strand of Alessia's hair and wind it around my finger. She was reluctant to let me buy her clothes, reluctant when she has nothing. She doesn't want me to buy her a phone, and she always chooses the cheapest item on the menu. This is not the modus operandi of a gold digger.

Is it?

And the other day she said that I have no rivals. I think she cares for me. If she does, I wish she'd tell me. It would make this so much easier. She's talented, bright, and brave—and eager. I smile thinking about her carnal appreciation. Yes. Eager. I lean over and kiss her hair.

And she can cook.

"I love you, Alessia Demachi," I whisper, and I lay my head on my pillow and gaze at her . . . this beguiling woman. My beautiful, precious girl.

I'm woken by my phone. It's morning, and too bloody early judging by the dim light seeping through the space between the blinds. Alessia is wrapped around me as I reach across and pick up my phone. It's Mrs. Beckstrom, my neighbor in London.

Why the hell is she calling me?

"Hello, Mrs. Beckstrom. Is everything all right?" My voice is low so I don't wake Alessia.

"Ah, Maxim. There you are. I am sorry to call you so early, but I think you've been burgled."

Chapter Twenty

"What?" A chill sweeps across my skin as every hair on my body stands to attention, and suddenly I'm fully awake. I run my fingernails over my scalp.

Burgled? How? When?

My mind and heart are racing.

"Yes. I was taking Heracles for a morning walk. I do so love a walk beside the river early in the morning, whatever the weather. It's so quiet and restful."

I roll my eyes. Get on with it, Mrs. B.

"Your front door is open. It may have been open for a few days. I don't know. But I thought it odd. So today I had a peek inside, and of course you're not there."

Did I lock the flat in my panic to leave and go search for Alessia?

I can't remember.

"I'm afraid the place is a frightful mess."

Fuck.

"I was going to call the police, but I thought I'd call you instead, dear."

"Well. Thank you. I appreciate it. I'll deal with this."

"I am so sorry to be the bearer of bad news."

"It's okay, Mrs. B. Thank you." I hang up.

Shit! Fuck! Bollocks!

What have the fuckers stolen? I don't have much—all the important stuff is in the safe. I hope they haven't found that.

Bugger. Bugger. Bugger.

What a fucking nuisance. I may have to go back to London, and I don't want to go. I'm having way too much fun with Alessia. I sit up in bed and look down at her. She's blinking up at me sleepily, and I give her a reassuring smile.

"I've got to make a call." I don't want to worry her with these details, so I get up, wrap the throw around my waist, and head into the spare room with my phone. I call Oliver as I pace the floor.

Why didn't the alarm go off?

Did I set it? Shit! I left in such a rush. I don't know.

"Maxim." He's surprised to hear from me. "Everything okay?"

"Good morning. My neighbor's just called me. She says I've been burgled."

"Oh, shit."

"Precisely."

"I'll get around there right away. Shouldn't take me more than fifteen minutes at this time."

"Great. I'll ring you back in about twenty."

I hang up. My mood has nosedived, and I start to think about what I'd really miss if it was taken. My cameras. My decks. My computer . . .

Shit! My father's cameras!

What a fucking pain in the arse this is—some fucking lowlife addict or maybe some feral teenage kids wrecking my place.

Fuck. A. Duck.

I had plans to spend the day with Alessia, maybe go down to

the Eden Project. Well, I might still be able to do so, but I need to assess the damage—and I don't want to do it from my phone. If I FaceTime Oliver from the iMac up at the great house, I'll get a better view; he can show me via his phone what's happened.

Feeling fucked off and with a heavy heart, I head back into the bedroom, where Alessia is still in bed.

"What is wrong?" she asks, sitting up, her hair falling over her breasts. She looks rumpled and sexy and eminently fuckable. The sight of her is a balm that immediately makes me feel better. But, sadly, I'll have to leave her for a short while. I don't want to burden her with this news. She's had enough to deal with over the last few weeks.

"I've got to pop out and take care of something. We may even have to go back to London. But you stay in bed. Sleep. I know you're tired. I'll be back soon." She pulls the quilt up, her brow furrowed in concern. I give her a swift kiss and go grab a shower.

When I come out of the bathroom, she's gone. I dress quickly in jeans and a white shirt. I find her downstairs in the kitchen, wearing only my pajama top and clearing up our dishes from the night before. She hands me a cup of espresso. "To wake you up," she says with an adoring smile, though her eyes are wide, wary. She's anxious.

I swallow it down. It's hot, strong, and delicious. A little like Alessia.

"Don't worry, I'll be back before you know it." I kiss her once more, grab my coat, and I'm out the door, dodging the raindrops and bolting up the steps. I climb into the car and speed off along the lane.

Alessia watches Maxim vault up the steps and close the gate behind him. He looks worried, and she wonders where he's going. Something bad has happened. A frisson skitters up her spine, but she's not sure why. She sighs. There's so much she doesn't know about him.

And he said they might have to return to London. She will have to face the reality of her situation.

Homelessness.

Zot.

She's pushed it all aside for the last few days, but so much is unresolved in her life. Where will she live? Will Dante have given up looking for her? How does Maxim feel about her? She sucks in a breath as she tries to shake off her concerns and hopes that he can deal with whatever the problem is quickly and return. Even now the house feels empty without him. The last few days have been blissful, and she hopes they don't have to go back to London. She's not ready to return to reality yet. She's never been happier than she is here, with him. In the meantime she'll finish loading the dishwasher. Then she'll shower.

I take a shortcut along the back roads to the great house that is Tresyllian Hall because it's faster than going up the main drive. The rain is growing heavier, drumming on the car windscreen and roof as I slice through the narrow lanes. Passing the gatehouse at the southern entrance to the estate, I slow as the car rattles over the cattle grid, then accelerate up the driveway through the south pasture. In this winter rain, the landscape is dreary and damp and dotted with the occasional sheep. Come spring, the cattle will be out to graze again. Through the leafless trees, I catch sight of the house. Nestled in the wide dale, slate gray and Gothic, it dominates the landscape as if plucked from a novel by one of the Brontë sisters. The original house was built on the site of an old Benedictine priory. But the land and the abbey were seized by Henry VIII during the dissolution of the monasteries. Over a century later, in 1661, following the restoration of the monarchy, the estate was bestowed, along with the title Earl of Trevethick, to Edward Trevelyan for his services to Charles II. The great house he built was all but destroyed by fire in 1862, and this neo-Gothic monstrosity, with all its finials and fake molded battlements, was built in its place. It's the seat of the earls of Trevethick, a huge rambling pile, and I've always loved it.

And now it's mine.

I am the custodian.

The car rocks over a second cattle grid as I drive around the back of the great house and pull up outside the old stables where Kit's car collection is housed. Abandoning the Jag, I dash up to the kitchen door, and I'm pleased to find it open.

Jessie is in the kitchen cooking breakfast, with Kit's dogs at her feet. "Good morning, Jessie," I call as I dash through. Jensen and Healey both jump up and scramble after me.

Jessie's voice follows me out into the corridor. "Maxim! I mean, my lord!"

I ignore her and head into Kit's study. Fuck. *My* study. The room feels and smells as if my big brother is still in residence, and I halt as an intense pang of grief bubbles up from nowhere.

Damn you, Kit. I miss you.

The truth is, the office looks as though my father is still in residence. Kit had not changed a thing apart from installing an iMac. This was my father's refuge. The walls are painted blood-red and covered with his photographs, landscapes and portraits, even a couple of my mother. The furniture dates back to before the war, the 1930s, I think. With canine enthusiasm—tails wagging and tongues licking—the dogs jump up at me while I make my way to the desk.

"Hello, boys. Hi. There. Hi. There. Steady." I pet them both.

"Sir, it's great to see you, but is everything okay?" Jessie asks as she enters behind me.

"The Chelsea flat has been burgled. I'm going to sort it out from here."

"Oh, no!" Jessie's hand flies to her mouth.

"No one's hurt," I reassure her. "Oliver's there and assessing the damage."

"That's terrible." She wrings her hands.

"It's a pain in the arse, is what it is."

"Can I get you anything?"

"I'd love some coffee."

"I'll fetch some straightaway." She bustles out of the room, and Jensen and Healey, with mournful looks at me, follow her out. I sit down at Kit's—no, my desk.

Firing up the iMac, I log in and open FaceTime, then click on Oliver's contact link.

Alessia stands under the powerful shower enjoying the hot water streaming over her. She will miss this when they leave to go back to London. As she washes her hair, the thought depresses her. She's loved this magical time in Cornwall, just the two of them. She will always treasure the memory of her stay in this extraordinary house with him.

Maxim.

As she soaps her hair, she opens one eye, unable to shake her anxiety. Even though she's locked the bathroom door, she's nervous. She's not used to being alone, and she's missing him. She's become accustomed to his presence. Everywhere. She blushes and smiles.

Yes. Everywhere.

Now, if she could just work up the courage to touch him . . . everywhere.

Much of my flat is unaffected by the burglary. The darkroom is undisturbed, so my camera gear is intact, and more important from a sentimental point of view, I still have my father's cameras. And I'm lucky the thieves didn't find the safe. They've stolen some of my shoes and some jackets from my wardrobe, though it's difficult to tell, as there are clothes thrown around my bedroom.

The drawing room, on the other hand, is a mess. All my photography has been ripped off the walls. My iMac is smashed on the floor. My laptop and mixing consoles are gone, and my vinyl is all over the floor. Fortunately, the piano is untouched.

"That appears to be the extent of it," Oliver says. He's holding up his phone and using the camera so I can inspect the damage on my computer screen.

"Fuckers. Any idea when they broke in?" I ask.

"No. Your neighbor didn't see anything. But it could have been anytime over the weekend."

"It could have been after I left on Friday. How did they get in?"

"You saw the state of the front door."

"Yeah. They must have forced it with something heavy. The fuckers. I must have forgotten to set the alarm in my haste to leave."

"It didn't go off. I think you probably did forget. But I don't think that would have deterred them."

"Hello . . . ?" A disembodied voice from somewhere else in the flat interrupts us.

"That will be the police," Oliver says.

"You called them? That was quick. Good. Let me know what they say. Call me back."

"Will do, sir." He rings off.

I stare despondently at the screen. I don't want to go back to London. I want to stay here, with Alessia.

There's a knock on the door, and Danny appears in the doorway. "Good morning, sir. I hear you've been robbed."

"Morning, Danny. Yes. Though it doesn't look like I've lost anything irreplaceable. It's just a mess."

"Mrs. Blake will be able to tidy up any mess. What a nuisance this is."

"Indeed."

"Where would you like your breakfast?"

"Breakfast?"

"Sir, Jessie's made you breakfast. French toast. Your favorite."

Oh. I wanted to get back to Alessia.

Danny, sensing my hesitancy, gives me The Look over her

glasses. The Look that made me, Kit, and Maryanne quail as young kids.

You settle down now, children, and eat your supper. Or I will tell your mother.

She always played the Mothership card.

"I'll take it in the kitchen with you and the rest of the staff, but I have to be quick."

"Very good, sir."

Alessia's wrapped in towels to dry off after her shower. In the walk-in closet, she rummages through the clothes that Maxim bought her a few days ago. She cannot seem to shake her apprehension. She jumps at every strange noise she hears. It's rare for her to be on her own. At home in Kukës, her mother was always around, and in the evenings her father, too. Even in the Brentford house, when she lived with Magda, Alessia was seldom alone; either Magda or Michal was there.

She wills herself to concentrate on the task at hand. After all, she has her new clothes. She decides on the black jeans with a gray top and a pretty pink cardigan. She hopes that Maxim will like what she's chosen.

Finally dressed, she picks up the hair dryer and switches it on, its high-pitched whir filling the silence.

When I enter the kitchen, it's crowded and humming with the early-morning banter of some of the staff, Jenkins among them. Seeing me, they all stand as one, a frankly feudal display of deference, which I find irritating. But I let it go. "Good morning, all. Please. Sit. Enjoy your breakfast."

There are various pleasant mutterings of "my lord."

During its heyday, Tresyllian Hall would have employed well over three hundred and fifty staff, but now we manage with twelve full-time and about twenty part-time employees. We also have eight tenant farmers, whom I met on my recent trip. They raise livestock and various arable crops across ten thousand acres. All organic. Thanks to my father.

By Trevethick tradition the outdoor and household staff eat at separate sittings. At this moment the assistant estate managers, the gamekeeper, assistant gamekeeper, and the gardeners are enjoying Jessie's cooked breakfast. I note that mine is the only plate with French toast.

"I hear you've had a break-in, sir," Jenkins says.

"Sadly, yes. It's a massive pain in the arse."

"I'm sorry to hear that, milord."

"Michael about?"

"Dentist this morning. He says he'll be in around eleven."

I bite into my breakfast. The melt-in-the-mouth goodness of Jessie's French toast takes me back to my childhood. Kit and I talking cricket scores or bickering about who was kicking who under the table, Maryanne's nose in a book . . . and Jessie's French toast served up with stewed fruits. Today it's apple with cinnamon.

"It's nice to have you here, my lord," Danny says. "I hope you don't have to rush back to London."

"Police just arrived. I'll find out a bit later."

"I've let Mrs. Blake know about the burglary. She and Alice can pop round from the house to your flat and clear up."

"Thanks. I'll ask Oliver to liaise with her."

"Are you enjoying the Hideout?"

I give her a swift grin. "Very much. Thank you. It's very comfortable."

"I hear you had a successful day yesterday."

"It was fun. Thank you again, Jenkins."

He gives me a nod, and Danny smiles. "That reminds me," she says. "There were two very unsavory characters who came calling for you yesterday."

"What?" She has my immediate attention, and everyone else's in the room. She pales.

"They were asking after you. I told them to bugger off, sir."

"Unsavory?"

"Rough-looking, sir. Aggressive. From Eastern Europe, I think. Anyway—"

"Fuck!" *Alessia!*

A lessia pulls the brush through her hair. It's finally dry enough. She switches off the hair dryer, feeling ill at ease and wondering if she heard something. But it's only the sound of the crashing waves in the cove below. She stands staring out the window down at the sea.

Mister Maxim gave her the sea.

She smiles remembering her antics on the beach. The rain is easing off. Perhaps they could go for another walk on the shore today. And back to that pub for lunch. That was a good day. Every day here with him has been a good day.

From downstairs she hears the scrape of furniture on the wooden floor and hushed male voices.

What?

Has Maxim brought someone back to the house?

"Urtë!" someone grates in a strangled whisper. It's her mother tongue! Fear and adrenaline sweep through her body as she stands frozen in the bedroom.

It's Dante and Ylli.

They've found her.

Chapter Twenty-One

I tear down the lane, clattering over the cattle grid and pushing the Jag to go faster. I have to get back to the house. I'm finding it hard to breathe. My anxiety is a weight pressing on my chest.

Alessia.

Why did I leave her at the house? If something has happened to her . . . I will never forgive myself.

My brain works feverishly.

Is it them? The bastards who trafficked her? I feel sick to my stomach. How the hell did they find us? How? Maybe they were the fuckers who burgled my flat. They found information on the Trevethick estate and Tresyllian Hall. And now they're here. Asking questions. The fucking nerve of them, coming to my house. I grip the steering wheel.

Hurry. Hurry. Hurry.

If they locate her at the Hideout . . . I'll never see her again.

My panic mushrooms.

She'll be dragged into a horrific underworld, and I'll never be able to find her.

No. Fuck. No.

I swerve down the lane toward the Hideout, spraying gravel into the hedgerows.

Alessia's heart is pounding, her pulse thumping in her ears even as the blood drains from her head. The room spins once, twice, and her legs start to shake.

She's in her worst nightmare.

The bedroom door is open, and she hears their whispers downstairs. How did they get in? A creak on the stair galvanizes her into action. She sprints into the bathroom and quietly shuts the door. With shaking, clammy hands, she locks it behind her while she gasps for air.

How did they find her?

How?

She's dizzy with fear. Feeling powerless, she quickly scans the room looking for something to use to defend herself. *Anything.* His razor? Her toothbrush? She picks up both and slips them into her back pocket.

But the drawers are empty . . . there's nothing there.

All she can do is hide. She can only hope that the door will hold until Maxim returns.

No. Maxim!

He is no match for them. He is one man—and they are two. They will harm him. Tears well in her eyes, and she sinks to the floor as her legs give out under her. She leans against the door as human ballast in case they try to break it down.

"I heard something." It's Ylli. He's in the bedroom. When did her own language become so terrifying? "Check that door."

"You in here, you fucking bitch?" Dante calls out, and rattles the bathroom door, testing the handle. Alessia puts her fist in her mouth to stop from screaming, and tears trickle down her cheeks. Her body starts shaking. Her terror is overwhelming. And she pants, taking in shallow breaths. She's never felt so frightened. Not even in the truck that brought her to England. She's completely impotent. She doesn't know how to fight, and there's no escape from this room. And, she has no way to warn Maxim.

"Come out!" Dante's voice makes her jump. It's inches from her ear on the other side of the door. "It will only be worse for you if we have to break the door down."

Alessia screws her eyes up tight and stifles her sobs. Suddenly there's a horrific thud, like a sack of grain falling to the floor, followed by loud cursing, and Alessia is jolted backward.

Zot. Zot. Zot.

He's trying to break down the door. But it holds. Alessia stands and puts her foot against the door, silently cursing that she's not wearing shoes and socks. Her feet grip the limestone floor, and she presses her full weight against the door in the hope that it might help hold him back.

"When I get in there, I'm going to kill you. You fucking bitch. Do you know how much you cost me? Do you?"

He slams into the door again.

And Alessia knows it's only a matter of time. She sucks in a sob as her despair takes hold. She never found the courage to tell Maxim she loves him.

The Jag hurtles down the lane toward the Hideout, and I spot an old BMW encrusted with at least a year's worth of dirt, and it's abandoned haphazardly outside the garage.

Fuck. They're here.

No. No. No.

My fear and rage race into overdrive, threatening to overcome me.

Alessia!

Calm down, mate. Calm the fuck down. Think. Think. Think.

I pull up and park the car hard against the gate. They won't get out that way. If I go down the entry steps, they'll see me, and I'll lose the element of surprise. I fling open the car door and run to the little-used and hidden side gate and down to the scullery-room door. My breath is coming in short, sharp bursts as adrenaline pumps into my bloodstream, doubling my heart rate.

Calm down, mate. Calm down.

The scullery door's ajar.

Fuck. Maybe this is how they got into the house. I gulp down a steadying breath, my heart hammering, and gently push open the door and creep in. The adrenaline has sharpened my senses. My breathing is deafening.

Quiet. Be fucking quiet.

There's shouting. Upstairs.

No. No. No.

If they touch one hair of her head, I will murder them. I turn to the gun cabinet high on the wall and unlock it. I'd stashed my shotguns there yesterday before Alessia and I went for a walk on the beach. Trying to remain calm, I concentrate on removing one of the Purdeys as quietly as I can. With smooth and deliberate movements, I lift it out, open up the barrel, and load two cartridges. I put four more into my coat pocket. I have never been so grateful as I am right now that my father taught me how to shoot.

Keep calm. You will only have a chance to save her if you keep calm.

I repeat this mantra in my head. Releasing the safety, I brace the gun against my shoulder and sneak into the main room. There's no sign of anyone downstairs, but I hear an almighty crash from upstairs, followed by shouting in a foreign tongue.

Alessia screams.

Alessia shrieks as the door gives way, and she's flung across the bathroom floor. Dante almost falls into the room. She curls up into a ball, sobbing, as fear paralyzes her body. Her bladder fails, and the telltale wetness seeps down her legs and into her new jeans.

Her fate is sealed.

She's breathing in short, shallow gasps as her throat constricts. She's dizzy. Dizzy with fear.

"There you are, you fucking bitch." He grabs her hair, pulling her head up.

Alessia cries out, and he slaps her hard across her face.

"Do you know how much you've cost me, you fucking whore? You're going to pay every fucking penny back to me with your body." His face is inches from hers. His eyes dark and feral and full of rage. Alessia gags. His breath is rank, as if something died on his tongue, and his body odor washes over her in a haze of squalor.

He slaps her hard again and drags her to her feet by her hair. The pain is indescribable—as though her scalp is being torn from her head.

"Dante! No! No!" she wails.

"Stop fucking sniveling, you filthy whore, and move!" He shakes her hard and throws her into the bedroom, where Ylli is waiting. She lands on the floor, sprawling out like a starfish. She curls up quickly.

This can't be happening.

She screws her eyes shut, waiting for the inevitable blows.

Just kill me. Just kill me. She wants to die.

"And you've pissed yourself. You dirty *piçka.* I'm going to fuck you up." Dante swaggers around her and kicks her hard in her belly.

She screams as pain shoots through her body, leaving her gasping for air.

"Step away from her, you fucking piece of shit!" Maxim's voice bellows through the room.

What?

Alessia opens bleary eyes. *He's here.*

Maxim is standing on the threshold, shrouded in his dark coat like an avenging archangel, his eyes flashing a deadly green, and he's brandishing his double-barreled shotgun.

He's here. With his gun.

The evil fucker whirls around to face me. He blanches in shock and jumps back, gaping at me, sweat beading on his pale bald pate. His thin-faced friend also steps back and holds up his hands, his lips twitching. He looks like a fucking rodent, drowning in his oversize parka. The urge to pull the trigger is overwhelming. I have to fight every instinct to stop myself. Baldy is watching me, his eyes focused, weighing me up. Will I shoot? Do I have the balls?

"Don't fucking tempt me!" I roar. "Keep your hands up or I'll fucking end you. Step away from the girl. Now!"

He takes another cautious step back, his eyes flying from me to Alessia as he considers his options.

He has none.

Fucker.

"Alessia. Get up. Now. Move!" I bark, as she's still within his reach. She scrambles to her feet. Her face is red on one side where the cunt must have hit her. I fight the compulsion to blast his head off. "Get behind me," I say through gritted teeth.

She slips around me, and I hear her panting with fear. "Both of you. On the floor, on your knees!" I shout. "NOW! And not a fucking word from either of you."

They exchange a quick look.

And I brace my finger on the trigger. "Two barrels. Both primed. I can take you both down. I will blow your fucking balls off." And I aim for Baldy's crotch.

His eyebrows shoot up his ashen forehead, and both men sink to their knees.

"Hands behind your heads."

They do as they're told. But I have nothing to restrain them with.

Bollocks.

"Alessia, are you okay?"

"Yes."

My phone starts buzzing in my pocket. *Shit.* I bet it's Oliver.

"Can you take the phone out of the back pocket of my jeans?" I ask Alessia while keeping my aim on the two gangsters. Deftly, she does. "Answer it." I can't see what she's doing, but after a moment I hear her.

"Hello?" she says, and there's a pause before she speaks again, in a hushed voice choked with fear. "I am Mister Maxim's cleaner."

Jesus. She's so much more than that.

Baldy spits words at his rat-faced colleague. *"Është pastruesja e tij. Nëse me pastruese do të thuash konkubinë."*

"Ajo nuk vlen asgjë. Grueja asht shakull për me bajt," Ratface replies.

"Shut the fuck up!" I roar at the two of them. "Who is it?" I ask Alessia.

"He says his name is Oliver."

"Tell him we've captured two intruders at the Hideout and to call the police. Now. Tell him to call Danny and ask her to send Jenkins here right away."

Haltingly, she does.

"Tell him I will explain later."

She repeats what I've said. "Mr. Oliver says he is doing it. . . . Good-bye." She hangs up.

"Lie down, both of you. On your front. Hands behind your back." Baldy gives Ratface a quick look. Is he going to try something? I step forward and lower the barrel, aiming for his head.

"Hello!" A voice from downstairs calls up. It's Danny. Already? That makes no sense.

"Upstairs, Danny!" I shout, not taking my eyes off the two lowlifes. I motion with the gun. *Fucking lie down.* They comply, and I approach the two prone figures on the bedroom floor. "Don't move a muscle." I press the muzzle of the gun into Baldy's back. "Try me. The shot will break your spine and enter your stomach, and you'll die a slow, agonizing death—which is more than you deserve, you fucking animal."

"No. No. Please," he whimpers like a beaten dog in his thick accent.

"Shut up and keep still. Do you understand? Nod if you do."

Both men give me quick, furious nods, and I chance a glance at Alessia who is wide-eyed, pale, and hugging herself in the doorway. Behind her, Danny appears—and Jenkins behind Danny.

"Oh, my God." Danny's hand goes to her mouth. "What's happening here?"

"Did Oliver reach you?"

"No, milord. We followed you after you leapt up from the breakfast table. We knew something was wrong. . . ."

Jenkins hovers in the background.

"These two kidnappers broke into the house. They were after Alessia." I press the barrel into Baldy's back.

"Do you have anything I can restrain them with?" I ask Jenkins, keeping my eyes trained on the men on the floor.

"I've some baling twine in the back of the Land Rover." He turns and hurries back down the stairs.

"Danny, take Alessia back to the Hall, please."

"No," Alessia protests.

"Go. You cannot be here when the police arrive. I'll be with you as soon as I can. You'll be safe with Danny."

"Come on, child," Danny says.

"I need a change of clothes," Alessia mumbles.

I frown. *Why?*

Alessia dashes into the walk-in wardrobe and comes out a few moments later carrying one of the bags from our shopping the other day. With one unreadable glance at me, she follows Danny down the stairs.

Alessia stares, unseeing, out the windshield, her hands
wrapped around her body as the old woman named Danny
drives the large, rattling car down a country lane.

Where are we going?

Her head aches, her scalp and face are throbbing. It also hurts
her side when she takes a breath. She tries to keep her breathing
shallow.

Danny has wrapped her in a blanket that she took from the
sofa in the holiday house.

"We don't want you catching cold, dear," she'd said.

She has a kind, gentle voice with an accent that Alessia cannot
place. She must be a good friend to Mister Maxim to take such
care of her.

Maxim.

She would never forget how he looked when he saved her,
in his long coat, brandishing a shotgun like a hero from an old
American movie.

And she had thought he would be at their mercy.

Her stomach roils.

She's going to be sick.

"Please stop the car."

Danny pulls to a stop, and Alessia almost falls out of the vehicle. She doubles over, retching on the side of the road, losing her
breakfast.

Danny comes to her aid, holding her hair back as Alessia
heaves and heaves until her stomach's empty. Finally she straight-
ens up, trembling.

"Oh, child." Danny offers her a handkerchief. "Let's get you
back to the Hall."

As they continue on their journey, Alessia hears sirens in the
distance and imagines that the police are arriving at the Hideout.
She trembles, knotting the handkerchief in her fingers.

"It's okay, child," the old woman says. "You're safe now."

Alessia shakes her head, trying to process all that has just happened.

He's saved her. Again.

How could she ever thank him?

Jenkins makes short work of tying the two thugs' hands behind their backs. He lashes their ankles together for good measure. "My lord," he says, and points to where Ratface's parka has ridden up to reveal a pistol butt in the waistband of his trousers.

"Armed breaking and entering. This gets better and better." I'm grateful he didn't try to use the weapon on me—or Alessia. I pass Jenkins the shotgun, and after a moment's hesitation, because he deserves it, I give Baldy a fast, forceful kick in his ribs. "That's for Alessia, you fucking scumbag." He grunts in pain as Jenkins looks on, and I kick him again, harder this time. "And all the other women you've sold into slavery."

Jenkins gasps. "Traffickers?"

"Yes. Him, too! After Alessia." I nod toward Ratface, who's glaring at me with hatred. Jenkins gives him a swift kick.

I kneel beside Baldy and grab his ear, wrenching his head back. "You are a blight on humanity. You're going to rot in jail, and I'll make sure they throw away the fucking key." He puckers his lips and tries to spit in my face, but he misses, his spit drizzling down his chin. I slam his head onto the floor with a loud thud. Hopefully he'll have a cracking headache. I stand up, fighting the renewed urge to kick him to a pulp.

"We could finish them off and dispose of the bodies, my lord," Jenkins offers, placing the barrel of the gun against Ratface's head. "No one would ever find them on the estate." For a moment I'm not sure if Jenkins is joking or not—but Ratface believes him, screwing his eyes up, his expression riddled with dread.

Good. Now you know how Alessia felt, you piece of shit.

"Tempting though that idea is, it would make an awful mess in here, and I don't think the cleaning crew would thank us."

We all look up when we hear the sirens.

"And there's the small matter of the law," I add.

D anny turns into a smaller lane, by a charming old-fashioned
house, and the antiquated car shakes as they go over some
metal rods in the road. The land here is green and lush even
though it's winter. They drive through an open and rolling pasture. It looks . . . groomed, not wild like the countryside she's
seen since she got here. It's dotted with well-fed sheep. As the car
rattles down the road, a large gray house looms before them. It's
imposing. The biggest house Alessia has ever seen. She recognizes
the chimney. It's the one she saw from the road when she was
walking with Maxim. He said it belonged to someone, but she
can't remember who. Perhaps this is where Danny lives.

Why is she cooking for Mister Maxim when she lives here?

Danny drives around to the rear of the house and pulls up by
the back door.

"We're here," she says. "Welcome to Tresyllian Hall."

Alessia tries but fails to give her a smile and climbs out of the
car. Still feeling unsteady on her feet, she follows Danny through
the door and into what looks like the kitchen. It's a large, airy
room, the most spacious kitchen Alessia has ever seen. Wooden
cupboards. Tiled floor. It's spotlessly tidy. Old and modern at the
same time. There are two stoves. Two! And a massive table that
seats at least fourteen people. Two tall dogs with auburn coats
come bounding toward them. Alessia recoils.

"Down, Jensen. Down, Healey!" Danny's command stops the
dogs in their tracks. They lie down, gazing up at both women
with big expressive eyes. Alessia regards them suspiciously. They
are handsome hounds . . . but where she comes from, dogs do not
live in the house.

"They are harmless, my dear. Just pleased to meet you. Come
with me," she says. "Would you like a bath?" Her tone is solicitous
and kind, but Alessia blushes, mortified.

"Yes," she whispers. *She knows!* She knows that she's wet herself.

"You must have had a terrible fright."

Alessia nods and blinks back the tears that well in her eyes.

"Ah, lassie, don't you be crying. His lordship wouldn't want that. We'll get you sorted."

Lordship?

She follows Danny along a wood-paneled corridor hung on both sides with old paintings of landscapes, horses, buildings, religious scenes, and a couple of portraits. They pass many closed doors and ascend a narrow wooden staircase to yet another long, paneled corridor. Eventually Danny stops and opens a door into a pleasant room with a white bed, white furniture, and pale blue walls. She walks through the room to an en suite bathroom and turns on the faucets. Alessia stands behind her, pulling the blanket around herself and watching as water thunders into the bath and steam rises. Danny adds some aromatic bubble bath that Alessia recognizes as Jo Malone, like in the Hideout.

"I'll bring some towels for you. If you put your clothes by the bed, I'll have them laundered in no time." She gives Alessia a sympathetic smile and slips out, leaving her alone.

Alessia stares at the water cascading into the bath; a foam forming and spreading over the surface. The bath is old. A tub with claw feet. Her body starts to shiver, and she clutches the blanket and pulls it tighter around her.

She is still standing there when Danny returns with fresh towels. Draping them over a white wicker chair, she shuts off the water, then turns her attention to Alessia, her sharp blue eyes shining with compassion. "Do you still want a bath, dear?"

Alessia nods.

"Would you like me to leave?"

Alessia shakes her head. She doesn't want to be alone. Danny lets out a sigh of sympathy.

"Okay, then. Would you like me to help you undress? Is that what you want?"

Alessia nods.

And we'll need to interview your fiancée," PC Nicholls says. She's around the same age as me, tall and willowy, bright-eyed and keen, scribbling down every word I utter. I drum my fingers on the dining-room table. How much longer are we going to be? I'm anxious to get to Alessia, *my fiancée.* . . .

Both Nicholls and her boss, Sergeant Nancarrow, have patiently sat through the sorry tale of Alessia's attempted kidnapping. Naturally, I've been economical with the truth, but I've kept as close to it as I can. "Of course," I respond. "Once she's recovered. Those bastards really roughed her up. If I hadn't arrived back here when I had ..." Briefly I close my eyes as a tremor runs down my spine.

I might never have seen her again.

"You've both been through a terrible experience." Nancarrow shakes his head in disgust. "Will you have her checked over by a doctor?"

"Yes." I hope Danny's had the foresight to organize one.

"I hope she makes a quick recovery," he says.

I'm glad Nancarrow's here. I've known him since I was a child. We've had the odd run-in over noisy, late-night parties and drinking on the beach. But he has always been fair. And of course it was he who came to the house to inform us of Kit's tragic accident.

"If these men have form, they'll be on our database. Petty crime, more serious offenses, they'll all show up, Lord Treve-thick," Nancarrow continues. "Got everything you need, Nicholls?" he asks his eager colleague.

"Yes, sir. Thank you, my lord," she says to me. She looks thrilled, and I suspect she's never had to deal with an attempted kidnapping before.

"Good." Nancarrow gives her an approving smile. "Lovely place you have here, my lord."

"Thank you."

"And how have you been keeping? Since your brother passed away?"

"Holding up."

"Sad business."

"Indeed."

"He was a good man."

I nod. "He was." My phone buzzes, and I check my screen. It's Oliver. I ignore the call.

"We'll be on our way, sir. I'll let you know how the investigation proceeds."

"I bet these arseholes were the ones who broke into my flat in Chelsea."

"We'll be sure to check on it, sir."

I escort them to the front door.

"Oh, and congratulations on your impending nuptials." Nancarrow offers me his hand.

"Thank you. I'll pass your well wishes on to my fiancée."

I just have to ask her to marry me first. . . .

The water is hot and soothing. Danny has left to wash Alessia's dirty laundry. She's promised to be back in a *wee* minute. She's going to fetch the rest of Alessia's clothes from the car and bring her some painkillers for her head. It's throbbing because Dante pulled her upright by her hair. Alessia's trembling has subsided, but her anxiety remains. She closes her eyes and all she can see is Dante's snarling face in front of hers. She opens them again immediately and shudders remembering the smell.

Zot. The stink of him. Fetid. Stale sweat. Unwashed. And his breath.

She gags. And splashes her face to rinse away the memory, but the hot water stings where he hit her.

Ylli's words sound in her head.

"Nëse me pastruese do të thuash konkubinë."

If by cleaner you mean concubine.

Concubine.

The word is apt. She doesn't want to acknowledge it, but it's the truth. She is Maxim's concubine—and his cleaner. Her mood grows bleaker still. What did she expect? The moment she defied her father, her fate was sealed. But she had no choice. If she had stayed in Kukës, she would be married to a volatile and violent man. Alessia shudders. She had begged her father to stop the betrothal. But he ignored her and her mother's pleas. He had given that man his word of honor.

His *besa*.

And there was nothing either of them could do. Baba would not go back on his word. He would bring great dishonor to the family name if he did. Her mother's solution was to unwittingly put her in the hands of those gangsters. But now that they are in police custody, they are no longer a threat to her, and she has to accept the reality of her situation. While she's been in Cornwall, laughing on the beach, drinking in the pub, eating in fine restaurants, having sexual intercourse and falling in love with Mister Maxim, she has lost sight of that reality. Being with him has filled her head with illusions. Just as her grandmother had done—giving her crazy ideas about independence and liberation. Alessia had left her homeland to escape her betrothed but also, in good faith, expecting to find work. That's what she needed to do. To work, to be independent—not a kept woman.

She stares into the dissipating bubbles in the bath.

She hadn't expected to fall in love. . . .

Danny comes bustling back into the bathroom holding a large navy-blue bathrobe. "Come now. Let's get you out of there. We don't want you turning into a prune," she says.

Prune?

Alessia rises. On automatic. And Danny drapes the bathrobe around her and helps her step out of the bath. "Is that better?" she asks.

Alessia nods. "Thank you, missus."

"My name's Danny. I know we haven't been formally intro-
duced. But that's what everyone calls me here. I've brought a glass
of water, some tablets, and an ice pack for your head and some
arnica cream for your cheek. It will help with the bruising, and
I've called the doctor to come look at that nasty bruise on your
side. Let's get you into bed. You must be exhausted." She ushers
Alessia into the bedroom.

"Maxim?"

"His lordship will be along as soon as he's dealt with the police.
Come now."

"His lordship?"

"Yes, dear."

Alessia frowns, and Danny's expression echoes hers.

"Did you not know? Maxim is the Earl of Trevethick."

Chapter Twenty-Two

Earl of Trevethick?

"This is his house," Danny says gently, as if talking to a child. "All the land surrounding the house. The village—" She stops. "He didn't tell you?"

Alessia shakes her head.

"I see." Danny's white brows knit together, but she shrugs. "Well, I'm sure he had his reasons. Now, shall I leave you to get dressed? Your bag of clothes is on the chair."

Alessia nods, and Danny takes her leave, shutting the door behind her. Stunned, Alessia stares at the closed door, her mind imploding. Her knowledge of the English peerage is limited to two Georgette Heyer books her grandmother had smuggled into Albania. As far as Alessia knows, there is no aristocracy in her country. In ancient times yes, but since the Communists had seized all land after the Second World War, the nobles that lived there had fled.

But here . . . Mister Maxim is an earl.

No. Not Mister. He's *Lord Maxim*.

Milord.

Why didn't he tell her?

And the answer echoes loudly and painfully through her head.

Because she is his cleaner.

Nëse pastruesi do të thotë konkubinë.

If by cleaner you mean concubine.

She sucks in a breath, wrapping the bathrobe tighter around herself against the winter chill and this distressing news.

Why did he keep this from her?

Because she is not good enough for him, of course.

She is only good for one thing. . . .

Her stomach lurches at his betrayal. How could she be so gullible? Feeling raw and wounded by his dishonesty, she wipes away the tears that spring to her eyes. She's been in denial.

Her relationship with him has been too good to be true.

Deep down she suspected this. And now she knows the truth.

But he never made any promises to her. Those were all in her head. He's never told her he loves her. . . . He's never pretended to love her. Yet in the short time she's known him, she's fallen for him. Fallen from a great height.

I am a fool. A misguided fool in love.

She closes her eyes in anguish as hot tears of shame and regret course down her cheeks. Furious, she dashes them away and begins to dry herself briskly.

This is her wake-up call.

She takes a long breath—she's cried enough. Her deepening anger gives her momentum. She's not going to cry over him. She's mad at him, and at herself for being so stupid.

In her heart she knows that her fury is masking her hurt, and she's grateful for it. It's less painful than his betrayal.

She drops the robe on the floor, grabs the bag of clothes off the blue chair, and empties the contents onto the bed. Thankful that she had acted on impulse to bring her old clothes, too, she tugs on her pink panties, bra, her own jeans, her Arsenal FC top, and her sneakers. That's the extent of her own stuff. She's not brought her coat, but she grabs one of the sweaters that Mister Maxim—Lord Maxim—bought her, and the blanket that Danny had grabbed from the Hideout.

Dante and Ylli will be arrested, and surely once the police establish the extent of their crimes, they'll be incarcerated and those brutes will no longer be a threat to her.

She can leave.

She's not going to stay here.

She doesn't want to be with a man who has deceived her. A man who will cast her aside when he tires of her. She would rather leave than be sent away.

She has to get out. Now.

Swiftly she downs the two tablets Danny has left for her. Then, with one last glance around the elegant bedroom, she opens the door a crack. There's no one on the landing. She slips out of the room, closing the door behind her. Somehow she needs to find her way back to the Hideout to retrieve her money and her belongings. She cannot leave the house the way she came in— Danny might be in the kitchen. She turns right and heads down the long corridor.

The Jag skids to a halt by the old stables. I fling open the door and abandon the car, flying into the house. I'm desperate to see Alessia.

Danny, Jessie, and the dogs are in the kitchen. "Not now, boys," I instruct the dogs as they leap up to greet me and be petted.

"Welcome back, my lord. The police gone?" Danny asks.

"Yes. Where is she?"

"In the blue room."

"Thanks." In haste I make for the door.

"Oh, my lord . . ." Danny calls after me and there's a waver in her voice that brings me to a halt.

"What? How is she?"

"Shaken, sir. She threw up on the way over here."

"Is she okay now?"

"She's had a bath. And she's changing into fresh clothes. And . . ." Danny glances with uncertainty at Jessie, who goes back to peeling spuds.

"What is it?" I demand.

Danny pales. "I mentioned that you're the Earl of Trevethick."

What?

"Shit!" I race out of the kitchen, along the west hallway, and bound up the back stairs toward the blue room with Jensen and Healey at my heels. My heart is pounding.

Bugger. Bugger. Bugger. I wanted to tell her. What must she be thinking?

Outside the blue room door, I stop and take a deep breath, ignoring the dogs, who have chased after me convinced some new game is afoot.

Alessia's had a horrific scare today. Now she's in a place she doesn't know, with people she doesn't know. She's probably utterly overwhelmed.

And she's going to be really fucking angry I didn't tell her . . .

I knock on the door, briskly.

And wait.

I knock again. "Alessia!"

There's no answer.

Fuck. She's really pissed off with me.

With caution I open the door. Her clothes are scattered on the bed—her robe discarded on the floor, but there's no sign of her. I check the bathroom. It's empty except for the trace of her scent. Lavender and roses. For an instant I close my eyes and inhale. It's soothing.

Where the hell is she?

She's probably gone off to explore the house.

Or she's left.

Shit.

I storm out of the room and bellow her name down the corridor. My voice echoes off the walls hung with portraits of my ancestors, but it's met with a resounding silence. Dread seeps into my bones. Where is she? Has she passed out somewhere?

She's fled.

This is all too much for her. Or maybe she thinks I don't care....

Fuck.

I pace down the hallway, throwing open each door, with Jensen and Healey as my wingmen.

Alessia is lost. She's trying to find a way out. On tiptoe, she walks past door after door, painting after painting, along yet another wood-paneled corridor, until she eventually reaches a pair of double doors. She pushes through and finds herself at the top of a grand, wide staircase carpeted in scarlet and blue, which leads to a cavernous dark hallway below. On the landing there's a mullioned bay window, beside which stand two suits of armor holding what look like pikes. On the wall over the staircase is a massive faded tapestry, bigger than the kitchen table she saw earlier, that depicts a man on bended knee to his sovereign. Well, Alessia *assumes* he must be the sovereign, judging by the crown he's wearing. On the opposing walls above the staircase, there are two portraits. Huge. Both men. One is from an ancient time, the other far more recent. She sees the family resemblance in their faces and has a flash of recognition. They each stare at her with the same imperious green eyes. *His* green eyes.

This is Maxim's family. His heritage. She finds it almost impossible to grasp.

But then her gaze falls on the carved twin-headed eagles that sit on the newel posts at the top, the turns, and the bottom of the staircase.

The symbol of Albania.

Suddenly she hears him shout out her name. It startles her.

No.

He's back.

He shouts again. He sounds panicked. Desperate. Alessia freezes at the top of the impressive staircase, staring at the history that surrounds her. She's torn. From far off beneath her, a clock with a booming chime signals the hour, making her jump. Once, twice, three times . . .

"Alessia!" Maxim calls again, nearer this time, and she can hear his footsteps. He's running—running toward her.

The clock is still chiming. Loud and clear.

What should she do?

She grips the ornate eagle at the corner of the staircase as Maxim and the two dogs burst through the double doors. He stops when he sees her. His eyes sweep from her face to her feet, and he frowns.

I've found her. But my relief is tempered by her aloof yet inscrutable expression and the fact that she's wearing her old clothes and carrying a sweater and a blanket.

Shit. This does not look good.

Her stance reminds me of the first time I encountered her in my hallway, all those weeks ago. She's clutching the newel post like she clutched that broom. My senses are on high alert.

Tread warily, dude.

"There you are. Where are you going?" I ask.

She tosses her hair over her shoulder with that careless grace she has and tilts her chin in my direction. "I'm leaving."

No! It's like she's kicked me in the stomach.

"What? Why?"

"You know why." She sounds haughty, her expression etched with righteous indignation.

"Alessia. I'm sorry, I should have told you."

"But you did not."

I can't argue with that. I stare at her while the hurt in her dark eyes burns a hole in my conscience.

"I understand." She lifts one of her shoulders. "I am only your cleaner."

"No. No. No!" I stalk toward her. "That's not the reason."

"Sir. Is everything okay?" Danny's voice echoes off the stone walls and up the staircase from beneath us. I lean over the balustrade, and she appears with Jessie and Brody, one of the estate hands, in the hallway below. The three of them gape up at us openmouthed, like curious carp from the fish pond.

"Go. Now. All of you. Go!" I wave them away. Danny and Jessie exchange anxious glances, but they scatter.

Thank fuck.

I turn my attention back to Alessia. "This is why I didn't bring you here. There are just too many people in this house."

She tears her gaze away from me, her brow furrowed, her mouth a tight line.

"This morning I had breakfast with nine staff, and that was just the first sitting. I didn't want to intimidate you with all . . . this." I wave at the portraits of my father and the first earl while she traces the intricate carvings on the eagle with one finger. She remains mute.

"And I wanted you to myself," I whisper.

A tear slides down her cheek.

Fuck.

"Do you know what he said?" she whispers.

"Who?"

"Ylli."

One of those fucking intruders at the Hideout. "No." *Where is she going with this?*

"He said that I am your concubine." Her voice is hushed, full of shame.

No!

"That's . . . absurd. It's the twenty-first century. . . ." It takes all my self-restraint not to pull her into my arms, but I inch closer, so close that the warmth from her body seeps into mine. Somehow I manage not to touch her. "I would say that you're my girlfriend. That's what we say here. Though I don't want to presume. We've not discussed our relationship, as this has all happened so quickly. But that's what I want to call you. Girlfriend. My girlfriend. Which means that we are together in a relationship. But that's only if you'll have me."

Her eyelashes flutter over her dark, dark eyes, but she gives nothing away.

Shit.

"You're a bright, talented woman, Alessia. And you're free. Free to make your own choices."

"But I'm not."

"You are *here*. I know you're from a different culture, and I know we're not economic equals, but that's just an accident of birth. . . . We are equals in every other way. I've fucked up. I should have told you, and I'm sorry, deeply sorry. But I don't want you to go, I want you to stay. Please."

Her fathomless eyes strip me bare as she studies my face, and then she turns her attention to the carved eagle.

Why is she avoiding me? What is she thinking?

Is it the trauma she's just been through?

Or is it because those fuckers are out of the picture, so she no longer needs me?

Shit. Maybe that's the reason.

"Look, I can't keep you here if you want to leave. Magda is moving to Canada. So where you'll go, I don't know. If nothing else, stay until you know where. But please don't go. Stay. With me."

She can't run . . . she can't.

Forgive me! Please.

I hold my breath. Waiting.

It's excruciating. I'm the defendant in the dock waiting for the verdict.

She turns her tearstained face to me. "You are not ashamed of me?"

Ashamed? *No!*

I can bear it no longer. I skim the back of my index finger across her cheek, capturing a tear. "No. No. Of course not. I . . . I . . . I've fallen in love with you."

Her lips part, and I hear her just-audible gasp.

Shit. Am I too late?

Her eyes glisten with fresh tears, and my heart clenches with a new and intimidating sensation. Perhaps she'll reject me. My anxiety level ratchets up several notches, and I've never felt as vulnerable as I do now.

What's the verdict, Alessia?

I open my arms, and she looks from my hands to my face. Her expression uncertain. It's killing me. She bites her lower lip and takes one small hesitant step, and she's in my embrace. I wrap my arms around her and press her to my chest. I never want to let her go. Closing my eyes, I bury my nose in her hair and inhale her sweet scent. "My love," I whisper.

She shudders and starts to sob.

"I know. I know. I've got you. You've had a terrible fright. I'm sorry I left you on your own. It was a stupid thing to do. Forgive me. But those arseholes are in police custody. They're gone. They won't harm you again. I've got you." Her arms slide around me, and she grabs my coat at the back. She holds me as she weeps.

"I should have told you, Alessia. I'm sorry."

We stand for seconds, minutes, I don't know. Jensen and Healey give up on us and wander down the stairs.

"You can cry on me anytime," I tease. She sniffles, and I tip her chin up and stare down into beautiful, red-rimmed eyes. "I thought . . . oh, God, I thought if they got their hands on you . . . I'd never see you again."

Swallowing, she gives me a weak smile.

"And you must know," I continue, "I'd be honored to call you mine. I need you." And loosening my hold, I gently caress her face, avoiding the slight red mark on her right cheek. The sight of her bruise fills me with anger, but, taking great care not to touch it, I smooth away her tears with my thumbs. She places her hand on my chest. Through my shirt I feel the warmth. It spreads. Everywhere.

Alessia clears her throat. "I was so scared. I thought I'd never see you again. But my biggest . . . um, sorrow . . . um, regret," she whispers, "was that . . . was that I never told you that I love you."

Chapter Twenty-Three

Joy bursts like a million fireworks within me from head to foot. Its intensity leaves me breathless. I can't quite believe it. "You do?"

"Yes," Alessia whispers with a timid smile.

"Since when?"

She pauses and lifts a shoulder in a coy shrug. "Since you gave me the umbrella."

I beam at her. "I felt so good about that. Your wet footprints were all over my hall. So . . . are you saying you'll stay?"

"Yes."

"Here?"

"Yes."

"I'm so very glad to hear that, my love." I brush her bottom lip with my thumb and lean down to kiss her. I place my lips on hers, gently, but she ignites around me, her fervor taking me by surprise. Her lips and tongue are greedy, urgent, her hands are in my hair, tugging and twisting. She wants more. So much more. I groan as my body comes alive, and I deepen the kiss, taking everything she has to offer. There's a desperate quality to her demanding mouth. She's needy. And I want to be the one to fulfill her need. My hands move into her hair, holding her still, steadying her, slowing our pace. I want to take her, here, now, on the landing.

Alessia.

My arousal is instant.

I want her.

I need her.

I love her.

But . . . she's been through hell. She winces when I run my hand down her side. And her reaction brings me to my senses.

"No . . ." I whisper, and she pulls back, giving me a carnal but bewildered and disappointed look.

"You're hurt," I explain.

"I'm okay." She's breathless, and she cranes her neck to kiss me again.

"Let's just take a moment," I whisper, and I rest my forehead on hers. "You've had a horrible morning." She's extremely emotional, and her ardor may be a direct reaction to being roughed up by those arseholes.

The thought is sobering.

Or maybe it's because she loves me.

I like that idea better.

We stand forehead to forehead as we each catch our breath.

She strokes my cheek, then tilts her head to one side, and a hint of a smile plays on her lips. "*You* are the Earl of Trevethick?" she teases. "When were you going to tell me?" There's a mischievous twinkle in her eye, and I laugh out loud, knowing that she's echoing my question from the other night.

"I'm telling you now."

She grins and taps her lip with her finger. I turn and wave theatrically to the portrait that dates from 1667. "May I introduce

Edward, the first Earl of Trevethick. And that gentleman"—I point to the other painting with my thumb—"that's my father, the eleventh earl. He was a farmer and a photographer, too. And he was an ardent Chelsea supporter, so I'm not sure what he would have made of your Arsenal top."

Alessia gives me a puzzled look.

"They are rival London football teams."

"Oh, no." She laughs. "Where is your portrait?"

"I don't have one. I haven't been the earl for very long. My older brother, Kit. He was the real earl. But he never got around to having his portrait painted."

"Your brother who died?"

"Yes. The title and everything that comes with it were his responsibility until a few weeks ago. I wasn't meant for the role, for all . . . this." I tilt my head toward the suits of armor. "Running this place—this museum—it's all new to me."

"Is that why you didn't tell me?" Alessia asks.

"It's one of the reasons. I think part of me is in denial. All this, and the other estates, it's a lot of responsibility, and I've not been trained for it."

Whereas Kit was. . . .

This conversation is getting too deep and too close to home. I continue with a slight smile. "I'm very lucky. I've never really had to work before, and now all this is mine. And I have to maintain it for the next generation. It's my duty." I give her an apologetic shrug. "This is who I am. And now you know. And I'm glad you've decided to stay."

"My lord?" Danny calls up from below.

Maxim's shoulders sag a little. Alessia senses that he wants to be left alone. "Yes, Danny?" he answers.

"The doctor is here to see Alessia."

Maxim turns an anxious gaze to her. "Doctor?"

"I'm okay," Alessia says, hesitantly.

He frowns. "Send her up to the blue room."

"It's not Dr. Carter, it's Dr. Conway, sir. I'll send *him* up right away, my lord."

"Thank you," Maxim calls down to Danny, and he takes Alessia's hand. "What did that bastard do to you?"

Alessia can't look him in the eye. She feels ashamed, ashamed that she's brought this horror into Maxim's life. "He kicked me," she whispers. "Danny wanted the doctor to see this." She lifts the side of her Arsenal shirt to reveal a vivid red mark that's the size of a woman's fist.

"Fuck." Maxim's expression hardens, his mouth pressing into a thin line. "I should have killed that scum," he hisses. He takes her hand, and they walk back to the blue room, where an elderly man with a large leather bag is waiting. Alessia is surprised to see that the clothes she'd left on the bed and the floor have been tidied away.

"Dr. Conway. It's been a while." Maxim shakes hands with him. The doctor has wild white hair, a wispy mustache, and a beard to match. His keen blue eyes are the same color as his crooked bow tie. "Have we brought you out of retirement?"

"My lord, you have. But only for today. Dr. Carter is on holiday. It's good to see you looking so well." He places a hand on Maxim's shoulder, and a look passes between them.

"And you, Doctor," Maxim answers, his voice gruff, and Alessia suspects the doctor is checking on Maxim's well-being following the death of his brother.

"How's your mother?"

"The same." Maxim's lips quirk up.

Dr. Conway's laugh is deep and gravelly. He turns his attention to Alessia, who tightens her hold on Maxim's hand. "Good day, my dear. Ernest Conway at your service." He gives her a little bow.

"Dr. Conway, this is my girlfriend, Alessia Demachi."

Maxim looks at her, his shining eyes full of pride. As he turns back to the doctor, his expression hardens. "She's been assaulted and was kicked in the side by someone who is now in police custody. Miss Campbell thought it best that a doctor examine her."

Miss Campbell?

"Danny," he answers her unspoken question. He gives her hand a quick squeeze. "I'll leave you to it," he adds.

"No. Please don't go," Alessia blurts out. She does not want to be alone with this strange man.

Maxim nods in understanding. "Of course, if you'd like me to stay." He sits down in a small blue armchair, stretching out his long legs. Reassured, Alessia turns her attention to the doctor. His expression is serious. "Assaulted?"

Alessia nods and feels her face flush with mortification.

"Would you like me to take a look?" Dr. Conway asks.

"Okay."

"Please sit."

The doctor is kind and patient. He runs through several questions before he asks her to lift her shirt, and keeps up a steady stream of chatter while he examines her. His kind manner helps her relax, and she learns that he brought Maxim and his siblings into the world. Alessia glances at Maxim, who gives her a comforting smile.

Her heart expands.

Mister Maxim loves her.

She smiles back at him.

And he grins.

The doctor prods Alessia around her stomach and ribs, and the spell between her and Maxim is broken. She winces at Dr. Conway's touch.

"There's no permanent damage. And you're lucky not to have any cracked ribs. Just take it easy. And try some ibuprofen if it's painful. Miss Campbell will have some." Dr. Conway gives her a gentle pat on her arm. "You'll live," he says.

"Thank you," Alessia says.

"I should just take a quick photograph of the bruise. The police might need it for their records."

"What?" Alessia's eyes widen.

"Good idea," says Maxim.

"Lord Trevethick, would you mind?" He hands Maxim his phone. "Just the bruise."

"Darling, I'll only photograph the bruise. Nothing else."

She nods and lifts her shirt once more, and Maxim takes a few quick snaps.

"Done." He hands the phone back to the old man.

"Thank you," Dr. Conway replies.

With a look of relief, Maxim says, "I'll show you out, Doctor."

Alessia quickly rises to her feet and takes Maxim's hand. He smiles down at her and laces his fingers through hers. "We'll both see you out." Maxim gestures to the door, and they follow Dr. Conway into the corridor.

They watch as the doctor drives off in his old car. Maxim has his arm around Alessia's shoulders, and she's nestled into his side. It feels . . . natural. They are standing in the wide hallway at the front of the house. "You know, you can hold me, too," Maxim says, his tone warm and encouraging. Shyly she snakes an arm around his waist. He grins. "See how well we fit together?" And he kisses the top of her head. "I'll give you the tour later. Right now I want to show you something." They turn around, but Alessia stops when she notices the large sculpture above the stone fireplace that dominates the hall. It's the shield that Maxim has tattooed on his biceps, but it's more decorative. There are two stags on each side, a knight's helmet above it, and above that, in a swirl of yellow and black, a small coronet bearing a lion. Beneath the shield there's a scrolled caption: FIDES VIGILANTIA.

"My family's coat of arms," Maxim explains.

"And on your arm." She asks, "What do the words mean?"

"It's Latin. 'Loyalty in vigilance.'"

She looks puzzled, and Maxim shrugs. "Something to do with the first earl and King Charles II. Come." It seems he doesn't wish to say any more. He's buoyant, eager to show her something, and his excitement is infectious. From somewhere deep in the house, the clock that Alessia heard earlier announces the hour, one chime echoing through the Hall. He grins, looking boyish and adorable. She can't quite believe he's fallen for her; he's talented, handsome, kind, wealthy, and he's saved her from Dante and Ylli once more.

Hand in hand they walk through a lengthy hallway that's lined with paintings and the occasional ornate console table laden with statues, busts, and ceramics. They ascend the great staircase where they had their conversation earlier and cross to the other side of the landing from the double doors.

"I think you might like this," Maxim says, and he opens the door with a flourish. Alessia walks into a large chamber with wood-paneled walls and an elaborate plaster ceiling. At one end is a bookcase that covers the entire wall, but at the other, bathed in light from a huge mullioned window, is a full-size grand piano, the most ornate piano Alessia has ever seen.

She gasps and whips her head around to Maxim.

"Please. Play," he says.

Alessia claps her hands and bolts across the wooden floor, the sound of her quick footsteps echoing off the walls.

She stops a pace away from the piano to take in its majesty. It's made of a highly polished wood with a rich grain that gleams in the light. The legs are solid and intricately carved with leaves and grapes, the sides inlaid with a complex marquetry of golden ivy leaves. She runs her finger along the cartouche. It's splendid.

"She's old," Maxim says over Alessia's shoulder. Lost in wonder, she hadn't heard him approach. She doesn't understand why he sounds apologetic.

"It's magnificent. I have never seen a piano like this," she whispers in admiration.

"It's American. From the 1870s. My great-great-grandfather

married a railroad heiress from New York. This came here with her."

"It's beautiful. How does it sound?"

"Let's find out. Here." Maxim makes quick work of lifting the top board and using the longer prop to hold it open. "I don't think you'll need this, but I thought you might like to see it." Raising the music rack, he sets it in place. It's etched in a fine filigree. "Cool, huh?"

Alessia nods in awe.

"Sit. Play."

Alessia flashes him a delighted grin and pulls the carved piano stool forward. Maxim steps out of her sight line, and she closes her eyes to collect herself. She places her hands on the keys, relishing the feel of the cool ivory beneath her fingertips. She presses down, and the D-flat major chord sings into the room, resonating off the wooden paneling. The tone is rich, like the dark green of a forest fir, but the action is light—surprisingly light for such an old piano. Opening her eyes, she stares down at the keys, wondering how this instrument could have survived for so long and made it through such an epic journey from America. Maxim and his family must cherish their possessions. Shaking her head with incredulity, she places her hands on the keys once more and, not bothering with her warm-up piece, begins to play her favorite Chopin prelude. The notes of the first four bars dance across the room in a verdant spring green—the color of Maxim's eyes. But as she plays, the colors become darker and more ominous, filling the room with portent and mystery. Consumed by the music, she surrenders herself to each precious note. It drives away her anxiety and her fear. All the horror of the morning fades and then disappears in the dark and emerald greens of Chopin's remarkable, stirring masterpiece.

I watch, enthralled, as Alessia plays the "Raindrop" Prelude. With her eyes closed, she's lost in the music, her face expressing every thought and feeling that Chopin evokes in the piece. Her hair flows down her back, glinting like a raven's wing in the light of the winter sun that streams through the window. She's captivating. Even in that football shirt.

The notes swell and fill the room . . . and my heart.

She loves me.

She said so.

I'll have to get to the bottom of why she thought she'd be better off leaving. But for the moment I'll listen and watch her play. Hearing a muffled cough from outside the room, I look up. Danny and Jessie are poised on the threshold, listening. I wave them in. . . .

I want to show Alessia off.

This is what my girl can do.

They tiptoe into the room and stand watching Alessia with the same look of amazement that I'm sure I had when I first heard her play. And they can see she doesn't have the sheet music—she's performing this from memory.

Yeah. This is what she does best.

Alessia plays the final two bars, and the notes fade into the air . . . leaving us entranced. As she opens her eyes, Danny and Jessie burst into applause, as do I. She smiles shyly at them.

"Brava, Miss Demachi! That was exceptional," I exclaim as I walk over and bend to kiss her, my lips grazing hers. When I look up, Danny and Jessie have gone, as discreetly as they appeared.

"Thank you," Alessia whispers.

"What for?"

"Saving me. Again."

"It is you who has saved me."

She frowns as if she doesn't believe me, and I sit down beside her on the piano stool. "Trust me, Alessia, you've saved me in ways I can't even begin to fathom, and I don't know what I would have done if they'd taken you." I kiss her once more.

"But I've brought such trouble into your life."

"You have done nothing of the kind. This is not your fault. For God's sake. Never think that."

Her lips thin for a moment, and I know she doesn't share my point of view, but she reaches up and strokes my chin.

"And for this," she whispers, and glances at the piano. "Thank you." She leans up and kisses me. "Can I play some more?"

"All you want. Always. I'm going to make some calls. My flat was burgled over the weekend."

"No!"

"I suspect it was the same two bastards who are now in the custody of the Devon and Cornwall Police. I think that's how they found us. I need to talk to Oliver."

"The man I spoke to on the phone?"

"Yes. He works for me."

"I hope they did not take much."

I caress her face with one hand. "Nothing that can't be replaced—unlike you." Dark eyes shine at me, and she leans her face into my hand. I brush my thumb over her bottom lip and ignore the fire that lights low in my belly.

Time for that later.

"I won't be long." I give her a swift kiss and head toward the door. Alessia launches into Louis-Claude Daquin's piece "Le Coucou," which I learned when doing my grade six, and the bright and breezy notes follow me out of the room.

From *my* study—not Kit's—I call Oliver. Our conversation is all business. He's handling the fallout from the burglary. Mrs. Blake and one of her assistants are at the flat clearing up, two members of the construction crew in Mayfair have been dispatched to repair the front door, and a locksmith will change the locks on the entry to the street. The alarm is untouched and working fine, but we decide to change the code. I choose Kit's birth year as the new number. Oliver is keen for me to return to London; he has documents that I need to sign for the Crown Office to register my succession to the earldom and entry onto the Roll of the Peerage. With Alessia's assailants under arrest and in custody, there's no reason for us to stay in Cornwall. When I finish with Oliver, I call Tom to see how Magda and her son are faring. I tell him about the attempted kidnapping.

"Well, that's fucking audacious," Tom splutters. "How's your young lady? Is she okay?"

"She's tougher than all of us."

"Good to hear. I think I should keep an eye on Mrs. Janeczek and her son for a couple of days. Until we find out what the police are going to do with those scumbags."

"Agreed."

"I'll report anything suspicious."

"Thanks."

"You okay?"

"Peachy."

Tom laughs. "Good to hear. Over and out." Moments after I hang up on Tom, my phone buzzes. It's Caroline.

Damn. I told her I'd call next week.

Shit—it is *next week.*

I've lost track of time.

Sighing, I answer the phone with a terse "Hey."

"There you are," she snaps. "What the hell are you playing at?"

"Hello, Caroline, it's nice to talk to you, too. Yes, thanks, I've had a great weekend."

"Don't start with your bullshit, Maxim. Why haven't you called me?" Her voice cracks, and I know she's hurt.

"I'm sorry. Events have been a little beyond my control down here. Please let me explain when I see you. I'll be back in London tomorrow or the day after."

"What events? The burglary?"

"Yes and no."

"Why all this subterfuge, Maxim?" she whispers. "What's going on?" Her voice drops lower. "I've missed you." Her grief echoes through each syllable of her response. And I feel like shit.

"I'll tell you when I see you. Please."

She sniffs, and I know she's crying.

Fuck.

"Caro. Please."

"You promise?"

"I promise. As soon as I'm back. I'll come see you."

"Okay."

"Bye for now." I hang up and ignore the sinking feeling in my stomach. I have no idea how she'll react to what's been happening here.

Yes, I do. It's going to get ugly.

I sigh once more. My life has been complicated beyond recognition by Alessia Demachi, but even as the thought pops into my head, I smile.

My love.

We could head back to London tomorrow. I can see for myself the damage done to my flat.

There's a knock on the door.

"Come in."

Danny enters. "Sir, Jessie's prepared some lunch for you and Alessia. Where would you like us to serve it?"

"In the library. Thank you, Danny." I think the formal dining room might be a little overwhelming just for the two of us, and the breakfast room is a little dull. She likes books, so . . .

"If it suits your lordship, we'll be set up in five minutes."

"Great." I realize how hungry I am. A quick glance at the Georgian wall clock above the door tells me it's two fifteen. Its steady tick reminds me of the times I waited in this office for the bollocking my father administered whenever I'd transgressed—which was often. Right now the clock says . . . way past lunchtime.

"Oh, Danny," I call her back.

"My lord?"

"After lunch can you go to the Hideout and retrieve all our belongings and bring them here? Put everything in my room, including the dragon night-light that's beside the bed."

"Will do, sir." With a nod she departs.

As I approach the bottom of the staircase, I hear the music. Alessia is deep into another complex piece—one I don't know. Even down here it sounds amazing. I quickly head up the stairs and stand just inside the room watching her from afar. I think this composition is by Beethoven. I haven't heard her play any of his work before. A sonata, maybe? The music is rousing and passionate one moment and then quieter and softer the next. Such a lyrical piece. And she plays it exquisitely. She should be filling concert halls.

The music spirals down to its close, and Alessia sits for a second, her head lowered, eyes closed. When she looks up, she's surprised to see me.

"Another great performance. What was it?" I ask as I stroll across the floor toward her.

"It is Beethoven. 'Tempest,'" she says.

"I could watch and listen to you play all day. But lunch is served. Rather late. You must be hungry."

"Yes. I am." She jumps up off the stool and accepts my outstretched hand. "I love this piano. It has a rich . . . um . . . tone."

"Tone. That's the correct word."

"You have so many instruments here. I only had the eyes for the piano at first."

I grin. "Only had eyes for. No 'the.' You really don't mind me correcting you?"

"No. I like to learn."

"Cello is my sister Maryanne's instrument. My father played the double bass. The guitars are mine. The drums over there were Kit's."

"Your brother's?" she asks.

"Yes."

"It is an unusual name."

"Kit is short for Christopher. He was a demon on drums." I stop by the crash cymbal and run my fingers over the polished bronze. "Kit. Drum kit. Get it?" I flash her a smile. Alessia gives me a puzzled look.

"We used to joke about it." I shake my head, remembering Kit's shenanigans on the drums. "Come on. I'm hungry."

Maxim's eyes gleam a brilliant green as he looks at her, but she can see from the tension across his forehead that his grief is still raw and he misses his brother.

"So that's the music room," he says as they leave and head back down the great staircase, stopping at the bottom. "The main drawing room is through those double doors, but today we're having lunch in the library."

"You have a library?" Alessia asks, excited.

He smiles. "Yes, we have a few books. Some of them are quite old." They head back toward the kitchen, but Maxim stops outside one of the doors in the corridor. "I should warn you, my grandfather was keen on all things Egyptian." He opens the door, standing aside for Alessia to enter. She pauses a few steps into the room. It's like she's entered another world—a treasure trove of literature and antiquities. On every available wall, there are floor-to-ceiling bookshelves stuffed with books. At each corner is either a plinth or a cabinet holding treasures from Egypt: canopic jars, statues of pharaohs, sphinxes, a full-size sarcophagus!

A fire rages in the grate beneath an ornate marble fireplace that's set between two tall but narrow windows overlooking a courtyard. Hanging above the mantelpiece is an old painting of the pyramids.

"Oh, boy, the staff have gone all out," Maxim says, as if to himself. Alessia follows his gaze. Before the fire a small table covered in a fine linen cloth is elaborately set for two: silver cutlery, cut glasses, and delicate china plates decorated with small thistles. He holds out a chair for her. "Sit." He nods at her seat. Alessia feels like the noblewoman Donika Kastrioti, the wife of Skënderbeu, Albania's fifteenth-century hero. She gives him a gracious smile and sits down at the table facing the fire. Maxim sits at the head.

"As a young man in the early 1920s, my grandfather worked with Lord Carnarvon and Howard Carter, excavating various sites in Egypt and stealing all these antiquities. Maybe I should send them back." He pauses. "Until very recently that was Kit's dilemma."

"You have so much history here."

"Yes, we do. Rather too much of it, perhaps. It's my family's legacy."

Alessia cannot imagine the responsibility of dealing with such a heritage.

There's a knock at the door, and without waiting for an answer, Danny enters, followed by a young woman carrying a tray.

Maxim reaches for his linen napkin and drapes it on his lap. Watching him, Alessia follows suit. Danny takes two plates from the tray and serves each of them what looks like a salad with meat and avocado and pomegranate seeds.

"Pulled pork from one of the local farms, with a salad of fresh leaves, finished with a pomegranate jus," Danny says.

"Thanks," Maxim responds, and gives Danny a quizzical look.

"Would you like me to pour the wine, my lord?"

"I've got this. Thanks, Danny."

She gives him a little nod and discreetly ushers the young woman out the door.

"A glass of wine?" Maxim picks up the bottle and studies the label. "It's a good Chablis."

"Yes. Please." She watches as he half fills her glass. "I have never been . . . waitered on, except when I am with you."

"Waited on," he says. "While we're here, you might as well get used to it." He winks at her.

"You do not have staff in London."

"No. Though that may have to change." His brow furrows for a moment, and then he raises his glass. "To narrow escapes."

She raises hers. "*Gëzuar*, Maxim. My lord."

He laughs. "I'm still not used to the title. Eat up. You've had a horrible morning."

"I think the afternoon will be much better."

Maxim's look is heated—and Alessia smiles and takes a cautious sip of her wine.

"Mmm . . ." It is so much better than the wine she tasted with her grandmother.

"You like?" Maxim asks.

She nods and studies her cutlery. She has an array of knives and forks to choose from. Glancing at Maxim, she sees him smile and pick up the outermost knife and fork. "Always start from the outside and work inward with each course."

Chapter Twenty-Four

After lunch we head outside. Alessia's hand is warm in mine. The day is crisp and cold, and the sun is low in the sky as we walk together down the beech-lined avenue that leads to the front gates. Jensen and Healey scamper along behind, beside, and in front of us, grateful to be outdoors. After the trauma of this morning, I think we're both enjoying this quiet and peaceful walk in the late-afternoon sunshine.

"Look!" Alessia exclaims as she points to the herd of fallow deer grazing on the horizon of the north pasture.

"We've had deer here for centuries."

"The one we saw yesterday. It was from here?"

"No. I think it was wild."

"The dogs do not bother them?"

"No. But we keep the dogs out of the south pasture near lambing time. We don't want them worrying the sheep."

"There are no goats here?"

"No. We're more sheep and cattle people."

"We are goat people." She grins at me. Her nose is pink from the cold, but she's bundled up in her coat, hat, and scarf. She looks adorable. And I find it hard to believe that she was the victim of an attempted kidnapping this morning.

My girl is stoic.

But there's one thing that's been bugging me. I have to know. "Why did you want to leave? Why didn't you want to stay and have it out with me?" I hope she doesn't hear the apprehension in my voice.

"Have it out with you?"

"Talk to me. Argue with me," I explain.

She stops beneath one of the beech trees and looks down at her boots, and I don't know if she's going to answer me.

"I was hurt," she says after an age.

"I know. I'm sorry. I didn't mean to hurt you. I never want to hurt you. But where would you have gone?"

"I don't know." She turns to face me. "I think it was . . . how do you say? Instinct. You know, Ylli and Dante . . . I've been running for so long. I was a little crazy."

"I can't imagine how terrifying that was for you." I cringe and close my eyes, thanking all the gods that I got to her in time. "But you can't run every time we have a problem. Talk to me. Ask me questions. About anything. I'm here. I'll listen. Argue with me. Shout at me. I'll argue with you. I'll shout at you. I'll get it wrong. You'll get it wrong. That's all okay. But to resolve our differences, we have to communicate."

A fleeting look of anxiety crosses her face.

"Hey." I tilt her chin up and draw her closer to me. "Don't look worried. If . . . if you're going to live with me . . . you know. You need to tell me how you feel."

"Live with you?" she whispers.

"Yeah."

"Here?"

"Here. And in London. Yes. I want you to live with me."

"As your cleaner?"

I laugh and shake my head. "No. As my girlfriend. I meant what I said on the landing. Let's do this." I hold my breath. My heart is racing. And deep down, I don't know what choice she has—but I love her. I want her with me. Marriage seems too big a step to throw at her right now. I don't want her to run again.

Bro, it's also a big step for you!

"Yes," she whispers.

"Yes?"

"Yes!"

With a shout of joy, I scoop her up and swing her around. The dogs start barking and jump up at us with tails wagging, eager to join in the fun. She's giggling, but suddenly she winces.

Shit.

I set her down immediately.

"Did I hurt you?"

"No," she says, and I take her face between my palms, and she sobers, her eyes shining with love and maybe desire.

Alessia.

Leaning down, I kiss her. And what's meant to be a gentle I-love-you kiss becomes something . . . other. She opens up like an exotic flower, kissing me back with a passion that's staggering and I revel in all she has to give.

Her tongue in my mouth.

Her hands moving over my back and clutching at the material of my coat.

All the stress of this morning—the sight of her with those lowlifes, the fact that I might never have seen her again—all of that vanishes, and I pour my fears and my gratitude that she's still with me into our kiss. When we come up for air, our breath mingles in a steamy fog in the cold around us, and her fingers are wrapped around the lapels of my coat.

Jensen sticks his muzzle into my thigh. Ignoring him, I lean back to look at Alessia's dazed expression. "I think Jensen wants to join in."

Her giggle is breathy, and it speaks directly to my groin.

"I also think we're wearing too many clothes." I rest my forehead on hers.

"Do you want to take them off?" She chews on her lip.

"Always."

"I am warm. Too warm," she whispers.

What?

I look down at her once more. My remark was flippant and meant to be amusing—not a come-on.

What is she saying?

"Oh, *sweetheart*, you've just been through a terrible ordeal."

She lifts one shoulder in a "so what?" manner and averts her eyes.

"What are you telling me?" I ask.

"I think you know."

"You want to go to bed?"

Her broad grin is all the encouragement I need, and against my better judgment I grab her hand. Beaming and giddy, we trot back to the house with the dogs in hot pursuit.

T his is my room." Maxim stands aside for Alessia to enter. It's a few doors down from the blue room where Danny had brought her earlier.

A magnificent four-poster dominates the dark green room. Made of the same highly polished wood as the piano, the bed is just as intricately carved. The flames in the fireplace cast flickering shadows over the carvings. Above the mantelpiece there's a painting of the house and the surrounding countryside, and at the far end of the room stands an immense wardrobe in the same wood as the bed. On every wall are shelves covered in books and curios, but Alessia's gaze is drawn to the nightstand where the little dragon night-light sits.

Maxim throws several more logs on the fire until it blazes. "Good. I'm glad someone had the foresight to light the fire." Returning to stand in front of her, he points to a wicker basket perched on the ottoman at the end of the bed. "I've had your stuff brought here from the Hideout. I hope that's okay." His voice is low and soft, and his eyes glow. Intense. Growing larger and darker . . . full of his desire.

A tingle runs down Alessia's spine.

"It's okay," she whispers.

"You've had a rough day."

"I want to go to bed." She remembers their kiss on the stairs. She would have taken his clothes off then and there if she'd had the nerve.

He strokes her face. "Maybe you're still in shock."

"I am," she whispers. "I am shocked that you love me."

"With all my heart," Maxim says with real sincerity, but then he smiles and puts his arm around her. "And with this." He tilts his pelvis forward so she can feel his erection against her hip. His eyes alive with carnal humor. She returns his smile as the fire in her belly ignites. She's been longing to touch him—after all, he's touched her everywhere, with his hands . . . with his lips . . . with his tongue, just as he promised. Her gaze moves to his mouth, his skilled and sensual mouth, and the flames in her belly lick higher.

"What do you want, beautiful?" The backs of his fingers stroke her face, and his eyes sear her soul. She's wanted him since he said he loved her.

"I want you." The words are barely audible.

He groans. "You never cease to surprise me."

"Do you like surprises?"

"From you, very much."

Alessia tugs at his white shirt until it slips out of the waistband of his jeans. "Are you going to undress me?" Maxim's voice is hoarse, like he's stopped breathing.

She eyes him from beneath her lashes. "Yes." She can do this. And with brave but trembling fingers, she undoes the lowest of his shirt buttons. She glances up at him.

"Go on," he coaxes, his tone soft and seductive.

Alessia hears the burgeoning excitement in his voice. It feeds her desire. She undoes the next one up, revealing the top button of his jeans and the line of hair that points to his lean abs. The next button reveals his navel and his honed stomach muscles. Maxim's breathing alters. Rising. More rapid. The sound excites her, and her fingers fly up his shirt, unfastening it until it's hanging loose and open, revealing his sun-kissed chest. She longs to lean forward and place her lips against his flesh.

"What now, Alessia?" He's waiting. "Whatever you want," he says, arousing her. She leans forward and presses her lips against the warmth of his chest, where his heart thunders beneath his skin.

I am itching to touch her. But I can't. This is the most audacious she's been with me since we first made love. My body is straining. How can her innocent touch be so erotic? She's driving me wild. She eases my shirt over my shoulders and tugs it down to my elbows. I present her with my wrists. "Cuffs."

She flashes me a grin and undoes each one in turn, then drags my shirt off and drapes it over the armchair in front of the fire.

Now what are you going to do?" he says. Alessia steps back to admire his fine, toned physique in the dancing light of the fire. The gold in his hair glints, and his eyes are a luminous green. They watch her, full of promise as he stares.

Emboldened by his gaze, she reaches down and peels off her sweater, then tugs her football shirt over her head and shakes her hair loose. But her courage fails at the last minute, and she hesitates, holding the top to her breasts. Maxim steps forward and gently takes it from her. "You're lovely. I like looking at you. You won't be needing this." He tosses it on top of his shirt, then takes a strand of her hair and winds it around his finger. Bringing it to his lips, he kisses it. "You are so brave. In so many ways. And I've fallen for you. All of you. Madly. Passionately." His words heat her blood, and he tugs the lock, drawing her into his arms. He angles her head and kisses her like his life depends on it. "I could have lost you," he whispers.

His skin is warm against hers, and the desire within her burns brighter. She wants him. All of him. Greedily, she kisses him, her tongue twisting with his. Her hands rest on the back of his head, drawing him closer. His lips move to her jaw, her throat. And her hands travel down his body to the waistband of his jeans.

She wants to touch him. Every inch of him. But she stops. She doesn't know what to do. Maxim holds her chin tenderly between his fingers. "Alessia," he growls against her ear. "I want you to touch me." The need in his voice is arousing.

"I want to."

He grazes her earlobe with his teeth.

"Ah," she groans as the muscles tighten deep in her belly.

"Undo my jeans." He kisses a trail of butterfly kisses down her neck. Hastily her fingers scramble to his waistband, brushing against his hardened penis. She stops, fascinated by his body, and in a really bold move places her hand over his erection.

"Oh, God," he whispers.

Tentatively her fingers trace around him.

He gasps, and she stops. "I am hurting you?"

"No. No. No. This is good. Yeah." He's breathless. "Really good. Don't stop."

She grins, feeling more confident. With deft fingers she undoes his top button. He stands stock-still as she moves to the zipper.

I take a deep breath. She is going to unman me. Her delight is contagious and I love that she's finally plucking up the courage to undress me. In the firelight her skin is radiant, and the deep red and blue highlights glimmer in her hair. I want to throw her onto the bed and make easy, sweet love to her. But I need to slow down. Let her discover things at her own pace. While she undoes my fly, she seems less self-conscious. She's even forgotten she's not wearing her bra. She has beautiful, full breasts. I want to wor-ship each one until her nipples are rock hard and she's squirming beneath me. But I restrain myself and muffle my groan. She tugs my jeans down my legs, and I step out of them, so I'm standing before her in just my underwear.

"Your turn," I whisper, and make quick work of her fly and peel off her jeans. She steps out of them, and I cup her face gently and kiss her. "It's cold. Let's get into bed."

"Okay." She slides under the covers, her eyes on me.

"Oh—the bed is cold!" she squeaks.

"We'll warm it up."

Alessia's eyes flit to his straining shorts.

He grins. "What?" he asks.

She flushes.

"What?" Maxim insists.

"Take them off."

"My underwear?" Maxim's smile is lopsided.

"Yes."

He smirks—and removes one sock. Then the other. "There!"

"That is not what I was talking about." She giggles, marveling at how boyish he can be. He laughs and with one swift move slides off his shorts, freeing his erection—then tosses the underpants at her.

"Hey!" she cries out, playfully. She deflects them, but he leaps onto the bed, landing beside her.

"Brrr . . . move over." Maxim snuggles in beside her under the sheets, putting his arm around her and pulling her close. "I want to hold you for a moment. I can't believe I almost lost you today." He plants a soft kiss in her hair and squeezes her tight. She sees he's closed his eyes—as if he's in pain.

"You didn't. I am here. I would have fought them to stay with you," she whispers.

"They would have hurt you."

Sitting up suddenly, he lifts her hand to inspect the bruise on her side. His demeanor hardens. "Look at what they did to you." He hesitates, concerned.

"It's okay." She's suffered worse. . . .

"Maybe we should just nap." Maxim looks doubtful.

"What? No."

"I don't think—"

"Maxim! Don't think."

"Alessia—"

She reaches up and places a finger on his lips. "Please . . ." she says.

"Oh, baby." Taking her hand, he kisses each knuckle. Then he bends down and rings her bruise with tender kisses. Her fingers find his hair, and she tugs hard, so that he has to look up at her.

"Does it hurt?"

"No," she says hurriedly. "I want this. I want you." He sighs, and his mouth travels up to her breast and its nipple, teasing and sucking as he goes. She groans and writhes beneath him, closing her eyes and surrendering to the pleasure of his touch and his lips. Her fingers dig into his back, and she feels his erection against her hip. She's yearning to explore his body. All of his body.

He looks up at her. "What is it?"

"I . . . I . . ." She blushes.

"Tell me."

She laughs, embarrassed, and shuts her eyes.

"Tell me."

She opens one eye and squints at him.

"You're driving me crazy. What is it?"

"I want to touch you," she says, and hides her face with her hands.

Peeking through her fingers, she watches Maxim's eyes soften—amused, she thinks. He lies down beside her. "I'm all yours," he says. She leans up on one elbow, and they gaze at each other. "You're so lovely," he whispers.

She strokes his cheek, enjoying the feel of his rough stubble.

"Here, let me help you. . . ." Taking hold of her hand, he plants a kiss in her palm. He moves it to his chest, and she splays it out against his skin, feeling his warmth. His lips part as he takes a sharp breath. "I like you touching me."

Encouraged, she moves her hand down, her fingers tickling the fine hair that's sprinkled across his chest. She skims over one of his nipples, and it puckers under her touch.

"Oh," she breathes in delight.

"Oh," he responds, his voice hoarse, his eyes hooded and a dark, mossy green. He's watching her like a hawk. She bites her upper lip, and he groans. "Don't stop," he whispers. Feeling more wanton and enjoying the fact that she's turning him on, she moves her hand south over his smooth skin, over the bluffs and dips of his abdominal muscles. He tenses beneath her touch, and his breathing accelerates. She reaches the line of hair that leads down to her destination, and her courage falters.

"Here," he says, and, taking her hand, wraps it around his erection. She gasps, both shocked and thrilled in equal measure. It's big and hard and velvet smooth at once. Her thumb brushes the tip, and he closes his eyes, inhaling sharply. She tightens her hold, enjoying the feel of him beneath her fingers, feeling the pulse within him. He turns blazing eyes to her. "Like this," he whispers, and, guiding her hand, moves it slowly a fraction down and then up.

I've never had to show a woman what to do. It's possibly the most erotic thing I've ever done. Alessia's brow is furrowed as she concentrates, but her eyes are alive with wonder and desire, her mouth a little slack as she moves her hand, finally finding her rhythm and driving me wild. When she licks her lips, I want to come in her hand.

"Alessia, enough. I'm going to come."

She immediately removes her hand as if she's been burned, and I regret saying anything. I want to swoop over and into her—

but she's got that damned bruise, and I can't. I don't want to hurt her. She takes matters into her own hands, climbing onto me, her lips finding mine as she kisses me, pushing her tongue into my mouth. Tasting me. Her hair forms a lush curtain around us. And for a split second, we stare at each other in the firelight. Rich brown eyes to green. She's so bewitching. And giving. And sensual. And she's here with me.

She leans down and kisses me once more, and I reach over to the bedside table to grab a condom.

"Here." I show her the packet, and for a moment I wonder if she's going to take it and put it on me—but she blinks, uncertain.

"Move down. I'll show you what to do." I rip open the packet, take out the rubber, and, pinching the end, quickly roll it over my eager dick. "There. All done. We just have to get your knickers off."

She laughs as I roll her onto the mattress and hook my thumbs into her pink panties. *The* pink panties. I sweep them down her long legs and pitch them onto the floor. I'm kneeling between her thighs, but I sit back on my heels and pull her onto my lap with my arm around her waist, careful to avoid that bruise. "Is this okay?" She has her hands on my shoulders, and I lift her and position her over my straining cock. I'm waiting for her answer. She leans forward, her lips eager on mine, and I take that as my cue, and slowly . . . oh, so fucking slowly . . . I lower her onto me. Her teeth close around my bottom lip, and for a moment I think she's going to bite me.

When I'm fully inside her, she gasps and releases my lip.

"Okay?" I breathe.

"Yes." She nods. Enthusiastically. Her fingers are once more knotted in my hair, and she yanks hard, bringing my lips to hers. She's ravenous. Devouring me. Needy. Kissing me with the same intensity that she showed on the stairs. And I don't know if it's because of what happened to her earlier or if it's because I've told her that I love her, but she's on fire. She moves. Up and down. Again and again. Taking me . . . taking me . . .

It's heady. It's hot. But it's frantic.

This is going to end too soon!

"Hey." I tighten my hold around her, stilling her, and I smooth her hair from her face. "Easy, baby. Easy. We have the rest of the evening and all night. And tomorrow. And the day after that." Dark, dazed eyes blink at me. And my heart swells with a new and intoxicating feeling that consumes me. "I've got you," I whisper. "I love you."

"Maxim," she breathes, leaning forward and kissing me once more, her arms clasped around my neck. She starts to move again, more slowly, letting me savor her. Inch by inch. Steadier . . . easier . . . It's heaven.

Fuck.

And she rises and falls. Rises and falls. Taking me with her . . . climbing and climbing, until she stalls and cries out her orgasm, her mouth raised to the heavens and triggering my own shattering release.

"Oh, Alessia . . . !"

We lie still and quiet, facing each other. Not speaking. Just looking. Eyes. Noses. Cheeks. Lips. Faces. We gaze at each other. Absorbing each other. The only light is from the flickering flames of the fire, and all I hear is the spit and crackle of the burning logs and the thud of my heartbeat as it slows. Alessia raises her hand and traces my lips with her fingers. "I love you, Maxim," she whispers.

And I lean forward and kiss her once more. Her body rises to meet mine and we make sweet, sweet love again.

We are cocooned beneath the sheets in our own makeshift camp in my bedroom. Both of us are sitting cross-legged, knees touching, eyes intent on each other, and lit by the light of the little dragon that joins us in our secret, tented hideout.

She's talking.

And talking.

And I'm listening.

She's naked, her hair is loose and flowing down to her waist, preserving her modesty, and she's explaining how she learns a new piece for the piano.

"I will read the music for the first time, and I will see the colors. They . . . how do you say? Match a key."

"A color for each key?"

"Yes. D-flat major is a green. Like a fir tree. From Kukës. The 'Raindrop' Prelude. All greens. But some darker greens as the piece changes. Other keys are different colors. And sometimes a piece may have many colors. Like the Rachmaninoff. And they . . . um . . . print in my head. And I remember the piece." She shrugs and gives me an impish smile. "For a long time, I thought everyone sees all the colors in music."

"If only we were so lucky." I run a finger down her soft cheek. "You're special. Very special to me."

She blushes her lovely shade of pink.

"And who's your favorite composer? Bach?" I ask.

"Bach." She breathes his name with such veneration. "His music is . . ." She gestures and waves with her hands seeking inspiration, trying to capture the magnitude of what she wants to say, and she closes her eyes as if she's experiencing an ecstatic, religious moment. . . .

"Awe-inspiring?" I offer.

She laughs. "Yes." She sobers and lowers her lashes, then peeks up at me through them. "But my favorite composer is you."

I inhale sharply. I'm not used to her compliments.

"My composition? Wow. You flatter me. What colors do you see with that?"

"That was sad and solemn. Blues and grays."

"Fitting," I murmur, and my thoughts turn to Kit. She reaches up and caresses my cheek, bringing me back to her.

"I watched you play it at your apartment. I was supposed to be cleaning. But I had to watch you. And listen. It's beautiful music."

Her voice softens to a barely audible whisper. "I fell more in love with you then. . . ."

"You did?"

She nods, and my heart swells at her words.

"I wish I'd known you were listening. I'm glad you liked it. You played it so well at the Hideout."

"I loved it. You are a talented composer."

I take her hand and trace a pattern on her palm. "You're a very accomplished pianist."

She grins and flushes once more.

Surely she should be used to compliments.

"You're so talented. And beautiful. And brave." My fingers stroke her face and I draw her lips to mine. And beneath the sheet, we lose ourselves in a kiss. When Alessia pulls away to catch her breath, she gazes at me with longing once more. "Shall we . . . make love . . . again?" She leans forward and places her lips on my chest above my heart.

Oh, boy.

Alessia is lying across me, head on my chest, her fingers tapping out a melody over my stomach. I don't know what it is—but I'm enjoying it. I call the kitchen via the internal phone system. "Danny, I'd like some supper in my room. Can we have some sandwiches and a bottle of wine?"

"Very good, my lord. Beef?"

"Great. And a bottle of the Château Haut-Brion."

"I'll leave a tray outside the door, sir."

"Thank you." I smile at the blatant glee in her voice and hang up the phone. I don't know why, but Danny knows that Alessia is different. I've brought women here before, but Danny's never been as solicitous as she's been today. She must know that I'm in love. Head over heels. Completely. Utterly. Wholly. In love.

"You have a phone for inside the house?" Alessia looks up at me.

"It's a big house." I grin.

She laughs. "It is." She glances at the window; it's pitch-black outside. Is it seven o'clock? Ten o'clock? I've lost all track of time.

Alessia's curled up in one of the armchairs facing the fire, wrapped in a green throw, enjoying a roast beef and salad sandwich and drinking red wine. Her hair is a wonderful mess, spilling over her shoulders down to her waist. She's luminous. And lovely. And mine.

I toss another log on the fire, sit down in the armchair opposite her, and take a sip of the delicious wine. I've not felt this degree of peace since Kit died. . . . In fact, I can't remember ever feeling this way.

Maxim puts down his glass and picks up a sandwich. He looks glorious. Rumpled hair, stubble, wicked green eyes that glow with desire and love in the firelight. He's wearing his bulky cream sweater and his black jeans with a rip at the knee, and she spies his skin beneath. . . . Alessia drinks him in.

"Happy?" he asks.

"Yes. Very . . . muchly."

He grins. "I feel the same. I don't think I've ever been happier. I know you'd like to stay here, and so would I, but I think we should go back to London tomorrow. If that's all right. I have stuff I need to do."

"Okay." Alessia nibbles at her lip.

"What?"

"I like being in Cornwall. It is not as busy as London. There are less people. Less noise."

"I know. But I should get back to London and check on my flat."

Alessia examines her glass of wine. "Back to reality," she whispers.

"Hey. It's going to be okay."

She stares into the fire, watching one of the logs spit embers onto the hearth.

"Darling, what's wrong?" Maxim is concerned.

"I . . . I want to work."

"Work? Doing what?"

"I don't know. Cleaning?"

His brow creases. "Alessia, I don't think so. You don't need to clean anymore. You're a talented woman. Is that really what you want to do? We need to find something more interesting for you. And we need to make sure that it's legal for you to work here. I'll look into it. I have people who can help." His smile is sincere and encouraging.

"But . . . I want to earn my own money."

"I understand. If you're caught, though, you'll be deported."

"I don't want that!" Alessia's heartbeat spikes. She cannot go back.

"Neither of us wants that," Maxim reassures her. "Don't worry about this. We'll figure it out. Maybe you can do something with your music, eventually."

She studies him. "I will be your kept woman." Her voice is low. This is what she wanted to avoid.

His answering smile is rueful. "Only until it's legal for you to work here. Think of this as a redistribution of wealth."

"How socialist you are, Lord Trevethick," she teases.

"Who knew?" He raises his glass to her. She reciprocates, and as she takes a sip of wine, an idea forms in her head. But will he agree?

"What is it?" he asks.

Alessia draws a deep breath. "I will clean for you. And you will pay me."

Maxim frowns, taken aback. "Alessia. You don't need—"

"Please . . . I want this." She stares at him, silently begging for him to agree.

"Ales—"

"Please."

He rolls his eyes in exasperation. "Okay. If that's what you want. But on one condition."

"What?"

"Can I veto the housecoat and scarf?"

"I will think about it." She smirks, feeling more lighthearted.

He laughs, and she breathes a sigh of relief. She will have something to do while *his people* resolve her immigration status.

A warmth spreads through her body. This is not where she thought her life might lead, here in this old, grand house with this handsome, gentle, kind man. Of course she had fantasized about it—in a vague way. But she thought it was impossible.

She had challenged her destiny and taken a huge risk when she left Albania, and fate had not let go without a fight.

Yet her Mister had intervened, and now she's here with him. *Safe.*

He loves her, and she loves him. And the future stretches before her, full of possibility. Perhaps, after all this time, fortune has turned its benign smile on her.

Chapter Twenty-Five

A primal wail disturbs my dream, waking me in an instant.

Alessia.

In the soft light from the little dragon, I see that she's asleep beside me, but utterly still, her hands clenched into fists beneath her chin. She's like a statue petrified by some natural disaster. She parts her lips and cries out again, the most eerie and unearthly of sounds. I prop myself up on my elbow and gently shake her awake.

"Alessia. Sweetheart. Wake up."

Her eyelids fly open. She looks around wildly and immediately starts fighting me off.

"Alessia. It's me. Maxim." I grab her hands before she does either of us any harm.

"M . . . M . . . Maxim," she whispers, and stops struggling.

"You're having a bad dream. I'm here. I've got you." I gather her in my arms and pull her on top of me, kissing the crown of her head. She's trembling.

"I . . . I thought . . . I thought . . ." she stutters.

"It's okay. It's just a bad dream. You're safe." I hold her and tenderly stroke her back, wishing I could take all her fear and pain away. She shivers but seems to settle, and before long she's asleep again.

I close my eyes, one hand in her hair and the other on her back, enjoying her weight and her skin against mine. I could get used to this.

A lessia wakes in the gray light of early morning. She's nestled under Maxim's arm, her hand splayed on his belly. He's fast asleep, with his face turned toward her. His hair is tousled, his lips slightly parted, and his cheeks and jawline shaded with stubble. He looks relaxed and quite irresistible. She stretches out beside him, enjoying the pull of her muscles. Her side is a little sore, and her bruise is still tender, but she feels . . . good.

No. More than good.

Hopeful. Calm. Powerful. Safe.

Because of this wonderful man asleep beside her.

She loves him. With all her heart.

And what's more remarkable, he loves her, too. She can scarcely believe it.

He's given her hope.

Maxim stirs, and his eyelids blink open.

"Good morning," she whispers.

"It is now," he answers with a mischievous gleam in his eye. "You look lovely. Sleep well?"

"Yes."

"You had a nightmare."

"Me? Last night?"

"You don't remember?"

Alessia shakes her head. He skims her cheek with the backs of his fingers. "I'm glad you don't. How are you feeling?"

"Good."

"Good or *good*?" His tone is sultry.

"Very good." She grins.

Maxim rolls over, pinning her to the mattress, and stares down at her, his green eyes glowing. "God, I love waking up next to you," he whispers, and kisses her throat. She throws her arms around his neck and surrenders gladly to his skilled mouth.

"I suppose we should get up and go back to London," Maxim murmurs against her belly. Alessia's fingers play with his hair, but she's too relaxed to move. She's relishing the few moments of quiet after their passionate storm. Finally he interrupts her reverie. "Shower with me." He turns his head to look up at her with the broadest of smiles.

How can she resist?

Alessia towel-dries her hair while I shave. The bruise on her side looks smaller, but it's still a livid purple. A wave of guilt washes through me—she certainly gave me no indication last night or this morning that she was in any pain. She gives me a dazzling smile over her shoulder, and like a sea mist in the breeze, my guilt fades into the ether.

Part of me wants to stay here with her forever. But I'm also anxious to leave. I don't want Sergeant Nancarrow or his colleague coming to the Hall to interview Alessia. I need to keep her away from the police. If necessary, I'll inform him that business has taken me back to London.

It will be a shame to go. I'm enjoying our comfortable familiarity, and I marvel at the change in her. She seems far more confident, and it's been only a few days. Tossing her hair to the side, with a glance at me, she strolls out of the bathroom, naked as the day she was born. I peek around the doorframe; the view is too tantalizing not to enjoy, her hair swinging almost to her waist in a gentle counterpoint to her walk. She stops at the bed and rummages through the wicker basket on the ottoman, looking

for some clothes. When she glances up and catches me gawking, she smirks. And I move back to stare at my reflection in
the mirror with a smug grin. Her newfound confidence is sexy
as hell.

A few moments later, she appears in the doorway and leans
on the frame. She's wearing the clothes I bought her, and I know
it's going to be a good day. "In the bottom of the armoire, there
should be a bag you can use for your clothes. Or I can ask Danny
to pack them for you."

"I can do it." She folds her arms, studying me. "I like to watch
you shave."

"I like you watching me," I murmur as I finish up. Turning, I
brush her lips with a kiss, then wipe my face of the remaining
foam. "Let's have some breakfast and get on the road."

Alessia is animated on our drive back to London. We talk and
laugh and talk some more—she has the most infectious giggle.
When we hit the M4, she takes command of the music, and we
listen to the Rachmaninoff. As the first bars of the piano concerto
begin to play, I'm reminded of when she played this piece at the
Hideout—the memory is stirring. I watched her lose herself in
the music, and she took me with her. From the corner of my
eye, I notice Alessia's fingers pressing imaginary keys through
the cadenza. I'd love to see her play this again, but this time as a
performance with a full orchestra.

"Have you seen *Brief Encounter*?"

"No."

"It's a classic British film. The director uses this piece through-
out the movie. It's cool. It's one of my mother's favorite films."

"I'd like to see it. I love this music."

"And you play it so well."

"Thank you." She gives me a shy smile. "What is she like?"

"My mother? She's . . . ambitious. Clever. Funny. Not very
maternal." As I say it, I feel a stab of disloyalty, but the truth is,

Rowena always seemed bored or inconvenienced by her young children. She happily handed us over to our various nannies and sent us off to boarding school. It was only after our father died that we became more interesting to her.

Though she was always interested in Kit.

"Oh," says Alessia.

"My relationship with my mother is a little . . . strained. I suppose I never forgave her for leaving my father."

"She left him?" She sounds shocked.

"She left all of us. I was twelve."

"I'm sorry."

"She met someone younger—and broke my father's heart."

"Oh."

"It's okay. It was a long time ago. We have an uneasy truce now. Well, ever since Kit died." Talking about this is grim. "Choose another song," I prompt when the Rachmaninoff finishes. "Something cheerful."

She smiles and scrolls through the list. " 'Melody'?"

I laugh. "Rolling Stones? Yes. Play that." She taps the screen, and the countdown begins: *Two. One, two, three,* followed by the blues piano. Alessia grins. She likes it. Lord, I have so much music I'd like to share with her.

The roads are quiet and we make good time. We fly past the junction for Swindon, with a further eighty miles to go until we reach Chelsea. But I have to stop for petrol, so I take the slip road for Membury Services. Alessia's demeanor suddenly changes. Her hand grips the door handle and she casts large, apprehensive eyes at me.

"I know that service stations make you anxious. We'll just get petrol. Okay?" Reaching over, I give her knee a reassuring squeeze. She nods but looks unconvinced. I pull up by a petrol pump, and she hops out to stand beside me while I fill up. "You going to keep me company?"

She nods and dances from foot to foot to stay warm, her breath a gauzy cloud around her. Her eyes survey the locale and fix on the parked trucks. She's watchful. Wary. It's painful to see her this way, especially when she'd been so relaxed this morning.

"You know you're safe now. The police have them," I say to reassure her, but then the pump stops with a loud metallic clunk, startling us both. The tank is full. "Let's pay." Hooking the nozzle back in its holder, I slip my arm around her shoulders, and we head into the shop. She walks beside me, subdued.

"You okay?" We're in the queue, and she's radiating anxiety, taking furtive glances at everyone in the shop.

"It was my mother's idea," she blurts, quickly, quietly. "She thought she was helping me." It takes me a couple of seconds to realize what she's referring to.

Bloody hell. She's telling me *this story* now? A frisson runs up my spine. Why now? I have to pay for my petrol. "Hold that thought." I raise my index finger and hand the shop assistant my credit card. His eyes shift to Alessia, several times.

Man, she is so out of your league.

"Please enter your PIN," he says, smiling at Alessia, who barely gives him a glance. She's watching the petrol pumps, checking who's out there.

When I'm done, I take her hand. "Shall we continue talking in the car?"

She nods.

As we climb back into the Jag, I wonder why she picks service stations and car parks for her revelations. I drive away from the pumps, park the car facing woodland, and the engine idles off. "Okay. Do you still want to talk?"

Alessia stares out at the leafless trees in front of us and nods. "My betrothed. He is a violent man. One day . . ." Her voice falters.

My heart sinks. It is as I feared.

What the fuck did he do to her?

"He does not like me playing the piano. He does not like the . . . um . . . attention that I get."

I despise him even more.

"He is angry. He wants me to stop. . . ."

My hands tighten on the steering wheel.

Alessia's voice is practically inaudible. "He hits me. And he wants to break my fingers."

"What?"

She looks down at her hands. Her precious hands. She cups one with the other, holding it tenderly.

The fucking piece of shit hurt her.

"I had to get away."

"Of course you did."

And I have to touch her, so that she knows I'm on her side. Folding both her hands in one of mine, I squeeze gently. The temptation to haul her into my lap and just hold her is overwhelming, but I resist. She needs to talk. She gives me a hesitant look, and I let go. "I went in a small bus to Shkodër, and there we move into the big truck. Dante and Ylli are there with five other girls. One of them has . . . I mean—is only seventeen years."

I gasp. Shocked. *So young.*

"Her name is Bleriana. On the truck. We talked. A lot. She lives in the north of Albania, too. In Fierza. We became friends. We made plans to find work together." She stops—lost in the horror of her story, or maybe she's wondering what became of her friend.

"And they take everything from us. Except the clothes we are wearing and our shoes. There is only one bucket in the back. . . . You know." Her voice fades.

"That's awful."

"Yes. The smell." She shudders. "And all we have is a bottle of water. One bottle for each of us." Her leg starts jiggling, and her face pales—I'm reminded of how she looked when I first met her.

"It's okay. I'm here. I've got you. I want to know."

She turns dark, devastated eyes to me. "Do you?"

"Yes. But only if you want to tell me."

Her eyes move over my face, scrutinizing me. Exposing me, like that first time in my hallway.

Why do I want to know?

Because I love her.

Because she's the sum of all her experiences, and this, sadly, is one of them.

She takes a deep breath and continues, "We were in the truck for three, four days maybe. I don't know how long. We stopped before the truck went on a—what is the word?—ferry. For carrying cars and trucks. We were given bread. And black plastic bags. We had to put them over our heads."

"What?"

"It is to do with the immigration. They measure the, um . . . *dioksidin e karbonit?*" She flounders for the words.

"Carbon dioxide?"

"Yes. That is it."

"In the cab?"

She shrugs. "I don't know, but if there is too much, the authorities know there are people in the truck. They measure it. Somehow.

"We drove onto the ferry. The noise was loud. Too loud. The engines. The other trucks . . . and we were in the dark. My head in the plastic bag. And then the truck stopped. The engine was off, and all we could hear was the creaking and groaning of the metal and the tires. The sea was rough. So rough. We were all lying down." Her fingers move to the little cross at her neck, and she starts to fiddle with it. "It was hard to breathe. I thought I was going to die."

A lump forms in my throat. My voice is hoarse. "No wonder you don't like the dark. That must have been terrifying."

"One of the girls was sick. The smell." She stops and gags.

"Alessia . . ."

But she continues. She seems compelled. "Before we went on

the ferry, when we are eating the bread, I heard Dante say in English—he did not know that I understood the language—he said that we would be earning our money on our backs. And I knew our fate."

My fury is swift, burning through my blood. I wish I'd killed the fucker when I had the chance and dumped his body the way Jenkins suggested. I have never felt as inadequate as I do in this moment. Alessia drops her head, and I lift her chin gently with my fingers. "I'm so sorry."

She turns to face me, and there's a fire in her eyes. It's not sorrow reflected back at me, or self-pity—she's angry. Really angry. "I heard rumors, before. Girls missing from our town and from neighboring villages. And from Kosovo. It was in the back of my mind when I boarded the bus—but you always hope." She swallows, and beneath her anger I see the anguish in her eyes. She feels like a fool.

"Alessia, you are not to blame, and neither is your mother. She acted in good faith."

"She did. And I had to get away."

"I understand."

"I told the girls what Dante said. And three of them believed me. Bleriana, she believed me. And when we had the chance to escape, we did. We ran. I don't know if the others succeeded. I don't know if Bleriana got away." There's a trace of guilt in her voice. "I had Magda's address on a piece of paper. People here were celebrating Christmas. I walked for days. . . . I think it was six or seven days. I don't know. Until I reached her house. And she looked after me."

"Thank God for Magda."

"Yes."

"Where did you sleep while you were walking?"

"I didn't sleep. Not really. It was too cold. I found a shop, and I stole a map." She lowers her gaze.

"I can't begin to imagine this horror that you've been through, and I'm sorry."

"You do not have to be sorry." She gives me a slight smile. "This was before I met you. Now you know. Everything."

"Thank you for telling me." I lean over and kiss her forehead. "You brave, brave woman."

"Thank you for listening."

"I'll always listen, Alessia. Always. Shall we go home now?"

Seemingly relieved, she gives me a nod, and I restart the engine and reverse out of the space. I head for the slip road back to the motorway.

"There's one thing I want to know," I add, reflecting on the horrid tale she's just shared.

"What?"

"Does he have a name?"

"Who?"

"Your . . . betrothed." I spit the word out. I loathe him.

She shakes her head. "I never say his name."

"Like Voldemort," I mutter under my breath.

"Harry Potter?"

"You know Harry Potter?"

"Oh, yes. My grandmother—"

"Don't tell me, she smuggled the books into Albania?"

Alessia laughs. "No. She had them sent to her. By Magda. My mother read them to me as a child. In English."

"Ah, another reason you speak such good English. Is she fluent as well?"

"Mama? Yes. My father . . . he does not like it when we speak to each other in English."

"I bet." The more I hear about her father, the more I dislike him, too. But I keep that to myself. "Why don't you find another song?"

She scrolls through the screen, and her eyes light up when she finds RY X. "We danced to this song."

"Our first dance." I smile at the memory. It seems like a lifetime ago.

We settle into a comfortable silence, both of us listening to the music. She seems preoccupied by the rhythm, swaying gently to and fro. And I'm happy to see that she's recovered her equilibrium after telling her harrowing story.

While she chooses another song, I brood. This man, this fucker who harmed her, her *betrothed*, I want to know everything about him if I am to protect her from him. I need to sort out Alessia's legal status, urgently—but I have no idea how. Marrying her would help, but I think she needs to be here legally for me to do that. I resolve to call Rajah as soon as possible.

I smirk as we pass the junction for Maidenhead, and shake my head, amused by my own idiocy. I'm embracing my inner twelve-year-old boy. I glance at Alessia, but she hasn't noticed. She's deep in thought, tapping her finger against her lips.

"His name is Anatoli. Anatoli Thaçi," she says.

What? "He who must not be named?"

"Yes."

Mentally I file the arsehole's name away. "You decided to tell me?"

"Yes."

"Why?"

"Because he has more power without a name."

"Like Voldemort?"

She nods.

"What does he do?"

"I am not sure. My father owes him a big debt, something to do with his business, I think. But I don't know what. Anatoli is a powerful man. Rich."

"Really?" My voice is dry. I hope to God that my bank balance is bigger than his.

"I don't think his business is . . . um . . . legal. Yes?"

"Yep. That's how we'd say it. He's a crook."

"A gangster."

"What is it with you and gangsters?" I scowl. She chuckles, and it's the most disarming and unexpected sound. "What's so funny?"

"Your face."

"Ah." I grin. "That's reason enough."

"I love your face."

"I'm rather attached to it as well."

She laughs once more and then sobers. "You are right. He is not funny."

"He's not. But he's far away. He can't hurt you here. We'll be home soon. Can we listen to the Rachmaninoff again?"

"Sure," she says, scrolling through the screen once more.

I pull the F-Type up outside the office, and Oliver comes out to greet me and hand over new keys for my flat.

"This is my girlfriend, Alessia Demachi." I lean back, and Oliver reaches through the car window to shake Alessia's hand.

"How do you do," he says. "I'm sorry we're not meeting under better circumstances." He gives her a warm smile.

Her answering smile is dazzling.

"I hope you've recovered from your ordeal."

Alessia nods.

"Thanks for sorting all this out," I say. "I'll see you in the office tomorrow." He gives me a wave, and I ease the Jag into the traffic.

Maxim carries the bags from the car to the elevator. It's odd to be back here, knowing that she'll now be staying. The doors open, and they step in, and Maxim drops her bag and pulls her into his arms. "Welcome home," he whispers, and her heart skips a beat. She strains upward to kiss him. And his lips find hers, kissing her hard and long until she forgets her name.

When the doors open, they are both breathless.

An old lady is standing at the entrance to the elevator. She's wearing large dark sunglasses, a garish red hat, with earrings and coat to match, and she's clutching a diminutive hairball of a dog. Maxim releases Alessia. "Good afternoon, Mrs. Beckstrom."

"Oh, Maxim. How lovely to see you," she replies in a high-pitched voice. "Or should I address you by your title now?"

"Maxim is fine, Mrs. B." He maneuvers Alessia out of the elevator and holds the door back for the old lady. "This is my girlfriend, Alessia Demachi."

"How do you do?" Mrs. Beckstrom beams at Alessia but continues talking before Alessia can reply. "I see you've had the front door repaired. I hope you didn't lose much during the burglary."

"Nothing that can't be replaced."

"I hope they don't come back."

"I think the police have them already."

"Good. I hope they hang them."

Hang? They hang people here?

"I'm off to walk Heracles, now it's finally stopped raining."

"Enjoy your walk."

"I'll do just that. You, too!" And she looks sideways at Alessia, who cannot help but blush. The doors close, and Mrs. Beckstrom disappears.

"She's been my neighbor forever. She's about a thousand years old, and she's batty."

"Batty?"

"Crazy," he explains. "And don't be fooled by that dog. He's a vicious little bastard."

Alessia smiles. "How long have you lived here?"

"Since I was nineteen."

"I don't know how old you are."

He laughs. "Old enough to know better."

She frowns while Maxim unlocks the front door.

"I'm twenty-eight."

Alessia grins. "You are an old man!"

"Old. I'll give you old!" He bends suddenly, surprising her, and scoops her up over his shoulder, avoiding her bruised side. She squeals and laughs as he waltzes into the apartment.

The alarm bleeps, and Maxim turns around until Alessia is

facing the alarm panel. Breathless, she enters the new code that
he gives her, and when the beeping stops, Maxim slides her down
his front so that she's once more in his arms.

"I'm glad you're here with me," he says.

"I am glad, too."

From his pocket he draws the keys that Oliver gave him earlier.
"For you."

Alessia takes them. They're on a key chain with a blue leather
fob that reads ANGWIN HOUSE.

"The keys to the kingdom," she says.

Maxim grins. "Welcome home." He bends to kiss her, his lips
coaxing hers. She groans as she responds, and they lose themselves in each other.

Alessia screams as she climaxes. It's a cock-hardening sound.
Her fingers are clenched around the sheets. Her head tossed
back. Her mouth open. I kiss her clitoris as she writhes beneath
me, then her belly, her navel, her stomach, and her sternum as
she mewls, and taking her cries into my mouth, I ease into her.

My phone buzzes. And without looking at the caller ID, I know
it's Caroline. I'd promised to see her. Ignoring the phone, I gaze
down at Alessia, who is dozing beside me. She's becoming quite
demanding in bed—and I like it. Leaning down, I kiss her shoulder, and she stirs.

"I have to go out," I murmur.

"Where are you going?"

"I have to see my sister-in-law."

"Oh."

"I haven't seen her for days, and I need to talk some things
through with her. I won't be long."

Alessia sits up. "Okay." She glances out the window. It's dark.

"It's six P.M.," I tell her.

"Shall I make something for us to eat?"

"If you can find something. Please."

She smiles. "I'll do that."

"If you can't find anything, we'll go out. I'll be about an hour." Reluctantly I throw the quilt aside, get out of bed, and start to dress under Alessia's appreciative gaze.

I don't tell her that I'm dreading this meeting.

Chapter Twenty-Six

"Good evening, my lord," Blake says as he opens the front door to Trevelyan House.

"Hello, Blake." I don't correct him. After all, as much as it pains me, I am the earl. "Is Lady Trevethick at home?"

"I believe she's in the morning room."

"Great. I'll see myself up. Oh, and thank Mrs. Blake for clearing up after the burglary. She's done a great job."

"Will do, my lord. Very unfortunate business. May I take your overcoat?"

"Thanks." I slip out of my coat, and he folds it over his arm.

"Something to drink?"

"No. I'm good. Thanks, Blake."

I vault up the stairs, turn left, take a deep, steadying breath, and open the morning room door.

Alessia examines the chaos that is the walk-in closet off Maxim's bedroom. The drawers, the racks—they are all bursting with his clothes, leaving no room to store hers. She takes her duffel bag through to the spare room and proceeds to unpack, hanging her new clothes in the small armoire.

Placing her bag of toiletries on the bed, she wanders through the apartment. Everything is achingly familiar, but now she's viewing the place from a new perspective. She'd always thought of Maxim's home as a place of work. She had never dared to imagine that one day she might be living *here* with *him*. She'd never aspired to live in a place as grand as this. She does a twirl in the doorway of the kitchen, feeling giddy and grateful—and happy. It's a precious and rare feeling. She still has so much to figure out in her life, but for the first time in a long time she's hopeful. With Maxim at her side, she feels that no obstacle is insurmountable. She wonders if he'll only be an hour. . . . She's missing him.

She runs her fingers along the wall of the hallway. The photographs that had been hanging there have disappeared. Maybe they were stolen during the burglary.

The piano!

She races into the living room. It's still there, unscathed. Breathing a sigh of relief, she switches on the lights. The room looks fresh and clean, his record collection in place. But the desk is bare—the computer and the sound gear gone. Here, too, the photographs that used to hang on the walls are missing. She walks with trepidation toward the piano, scrutinizing all its parts. Under the glow of the chandelier, it's glossy and gleaming—newly polished, she thinks. Placing her hand on the ebony, she walks around it, stroking its sweeping curves. When she gets to the business end, she notices that his compositions are gone. Perhaps they've been tidied away. She lifts the lid and presses middle C: it's a golden sound that rings through the empty room, seducing her, calming her . . . centering her. She sits down on the stool, shakes off her feelings of solitude, and begins to play Bach's Prelude no. 23 in B Major.

Caroline is sitting by the fire, staring into the flames, huddled in a tartan throw. She doesn't look around when I walk in.

"Hi." My subdued greeting competes with the crackle of the fire. Caroline angles her head toward me, her expression forlorn, her mouth turned down in sorrow.

"Oh, it's you." she says.

"Who were you expecting?" She hasn't risen to greet me and I'm beginning to feel a little unwelcome.

She sighs. "I'm sorry. I was just thinking about what Kit would be doing now if he were here." From nowhere my grief emerges and smothers me like an itchy woolen blanket. I shrug it off, swallowing the lump that's sticking in my throat. When I get closer to her, I see she's been crying.

"Oh, Caro . . ." I murmur, and squat beside her chair.

"Maxim, I'm a widow. I'm twenty-eight, and I'm a widow. This wasn't part of the plan."

I take her hand in mine. "I know. It wasn't in any of our plans. Even Kit's."

Pained blue eyes meet mine. "I don't know," she says.

"What do you mean?"

She leans forward so she's facing me and in a conspiratorial whisper says, "I think he meant to kill himself."

I squeeze her fingers. "Caro. That's not true. Don't think that. It was just a horrid accident." My eyes meet hers, and I'm trying for my most earnest look, but the truth is—I've had the same thought. I can't let her know that, though, and I don't want to believe it either. Suicide is too painful for those of us left behind.

"I keep going over that day," she says, searching my face for answers. "But I have no idea why . . ."

Alas, neither have I.

"It was an accident," I reiterate. "Let me sit." Releasing her, I slump into the chair opposite hers, facing the fireplace.

"Do you want a drink? After all, this is your house." Her words have a bitter edge that I ignore. I don't want a fight.

"Blake already offered, and I declined."

She exhales and turns back to stare at the flames. We both do, each of us lost in the pain of losing Kit. I had expected the third degree from her, but she's not forthcoming at all, and we sit in an uneasy silence. After a while the fire dies down. I get up and place another couple of logs in the grate and stoke the flames.

"Do you want me to go?" I ask.

She shakes her head.

Okay, then.

I sit back down, and she tilts her head to the side, her hair falling across her face until she tucks it behind her ear. "I heard about the burglary. Did you lose anything important?"

"No. Just my laptop and my decks. I think they smashed my iMac."

"People are shitty."

"They are."

"What were you doing in Cornwall?"

"This and that...." I'm trying for humor.

"Well, that's illuminating." She rolls her eyes, and I glimpse a flash of the spirited Caroline I know. "What were you doing in Cornwall?"

"Escaping from gangsters, if you must know."

"Gangsters?"

"Yes . . . And falling in love."

Alessia explores the kitchen cupboards and drawers, looking for something to cook for supper. She's not examined their contents in any comprehensive way before. But as she goes through them, she notes that the utensils are all clean and the pots and pans are pristine. She suspects they've never been used. Two of the pans still have the price stickers attached. She finds a few groceries in the larder: pasta, pesto, sun-dried tomatoes, some jars of herbs and spices. Enough to make a meal, but these ingredients don't inspire her. She eyes the kitchen clock. Maxim will be a while yet. She has time to go to the local store to find something a little more enticing for her man.

A silly grin spreads over her face.

Her man.

Her Mister.

At the bottom of the armoire, she finds the Ziploc bag that she'd stuffed in Michal's old rugby sock—the bag that holds her precious savings. Taking out two twenty-pound notes, she slips them into the back pocket of her jeans, grabs her coat, sets the alarm, and leaves.

W̲hat?" splutters Caroline. "You? In love?"

"And why would that be so improbable?" I note that she doesn't continue her line of questioning about "gangsters."

"Maxim, the only thing you love is your dick."

"That's not true!"

She cackles. And it's good to hear her laugh, but not so good that it's at my expense. Noticing my less-than-enthusiastic reaction, she tries to bring her amusement under control. "Okay, so who's been on the sharp end of it?" she says indulgently.

"You don't have to be quite so crude."

"That's not an answer."

I gaze at her, and the warmth and humor slowly fade from her face.

"Who?" she presses me.

"Alessia."

She frowns for a split second, and then her eyebrows shoot up. "No!" She gasps. "Your daily?"

"What do you mean, no?"

"Maxim. She's your fucking daily—literally!" And a dark cloud crosses her face; a storm is brewing.

I shift in my seat, irritated by her response. "Well, she isn't my daily anymore."

"I knew it! That time when I met her. In your kitchen. You were so weird and attentive toward her." She spits each word out like venom. She's horrified.

"Don't be so dramatic. That's not like you."

"It *is* like me."

"Since when?"

"Since my bloody husband upped and killed himself," she hisses, her eyes glassy with animosity.

Shit.

She went there. She's using Kit's death in an argument.

I gulp down my shock and grief as we glare at each other, the air between us ripe with our unspoken thoughts.

Abruptly she turns her attention back to the fire, her contempt evident in the stubborn line of her chin. "You should just fuck her out of your system," she grumbles.

"I don't think I'll ever get her out of my system. I don't want to. I'm in love with her." My words are softly spoken, and they hang in the air as I wait for Caroline's reaction.

"You're crazy."

"Why?"

"You know why! She's your fucking *cleaner.*"

"Does that matter?"

"Yes, it matters!"

"No, it doesn't."

"QED. You're crazy if you don't think it matters."

"Crazy in love." I shrug. It's the truth.

"With the help!"

"Caro, don't be such a snob. You can't choose who you love. Love chooses you."

"Bloody hell!" She stands suddenly, looming over me. "Don't

give me some bullshit clichéd homily. She's just a grimy little freeloader, Maxim. Can't you see that?"

"Fuck off, Caroline!" I stand up, bristling with a sense of injustice, and we're practically nose to nose. "You know nothing about her—"

"I know her type."

"From where? From where do you Know. Her. Type, Lady Trevethick?" I enunciate each syllable, my words echoing off the blue-painted walls and framed artwork of this small drawing room.

I'm furious.

How dare she judge Alessia? Caroline, like me, has led a life of utter fucking privilege.

She blanches and steps back, looking at me as if I've just slapped her.

Fuck.

Mate! This is getting out of hand.

I run my fingers through my hair.

"Caroline, it's not the end of the world."

"It is to me."

"Why?"

She glares at me with a look that's both wounded and enraged. I shake my head. "I don't understand. Why is this such a big deal to you?"

"What about *us*?" she asks, her voice wavering, her eyes wide.

"There is no 'us.'" God, she's so annoying. "We fucked. We were grieving. We're still grieving. I've finally met someone who makes me step up and think about the life I lead, and—"

"But I thought—" She interrupts me, though her words dry up at the look I give her.

"What did you think? Us? Together? We had that! We tried that! And you chose my brother!" I'm shouting.

"We were young," she whispers. "And after Kit died . . ."

"No. No. No. You do not get to do that. Don't try to make

me feel guilty—it takes two, Caroline. You made the first move when we were both empty and aching with grief. Maybe it was just an excuse. I don't know. But we're not a good combination. We never have been. We had our chance but you went off and fucked my brother. You claimed him and his title. I am not your fucking consolation prize."

She gapes at me with horror writ large on her face.

Fuck.

"Get out!" she whispers.

"You're throwing me out of my own house?"

"You bastard! Get the fuck out. Go!" she screeches. Picking up an empty wineglass, she hurls it at me. It hits my thigh and falls to the wooden floor, where it shatters. We glare at each other in the ensuing and oppressive silence.

Tears pool in her eyes.

And I can bear it no more. I turn on my heel and exit, slamming the door behind me.

A lessia walks briskly down a side street toward the convenience store that she knows on Royal Hospital Road. It's a cold, dark night, and she pushes her hands deeper into her pockets, grateful for the warm coat that Maxim bought for her. A tingle runs up her spine, raising all the fine hairs on the back of her neck.

She glances behind her, suddenly uneasy. But under the streetlamps all is quiet; she is alone, except for a woman walking a large dog on the other side of the road. Alessia shakes her head, chiding herself for overreacting. In Albania, at night, she would be wary of the djinn—the demons that roam the earth after sundown. But she knows that this is superstition. She's still jumpy after her encounter with Dante and Ylli. All the same, she picks up her pace and trots to the end of the street and around the corner to the Tesco Express.

The store is busier than usual, and she's grateful that there are many customers milling through the aisles. Grabbing a shopping basket, she walks to the fresh produce section and begins to browse through the vegetables on sale.

"Hello, Alessia. How have you been?" It takes a fraction of a second for her to realize that the calm, familiar voice is speaking in Albanian. It takes another fraction of a second for fear to grip her heart and her soul.

No! He's here!

I stand outside Trevelyan House trying to get a hold of my temper. Furious, I button up my coat against the February chill.

That did not go well.

Fisting my hands, I thrust them into my pockets.

I am so fucking angry right now. Too angry to go home to Alessia. I need to walk off my temper. Consumed by my thoughts and beyond pissed off, I turn right and stride up Chelsea Embankment.

How could Caroline think she and I had a chance?

We know each other too well. We're supposed to be friends. She *is* my best friend. And she's my brother's widow, for fuck's sake.

This is one fine bloody mess, dude.

But truth be told, I had no idea that she had designs on me beyond the occasional fuck.

Shit. She's jealous.

Of Alessia.

Fuck.

My mind's a mess. I scowl as I cross Oakley Street and stalk past the Mercedes-Benz garage. Even the familiar grace and beauty of the *Boy with a Dolphin* statue on the corner cannot lift my mood. My anger is as dark as the night.

Alessia turns, her heart pounding, fear streaking like lightning through her veins. She's suddenly dizzy, her mouth dry. Anatoli is standing over her, invading her space. He's close. Too close. "I have been looking for you," he continues in their mother tongue. His full lips are twisted in a seemingly casual smile that doesn't touch his piercing, pale blue eyes. He scrutinizes her, looking for answers. His chiseled face is thinner and his fair hair longer than she remembers. He looms over her, bundled up in what looks like an expensive Italian coat, intimidating her even now.

She starts to tremble as she wonders how the hell he found her. "H-h-h-hello, Anatoli," she stutters, her voice shaky and full of fear.

"Surely you can do better than that, *carissima*. No smile for the man you are going to marry?"

No. No. No.

Alessia's feet seem frozen to the shop floor as despair rises through her body. Her mind races—how can she escape? She is surrounded by shoppers going about their business, but she's never felt so stranded and alone. They are oblivious to what is happening in front of them.

Gently Anatoli strokes her cheek with a gloved finger, and her stomach recoils.

Don't touch me.

"I've come to take you home," he says casually, as if they'd been talking only yesterday. Alessia stares at him, unable to speak. "No kind words? You are not pleased to see me?" His eyes flash with a spark of irritation—and something more, something darker. Speculation? Admiration? A challenge accepted?

Bile rises in Alessia's throat, but she swallows it down. He grasps her arm at her elbow and squeezes. "You are coming with me. I have spent a small fortune tracking you down. Your parents are devastated by your disappearance, and your father says you sent no word back to them that you were safe and well."

Alessia is confused. This is not what happened. Does he know that her mother helped her? Is her mother okay? What did her mother say?

He tightens his hold on her arm. "You should be ashamed of yourself. But we'll deal with that later. Right now let's go and collect your things, I'm taking you home."

Chapter Twenty-Seven

I storm down Cheyne Walk.

Fuck it. I need a drink to help me calm the fuck down. I snatch a look at my watch. Alessia's not expecting me back until seven. I have time. I do an about-face and head back to Oakley Street, with the Coopers Arms firmly set in my mind as my destination.

The wind whips around me, but I don't feel the cold. I'm too angry. I cannot believe Caroline's reaction.

Or maybe I knew it would be bad.

Did I? That bad? Throwing-me-out-of-the-house bad?

Bollocks to that.

Usually the only person who makes me this angry is my mother.

Both of them are appalling snobs.

As am I.

Fuck.

I'm not! No.

What will Caroline say when I tell her I want to marry Alessia?

What will my mother say?

Marry someone with money, darling.

Kit chose wisely.

My dark mood grows darker still as I stomp into the night.

I am not going with you," Alessia says, her voice shaking and betraying her fear.

"Let's discuss this outside." Anatoli tightens his grip on her elbow to the point of pain.

"No!" Alessia cries, and she wrenches her arm free from his hold. "Don't touch me!"

He glares at her, his neck reddening and his eyes narrowing to icy pinpricks. "Why are you behaving like this?"

"You know why."

His mouth presses into a hard line. "I came a long way for you. I am not leaving without you. You are promised to me by your father. Why are you dishonoring him?"

Alessia flushes.

"Is it the man?"

"Man?"

Alessia's heart beats faster. *Does he know about Maxim?*

"If it is, I'll kill him."

"There is no man," she whispers quickly, her fear spiraling out of control, sucking her down deeper into her despair.

"That friend of your mother. She sent an e-mail. She said there was a man."

Alessia is dumbfounded.

Magda?

Anatoli takes the basket from her and clasps her arm once more at the elbow.

"Let's go," he says, and he leads her toward the automatic door, dumping the shopping basket on the nearby stack. Alessia, still reeling from his sudden appearance, allows him to lead her out into the street.

I stand at the bar nursing a Jameson. The amber liquid sears my throat, but it calms the violent storm as it pools in my stomach.

I'm a fool.

A priapic fool.

I knew that bedding Caroline was going to come back and bite me on the arse.

Fuck.

She's right, though. I've never thought beyond my dick. Until Alessia. And then that all changed.

Changed for the better.

I've never met anyone like her, someone possessing nothing—except her talent, her resourcefulness, and her beautiful face. I wonder what I would have made of my life if I'd been born in lowlier circumstances. Maybe I'd be a struggling musician—if I'd even learned to play. *Shit.* There's so much that I take for granted. I've been coasting through my life, everything handed to me on a plate, nothing affecting me and doing exactly as I pleased. Now I have to work for a living, and several hundred people depend on me and my decisions. It's a daunting task and a huge responsibility that I have to accept if I want to maintain my lifestyle.

In the midst of this turmoil, I found Alessia, and in an indecently short time I've come to care for her more than I've ever cared for anyone. More than I've ever cared for myself. I love her, and she loves me and cares for me. She's a rare gift, a wonderful woman who needs me. And I need her. She's a woman who makes me step up my game.

A woman who makes me want to be a better man.

Isn't that what one wishes for in a life partner?

And then there's Caroline. As I stare despondently into my glass, I have to admit that I hate arguing with Caroline. She *is* my best friend. She has been forever. My world feels out of kilter if we're at loggerheads. It happened occasionally, when Kit was here to mediate, but she's never thrown me out of the house before.

What's worse is that I had meant to ask for her help sorting out Alessia's legal status in the UK. Caroline's father is a senior director in the Home Office. If anyone can help, he can.

But that's out of the question for the moment.

I drain my glass. Caroline will come around.

I hope she'll come around.

I slam the glass on the counter and nod to the barman. It's 7:15, it's time to go. I need to get back to my girl.

Anatoli keeps a firm grip on Alessia's elbow as he marches her back up the street toward Maxim's building. "You are his housekeeper?"

"Yes." Her answer is clipped. She's trying not to panic, thinking through her options.

What if Maxim is home?

Anatoli threatened to kill him.

The thought of what Anatoli might do to Maxim is terrifying.

Magda must have written to her mother. *Why?* Alessia had begged her not to.

She has to get away, but Alessia knows she cannot outrun him.

Think, Alessia, think.

"So he is your employer?"

"Yes."

"That is all?"

Alessia turns her head sharply. "Of course!" Her tone is vehement.

He stops, pulling her roughly, and regards her through hooded eyes that gleam with suspicion in the muted glow of the streetlamps. "He's not had what's mine?"

It takes a moment for Alessia to realize what he's referring to. "No," she says quickly, breathlessly, blushing so that her cheeks heat up in spite of the frigid February air. Anatoli nods once, as if accepting her answer, and she feels a momentary pang of relief.

He follows her into the apartment. The alarm beeps, and Ales-

sia is thankful that Maxim has not returned. Anatoli looks around
the hallway. Out of the corner of her eye, she watches his brows
rise. He's impressed.

"He has money, this man?" he mutters. She doesn't know if he's
directing a question at her or not. "And you live here?"

"Yes."

"Where do you sleep?"

"In that room." Alessia points to the door of the spare bedroom.

"Where does he sleep?"

She nods toward the master bedroom door. Anatoli opens the
door and marches inside. Alessia stands in the hallway, frozen
with panic. Can she escape? But he returns moments later holding the small wastebasket. "And this?" he growls.

Alessia manages to mobilize her features and screws her nose
up in disgust at the condom in the trash. She shrugs, trying desperately for nonchalance. "He has a girlfriend. They are out at
the moment."

He puts the basket down, seemingly satisfied with her answer.
"Get your things. I am parked outside."

She stands motionless, her heart racing.

"Go. Now. I don't want to wait for him to return. I don't want
a scene." He undoes his coat, slips his hand inside his jacket, and
pulls out a pistol. "I am serious."

Alessia blanches at the sight of the gun, and her breathing
shallows with panic. He'll kill Maxim, of that she has no doubt.
Her head begins to swim. Silently she begs her grandmother's
God to keep Maxim away.

"I came here to rescue you. I don't know why you are here. We
can talk about that later. But right now I want you to pack your
things. We are leaving."

Her fate is sealed. She will go with Anatoli. She must, to protect the man she loves. She has no choice. How did she think she
could escape her father's *besa*?

Tears of helpless anger pool in Alessia's eyes as she heads into
the spare bedroom. She packs quietly and efficiently, her hands

shaking as rage and terror war within her. She wants to go before Maxim returns. She has to—to protect him.

Anatoli appears on the threshold. His eyes sweep over her and the empty room. "You look very . . . different. Western. I like it."

Alessia says nothing as she zips up the duffel, but for some reason she's grateful she's still wearing her coat.

"I don't know why you are crying." He sounds genuinely perplexed.

"I like England. I would like to stay. I have been happy here."

"You have had your fun. It is time to come home and accept your responsibilities, *carissima*." Slipping the gun into his overcoat pocket, he grabs her bag.

"I have to leave a note," she blurts.

"Why?"

"Because it is the right thing to do. My employer will worry. He has been good to me." She almost chokes on her words.

Anatoli gazes at her, and she has no idea what he's thinking. Perhaps he's weighing what she's said. "Okay," he says eventually. He follows her into the kitchen, where a notepad and pen lie beside the phone. Alessia scribbles quickly, careful with her choice of words, hoping desperately that Maxim will read between them. She doesn't know how well Anatoli speaks or reads English. She cannot take the chance—she cannot write what she really wants to say.

Thank you for protecting me.

Thank you for showing me what love means.

But I cannot escape my destiny.

I love you. I will always love you. Until the day I die.

Maxim. My love.

"What does it say?"

She shows him and watches as his eyes scan the words. He nods. "Good. Let's go." She lays her new keys on top of the note. They'd been hers for only a few precious hours.

It's a still, cold night, and frost is beginning to form, sparkling ice-white under the light from the streetlamps. When I turn the corner, the road is quiet except in the distance a man is closing the door of a black Mercedes S-Class that's parked in front of my building.

"Maxim!"

I turn to see Caroline running down the street toward me.

Caroline? What on earth?

But something about the man with the Mercedes pulls my attention back. The scene is odd, because he's walking around to the near side of the car. It's wrong. I'm missing something. My senses are suddenly on high alert: I can hear the crisp clip of Caroline's heels as she gets closer, I can smell winter and the Thames on the chilly breeze, and I strain my eyes to stare at the license number of the car. Even from this distance, I can tell that it has foreign plates.

The man opens what must be the driver's door.

"Maxim!" Caroline calls again. I turn, and she runs up to me and throws her arms around my neck with such force that I have to put my arms around her to balance us both and stop us from falling to the ground. "I'm so sorry," she sobs.

I say nothing as my focus is drawn back to the car. The driver climbs in and slams the door while Caroline offers more apologies, but I ignore her as the indicator light starts blinking and the car pulls away from the curb into the light of a streetlamp.

And then I see it. The small red-and-black flag of Albania on the number plate.

Alessia hears Maxim's name shouted down the street. She turns around in the passenger seat as Anatoli opens his door. Maxim is standing at the end of the block—and a fair-haired woman runs into his arms, hugging him.

Who is she?

He cradles her head.

No!

He holds her waist.

And she remembers—the woman wearing his shirt, standing in his kitchen.

Alessia, this is my friend and sister-in-law, Caroline.

Anatoli slams the door shut, making Alessia jump and forcing her to look ahead.

His sister-in-law? His married sister-in-law—and his brother is dead.

Caroline is his widow.

Alessia chokes back a sob.

This is where he has been. With Caroline. And now they are hugging in the street and he's holding her. The betrayal is swift and cruel, slicing Alessia into tiny pieces and shattering her faith in herself—and in him.

Him. Her Mister.

A tear oozes down her cheek as Anatoli starts the engine. Smoothly he maneuvers the car out of the parking space and drives away from the only happiness Alessia has ever known.

F uck!" I shout as dread spawns dark and deadly in my gut.
Caroline startles. "What is it?"

"Alessia!" Abandoning Caroline, I race up the street, only to see the car disappear into the distance.

"Shit. Shit. Shit. Not again!" I grab my hair with both hands, helpless. Completely helpless.

"Maxim, what is it?" Caroline is now standing beside me outside the entrance to my building.

"They've got her!" I fumble for my keys to open the front door.

"Who? What are you talking about?"

"Alessia." I crash through the front door and don't bother with the lift. Leaving Caroline at the foot of the stairs, I race up all six flights to my flat. When I unlock the door, the alarm starts beeping, confirming the worst of my fears.

Alessia is not here.

I silence the alarm and listen, hoping beyond hope that I have this wrong. Of course I hear nothing except the wind rattling the skylight in the hallway and my blood pulsing through my ears.

Frantically I start running through each room, my imagination shifting into overdrive. They have her. They have her again. My sweet, brave woman. What will those monsters do to her? Her clothes are not in my bedroom. Nor the spare room . . .

In the kitchen I find her keys and the note.

> Mister Maxim
> My betrothed is here and he is
> taking me to my home in Albania.
> Thank you for everything.
>   Alessia

"No!" I scream, overwhelmed by my despair. Picking up the phone, I hurl it at the wall. It shatters into pieces as I sink to the floor, my head in my hands.

For the second time in less than a week, I want to cry.

Chapter Twenty-Eight

"Maxim, what the fuck is going on?"

I take my head out of my hands, and Caroline is standing at the doorway. She looks windswept and unkempt, but calmer than she did a few minutes ago.

"He's taken her." My voice is hoarse as I struggle to control my rage and despair.

"Who has?"

"Her fiancé."

"Alessia has a fiancé?"

"It's complicated."

She folds her arms and frowns, with what seems like genuine concern. "You look shattered."

I turn blazing eyes at her. "I am." Slowly I get to my feet. "I think the woman I want to marry has just been kidnapped."

"Marry?" Caroline blanches.

"Yes. Fucking marry!" My voice booms off the walls, and we glare at each other, the words hanging between us, ripe with regret and recrimination. Caroline closes her eyes and tucks her hair behind her ear. When she opens them, they are steely blue with resolve.

"Well, you'd better go after her, then," she says.

A lessia stares unseeing out the car window, drowning in tears she cannot stop. They flow freely as grief shrouds her misery. Maxim and Caroline.

Caroline and Maxim.

Was what she experienced with him all a lie?

No! She can't bring herself to think that. He said he loved her—and she had believed him. She still wants to believe him, but of course it doesn't matter anymore. She'll never see him again.

"Why are you crying?" Anatoli asks, but she ignores him. She doesn't care what he does to her now. Her heart is in shreds, and she knows that it will never heal. He switches on the radio, and an upbeat pop song blasts over the speakers, jarring Alessia's nerves. She suspects he's done it to distract himself from her silent sobbing. Anatoli turns the volume down and hands her a box of tissues. "Here. Dry your eyes. Enough of this nonsense, or I'll give you something to cry about."

She takes out a wad of tissues and continues to stare listlessly out the window. She can't even bring herself to look at him.

She knows that she will die at his hands.

And there's nothing she can do.

Maybe she can escape. In Europe. Maybe she can choose how she dies. . . . She closes her eyes and drifts into her own version of hell.

G o after her?" I ask, my mind racing.

"Yes." Caroline is emphatic. "But I have to ask, what makes you think she's been kidnapped?"

"Her note."

"Note?"

"Here." I hand her the crumpled piece of paper and turn away, rubbing my face, trying to gather my splintered thoughts.

Where will he take her?

Did she go willingly?

No. She only had revulsion for him.

He tried to break her fucking fingers!

He must have forced her to go.

How the hell did he find her?

"Maxim, this note doesn't read like she's been kidnapped. Have you thought that maybe she's decided to go home?"

"Caro, she did not leave of her own free will. Trust me."

I have to get her back.

Fuck.

I storm past Caroline and head into my drawing room.

"Fucking hell!"

"What now?"

"I don't have a working fucking computer!"

I need your passport," Anatoli says as they speed through London's streets.

"What?"

"We are driving to the Eurotunnel train. I need your passport."

Eurotunnel. No!

Alessia swallows. This is real. It's happening. He's taking her back to Albania.

"I don't have a passport."

"What do you mean you don't have a passport?"

Alessia stares at him.

"Why, Alessia? Tell me! Did you forget to pack it? I don't understand." He frowns.

"I was smuggled into this country by some men who took my passport."

"Smuggled? Men?" His jaw clenches, and a muscle twitches in his cheek. "What is going on?"

She's too tired and too broken to explain. "I don't have a passport."

"Fucking hell." Anatoli smacks the steering wheel with his palm. Alessia flinches at the sound.

"Alessia, wake up."

Something has changed. Alessia is confused.

Maxim?

She opens her eyes, and her heart sinks further into hell. She's with Anatoli, and the car is at a standstill, parked on the side of the road. It's dark, but by the glow of the headlights she can tell they are on a country road surrounded by frosted fields.

"Get out of the car," he says. Alessia stares at him, and a small blossom of hope flowers in her chest.

He's going to leave her here. She can walk back. She's done it once before.

"Out," he says more forcefully.

He opens his car door, climbs out, and comes around to her door, opening it wide. Taking her hand, he hauls her out of her seat and leads her to the back of the car, where he opens the trunk. It's empty but for a small rolling suitcase and her duffel.

"You'll have to get in here."

"What? No!"

"We have no choice. You don't have a passport. Get in."

"Please, Anatoli. I hate the dark. Please."

He frowns. "Get in or I'll put you in."

"Anatoli. Please. No. I don't like the dark!" He moves quickly, picking her up, dumping her in the trunk, and slamming the lid shut before Alessia can fight back.

"No!" she shouts. It's pitch-dark inside. She starts to kick and scream as the darkness bleeds into her lungs, suffocating her like the black plastic bag from the last time she crossed the Channel.

She can't breathe. She can't breathe. She screams.

Not the dark. No. Not the dark. I hate the dark.

Seconds later the lid pops open and a blinding light shines in her face. She blinks. "Here. Take this." Anatoli hands her a flashlight. "I don't know how long the battery will last. But we have no choice. Once we are on the train, I can open the trunk."

Stunned, Alessia takes the flashlight and holds it protectively to her chest. He moves her bag so that she can use it as a pillow, then shuffles out of his overcoat and lays it over her. "You may get cold. I don't know if the heating works in here. Go back to sleep. And be quiet." He gives her a stern look and shuts the trunk once more.

Alessia clutches the light and scrunches up her eyes, trying to regulate her breathing as the car starts to move. In her head she begins to play Bach's Prelude no. 6 in D Minor on repeat—the colors flashing brilliant hues of bright blue and turquoise in her mind—her fingers flexing, tapping out each note on the flashlight.

Alessia is shaken awake. She looks sleepily up at Anatoli, who towers over her as he holds open the lid of the trunk. His breath is a foggy cloud around him, lit by a solitary light from the parking lot. His face is stark and ashen. "What took you so long to wake up? I thought you were unconscious!" He sounds relieved.

Relieved?

"We're going to stay the night here," he says.

Alessia blinks, huddling down into the coat. It's cold. Her head is fuzzy from crying. Her eyes are swollen. And she doesn't want to spend the night with him.

"Out," he snaps, and extends his hand. Sighing, Alessia sits up. The cold wind whips around her, blowing her hair across her face. Stiffly she clambers out of the car, refusing Anatoli's help. She doesn't want his hands on her. He reaches past her for his coat, which he shuffles on. He grabs his case and hands her the duffel containing her clothes before shutting the trunk. The parking lot is deserted except for two other cars. Not far away stands a squat, nondescript building that Alessia assumes is a hotel.

"Follow me." He walks briskly toward the entrance. Alessia quietly sets her bag on the ground, turns, and runs.

I stare at the ceiling, my mind churning through all the plans I've put in place since Alessia was taken. Tomorrow I'll fly to Albania, and Tom Alexander will accompany me. Annoyingly, it's too-short notice for a private jet, so we're flying commercial. Thanks to Magda, we have the address of Alessia's parents. It's also thanks to Magda that Alessia's fiancé found her. I don't dwell on this tidbit of information, because it makes me incandescent with fury.

Calm down, mate.

We'll pick up a car, drive to Tirana, and overnight there at the Plaza hotel. Tom has arranged for us to meet up with a translator who will come with us to Kukës the following day.

And we'll stay there for however long it takes. We'll wait for Alessia and her kidnapper.

Not for the first time this evening, I wish I'd bought her that phone. It's so frustrating not being able to contact her.

I hope she's okay.

I close my eyes, imagining horrible scenarios.

My sweet girl.

My sweet, sweet Alessia.

I'm coming to get you. I've got you.

I love you.

A lessia flees blindly into the dark, fueled by her adrenaline rush. She's running over the asphalt, then onto rough grass. Behind her she hears a shout. It's him. She hears his footsteps pounding on the frozen ground. Getting closer.

Closer still.

Then silence.

He's on the grass.

No.

She pushes herself harder, hoping that her feet will carry her away from him. But he grabs her, and she's falling. *Falling.* Tackled to the ground so forcefully that she scrapes her face on the frosted grass. Anatoli lies on top of her back, panting heavily. "You stupid bitch. Where the hell do you think you're going to go at this time?" he hisses in her ear. He kneels up and drags her over until she's lying on her back, then sits astride her. He slaps her hard across her face, snapping her head to the side. He leans down over her, puts his hand on her throat, and squeezes.

He's going to kill her.

She doesn't struggle.

She stares at him. Her eyes on his. In their frigid blue, she sees the darkness of his heart. His hate. His anger. His inadequacy. His hand tightens, and he's choking the life from her. Her head begins to swim. She reaches up and clutches his arm.

This is how I am going to die. . . .

She sees her end. Here. Somewhere in France at the hands of this violent man. She wants it. She welcomes it. She doesn't want to live a life in fear, like her mother. "Kill me," she mouths.

Anatoli growls something incomprehensible—and lets go.

Alessia takes a huge breath and puts her hands up to her throat, coughing and spluttering, her body overruling her, fighting for life, sucking in precious air, and reviving her.

She gasps. "This is why I don't want to marry you." Her voice is husky and small, forcing sound through her bruised larynx.

Anatoli grabs her jaw and looms over her, his face close enough for her to feel his warm breath on her cheek . " 'A woman is a sack, made to endure,' " he snarls, with a cruel glint in his eye.

Alessia gazes at him as hot tears scald the sides of her face and pool in her ears. She hadn't been aware that she was crying. He is quoting from the ancient Kanun of Lek Dukagjini, the primitive feudal code that governed the mountain tribes in the north and east of her country for centuries. Its legacy lingers. Anatoli sits back.

"I would be better off dead than with you." Her voice is emotionless.

He frowns, nonplussed. "Don't be ridiculous." He slowly rises, standing over her. "Get up."

Alessia coughs once more and staggers painfully to her feet. He clasps her elbow and marches her back to where her abandoned bag sits in the parking lot. He picks it up and grabs his own suitcase several steps farther on.

He makes short work of checking in. Alessia hangs back while he hands over his passport and credit card. Anatoli speaks fluent French. She's too weary and too sore to be surprised.

Their spartan suite has two main rooms. The living room has dark gray furniture and a small kitchenette to the side. The wall behind the sofa is painted in cheerful mismatched stripes. Through the open door beyond, Alessia spies two double beds. She breathes a sigh of relief. Two beds. Not one. Two.

Anatoli dumps her duffel on the floor, shoves off his coat, and throws it on the sofa. Alessia watches him, listening to the thud of her pulse thrumming in her ears. In the silence of the room, it's deafening.

What now? What will he do?

"Your face is a mess. Go and clean yourself up." Anatoli points to the bathroom.

"And whose fault is that?" Alessia snaps.

He glowers at her, and for the first time she notices his red-rimmed eyes and his pale complexion. He looks exhausted. "Just do it." He even sounds exhausted. She heads into the bedroom, then the bathroom, slamming the door with such force that the loud bang makes her jump.

The bathroom is small and dingy, but in the insipid glow of the light above the mirror Alessia sees her reflection and gasps. One side of her face is red from his slap, and on the other there's a graze on her cheekbone from where she hit the ground. Around her throat there are vivid red marks in the shape of his fingers. Tomorrow they will be bruises. But what shocks her most is the lifeless eyes staring back at her from beneath swollen lids.

She is dead already.

With swift, automatic movements, she washes her face, wincing as the soapy water touches the scrape. She pats herself dry with a towel.

When she reenters the living room, Anatoli has hung up his jacket and is searching through the minibar.

"Are you hungry?" he asks.

She shakes her head.

He pours himself a drink—scotch, she thinks—and downs the entire glass in one gulp, closing his eyes to savor the taste. When he opens them again, he seems calmer. "Take off your coat."

Alessia doesn't move.

He pinches the bridge of his nose. "Alessia, I do not want to fight with you. I am tired. It's warm in here. Tomorrow we will go back out into the cold. Please take your coat off."

Reluctantly she removes her coat as Anatoli stares at her, making her feel self-conscious. "I like you in jeans," he says, but Alessia can't look at him. She feels like a prize sheep on the auction block as he appraises her. She hears the rattle of bottles, but this time Anatoli produces a Perrier out of the fridge. "Here, you must be thirsty." He pours it into a glass and offers it to her. After a moment's hesitation, she takes it and drinks.

"It's almost midnight. We should sleep."

Her eyes meet his, and he smirks. "Ah, *carissima*, I should make you mine after the stunt you pulled outside." He reaches for her chin, and she flinches as his fingers graze her skin.

Don't touch me.

"You are so beautiful," he murmurs, as if he's speaking only to himself. "But I don't have the energy to fight you. And I think it would be a fight. Yes?"

She closes her eyes, battling a wave of revulsion that unsettles her stomach. Anatoli chuckles, and his lips caress her forehead in a soft kiss. "You will grow to love me," he whispers. He picks up their bags and takes them into the bedroom.

Never.

The man is delusional.

Her heart belongs to another. It will always belong to Maxim.

"Go and change into your nightclothes," he says.

She shakes her head. "I will sleep like this." She doesn't trust him.

Anatoli cocks his head, his expression severe. "No. Take your clothes off. You won't run if you're naked."

"No." She crosses her arms.

"No you won't run, or no you won't take your clothes off?"

"Both."

He exhales, frustrated and tired. "I don't believe you. But I also don't understand why you are running."

"Because you are an angry, violent man, Anatoli. Why would I want to spend my life with you?" Her voice holds no emotion.

He shrugs. "I don't have the energy for this conversation. Get into bed." Seizing the moment, in case he changes his mind, she scuttles into the bedroom. There she slips off her boots and huddles on top of the bed farther away, turning her back on him.

She listens as he moves around the room, undressing and folding his clothes. Her anxiety mounts with each movement and with each sound. After an eternity the soft slap of his footsteps pad on the floor as he approaches her bed. He stands beside her, his breathing shallow, and she feels his eyes on her. Everywhere. She squeezes hers shut, pretending to sleep.

He tuts, and she hears the rustle of sheets and blankets, and to her surprise he drapes a blanket over her. He switches off the light, plunging the room into darkness, and the bed dips as he lies down.

No! He should be in the other bed.

She stiffens, but he's beneath the covers while she's on top. He puts his arm around her and shuffles closer. "I will know if you leave the bed," he says, and he kisses her hair.

She recoils and clutches her little gold cross.

Soon his even breathing tells her that he's asleep.

Alessia stares into the darkness she fears and wishes it would swallow her up. Her tears refuse to fall. She's all cried out.

What is Maxim doing?

Is he missing me?

Is he with Caroline?

She sees Caroline in Maxim's arms as he holds her close, and Alessia wants to scream.

Alessia is too warm, and someone is murmuring in the background. She cracks one eye open momentarily, bewildered as to where she might be.

No. No. No.

A wash of fear and despair fills her with anguish when she remembers.

Anatoli.

He's on the phone in the other room. Alessia sits up and listens.

"She's okay. . . . No. Far from it . . . She's reluctant to return home. I don't understand it." He's talking to someone in Albanian, and he sounds confused and upset. "I don't know. . . . Maybe . . . There was a man. Her employer. The one who was mentioned in the e-mail."

He's talking about Maxim!

"She says she is just his cleaner, but I don't know, Jak."

Jak! He's talking to my father!

"I love her so much. She's so beautiful."

What? He doesn't know the meaning of the word "love"!

"She hasn't told me yet. But I want to know, too. Why would she leave?" His voice cracks. He's emotional.

I left because of you!

She left to get as far away from him as she could.

"Yes. I will bring her back to you. I will make sure she's unharmed."

Alessia places her hands on her still-tender throat. What the hell? *Unharmed?*

He's a liar.

"She's safe with me."

Ha! Alessia almost wants to laugh at the supreme irony of that statement.

"Tomorrow night . . . Yes . . . Good-bye." She hears him move about the room, and suddenly he appears at the door wearing only his pants and an undershirt.

"You're awake?" he says.

"Sadly, it would appear so."

He gives her an odd look and chooses to ignore her comment. "There is some breakfast for you out here."

"I'm not hungry." Alessia feels reckless and bold. She doesn't care anymore. Now that Maxim is out of harm's way, she can behave as she wishes.

Anatoli rubs his chin and regards her thoughtfully. "Suit yourself," he says. "We leave in twenty minutes. We have a long way to go."

"I'm not going with you."

He rolls his eyes. "*Carissima*, you have no choice. Don't make this painful for both of us. Don't you want to see your father and mother?"

Mama.

His eyebrows rise a fraction. He's noticed the chink in her armor and, sensing victory, swoops in for the kill. "She misses you."

She rises out of bed and sullenly grabs her bag and, skirting him as widely as she can, heads into the bathroom to wash and change.

Under the shower an idea begins to form in her head.

She has her money. Maybe she *should* return to Albania. She can get a new passport—and a visa—and return to England.

Maybe I should stay alive.

And as she briskly towel-dries her hair, she feels a new sense of purpose.

She will get back to Maxim. And see for herself. See if everything they shared was a lie.

Chapter Twenty-Nine

Alessia dozes in the front seat. They are on an autobahn travel-ing way too fast. They've been driving for hours, through France, through Belgium, and she thinks they're now somewhere in Ger-many. It's a cold, wet, winter day, and the landscape is flat and bleak, reflecting Alessia's mood. No. She feels more than bleak—she's desolate.

Anatoli seems grimly determined to get to Albania as fast as possible. At the moment he's listening to a German talk show on the radio, which Alessia doesn't understand. The monotony of the voices, the constant rumble of road noise, and the dreary countryside are all dulling her senses. Sleep is what she wants. When she's asleep, her anguish is a low hum, like static on the radio. It's not the searing pain that tears at her heart when she's conscious.

She turns her mind to Maxim.

And the pain amplifies.

Stop. It's too much.

She looks through tired eyes at her "betrothed," studying him. His face is hardened in concentration as the Mercedes eats up the miles. His complexion is fair, betraying his northern Italian roots—his nose straight, his lips full, and his blond hair, uncommon in her town, is long and unkempt. Alessia can look at him dispassionately and judge him to be a handsome man. But those lips have a cruel twist to them, and those eyes are piercing and cold when he's glaring at her.

She remembers when she first met him. How charming he'd been. Her father had told her that Anatoli was an international businessman. During that first meeting, he'd seemed so dashing and knowledgeable. He was well traveled, and she'd listened rapt to his stories of Croatia, Italy, and Greece—these faraway places. She'd been shy, but pleased that her father had selected such an erudite man for her.

Little had she known.

After she had met him a few times, she started to see flashes of the man he really was. His irrational anger at the local children who'd surrounded his car out of curious wonder when he came to visit, his temper when arguing with her father about politics, and his sly admiration when her father scolded her mother for spilling some raki. The signs were there, and he'd rebuked Alessia a few times, too, but his true nature had been constrained by social etiquette.

It was at a local dignitary's wedding, where Alessia was playing the piano, that Anatoli finally revealed his dark side. Two young men, whom she had known at school, lingered when she finished playing. They flirted with her until Anatoli managed to usher her into a side room, away from them and the festivities. Alessia, secretly thrilled, had thought he wanted to steal a kiss, since it was the first time they'd been alone together. But no—Anatoli was furious. He slapped her hard across her face, twice. It was a shock, even though living with her father had prepared her for physical anger.

The second time it happened, she was at the school. A young man came to ask her a couple of questions after her recital. Anatoli chased him away and dragged her into the cloakroom. There he hit her a couple of times and grabbed her hands and pulled back her fingers and threatened to break them if he ever caught her flirting again. She'd begged him to stop, and mercifully he had, but he'd pushed her to the floor and left her sobbing in that room, alone.

That first time, she kept his attack a secret. She excused it. It was a one-off. She had misbehaved. She had encouraged the young men by smiling at them.

The second time Alessia was devastated.

She'd thought that maybe she could break the cycle of violence that beset her mother, but it was her mother who'd found her while she lay curled up, sobbing and trembling, on the floor.

I don't want you to go through your life with a violent man.

They'd wept together.

And her mother had taken action.

But it was all for naught.

Now here she is—with *him*.

Anatoli gives her a sideways look. "What is it?"

Alessia averts her eyes, ignoring him, and stares out the window.

"We should stop. I'm hungry, and you've not eaten," he says.

She continues to ignore him, though hunger claws at her stomach, reminding her of her six-day walk to Brentford.

"Alessia!" he barks, making her jump.

She turns to him. "What?"

"I'm talking to you."

She shrugs. "You've kidnapped me. I don't want to be with you, and you expect conversation?"

"I didn't know you could be this disagreeable," Anatoli mutters.

"I'm just getting started."

Anatoli's mouth twitches—and to her surprise he seems

amused. "I can say this about you, *carissima*, you are not boring." He flicks the turn signal, and they pull off the autobahn into a service area. "There's a café here. Let's get something to eat."

Anatoli places a tray bearing a black coffee, several sachets of sugar, a bottle of water, and a cheese baguette in front of her. "I cannot believe *I* am serving *you*," he utters as he sits. "Eat."

"Welcome to the twenty-first century," Alessia retorts, folding her arms in an act of defiance.

His jaw hardens. "I will not tell you again."

"Oh, do your worst, Anatoli. I'm not eating. You bought it, you eat it," she snaps, ignoring her growling stomach. His eyes flare in surprise, but he presses his full lips together, and Alessia suspects he's trying not to smile. He sighs, reaches over, picks up her baguette, and takes a theatrically large bite out of it. With his mouth full, he looks both absurd and ridiculously pleased with himself, so much so that an involuntary snicker escapes from Alessia.

Anatoli smiles—a proper smile that travels all the way to his eyes. They regard her warmly, and he no longer tries to hide his amusement. "Here," he says, and he hands her the remaining part of the baguette. Her stomach chooses this moment to rumble, and when he hears it, his smile broadens. She eyes the baguette and him and sighs. She's so hungry. Against her better judgment, she takes it from him and begins to eat.

"That's better," he says, and starts on his own meal.

"Where are we?" Alessia asks after a few bites.

"We've just passed Frankfurt."

"When will we reach Albania?"

"Tomorrow. I hope to be home by tomorrow afternoon."

They eat the rest of their food in silence.

"Finish up. I want to get going. Do you need to use the restroom?" Anatoli stands over her, keen to move on. Alessia takes her coffee without adding sugar.

Like Maxim.

It's bitter but she downs it anyway and grabs her water bottle. The service station, with its large parking lot and smell of diesel fumes, is hauntingly familiar and reminiscent of the journey she made with Maxim—but the difference is, she wanted to be with Maxim. Alessia's heart aches. She is getting farther and farther away from him.

I'm sitting in the British Airways business-class lounge at Gatwick Airport, waiting for the afternoon flight to Tirana. Tom is leafing through *The Times* and sipping a glass of champagne while I'm brooding. I've been in a state of high anxiety since Alessia was taken from me.

Maybe she went with him willingly.

Maybe she's changed her mind about us.

I don't want to believe that, but doubt is creeping into my mind.

It's insidious.

If that's what's happened, at least I'll get to confront her about her change of heart. To distract myself from my unsettling thoughts, I snap and upload a few photos to my Instagram. Once that's done, I think back over the morning's events.

First I'd bought Alessia a phone, which is now in my backpack. I'd met with Oliver and gone through a quick agenda of all estate business; to my relief everything seemed to be running just fine. I'd signed the papers required by the Crown Office for my inclusion onto the Roll of the Peerage, with Mr. Rajah, my solicitor, acting as my witness. I'd given both men a redacted version of the weekend's events with Alessia and asked Rajah to recommend a lawyer specializing in immigration services, so we could begin the process of securing some kind of visa for Alessia to be in the UK.

Afterward, on a whim, I'd visited my bank in Belgravia, where the Trevethick Collection is secured. If I find Alessia and all is not lost, I will ask her to marry me. Over the centuries my ancestors have amassed quite a haul of fine jewelry crafted by the most prominent artisans of their day. When the collection is not on loan to museums around the world, it is safely stored in the bowels of Belgravia.

I needed a ring, one that would do justice to Alessia's beauty and talent. There were two in the collection that might have been suitable, but I chose the 1930s Cartier platinum-and-diamond ring that my grandfather, Hugh Trevelyan, bestowed on my grandmother, Allegra, in 1935. It's an exquisite, simple, and elegant ring: 2.79 carats and currently valued at forty-five thousand pounds.

I hope Alessia likes it. If all goes to plan, she'll return to the UK wearing it—as my fiancée.

I pat my pocket yet again, checking that the ring is safe, and scowl at Tom, who's stuffing his face with nuts. He looks up. "Hang in there, Trevethick. I can tell you're fretting. She'll be fine. We'll rescue the girl." He'd insisted on accompanying me when I called him and told him what had happened. He's left one of his guys to keep watch on Magda, and he's here with me. Tom loves an adventure. It's why, back in the day, he joined the army. He's up on his metaphorical white charger, ready for the fray.

"I hope so," I answer. Will Alessia see us that way—as rescuers, not as an inconvenience? I don't know. I'm itching to get on the plane and get to her parents' home. I have no idea what I'll find there, but I hope I find my girl.

W hy did you leave Albania?" Anatoli asks when they're back on the autobahn. His voice is soft, and Alessia wonders if he's trying to lull her into a false sense of security. She's not that stupid.

"You know why. I've told you." Though as the words leave her mouth, she realizes she doesn't know what story he's been told. Perhaps she can embellish the truth. It might make it easier on her and on her mother. But it depends on what Magda said. "What did my mother's friend say?"

"Your father intercepted the e-mail. He saw your name and asked me to read it for him."

"What did it say?"

"That you were alive and well and were going away to work for a man."

"Is that all?"

"More or less."

So Magda had not mentioned Dante and Ylli. "What did my father say?"

"He asked me to come get you."

"And my mother?"

"I didn't speak to your mother. This does not concern her."

"Of course it concerns her! Stop being prehistoric!"

He gives her a sideways look, taken aback by her outburst. "Prehistoric?"

"Yes. You are a dinosaur. She deserves to be consulted."

Anatoli's puzzled frown speaks volumes; he has no idea what she's talking about. Alessia continues, warming to her subject, "You are a man from another century. From another time. You and all the men like you. In other countries your Neanderthal attitude to women would be unacceptable."

He shakes his head. "You have been in the West too long, *carissima*."

"I like the West. My grandmother was from England."

"Is that why you went to London?"

"No."

"Why, then?"

"Anatoli, you know why. I want to make it clear to you. I don't want to marry you."

"You will come around, Alessia." He waves his hand as if to brush off her rejection as trivial.

Alessia huffs, feeling aggrieved but feeling brave, too. After all, what can he do while he's driving? "I want to choose who I marry. It's a simple enough request."

"You would dishonor your father?"

Alessia flushes. Of course her attitude—her defiance, her *willfulness*—brings great shame to her family.

She turns back to the window, but in her mind this conversation is not over. Perhaps she can appeal to her father once more.

She allows herself a moment to think about Maxim, and her grief rises, raw and real. Her bravado evaporates, and her mood plummets once more into despair. Her heart is beating but empty.

Will she ever see *him* again?

Somewhere in Austria, Anatoli stops at the services again, but this time only for gas. He insists Alessia accompany him into the store. Reluctantly she trails after him, oblivious to her surroundings.

Back on the autobahn, he announces, "We'll be in Slovenia soon. When we get to Croatia, you'll need to go into the trunk."

"Why?"

"Because Croatia is not part of the Schengen Agreement, and there's a border."

Alessia blanches. She hates being in the trunk. She loathes the dark.

"When we stopped for gas, I bought more batteries for the flashlight."

She glances at Anatoli, and he catches her eye. "I know you don't like it. But it can't be helped." He turns his attention back to the road. "And it shouldn't be for so long this time. When we stopped in Dunkirk, I thought you were unconscious from carbon monoxide poisoning or something." He frowns, and if Alessia is not mistaken, she would swear he's concerned. This afternoon at the restaurant, he had regarded her with warmth.

"What is it?" he asks, snapping her out of her reverie.

"I'm not used to concern from you," she states. "Only violence."

Anatoli's hands tighten on the steering wheel. "Alessia, if you don't do as you're told, there are consequences. I expect you to be a traditional Gheg wife. That's all you need to know. I think you have become too opinionated while you've been in London."

She doesn't answer him but turns away and stares out at the passing countryside, nursing her misery as they drive on into the afternoon.

Our flight lands in Tirana at 20:45 local time in pouring, icy rain. Tom and I are traveling with hand baggage only, so we go straight through customs and emerge into a modern, well-lit airport terminal. I don't know what I'd been expecting, but the place looks like any small airport in Europe, with all the facilities one might need.

Our rental car, on the other hand, is a revelation. My travel agent had warned me that there were no prestige cars for hire, so I find myself at the wheel of a car whose make I have never heard of: a Dacia. It's the most basic and analog car I've ever driven, though it does have a USB port in the radio so we can plug in my iPhone and use Google Maps. I'm surprised to find myself liking the car; it's practical and sturdy. Tom christens it "Dacy," and after some negotiation at the exit to the car park and a small bribe to the parking attendant, we are off.

Driving at night—in torrential rain, on the wrong side of the road, in a country where private car ownership was unheard of until the mid-1990s—is a challenge. But forty minutes later, Dacy and Google Maps get us in one piece to the Plaza hotel in the center of Tirana.

"Fuck, that was hairy," Tom announces as we pull up in front of the hotel.

"Damn right."

"Though I've driven in worse conditions," he mutters. I turn off the ignition, knowing that he's making an oblique reference to his time in Afghanistan. "How far did you say this girl's hometown is?"

"Her name's Alessia," I growl, for what feels like the tenth time, and wonder about the wisdom of agreeing to let Tom accompany me. "I think it's about a three-hour drive." He's a good man in a pinch, but diplomacy has never been his strong point.

"Sorry, old man. Alessia." He taps his forehead. "I've got it. I hope the rain holds off tomorrow. Let's check in and find somewhere to have a drink."

In the trunk of the Mercedes, Alessia clutches the flashlight as the car lurches to a stop. They must have reached the border with Croatia. She closes her eyes, pulls Anatoli's coat over her head, and switches off the flashlight. She doesn't want to get caught. She just wants to get home. She hears voices—they're quiet and in control. And the car starts to move. She breathes a sigh of relief and flicks on the bright beam once more. She's reminded of the makeshift hideaway beneath the sheets that she shared with Maxim and the little dragon. They were sitting and talking on his vast, baronial bed, their knees touching and . . . Her pain is swift and sudden. She aches to the bottom of her soul.

Before long the Mercedes slows and stops. The engine idles, and moments later Anatoli opens the trunk. Alessia switches off the flashlight and sits up, blinking in the darkness.

They are on a deserted rural road; a small bungalow squats darkly opposite them. Anatoli is lit by the car's tail-lights, his face cast in demonic red, his breath an ominous cloud around him. He offers his hand to help her out, and because she's tired and stiff, she accepts. She stumbles as she steps out of the trunk, and he yanks her forward, into his arms.

"Why are you so hostile?" he breathes against her temple. Tightening his hold around her waist, he grasps the back of her head with his hand and grips her hair. In spite of the cold, his breath is hot and heavy between them. As Alessia registers what's happening, his lips swoop down hard on hers. He tries to force his tongue into her mouth, and she struggles, fear and loathing careening through her body in a potent mix. She pushes ineffectually at his arms and frantically twists, trying to struggle out of his hold. He leans back to look down at her, and before she can stop herself, she slaps him across his face, her palm ringing from the blow, and he retreats. Shocked. She's breathing gulps of air, adrenaline coursing through her veins, chasing away her fear and leaving anger in its stead. Anatoli glares at her, rubbing his cheek, and before she can blink, he slaps her hard across her face. Once. Twice. Her head jerks from the right to the left, and she staggers at the force of each blow. With little care he picks her up and drops her back into the trunk so that she hits her shoulder, her backside, and her head. And before she can protest, he slams the lid shut.

"Until you learn to behave and be civil, you can stay in there!" he shouts. Alessia clutches her throbbing head as anger burns in her throat and behind her eyes.

This is her life now.

I take a sip of Negroni. Tom and I are in a bar next door to the hotel. It's contemporary, sleek, and comfortable, and the staff are friendly and attentive, but not overly so. What's more, they serve a bloody good Negroni.

"I think we fell on our feet with this place," Tom says as he takes another slug of his drink. "I don't know what I was expecting. Goats and wattle-and-daub shacks, I think."

"Yes. I had the same idea. This place exceeds all expectations."

He eyes me speculatively. "Forgive me, Trevethick. But I have to know. Why are you doing this?"

"What?"

"Chasing this girl all over Europe? Why?"

"Love," I state, as if it's the most understandable reason in the world.

Why doesn't he get this?

"Love?"

"Yep. It's that simple."

"For your daily?"

I roll my eyes. What is it about the fact that Alessia used to clean for me? *And still wants to clean for me!* "Just deal with it, Tom. I'm going to marry her."

He splutters into his drink, spitting red liquid over the table, and I wonder again at the wisdom of bringing him on this journey. "Steady on, Trevethick. She's a pretty girl, from what I remember, but is that wise?"

I shrug. "I love her."

He shakes his head, bemused.

"Tom, just because you haven't got the nerve to do the decent thing and pop the fucking question to Henrietta—who is a saint to put up with you—don't judge."

He frowns, and a pugnacious gleam lights up his eyes. "Listen, old boy, I wouldn't be doing my duty as a friend if I didn't state the fucking obvious."

"The fucking obvious?"

"You're in mourning, Maxim." His voice is surprisingly gentle. "Have you considered that this sudden infatuation is part of your way of dealing with your brother's death?"

"This has nothing to do with Kit, and I'm not fucking infatuated. You don't know her like I do. She's an exceptional woman. And I've known countless women. She's different. She's not bothered by trivial shit. . . . She's smart. Funny. Courageous. And you should hear her play the piano. She's a fucking genius."

"Really?"

"Yes. This is the real deal. I'm seeing the world in a whole different light since I met her. And questioning my place in it."

"Steady on."

"No, Tom. You steady on. She needs me. It's good to be needed, and I need her."

"But that's no basis for a relationship."

I grit my teeth. "It's not just that. You've fought for your country. You now run a successful business. What the fuck have I ever done?"

"Well, you're about to take your place in the history of the Trevethick family, and preserve that legacy for generations to come."

"I know." I sigh. "It's daunting, and I want someone I trust beside me. Someone who loves me. Someone who appreciates me for more than my wealth and title. Is that too much to ask?"

He frowns.

"You've found that person," I add. "And you take Henrietta for granted."

He exhales and stares down at the remains of his drink.

"You're right," he mumbles. "I love Henry. I should do the decent thing."

"You should."

He nods. "Okay. Let's order another." He signals to the waiter for another round of drinks, and I wonder if I'll have to deal with this level of doubt about Alessia from all my friends . . . from my family.

"Make them doubles," I call.

Alessia wakes and realizes the car has stopped. The engine is off. The lid of the trunk lifts, and Anatoli is standing over her once more. "Maybe you have learned some manners?"

Alessia gives him a venomous look and sits up, rubbing her fists in her eyes.

"Get out. We'll spend the night here." He doesn't offer her his hand this time but reaches in and grabs his coat from her and slips it on. The biting wind wraps around her, and she shivers. She aches everywhere, but she climbs out of the trunk and, feeling gloomy, stands to one side, waiting for his next move.

Anatoli's gaze follows her, and his lips press into a thin, angry line. "Feeling a little more docile now?" he sneers.

Alessia says nothing.

He snorts and reaches for their luggage. Alessia glances around. They are in a parking lot in the center of a city. An imposing hotel looms in the near distance. It's several stories high and lit up like a Hollywood movie with the word WESTIN crowning its façade. Abruptly Anatoli grabs her hand and tugs her toward the entrance. He doesn't break his stride, so she has to scurry to keep up.

The foyer is all marble, mirrors, and modernity, and Alessia spots the discreet sign: they are in the Westin Zagreb. Anatoli checks them in to the hotel in what sounds like flawless Croatian, and a few minutes later they are riding up to the fifteenth floor in the elevator.

Anatoli has booked them a luxurious suite that is furnished in creams and browns. There's a couch, a desk, and a small table, and through the sliding doors Alessia can see one bed.

One.

No!

She remains standing, tired and helpless, just within the threshold.

Anatoli shrugs off his coat and throws it onto the couch. "Are you hungry?" he asks, opening the doors of the dresser beneath the TV. Eventually he finds the minibar. "Well?" he snaps.

Alessia nods.

Anatoli motions with his head toward a leather-bound book on the desk. "We'll get room service. Choose something. And take off your coat." Alessia picks up the book and leafs through the pages to the in-room-dining section. The entries are in Croatian and English; she scans the selections and immediately chooses the most expensive item on the menu. She has no compunction about having Anatoli spend his money. She frowns, remembering how she resisted Maxim's attempts to pay. . . . Anatoli has retrieved two small bottles of scotch and is unscrewing the top from each in turn. Yes, Alessia has no compunction at all. She's a kidnap victim, and he's meted out enough physical abuse on her body already. He owes her. But with Maxim . . . the balance was all wrong. She had owed him. So much. Her Mister. She lets him slip quietly from her mind, to be mourned later.

"I'll have the New York steak," she declares. "With an extra salad. And fries. And a glass of red wine." Anatoli turns to regard her with surprise.

"Wine?"

"Yes. Wine."

He considers her for a moment. "You have become very Western."

She stands taller. "I would like a glass of French red wine."

"French now?" He raises a brow.

"Yes." And as an afterthought she adds, "Please."

"Okay, we'll get a bottle." He lifts his shoulder in a nonchalant shrug, and he sounds *so reasonable*.

But he's not. He's a monster.

He pours both whiskeys into a glass and watches her as he reaches for the phone. "You know, you're a very attractive woman, Alessia."

She freezes. *What now?*

"Are you still a virgin?" His voice is soft, cajoling.

She gasps and feels a little faint. "Of course," she breathes, attempting to look outraged and embarrassed at once.

He cannot know the truth.

His gaze hardens. "You seem different."

"I am. I've had my eyes opened."

"By someone?"

"Just . . . by my experiences," she whispers, wishing she had never responded. She's antagonizing a snake.

Anatoli dials room service and orders their meal while Alessia removes her coat and sits down on the couch to watch him warily. When he finishes his call, he grabs the TV remote, switches on the local news, and sits at the desk with his drink. For a while he watches the news, ignoring her, occasionally sipping his whiskey. Alessia is relieved that his attention is elsewhere. She watches the TV as well, trying to understand the newscaster, and she catches a few words. She concentrates; she doesn't want her mind to wander. It will only wander back to Maxim, and she refuses to grieve his loss in front of Anatoli.

When the program is over, he turns his attention back to Alessia. "So you ran away from me?" he says.

Is he talking about yesterday?

"When you left Albania." He takes a last swig of scotch.

"You threatened to break my fingers."

He rubs his chin, thoughtful for a moment. "Alessia . . . I—" He stops.

"I don't want excuses, Anatoli. There's no excuse for treating another human being the way you have treated me. Look at my neck." She pulls down her sweater, revealing the bruises he left yesterday, and raises her chin, making them conspicuous.

He flushes.

There's a discreet knock on the door, and with a frustrated glance at Alessia, Anatoli retreats to open it. A young man dressed in Westin livery is outside with a dining cart. Anatoli beckons him in and stands back as the server transforms the cart into a table. It's covered in a white linen tablecloth and plush place settings for two. There's a jaunty single yellow rose in a ceramic vase, striving to represent a little romance.

Ironic.

Alessia's sorrow surfaces, eating at her insides, and she has to fight back tears while the waiter opens the wine. Placing the cork in a ceramic dish, he pulls several plates from a warming drawer beneath the cart and removes their metallic covers with a flourish. The aroma is tantalizing. Anatoli says something in Croatian and slips the waiter what looks like a ten-euro note, for which he seems extremely grateful. Once the young man has left the room, Anatoli summons Alessia to the table. "Come and eat." He sounds like he's sulking.

Because she's hungry and tired of fighting, Alessia sits down at the makeshift table. This is how it will be, a slow, grinding erosion of her will, so that in time she will submit to this man.

"This is most Western, yes?" he says as he sits opposite her and picks up the bottle of wine. He pours her a glass.

Alessia mulls over his earlier statement. If Anatoli wants a traditional Albanian wife, then that's what he will have. She will not eat with him. Or sleep with him, except when he wants sex. Surely that's not really what he wants. She stares down at her dinner as the walls of the room close in, suffocating her.

"*Gëzuar*, Alessia," he says, and she looks up. Anatoli has raised his glass in a quiet salute to her, his eyes wide, his expression warm. Her scalp tingles. She wasn't expecting this . . . honor! Picking up her glass, she offers it in a reluctant toast to him and takes a sip.

"Mmm," she says, closing her eyes, seduced by the taste of the wine. When she reopens them, Anatoli is watching her, his eyes darkening, and in his gaze she sees a promise of something she doesn't want.

Her appetite vanishes.

"You won't run from me again, Alessia. You will be my wife," he murmurs. "Now, eat."

She stares down at the steak on her plate.

Chapter Thirty

Anatoli refills her glass again. "You've hardly touched your food."

"I'm not hungry."

"In that case I think it's time we went to bed." The tone of his voice makes her look up sharply. He's sitting back in his chair, watchful. Waiting. Like a predator. He taps his bottom lip with his index finger as if deep in thought, his eyes gleaming. He's had at least three glasses of wine. And the whiskey. He tosses the remaining contents of his glass down his throat and rises from his seat, slowly. His eyes on her, intense, darker. She's paralyzed by his stare.

No.

"I don't see why I should wait for our wedding night." He steps closer.

"No. Anatoli," she breathes. "Please. No." She clutches the table.

He runs a finger down her cheek. "Beautiful," he whispers. "Get up. Don't make this hard for both of us."

"We should wait," Alessia whispers, her brain churning through her options.

"I don't want to wait. And if I have to fight you, so be it." He moves suddenly, grabbing her by her shoulders and yanking her upright and out of her seat so forcefully that she knocks her chair to the floor. Fear and anger surge through her body. She twists and kicks, her foot striking his shin and then the table, rattling the crockery and cutlery and knocking over her glass so that it spills the remaining wine.

"Ow. Fuck," he whines.

"No!" she shouts, lashing out with both her feet, her fists flailing, hoping to strike him. He lunges at her and grabs her around the waist, jerking her into his arms. He lifts her off her feet while she kicks out at anything and everything in their path in an effort to strike him.

"No!" she screams. "Please, Anatoli!"

Ignoring her cries, he tightens his arms around her and half drags, half carries her into the bedroom.

"No. No. Stop!"

"Quiet!" he shouts as he shakes her and throws her facedown onto the bed. He sits beside her, holding her still, pressing down on her back with one hand while the other starts tugging at her boots.

"No!" she screams again. She twists, kicking him, once, twice, trying to struggle out of his hold as she pummels him with her fists.

"For fuck's sake, Alessia!"

She's wild, her anger and loathing giving her a strength she didn't know she possessed. She fights, consumed by her rage and directing it at the man she hates.

"Fucking hell." Anatoli throws himself on top of her, crushing her into the mattress and knocking the breath from her body. She tries to buck him off, but he's too heavy.

"Calm down," he pants in her ear. "Calm down."

She stills, marshaling her resources and struggling to gulp air into her lungs. Anatoli shifts his weight and flips her over so that they're nose to nose. Keeping his leg over her thighs, he grabs her hands and pulls them above her head, pinning them there with one hand.

"I want you. You are my wife."

"Please. No," she whispers, staring into his wild, wide eyes. In them she sees his excitement—his lean body vibrates with it. She feels it against her hip. He stares down at her, breathing hard, and one of his hands moves over her body, over her breast and belly to her fly.

"No. Anatoli, please. I'm bleeding. Please. I'm bleeding." She's lying, but it's a last desperate attempt to stop him. He frowns, as if not understanding, and then his expression changes from lust to distaste.

"Oh," he says.

Releasing her hands, he rolls off her and stares up at the ceiling. "Maybe we should wait," he grumbles.

Alessia twists onto her side, drawing up her knees and curling into a ball, making herself as small as possible. Despair, revulsion, fear—these are her bedfellows now. Her tears start to choke her, and she feels the bed move as Anatoli rises and walks back into the living room.

How long can she cry before her tears dry up?

Moments. Seconds. Hours.

Later Anatoli drapes a blanket over her. She feels the bed dip as he climbs in, beneath the covers. He shuffles over, wraps his arm around her, and tugs her unyielding body closer. "You will suit me well, *carissima*," he murmurs, and his lips brush her cheek in a surprisingly gentle kiss.

Alessia puts her fist to her mouth, stifling her silent scream.

She wakes suddenly. The room is in semidarkness, lit only by the gray light of the coming dawn. Beside her, Anatoli is fast asleep. His face is relaxed and less stern in repose. Alessia stares at the ceiling, her mind on full alert. She's still dressed and wearing her boots. She could run.

Go. Now. She wills herself.

Slowly, stealthily, she rolls off the bed and tiptoes out of the room.

The detritus of their meal from the previous night is still on the table. Alessia eyes the cold fries, hastily grabs a few, and stuffs them into her mouth. While she eats, she rummages through her bag and finds her money. She slips the notes into her back pocket.

She stops and listens.

He's still asleep.

Beside her duffel she spies Anatoli's suitcase. Maybe he keeps his money in there.... If he does, it could help her escape. Carefully she unzips it, not knowing what she'll find inside.

It's neatly packed. There are some clothes—and his gun.

The gun.

She fishes it out.

She could kill him.

Before he kills her.

Her heart starts pounding, and her head begins to spin.

She has the power. The means. The pistol is weighty in her hand.

Standing up, she sidles toward the bedroom door and watches Anatoli sleep. He hasn't moved. A tremor runs up her spine, and her breathing shallows. He's kidnapped her. Beaten her. Choked her. Nearly raped her. She despises him and everything he stands for. She's terrified of him. She raises her trembling hand and takes aim. Quietly she releases the safety. Her head is throbbing, sweat beading on her brow.

This is it.

Her moment.

Her hand wobbles, and her vision blurs with her tears.

No. No. No. No.

She dashes them away and drops her hand.

She's not a murderer.

She turns the gun around. And stares down the barrel. She's seen enough American television to know what to do.

She doesn't want to blindly accept her fate. This is one way out.

She could end it all, now. Her misery would be over.

She will feel nothing. Ever again.

Her mother's anguished face comes to her mind.

Mama.

How devastated would she be . . . ?

She thinks of Maxim. And dismisses the thought of him immediately.

She'll never see him again.

Her throat is closing. Choked with emotion. She screws up her eyes. Panting.

She can die at her own hand. Not Anatoli's . . .

And someone will have to clean up afterward.

No. No. No.

She crumples to the floor. Defeated. A failure. She cannot take her own life. She doesn't have the gumption. And deep down she wants to stay alive in the vague hope of seeing Maxim again. She can't run. She needs to get home. Zagreb is not five days' walk from London, it's so much farther. She's helpless. She rocks quietly to and fro, holding herself and cradling the gun, while she silently surrenders to her grief. She's never been so distraught. She's never wept this many tears. Ever. Even after her traumatic escape and on her long walk to Magda's. She'd mourned her grandmother and felt her loss—but she never felt this desolate. This sorrow is overwhelming. She cannot kill him, and she cannot kill herself. She's lost the man she loves, and she's bound to a man she loathes.

Her heart is broken. *No.* Her heart has disappeared.

As the sun peeks over the horizon, she stifles her sobs and through her tears she examines the gun. It's similar to one of her father's.

There is something she *can* do; she's seen her father do it often enough. She unclips the magazine and is surprised to find only four bullets in it. She removes them and then sharply pulls the slide back and catches the remaining round as it's ejected from the chamber. She reloads the magazine into the gun and pockets the bullets. Then she places the pistol back in Anatoli's case and zips it up.

Standing, she wipes away her tears. *Enough with the crying*, she scolds herself. She glances toward the window as the skyline of Zagreb materializes in the early-morning light. From the fifteenth floor of the Westin hotel, the city is spread out beneath like a terra-cotta patchwork quilt. It's an arresting vista, and in a distracted moment she wonders if Tiranë is similar.

"You're awake." Anatoli's voice startles her.

"I was hungry." She glances at the table of leftover food. "Now I'm going to have a shower."

Grabbing her bag, she scuttles into the bathroom and locks the door.

When she emerges, Anatoli is up and dressed. Their crockery and the leftover food have been cleared away, and there's fresh linen on the table, with a continental breakfast laid out for them.

"You stayed," Anatoli says quietly. He seems subdued, though he's as watchful as ever.

"Where would I go?" Alessia replies wearily.

He shrugs. "You left once before."

Alessia stares at him. Mute. Despondent. Exhausted.

"Is it because you care for me?" he whispers.

"Don't flatter yourself," she says, and, sitting down, picks out a pain au chocolat from the bread basket.

He takes his seat opposite her, and she can tell he's hiding a slight and hopeful smile.

Tom and I wander across the vast Skanderbeg Square, which is close to the hotel. It's a clear, chill morning, with the sun reflecting off the multicolored marble tiles that pave the gargantuan space. It's dominated on one side by a bronze statue of Albania's fifteenth-century hero on horseback, and on the other by the National History Museum. Although I'm anxious to get to Alessia's town and find her home, we have to wait to meet our interpreter.

I'm unsettled and jittery and unable to keep still, so to kill time Tom and I take a quick walk through the museum. I distract myself by snapping numerous photographs and posting the odd one online. I get told off twice, but I ignore the officials and continue to take photographs surreptitiously. It's hardly the British Museum, but I'm fascinated by the Illyrian artifacts. Tom, of course, is preoccupied with the displays of medieval weaponry; Albania has a rich and bloody history.

At ten we stroll down one of the tree-lined boulevards toward the coffeehouse where we've arranged to meet our translator. I am struck by how many men are sitting around drinking coffee outside, even though it's cold.

Where are the women?

Thanas Ceka is dark-haired and dark-eyed, a postgrad student at the University of Tirana doing his doctorate in English literature. His English is excellent, he has a ready smile and an easygoing nature—and he's brought his girlfriend. Her name is Drita, and she's an undergrad studying history. She's petite and pretty, and her spoken English is not as good as Thanas's. She wants to come with us.

Well, this could get complicated.

Tom glances at me and shrugs. I haven't got time to argue. "I'm not sure how long we're going to be," I state as I finish my coffee. It could double as paint stripper—I don't think I've ever drunk coffee this strong.

"It's cool. I've cleared my schedule for the week," Thanas responds. "I've never been to Kukës myself, but Drita has."

"What do you know of Kukës?" I ask Drita directly.

She gives Thanas a nervous glance.

"That bad?" I eye them both.

"It has a reputation. When the Communists fell, Albania was . . ." Thanas pauses. "It went through a difficult time."

Tom rubs his hands. "I love a challenge," he says, and Thanas and Drita have the grace to laugh.

"We shall be okay with the weather," Thanas says. "The motorway is open, and it hasn't snowed for a couple of weeks."

"Shall we get going?" I ask, eager to leave.

The landscape has changed. Gone are the dreary, fallow fields of Northern Europe; the terrain is stark, rocky, and barren in the winter sunshine. Under any other circumstances, Alessia might have enjoyed this journey. She's had a lightning tour of Europe's highways. But she's with Anatoli, the man she'll be forced to marry—and she still has to face her father when they reach Kukës. She is not looking forward to the inevitable confrontation, and deep down she knows it's because her mother will bear the brunt of his anger.

They tear across another bridge at an alarming speed. Below them is a vast body of water, reminding Alessia of the Drin—and reminding her of the sea.

The sea.

And Maxim.

He gave me the sea.

Will she ever see him again?

"The coastline in Croatia is very picturesque. I do a lot of business here," says Anatoli, breaking the silence that's hung between them since they left Zagreb.

Alessia glances at him. She doesn't care about his business. She doesn't want to know what he does. There was a time when she was curious, but that time has passed. Besides, as his wife—a *good* Albanian wife—she will ask no questions.

"I have several properties here." He gives her a wolfish grin, and she realizes he's trying to impress her, like he did when she first met him.

She turns away, staring out at the sea, and her mind spirals back to Cornwall.

The drive out of Tirana is frankly terrifying. Pedestrians have an unnerving habit of just stepping out into the road, and the roundabouts are free-for-alls—cars, trucks, buses all jostling for priority. It's like a giant game of chicken, and at this rate my nerves will be in shreds by the time we reach Kukës. Tom is constantly slamming his hand on the dashboard, yelling at pedestrians and drivers alike. It's bloody annoying.

"For fuck's sake, Tom, shut the fuck up! I'm trying to concentrate."

"Sorry, Trevethick."

By some miracle we make it out of the city center unscathed. Once we reach the main road, I start to relax a little, but I drive slowly; drivers here are unpredictable.

There are several car dealerships and countless petrol stations on the roadside. As we leave Tirana behind, we pass a grand, imposing neoclassical building that looks rather like a wedding cake.

"What's that place?" I ask.

"It's a hotel," Thanas says. "It's been under construction for many years." He shrugs when our eyes meet in the rearview mirror.

"Oh."

The lowlands look fertile and green considering it's February. There are squat, red-roofed houses dotted among the fields. While I drive, Thanas gives us a potted history of Albania and shares more information about himself. His parents lived through the fall of Communism, and both of them learned English via the BBC World Service, even though it was banned under Communist rule. It transpires that the BBC, and most things British, are held in high regard by Albanians. It's where they all want to go. There or America.

Tom and I exchange a glance.

Drita speaks quietly to Thanas, and he translates. Kukës was nominated for the Nobel Peace Prize in 2000, after the town accepted hundreds of thousands of refugees during the Kosovan conflict.

This I knew. I remember Alessia's look of pride when she regaled me about Kukës and all things Albanian in the pub in Trevethick.

It's been two days since she left, and I feel like I'm missing a limb.

Where are you, my love?

We join the main motorway to Kukës, and soon we are flying into the chilliest of blue skies, steadily climbing higher and higher toward the majestic, snowcapped peaks of the Albanian Alps, and the Shar and Korab mountain ranges that dominate the landscape. There are gorges with clear white-water rivers, craggy canyons, and steep, jagged cliffs. It's stunning, and apart from this modern motorway the land around us seems untouched by time. There's an occasional hamlet with terra-cotta-tiled houses, smoke rising from chimneys, stooks of hay flecked with snow, washing on lines, goats free, goats tethered—this is Alessia's country.

My sweet girl.

I hope you're okay.

I'm coming to get you.

The temperature drops the higher we go. Tom has taken the wheel so that I can play DJ and take photographs with my phone. Thanas and Drita are quiet, enjoying the views and listening to Hustle and Drone, who are streaming through the car stereo system from my iPhone. We emerge from a long mountain tunnel to find we're right among the peaks. They're covered with snow but are surprisingly bare, with very few trees. Thanas explains that after the Communist regime fell, there were fuel shortages, and in some places the locals cut down all the trees for firewood.

"I thought we were high enough to be above the tree line," Tom says.

In the middle of this rocky wilderness, we encounter a toll-booth, and while we queue up behind a few battered cars and trucks, my phone buzzes. I'm amazed I can get a signal in these mountains on top of Eastern Europe.

"Oliver, what's up?"

"I'm sorry to interrupt your day, Maxim, but the police have been in touch. They were rather hoping to interview your . . . um . . . fiancée, Miss Demachi."

Ah . . . so now he knows. I ignore the fiancée part of his state-ment. "As you know, Alessia has returned to Albania, so they'll have to wait until she comes back to London."

"I thought as much."

"Did they say anything else?"

"They have recovered your laptop and some sound equipment."

"That's good news!"

"And the case is now in the hands of the Metropolitan Police. It appears that Miss Demachi's assailants are known to the police and wanted in connection with other crimes."

"The Met? Good. Sergeant Nancarrow said those arseholes might have form."

Tom gives me a sideways glance.

"Have they been charged?"

"As far as I know, not as yet, sir."

"Keep me up to date with these proceedings if you can. I want to know if they're charged and if they make bail."

"Will do."

"Just relay my message to the police about Miss Demachi. Say she's had to return to Albania for a family matter. Everything else okay?"

"Tickety-boo, sir."

"Tickety-boo?" I snort. "Great." I hang up and pass Tom five euros to pay for the toll.

If Dante and his accomplice are still in custody, the police must be treating this seriously. Maybe they've got them for trafficking; I hope so. I hope they lock the fuckers up and throw away the key.

A short while later, we see a sign for Kukës and my spirits lift. We're nearly there. Soon we're driving alongside a huge lake, which, when I consult my Google Maps, turns out to be a river—the Drin which feeds Fierza Lake. I remember Alessia talking with such passion about the landscape around her town. My anticipation is growing exponentially. I urge Tom to drive faster. I am going to see her. I am going to save her. I hope.

She might not need saving.

She might want to be here.

Don't think that!

As we round a sweeping curve of the motorway, Kukës finally comes into view. It's nestled in the valley, with a wide, blue-green river-lake in front of it and ringed by dramatic mountains. The vista is spectacular.

Wow.

This was Alessia's view, every day.

We cross a sturdy bridge over the water. On a bluff above, a ghostly abandoned building stands sentinel, and I wonder if it's another unfinished hotel.

O n the outskirts of Nikšić, in Montenegro, Anatoli pulls in to the parking lot of a roadside café. Alessia stares listlessly out the window.

"I'm hungry. You must be, too. Let's go," he says. Alessia doesn't bother to argue but follows him into the pleasant, clean space. It's relatively new and decorated with a fun theme—automobiles—a cherry-red hot rod is painted above the bar. It's an inviting place. But not for Anatoli; he's irritable. He's slapped the steering wheel several times and sworn loudly in the last couple of hours, infuriated by other drivers. He is not a patient man.

"Order something for both of us. I'm going to the restroom. Don't run. I'll find you." He scowls at Alessia and leaves her to choose a table.

She's now keen to make it home. Given how Anatoli behaved yesterday evening, she doesn't want to spend another night with him. She'd rather face her father. She skims the menu, trying to find common words that she might recognize in either English or Albanian, but she's tired and can't seem to concentrate. Anatoli returns. He looks tired. Of course, he's been driving constantly for several days now, but Alessia refuses to feel any sympathy for him.

"What did you order?" he snaps.

"I haven't. Here's the menu." She hands it to him before he can gripe. A waiter joins them, and Anatoli orders without asking her what she wants. She's amazed that Montenegrin seems to be yet another language he speaks fluently. The waiter scuttles away, and Anatoli pulls out his mobile phone.

Cool blue eyes meet hers. "Keep quiet," he says, and he dials a number. "Good afternoon, Shpresa, is Jak there?"

Mama!

Alessia sits up. Fully engaged. He's talking to her mother.

"Oh . . . Well, tell him we'll be home around eight this evening. . . ." Anatoli's eyes slide to Alessia. "Yes, she's with me. She's well. . . . No . . . She's in the restroom."

"What!"

Anatoli puts his index finger to his lips.

"Anatoli, let me talk to my mother," Alessia insists, holding out her hand for the phone.

"We'll see you then. Good-bye." He hangs up.

"Anatoli!" Tears of anger threaten as a lump swells in her throat. She's never felt as homesick as she does now.

Mama.

How could he begrudge her a few words to her mother?

"If you were a little more docile and grateful, I would have let you talk to her," he says. "I have come a long way for you."

Alessia glares at him, then drops her eyes. She doesn't want to meet the challenge in his; she cannot bear to look at him after this latest outrage. He's cruel and vindictive and petulant and childish. Fury quietly seeps into every vein in her body.

For all that he's done, she will never forgive him.

Ever.

Her only hope is to plead with her father and beg him not to force their marriage.

Close up, Kukës is not what I thought it would be. It's a nondescript town of weathered Soviet-style apartments built in blocks. Drita informs us via Thanas that it was constructed during the 1970s. The original old town of Kukës is now at the bottom of the lake; the valley was flooded to feed the hydroelectric dam that provides power to the surrounding region. The roads are lined with fir trees, there's a blanket of snow on the ground, and the streets are quiet. There are a few shops, selling household goods, clothes, and farm equipment, and a couple of supermarkets. There's a bank, a pharmacy, and many cafés, where, as is customary, men sit outside in the afternoon sunshine wrapped up against the chill, drinking coffee.

Again, where are all the women?

The most distinctive feature of the town is that at the end of each street, wherever I look, the mountains stand tall and proud in a dramatic backdrop. We are surrounded by their majestic beauty, and I find myself wishing I'd brought my Leica.

My travel agent has booked us into a hotel called, of all things, Amerika. Google Maps guides us through the backstreets to the hotel itself. It's a curious mix of old and modern, with an entrance that looks like a Christmas grotto, especially now, as it's dusted with snow.

Inside, it has to be one of the kitschiest places I've ever seen, crammed with touristy knickknacks procured from the USA, including several plastic Statues of Liberty. The decor is impossible to define, a mishmash of styles, but the overall effect is . . . cheery and friendly. The host, a wiry, bearded man in his thirties, is warm and welcoming and greets us in a broken version of English before ushering us upstairs to our rooms via a tiny lift. Tom and I take the twin room, leaving the double for Thanas and Drita.

"Will you ask him for directions to this place?" I hand Thanas a crumpled piece of paper with Alessia's parents' address.

"Yes. What time would you like to go?"

"Five minutes. Just give us time to unpack."

"Steady on, Trevethick," butts in Tom. "Can't we have a drink first?"

Hmm . . . As my father would say, some Dutch courage always helps.

"A quick one. And just one. Okay? I'm going to meet my future wife's parents—I don't want to be stocious." Tom nods enthusiastically and claims the bed nearer the door. "I hope to God you don't snore," I say as I unpack.

An hour later we are parked in a small layby that leads to two open, rusty metal gates. Beyond, down a concrete driveway, is a solitary, terra-cotta-roofed house on the banks of the Drin. Only the roof is visible.

"Thanas, you'd better come with me," I say, and we leave Drita and Tom in the car. The glow of the setting sun casts tall shadows across the driveway. We're on a large plot, surrounded by naked trees, though there are a few firs and a sizable, well-kept vegetable patch. The house is painted a pale green and has three stories and two balconies that face the water, from what I can see. It's larger than the other houses we saw on our way here. Perhaps

Alessia's folks are affluent. I have no idea. The lake looks magnificent, lit up with the hues of a fading winter sunset.

On the outside of the house, there's a satellite dish, and it
reminds me of a conversation I had with Alessia.

And I've been to America by watching TV.

American TV?

Yes. Netflix. HBO.

I knock on what I assume is the front door. It's made of a good
solid wood, so I knock again, harder this time, to be sure to be
heard. My heart is pounding, and in spite of the cold a trickle of
sweat runs down my back.

This is it.

Game face on, dude.

I'm about to meet my new in-laws—though they don't know
that yet.

The door half opens, and a chink of light behind her reveals
a slight, middle-aged woman in a headscarf. In the fading evening light, I see that she's giving me a quizzical look, a little like
Alessia.

"Mrs. Demachi?"

"Yes." She looks bewildered.

"My name's Maxim Trevelyan, and I've come about your
daughter."

She gapes at me, blinking furiously, then opens the door a little
wider. She's trim with slight shoulders, and she's rather dowd-
ily dressed in a voluminous skirt and blouse. Her hair is hidden
beneath her headscarf, reminding me of the moment when I first
saw her daughter standing like a frightened rabbit in my hallway.

"Alessia?" she whispers.

"Yes."

She frowns. "My husband . . . is not here." Her English sounds
rusty and her accent much thicker than her daughter's. She peers
anxiously past me, scanning the driveway—for what, I don't
know—and then she looks directly at me. "You cannot be here."

"Why?" I ask.

"My husband is not at home."

"But I need to talk to you about Alessia. I think she's on her way back here."

She tilts her head, suddenly alert. "We are expecting her soon. You have heard she is returning?"

My heart leaps in response.

She's coming home. I was right.

"Yes. And I've come to ask you and your husband for . . ." I swallow. "For . . . permission to marry your daughter."

Our final border crossing, *carissima*," Anatoli says. "Back to your home country. Shame on you for leaving it and skulking away like a thief and dishonoring your family. When we return, you can apologize to your parents for the worry you have caused them."

Alessia averts her eyes, inwardly cursing him for making her feel guilty for running away. She was running from him! She knows that many Albanian men leave their country to work abroad—for women it's not so easy.

"This is the last time you have to go in the trunk. But wait, I need to retrieve something first." She stands back and looks west to where the sun has finally disappeared behind the hills. The chill in the air reaches through her clothes and entwines around her heart. And she knows it's because she's pining for the only man she'll ever love. Tears rise unexpectedly into her eyes, and she blinks them back.

Not now.

She doesn't want to give Anatoli the satisfaction.

She will cry tonight.

With her mother.

She inhales deeply. This is what freedom smells like—chilly, foreign. When she next takes a deep breath, she'll be in her home-land, and her adventures will become a . . . what did Maxim call it? A *folly* from the past.

"Get in. It will be night soon," Anatoli snaps as he holds open the lid.

The night belongs to the djinn.

And she's staring at one now. That's what he is. The djinn personified. She climbs in without complaint and without touching him. She's getting closer to home, and for the first time, she's looking forward to seeing her mother.

"Soon, *carissima*," he says, and there's a troubling glint in his eye.

"Shut the trunk," she responds as she clutches the flashlight.

His lips lift in a sardonic smile, and he slams the lid down, leaving her in darkness.

M rs. Demachi gasps, and with another quick and anxious glance past me, she steps aside. "Come in."

"Wait in the car," I say to Thanas, and I follow her into a confined vestibule, where she points to a shoe rack.

Oh. Quickly I slip off my boots, relieved that I'm wearing matching socks.

And that would be because of Alessia. . . .

The hall is painted white, its shiny tiled floor topped by a brightly colored kilim rug. She waves me on into an adjoining room, where two old sofas covered in bold and colorful patterned blankets face each other across a small table that's also covered in a rich printed cloth. Beyond is a fireplace, its mantelpiece peppered with old photographs. I squint, hoping to see one of Alessia. There's one of a young girl with large, serious eyes, seated at a piano.

My girl!

The grate is piled with logs, but they remain unlit in spite of the cold, and I suspect that this is the drawing room used to receive company. Pride of place is given to the old upright piano that sits against the wall. It's plain and shabby, but I bet it's tuned to perfection. This is where she plays.

My talented girl.

Beside the piano is a tall shelf stacked with well-thumbed books.

Alessia's mother has not asked me to remove my coat. I don't think I'm going to be here for long.

"Please. Sit," she instructs.

I take a seat on one of the sofas, and she perches on the edge of the one opposite, radiating tension. Clasping her hands together, she stares at me expectantly. Her eyes are the same dark shade as Alessia's—but whereas Alessia's are full of mystery, her mother's hold only sadness. I guess it's because she's anxious about her daughter. But from her lined face and the sprinkling of gray in her hair, it's obvious she's not led an easy life.

Life in Kukës is hard for some women.

Alessia's quietly spoken words come back to me.

Her mother blinks a couple of times. I suspect I'm making her nervous or uncomfortable, and for that I feel a little guilty.

"My friend Magda, she writes to me about a man who helps my Alessia and also Magda herself. Is that you?" Her voice is hesitant and soft.

"Yes."

"How is my daughter?" she whispers. She's studying me intensely, clearly desperate for news of Alessia.

"When I last saw her, she was fine. More than fine, she was happy. I met her when she worked for me. She came to my house to clean." I simplify my English, hoping Alessia's mother can keep up.

"You have come all the way from England?"

"Yes."

"For Alessia?"

"Yes. I've fallen in love with your daughter, and I believe she loves me, too."

Her eyes widen. "She does?" She looks alarmed.

Okay . . . this is not the reaction I'd been expecting.

"Yes. She told me she does."

"And you want to marry her?"

"Yes."

"How do you know that she wants to marry you?"

Ah!

"In truth, Mrs. Demachi, I don't know. I haven't had the chance to ask her. I believe that she's been kidnapped and is being brought to Albania against her will."

She leans her head back, her eyes intense, assessing me.

Shit.

"My friend Magda speaks well of you," she says. "But I don't know you. Why would my husband let you marry our daughter?"

"Well, I know she doesn't want to marry the man her father has chosen for her."

"She says this to you?"

"She's told me everything. And what's more, I listened. I love her."

Mrs. Demachi bites her upper lip, and the mannerism is so reminiscent of her daughter that I have to hide my smile. "My husband will return soon. And it is for him to decide what will become of Alessia. His mind is set on her betrothed. He has given his word." She looks down at her clasped hands. "I let her go once, and it broke my heart. I don't think I can let her go again."

"Do you want her to be trapped in a violent, abusive marriage?"

Her eyes whip to mine, and in them I see a glimpse of her pain and her insight, swiftly followed by her shock that I know—this is her life.

Everything that Alessia ever said about her father comes back to me.

Mrs. Demachi whispers, "You must go. Go now." She stands up.

Fuck.

I've offended her.

"I'm sorry," I say as I stand, too.

She frowns, looking momentarily confused and undecided.

Then, suddenly, she blurts out, "Alessia will return here at eight o'clock this evening, with her betrothed." She averts her eyes from mine for a moment, probably wondering if it was a good idea to impart this state secret.

Reaching out, I want to squeeze her clasped hands in gratitude, but I stop myself, as my touch may not be welcome. Instead I give her my most sincere and grateful smile. "Thank you. Your daughter means the world to me."

She thaws briefly, rewarding me with a hesitant smile of her own, and again I see a little of Alessia in her.

She shows me to the door, where I slip on my boots and she ushers me out. "Good-bye," she says.

"Are you going to tell your husband that I've been here?"

"No."

"Okay. I understand." I offer what I hope is a reassuring smile, and I head back to the car.

Back at the hotel, I'm restless. We've tried watching TV. Neither Tom nor I understand what we're watching. We've tried reading, and now we're in the bar. It's on the roof and would offer an impressive daytime view of Kukës, the lake, and the surrounding mountains. But it's dark and the dimly lit vista offers no solace for me.

She's on her way home.

With him.

I hope she's okay.

"Sit down. Maybe have a drink," Tom says. I give him a sideways look. It's at times like this that I wish I smoked. The anticipation and the tension are almost unbearable. After one slug of whiskey, I can bear no more.

"We're going."

"It's too early!"

"I don't care. I can't stay cooped up here waiting. I'd rather wait with her folks."

· · ·

At 7:40 we return to the Demachi house.

Time to be a grown-up.

Tom waits in the car once more with Drita while Thanas and I walk down the driveway. "And remember, I've not been here before. I don't want to get Mrs. Demachi into trouble?" I say to Thanas.

"Trouble?"

"With her husband."

"Oh. I understand." Thanas rolls his eyes.

"You understand?"

"Yes. Life is different in Tiranë. Here it's much more traditional. Men. Women." He grimaces.

I wipe my sweaty palms on my coat. I haven't felt this nervous since my interview for Eton. I have to make a favorable impression on Alessia's father. I need to persuade him that I'm a better option for his daughter than the arsehole he's chosen.

That's if she wants me.

Shit.

I knock on the door and wait.

Mrs. Demachi answers the door. Her eyes flit from Thanas to me.

"Mrs. Demachi?" I ask.

And she nods.

"Is your husband at home?"

She nods once more, and in case we're overheard, I replay the introduction I made to her earlier in the day as if it hadn't happened. "Come in," she says. "You must speak to my husband." Once we've removed our shoes, she takes our coats and hangs them in the hall.

Mr. Demachi stands when we enter a larger room at the back of the house. It's an airy, spotless kitchen–cum–living room, the two areas separated by an arch. A pump-action shotgun hangs ominously on the wall above Mr. Demachi's head. I note that it's within easy reach.

Demachi is older than his wife; his face is weather-beaten, his hair more gray than black. He wears a somber dark suit that lends him the air of a Mafia don. His eyes give nothing away. I'm glad he's half a head shorter than me.

As Mrs. Demachi quietly explains who we are, his expression becomes more and more mistrustful.

Shit. What is she saying?

Thanas whispers a running commentary. "She's telling him that you wish to speak to him about his daughter."

"Okay."

Demachi gives us both an uncertain smile as he shakes our hands in turn, then waves at an old pine couch, inviting us to sit. He appraises me with shrewd eyes the same shade as Alessia's, while Mrs. Demachi wanders through the arch into the kitchen.

Demachi looks from me to Thanas and starts to speak. His voice has a rich, deep timbre that's almost soothing to listen to. Thanas immediately starts to translate for both of us.

"My wife tells me you are here because of my daughter."

"Yes, Mr. Demachi. Alessia worked for me, back in London."

"London?" He looks impressed for a moment, but the shutters come down quickly. "What did she do, exactly?"

"She was my cleaner."

He closes his eyes for a moment, as if this news is too painful to hear, which surprises me. Or perhaps he thinks this is beneath her . . . or maybe he misses her, I don't know. I take a deep breath to calm my spiraling nerves and continue. "I have come to ask for her hand in marriage."

His eyes pop open in surprise, and he scowls. It's an exaggerated expression. But I don't know to what end. "She's already promised to another," he says.

"She does not wish to marry that man. He is the reason that she left here."

Demachi's eyes widen at my outspoken candor, and I hear a small gasp from the kitchen.

"Did she tell you this?"

"Yes."

Demachi's expression is inscrutable.

What the hell is he thinking?

The creases in her father's forehead deepen. "Why do you wish to marry her?" He seems perplexed.

"Because I love her."

K ukës is achingly familiar. Even in the dark. Alessia is both excited and apprehensive about seeing her parents. Her father will beat her. Her mother will hold her in her arms, and they will cry together.

Like they always do.

Anatoli drives over the bridge to the Kukës peninsula and turns left. Alessia sits up, straining to catch a first glimpse of home. Less than a minute later, she sees the lights of her parents' house and frowns. There's a car parked near the end of the drive with two people leaning against it, facing the river and smoking. Alessia thinks it's odd but dismisses the thought, too preoccupied by her imminent reunion with her parents. Anatoli steers the Mercedes around the parked car and down the driveway.

Before the car has come to a complete stop, Alessia flings open the passenger door and flies up the path and through the front door. Without taking off her shoes, she races down the main hallway.

"Mama!" she calls, and she bursts into the living room, expecting to see her mother.

Maxim and another man she barely notices stand. They had been sitting with her father, who is now staring up at her.

Alessia's world stops, and she freezes as she tries to process what she's seeing.

She blinks a couple of times as her empty, aching heart kick-starts back into life. She has eyes for only one man.

He's here.

Chapter Thirty-One

My heart is beating a frantic tattoo. Alessia stands in the middle of the room. Astounded.

She's here.

She's finally here. Dark, dark wide eyes stare back at me in disbelief.

Yes. I came to get you.

I've got you. Always.

She looks stunning. Slender. Sweet. Her hair wild. But her skin is pale. Paler than I've ever seen her before, and she has a graze on one cheek and a bruise on the other. There are dark circles beneath her eyes that are shining with unshed tears.

A lump forms in my throat.

What have you been through, sweetheart?

"Hello," I whisper. "You left without saying good-bye."

Maxim is here. For her. Everyone else in the room disappears. She can see only him. His hair is tousled. He looks pale and tired, but relieved. His startling green eyes drink her in, and his words touch her soul. The same words he used when he came to find her in Brentford. But there's a question on his face, beseeching her. It's asking why she left. He doesn't know how she feels about him. But he came anyway.

He's here.

He's not with Caroline.

How could she doubt him? How could he doubt her?

She lets out a small, sharp cry and races into his waiting arms. Maxim cradles her against his chest, holding her tightly. She inhales his scent. It's clean and warm and familiar.

Maxim.

Never let me go.

A movement at the periphery of her vision catches her attention. Her father has risen from his seat, and he's gaping at the two of them. He opens his mouth to say something—

"We're home!" calls Anatoli from the hall, and he swaggers into the room carrying her duffel bag, expecting a hero's welcome.

"Trust me," Alessia whispers to Maxim.

He stares into her eyes, his face full of love, and he kisses the top of her head. "Always."

Anatoli halts at the doorway. Stunned into silence.

Alessia turns to her father, who's looking from us to the arsehole who kidnapped her. Anthony? Antonio? I don't remember his name, but he's a good-looking bastard. His glacial blue eyes are wide with bewilderment at first, but they narrow, coolly assessing me and the woman in my arms. I tuck Alessia under my arm, protecting her from him and her father.

"*Babë,*" Alessia says to her dad, "*më duket se jam shtatzënë dhe ai është i ati.*"

There is a collective gasp of shock that rattles through the room.

What the fuck did she say?

"What?" roars the arsehole in English, and he drops her bag as his face contorts with anger.

Her father glowers dumbfounded at her and me, his complexion becoming more florid.

Thanas leans toward me and whispers. "She's just told her father she thinks she's pregnant and that you're the father."

"What?"

I feel a little dizzy. But wait . . . She can't possibly . . . We only . . . We used . . .

She's lying.

Her father reaches for his shotgun.

Fuck.

Y ou told me you were bleeding!" Anatoli screams at Alessia, and a vein in his forehead pulses with wrath.

Mama starts crying.

"I lied! I didn't want you to touch me!" She turns to her father. "Babë, please. Don't make me marry him. He is an angry, violent man. He will kill me."

Baba stares at her, both bemused and angry, while beside Maxim a man Alessia doesn't know quietly translates everything she's just said into English. But she has no time for this stranger now. "See," she says to Baba, and opening her coat, she yanks down the neck of her sweater, revealing the dark bruises around her throat.

Mama sobs out loud.

"What the fuck!" Maxim bellows, and he lunges at Anatoli, grabbing him by the neck and throwing them both onto the floor.

He's fucking dead.

Adrenaline coursing through my body, I take the fucker by surprise, knocking the breath out of him as he hits the floor with me on top of him.

"You fucking arsehole!" I roar, and punch his face, smacking his head to one side as I sit astride him. I hit him again as he struggles, taking a swipe at my face, which I dodge. But he's strong, and he writhes beneath me, so I close my fingers around his throat and squeeze. He grabs my hands, trying to shake me off. He puckers his lips and spits at my face, but I dodge that, too, and his spittle falls back onto his cheek, so he's covered in his own slime. This only enrages him more. And he bucks and bucks. He's shouting at me in his own language. Words I don't understand—but I don't fucking care.

I squeeze harder.

Die, you fucker.

His face reddens. His eyes bulge.

I lift my hands, bringing his head up, and then slam it down on the kitchen tiles. Grateful to hear the loud thud.

Somewhere behind me I hear a scream.

Alessia.

"Get. Off. Me!" the arsehole gasps in broken English.

And suddenly there are hands on me, trying to pull me away. Fighting them off, I lean in close, close enough to smell his stale breath. "You touch her again and I'll fucking kill you!" I snarl.

"Trevethick! Trevethick! Maxim! Max!" It's Tom. He's grabbing my shoulders, hauling me off. I drag air into my lungs as I stand, my whole body vibrating with fury and a lust for revenge. The arsehole glares up at me, and I find Alessia's father standing between us holding his shotgun. With a venomous look, he waves the barrel, motioning for me to back off.

Reluctantly I oblige.

"Calm down, Maxim. You don't want to cause an international incident," Tom says as he and Thanas tug me back. The arsehole scrambles to his feet, pure loathing in his scowl.

"You're like all Englishmen," the arsehole snarls. "You're soft and weak, and your women are hard."

"Soft enough to beat the shit out of you, you piece of crap," I snap.

As the red mist clears, I can hear Alessia fretting behind me. *Shit.*

A lessia's father stands between the two men, looking at each of them in consternation.

"You come into my house bringing violence? In front of my wife and my daughter?" he addresses Maxim and his friend Tom.

Where did Tom appear from? Alessia wonders. She remembers meeting him in Brentford and recalls him in Maxim's kitchen with the scars down his leg. Tom runs a hand through his rust-red hair as he gazes at her father.

The translator leans forward and murmurs her father's words to Maxim in English. Maxim holds up his hands and steps back. "I apologize to you, Mr. Demachi. I love your daughter, and I don't wish to see any harm come to her. Especially at the hands of a man." Maxim gives Baba a pointed look. Baba frowns and turns his attention to Anatoli.

"And you. You bring her back to me covered in bruises?"

"You know how spirited she is, Jak. She needs to be broken."

"Broken? Like this?" Baba points to her neck.

Anatoli shrugs. "She's a woman." His tone implies that she's of no consequence.

As the words are translated for Maxim, his jaw tightens and his fists clench. He bristles with tension and anger.

"No," Alessia murmurs, reaching out and touching Maxim's arm to calm him.

"Quiet, you!" her father snaps, whirling around to face her. "You brought this shame on us. You run. And you return a whore. Spreading your legs for this Englishman."

Alessia hangs her head, her cheeks ashen.

"Babë, Anatoli will kill me," she whispers. "And if you want me dead, I'd rather you shot me with that gun you're holding, so I might die at the hands of someone who is supposed to love me."

She glances at Baba, who blanches at her words while Thanas quietly translates them.

"No," Maxim says, with such heartfelt conviction that all eyes turn to him. He moves quickly, ushering Alessia behind him. "Don't touch her. Either of you."

Baba stares at him, but Alessia doesn't know whether her father is outraged or impressed.

"Your daughter is soiled goods, Demachi," Anatoli says. "Why would I want another man's leftovers and her bastard? You can keep her, and kiss good-bye to the loan I promised you."

Baba scowls at him. "You would do this to me?"

"Your word is worthless," Anatoli growls.

The translator quietly relays the words in English. "Loan?" Maxim says. He turns his head slightly and speaks so that only Alessia can hear him. "This arsehole *paid* for you?"

Alessia flushes.

Maxim faces her father. "I will match any loan," he says.

"No!" Alessia exclaims.

Her father glares at Maxim, furious.

"You dishonor him," Alessia whispers.

"*Carissima*," Anatoli declares from the doorway. "I should have fucked you when I had the chance." He uses English so that Maxim can understand.

Maxim lurches at him, bristling with anger once more, but Anatoli is ready this time. From his coat pocket, he whisks out his revolver and takes aim at Maxim's face.

"No!" Alessia shrieks, and she darts quickly in front of Maxim, shielding him.

"I don't know whether to shoot you or him," Anatoli snarls at her in his mother tongue, and he looks to her father for permission.

Baba stares back at Anatoli and then at Alessia.

Everyone quiets. The tension is a thick blanket over the whole room. Alessia leans forward. "What are you going to do, Anatoli?" She jabs her index finger at him. "Shoot him or me?" Thanas translates.

Maxim grabs her arms, but she shakes him off.

"Who hides behind a woman?" Anatoli sneers in English. "I have enough bullets for both of you." His look of triumph makes her nauseated.

"No, you don't," Alessia retorts.

Anatoli frowns. "What?" And he measures the weight of the gun in his hand.

"This morning in Zagreb, I took the bullets out while you were sleeping."

Aiming the gun at Alessia, Anatoli tightens his finger on the trigger.

"No!" roars her father, and he rams Anatoli with the butt of the shotgun so hard that he falls to the floor. Seething, Anatoli takes aim again, this time at her father, and pulls the trigger.

"No!" Alessia and her mother shout in unison. But nothing happens. The hammer clicks and echoes against an empty chamber.

"Fuck!" Anatoli shouts, and he glares up at Alessia, a bizarre combination of admiration and contempt on his face. "You are one fucking annoying woman," he mutters, and he staggers to his feet.

"Go!" Baba bellows. "Go now, Anatoli, before I shoot you myself. You want to start a blood feud?"

"Over your whore?"

"She is my daughter, and these people are guests in my house. Go. Now. You are no longer welcome here."

Anatoli gazes at her father, his fury and impotence written in every tense muscle on his face. "You've not heard the last of this," he snarls at Baba and Maxim. Turning on his heel, he pushes past Tom and heads out of the room. Moments later they hear a loud bang as he slams the front door.

When Demachi slowly turns to face Alessia, his eyes are blazing. Ignoring me, he concentrates his menacing look on his daughter. "You have dishonored me," Thanas translates. "Your family. Your town. And you return here in this state?" Her father waves a hand up and down her body. "You have dishonored yourself."

And I watch Alessia hang her head with shame, and a tear slides down her cheek. "Look at me," he growls. When she looks up, he pulls back his arm to backhand her face, but I grab her and tug her out of his reach. She's shaking.

"Don't you dare touch a hair on her head," I snarl, towering over him. "This woman has been through hell. And all because of you and your shit choice of a husband for her. She's been kidnapped by sex traffickers. She's escaped. She's gone without food. She's walked for days with nothing. And after all that, she was resilient enough to get herself a job and hold body and soul together with barely any help. How can you treat her this way? What kind of father are you? Where is *your* honor?"

"Maxim! This is my father." Alessia grabs my arm, a look of horror on her face, as I lay into her so-called father. But I'm on a roll, and Thanas sounds like he's keeping up with me.

"How can you speak of honor if this is the way you treat her? And, what's more, she may be carrying your grandchild—and you threaten her with violence?"

Out of the corner of my eye, I spot Alessia's mother, who is clutching her apron, her expression full of horror. It's chastening.

Demachi is staring at me as if I'm completely crazy. He looks to Alessia and then back to me, his fury and disgust clear in his dark eyes. "How dare you come into my house and tell me how to behave? You. You who should have kept his pecker zipped in his pants. Don't talk to me of honor." Thanas blanches as he translates. "You dishonor us all. You dishonor my daughter. But there's one thing you can do," he growls through gritted teeth, and in one swift move he cocks his shotgun with a loud click.

Shit.

I've gone too far.

He's going to kill me.

I feel rather than see Tom tense in the doorway.

Demachi points the gun at me and shouts, *"Do të martohesh me time bijë!"*

The Albanians look flabbergasted. Tom is ready to pounce. And all eyes are on me: Mrs. Demachi's. Alessia's. Thanas's. They all gape in shock. And Thanas quietly translates, "You're going to marry my daughter."

Chapter Thirty-Two

Oh, Babë, no!

Alessia realizes that she hadn't thought through her lie about the pregnancy. In a panic she whirls away from her shotgun-wielding father, desperate to explain the truth to Maxim. She doesn't want to force him into marriage!

But Maxim is sporting the biggest grin.

Joy shines in his eyes, evident for all to see.

His expression takes her breath away.

Slowly he sinks onto one knee, and from the inside pocket of his jacket he produces ... a ring. A beautiful diamond ring. Alessia gasps, and her hands fly to her face in utter amazement.

"Alessia Demachi," Maxim says, "please do me the honor of becoming my countess. I love you. I want to be with you always. Spend your life with me. At my side. Always. Marry me."

Alessia's eyes fill with tears.

He brought a ring.

This is what he came here to do.

To marry her.

She's breathless with shock.

And then it hits her. Like a freight train. Her elation. He really does love her. He wants to be with her. Not Caroline. He wants her with him, always.

"Yes," she whispers, tears of joy running down her face. All watch, speechless and as amazed as Alessia, while Maxim slides the ring onto her finger and kisses her hand. Then, with a whoop of happiness, he springs up and sweeps her into his arms.

I love you, Alessia Demachi," I whisper. Setting her down, I kiss her. Hard. Closing my eyes. I don't care that we have an audience. I don't care that her father is still holding his shotgun pointed in my direction or that her mother is still in the kitchen wide-eyed and weeping. I don't care that one of my closest friends is looking at me in shock and alarm as if I'm crazy.

Right now. Here. In Kukës, Albania, I'm the happiest I've ever been.

She said yes.

Her mouth is soft and yielding. Her tongue caressing mine. It's been only days, but I've missed her so much.

Her tears rub off on my face. Wet and cooling.

Fuck. I love this woman.

Mr. Demachi coughs loudly, and Alessia and I surface, winded and giddy from our kiss. He waves the muzzle of his shotgun between us, and we both step back, but I grasp her hand firmly. I'm never letting her go. Alessia is grinning and blushing, and I'm light-headed with love.

"*Konteshë?*" her father, his brow creased, asks Thanas. Thanas looks to me, but I have no idea what Demachi said.

"Countess?" Thanas clarifies.

"Oh. Yes. Countess. Alessia will be Lady Trevethick, Countess of Trevethick."

"*Konteshë?*" her father says again, and it seems like he's feeling his way around the word and its meaning.

I nod.

"*Babë, zoti Maksim është Kont.*"

Three Albanians turn to stare at me and Alessia as if we've each grown an extra head.

"Like Lord Byron?" Thanas asks.

Byron?

"He was a baron, I think. But he was a peer. Yes."

Mr. Demachi lowers his gun, continuing to gape at me. No one else in the room moves or says anything.

Well, this is awkward.

Tom shuffles forward. "Congratulations, Trevethick. Didn't expect you to propose on the spot." He puts his arms around me and claps me on the back.

"Thanks, Tom," I reply.

"This'll make a great story for the grandchildren."

I laugh.

"Congratulations, Alessia," Tom adds, giving her a little bow, and she rewards him with a glorious smile.

Mr. Demachi turns to his wife and barks an instruction. She heads deeper into the kitchen and returns with a bottle of clear spirits and four glasses. I glance at Alessia—she's radiant. Gone is the harrowed woman who walked into this room earlier.

She shines. Her smile. Her eyes. She takes my breath away.

I'm a lucky guy.

Mrs. Demachi fills the glasses and distributes them—only to the men. Alessia's father lifts his glass. "*Gëzuar,*" he says, and there's a look of relief in his shrewd, dark eyes.

This time I know what that means. I raise my own glass.

"*Gëzuar,*" I repeat, and Thanas and Tom echo the toast. We all upend our glasses and down our drinks. It's the fieriest, most lethal liquid that I've ever poured into my throat.

I try not to cough. And fail.

"That's great," I lie.

"Raki," Alessia whispers, and she's trying to hide her smile.

Demachi sets down his glass and refills it, then refills the rest. *Another? Shit.* I mentally prepare myself.

Alessia's father raises his raki once more. *"Bija ime tani është problem yt dhe do të martoheni, këtu, brenda javës."* He downs his shot and brandishes his gun with a look of glee.

Thanas quietly translates. "My daughter is your problem now. And you'll be married, here, within a week."

What?

Fuck.

Chapter Thirty-Three

A week!

I give Alessia a bemused smile, and she grins and releases my hand.

"Mama!" she blurts, and I watch her run to her mother, who's been standing patiently in the kitchen. They embrace and cling to each other as if they'll never let go, and both begin to silently weep in that way that women do.

It's . . . affecting.

It's obvious they've missed each other. More than missed each other.

Her mother wipes away her daughter's tears, speaking rapidly in her native tongue, and I have no idea what they are saying. Alessia's laugh is more of a gurgle, and they hug each other again.

Her father watches them and turns to me.

"Women. They are so emotional." Thanas translates his words, but Demachi looks relieved, I think.

"Yes," I answer, my voice gruff, and I hope I sound manly. "She's missed her mother."

But not you.

Alessia's mother relinquishes her, and Alessia steps toward her father. "Baba," she murmurs, her eyes wide once more.

I hold my breath, poised to intervene if he so much as lays a finger on her.

Demachi raises his hand and gently holds her chin. *"Mos u largo përsëri. Nuk është mirë për nënën tënde."*

Alessia gives him a timid smile, and he leans down and kisses her forehead, closing his eyes as he does. *"Nuk është mirë as për mua,"* he whispers.

I look at Thanas, waiting for his translation, but he's turned away, giving them this moment—and I think maybe I should, too.

It's late, I'm exhausted but I can't sleep. Too much has happened, and my mind is racing. I lie awake staring at the dancing, watery reflections on the ceiling. The patterns that form are so comforting in their familiarity that I grin. They mirror my ecstatic mood. I'm not in London, I'm at my soon-to-be-in-laws', and the reflections are from the full moon, skipping over the deep, dark waters of Fierza Lake.

I didn't have a choice about where I stayed—Demachi insisted it should be here. My room is on the ground floor, and though sparsely furnished, it's comfortable and warm enough and has a splendid view of the lake.

There's a rustle at the door, and Alessia sneaks in and closes it behind her. All my senses come alive, and my heart starts pounding. She tiptoes toward the bed, her body swathed in the most virginal, all-covering, Victorian-style nightdress I have ever seen. Suddenly I feel that I'm in a gothic novel, and I want to laugh at the ridiculousness of this situation. But she places her finger to her lips and then in one swift move draws her nightgown over her head and drops it onto the floor.

I stop breathing.

Her beautiful body is bathed in the pale light of the moon.

She's perfect.

In every way.

My mouth dries, and my body stirs.

I toss back the covers, and she slides into bed beside me, gloriously naked.

"Hello, Alessia," I whisper, and my lips find hers.

And without words we embrace our reunion, her passion taking me by surprise. She's unleashed; her fingers, hands, tongue and lips are on me. And mine on her.

I'm lost.

And found.

Oh, the feel of her.

And when she throws her head back in ecstasy, I cover her mouth to stifle her cries and bury my face in her soft, lush hair and join her.

When we're quiet once more, she nestles in my arms, her body entwined with mine as she dozes. She must be exhausted.

I let my contentment seep into my bones.

I've got her back. The love of my life is with me, where she belongs. Although if her father knew she was here, he'd shoot us both, I'm sure.

Watching her with her parents these last few hours, I've learned so much about her. Her emotional reunion with her mother—and her father—was affecting. I think he does love her. Very much.

But it seems like she's been fighting against her upbringing since before I met her, fighting to be her own person. And she's succeeded. Plus, she's taken me on an epic journey of self-discovery with her. I want to spend the rest of my life with this woman. I love her so much, and I want to give her the world. She deserves nothing less.

She stirs, and her eyes open. She beams up at me, her smile illuminating the room.

"I love you," I whisper.

"I love you," she responds, reaching up to caress my cheek, her fingers tickling my stubble. "Thank you for not giving up on me." Her voice is as soft as a summer breeze.

"Never. I've got you. Always."

"And I've got you."

"I think your dad will shoot me if he finds you here."

"No, he'll shoot *me*. I think he likes you."

"He likes my title."

"Maybe."

"Are you okay?" I'm serious now, my voice dropping as I search her face for clues of what she's endured for the past couple of days.

"Now that I'm with you, I am."

"I'll kill him if he ever comes near you again."

She puts her finger on my lips. "Let's not speak of him."

"Okay."

"I am sorry. For the lie."

"Lie? About the pregnancy?"

She nods.

"Alessia, it was genius. Besides, I wouldn't mind some kids."

An heir and a spare.

She smiles and, leaning up, kisses me, tempting and teasing my lips with her tongue, and I'm hungry for more.

I ease her onto her back to make love to her once again.

Mindful. Beautiful. Fulfilling. Love.

As it should be.

Later this week we'll be married.

I can't wait.

I just have to tell my mother. . . .

Alessia's Music

Chapter Two
"Le Coucou" by Louis-Claude Daquin (Alessia's warm-up piece)
Prelude no. 2 in C Minor, BWV847, by J. S. Bach (Alessia's angry
   Bach prelude)

Chapter Four
Prelude no. 3 in C-sharp Major, BWV848, by J. S. Bach

Chapter Six
Prelude and Fugue no. 15 in G Major, BWV884, by J. S. Bach
Prelude no. 3 in C-sharp Major, BWV872, by J. S. Bach

Chapter Seven
Années de Pèlerinage, 3ème année, S. 163 IV, "Les jeux d'eaux à la
   Villa d'Este," by Franz Liszt

Chapter Twelve
Prelude no. 2 in C Minor, BWV847, by J. S. Bach

Chapter Thirteen
Prelude no. 8 in E-flat Minor, BWV853, by J. S. Bach

Chapter Eighteen
Piano Concerto no. 2 in C Minor, op. 18-1 by Sergei Rachmaninoff

Chapter Twenty-Three
Prelude no. 15 in D-flat ("Raindrop") by Frédéric Chopin
"Le Coucou" by Louis-Claude Daquin
Piano Sonata no. 17 in D Minor, op. 31, no. 2 ("Tempest" III) by
    Ludwig van Beethoven

Chapter Twenty-Six
Prelude no. 23 in B Major, BWV868, by J. S. Bach

Chapter Twenty-Eight
Prelude no. 6 in D Minor, BWV851, by J. S. Bach

Acknowledgments

To my publisher, editor, and dear friend, Anne Messitte, thank you. For Everything.

I am indebted to all the team at Knopf and Vintage. In your attention to detail, your dedication, and your support, you go above and beyond. You do a fantastic job. Special thanks to Tony Chirico, Lydia Buechler, Paul Bogaards, Russell Perreault, Amy Brosey, Jessica Deitcher, Katherine Hourigan, Andy Hughes, Beth Lamb, Annie Lock, Maureen Sugden, Irena Vukov-Kendes, Megan Wilson, and Chris Zucker.

To Selina Walker, Susan Sandon, and all the team at Cornerstone, thank you for all your excellent work, enthusiasm, and good humour. It is much appreciated.

Thank you to Manushaqe Bako for the Albanian translations.

Thank you to my husband and my rock, Niall Leonard, for first edits and countless cups of tea.

Thank you to Valerie Hoskins, my unprecedented agent, for your mindful counsel and all the jokes.

Thank you to Nicki Kennedy and the crew at ILA.

Thank you to Julie McQueen for having my back.

Thank you to Grant Bavister from the Crown Office, Chris Eccles from Griffiths Eccles LLP, Chris Schofield, and Anne Filkins for advice on earldoms, heraldry, trusts, and property matters.

Huge thanks to James Leonard for his tuition in the language of posh young Englishmen.

For all the advice on clay pigeon shooting, thank you, Daniel Mitchell and Jack Leonard.

To my beta readers, Kathleen Blandino and Kelly Beckstrom, and to my pre-readers Ruth Clampett, Liv Morris, and Jenn Watson—thank you all for the feedback, and for being there.

To the Bunker—it's been nearly ten years now—thank you for joining me on this journey. My author friends—you know who you are. Thank you for inspiring me every day. And to the residents of Bunker 3.0, thank you for your constant support.

Major and Minor, thank you, for the help with the music, and for being exceptional young men. Shine bright, you beautiful boys. You make me so proud.

And finally, I will forever be grateful to everyone who has read my books, watched the movies, and enjoyed my stories. Without you this amazing adventure would not have been possible.

ABOUT E L JAMES

E L James is an incurable romantic and a self-confessed fangirl. After twenty-five years of working in television, she decided to pursue a childhood dream and write stories that readers could take to their hearts. The result was the controversial and sensuous romance *Fifty Shades of Grey* and its two sequels, *Fifty Shades Darker* and *Fifty Shades Freed*. In 2015, she published the #1 bestseller *Grey*, the story of *Fifty Shades of Grey* from the perspective of Christian Grey, and in 2017, the chart-topping *Darker*, the second part of the Fifty Shades story from Christian's point of view. Her books have been published in fifty languages and have sold more than 150 million copies worldwide.

E L James has been recognized as one of *Time* magazine's "Most Influential People in the World" and *Publishers Weekly*'s "Person of the Year." *Fifty Shades of Grey* stayed on *The New York Times* Best Seller List for 133 consecutive weeks. *Fifty Shades Freed* won the Goodreads Choice Award (2012), and *Fifty Shades of Grey* was selected as one of the 100 Great Reads, as voted by readers, in PBS's *The Great American Read* (2018). *Darker* has been long-listed for the 2019 International DUBLIN Literary Award.

She coproduced for Universal Studios the Fifty Shades movies, which made more than a billion dollars at the box office. The third installment, *Fifty Shades Freed*, won the People's Choice Award for Drama in 2018.

E L James is blessed with two wonderful sons and lives with her husband, the novelist and screenwriter Niall Leonard, and their West Highland terriers in the leafy suburbs of West London.

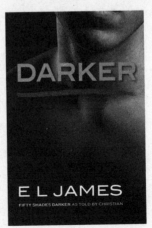